THE COMPLETE FILES OF DETECTIVE THOMAS MECANA

THE COMPLETE FILES OF DETECTIVE THOMAS MECANA

HORSE OF A DIFFERENT COLOR
WHEN THE NIGHT BIRD SINGS
TWISTED JUSTICE
THE BOX

JOHN L. LANSDALE

BOOKVOICE PUBLISHING

THE COMPLETE FILES OF DETECTIVE THOMAS MECANA
by John L. Lansdale Copyright © 2021
Originally published as:
HORSE OF A DIFFERENT COLOR Copyright © 2017
WHEN THE NIGHT BIRD SINGS Copyright © 2018
TWISTED JUSTICE Copyright © 2018
THE BOX Copyright © 2019
by John L. Lansdale
All rights reserved.

Design Copyright © 2021
by BookVoice Publishing
All rights reserved.

First BookVoice Paperback Edition 2021

ISBN
978-1-949381-32-0 Paperback
978-1-949381-33-7 eBook

BookVoice Publishing
PO Box 1528
Chandler, TX 75758
www.bookvoicepublishing.com

THE MECANA SERIES by JOHN L. LANSDALE
- Book One - Horse of a Different Color
- Book Two - When the Night Bird Sings
- Book Three - Twisted Justice
- Book Four – The Box

OTHER WORKS by JOHN L. LANSDALE
- The Last Good Day
- Broken Moon
- Slow Bullet
- Long Walk Home
- Beyond Imagination
- Zombie Gold
- Kissing the Devil
- Hell's Bounty (with Joe R. Lansdale)
- Shadows West (with Joe R. Lansdale)
- Tales from the Crypt (Comic Series)
- Robert Bloch's That Hellbound Train
  (Comic Series with Joe R. Lansdale)
- Robert Bloch's Yours Truly, Jack the Ripper
  (Comic Series with Joe R. Lansdale)

What Others are Saying about John L. Lansdale

"Mickey Spillane fans will welcome this page-turner...Lansdale effectively delays revealing the novel's big secret until the end. Those who like their thrillers with a heavy dose of violent action will be satisfied." - Publishers Weekly review of *Slow Bullet*

"This is an entertaining, science fiction-historical-horror blend with resourceful protagonists and a solid cast of secondary characters."
- Booklist review of *Zombie Gold*

"*Slow Bullet* is a straight-ahead thriller...it's about action, and there's plenty of that. Check it out." – author Bill Crider

"...the author's innate ability to spin a complex tale painted with vivid characters and intense suspense provides readers with a well-paced book that they may find difficult to set down...a worthwhile suspenseful ride."
- Amazing Stories review of *Horse of a Different Color*

"*Zombie Gold* has something for everyone... It's exciting, entertaining and educational. A fun ride." – author Joan Hallmark

"...something unique and comfortable and difficult to put down. Highly recommended." – Cemetery Dance review of *Hell's Bounty*

"True to Lansdale tradition, John L. Lansdale has compiled a piece of work that should appeal to a wide range of readers."
– Amazing Stories review of *Zombie Gold*

"*Long Walk Home* really touched and gripped me. A great bittersweet story of light and shadow about growing up in a time gone by. I loved it." – author Joe R. Lansdale

TABLE OF CONTENTS

BOOK ONE
HORSE OF A DIFFERENT COLOR

For Pam,
A real detective.

"Who knows what evil lurks in the hearts of men."
The Shadow radio drama

PART ONE
Officer Down

PROLOGUE

Fifth Ward Projects
Houston, Texas
12:05 A.M.

She lay on the bare mattress, naked, in a spread-eagle position on her back; her beautiful body drenched in sweat and her wet green eyes wide with fear. Her mouth was covered with duct tape and her hands and feet bound to the bed post with leather straps. A foul smell of dampness and decay filled the empty room.

Rain drops tapped on the dirty windows and the car lights made the rain drops look like sparkling rhinestones as they slid down the windows in the wee hours of the night.

A door opened and a tall, wet shadow appeared in the open doorway. She could make out the vague image of a gun. Tears ran down her cheeks; she fought at the straps.

She screamed but no sound came out. The shadow stepped inside the door and shined a flashlight on her.

"It's alright, I'm a cop," he said.

She closed her eyes and sighed. They found her. She had been rescued. Her prayers were answered.

Suddenly, a second shadow appeared in the doorway behind the first, holding something long and shiny. She squirmed and darted her eyes back and forth, shook her head up and down as a warning, but the dark night betrayed her and the cop kept moving toward her.

Then she saw it. It was a knife, a killing knife, in the hand of the dark figure behind the cop. In the blink of an eye, the knife plunged into his body. Blood gushed out and ran down his back. He crumbled to the floor, his gun sliding from his hand.

Houston Memorial Hospital
One Month Later

In Room 649 of the physical rehabilitation ward, Rustin Kemp struggled to raise his thirty-year-old, six-foot-three body up in bed on the pull-up bar. His blue eyes showed the pain as he tugged on the bar.

Sunlight splashed across the walls of the room through a window on a bright autumn day, painting them with a multi-colored pattern. A red porcelain vase with a dozen red roses in it and a card propped against it read, "Get well soon - from all the gang."

Rustin's boss, Captain Bill Lucas, stood beside the bed, his thin brown hair showing a shiny bald spot. Sagging jaws rested on the collar of a white shirt under a dark blue suit coat and a red tie draped over a pudgy belly swung back and forth like a pendulum.

"Everyone wanted to let you know they were thinking of you," he said. "Thought I would deliver the flowers and see how you were doing. The son of a bitch left you for dead."

Rustin dropped his hands from the pull bar, adjusted his pillow and looked at Bill Lucas.

"Can't walk yet," he said, "but the Doc thinks I will. I won't be doing any dancing, but I may be able to get around good enough to find that bastard if it's the last thing I ever do."

"I hope so, Rustin, but as my daddy used to say on the farm, 'We got a hard row to hoe.' No DNA, nothing except the horrific things he did to her. Homicide has had a crew on the case ever since you went down. It looks like she partied too hard and ran into the wrong guy. He may be in jail for something else, or laying low for a while."

"He'll show up," Rustin said. "The sick ones always do. I have to get out of this bed. There's something in the back of my mind that keeps bugging me. Something I need to remember that won't come to me."

"Rustin, if you hadn't been chasing that crackhead and stumbled in on her she may have disappeared like a lot of the others, and then no one would have known what happened to her. Unfortunately, it didn't turn out good. But at least her family got to bury her."

"All the more reason I have to find him, Bill."

"What you need to do is concentrate on getting well."

"I am, and I'll be planning how I'm going to catch that son of a bitch, too."

"You're a hard-headed man, Rustin."

"Been told that before."

Bill laughed and patted Rustin on the arm.

"Oh, I'm going to walk again. You can count on that."

"If you need anything let me know."

"I will. Tell everyone at the station I said thanks."

1

One Year Later

Julie Crawford just turned twenty-one. She was celebrating her adulthood on a Saturday night in downtown Warfield, Texas with friends and some of the club regulars at Griffin's Bar and Grill. Griffin's looked like a bastard cousin to Applebee's, with a smaller menu and a longer bar.

"Hey everybody," Julie said, standing up. "This is my last night at Griffin's. My grandpa left me a bundle; I'm headed to Hollywood to be an actress! I don't have to worry about going to law school anymore to please mommy and daddy."

A tall, thin, elderly gentleman in the back of the room with white hair to his shoulders stood up holding a glass of beer. "I propose a toast to the birthday girl," he said. "She's certainly pretty enough to be a movie star.

I'm old enough to remember June Allison. Julie reminds me of her, and the world could use another June Allison."

Everyone stood up, raised their glasses, gave a cheer and drank.

"Thanks everybody!" Julie said. "That's Mr. Rod Burger, my private drama coach who proposed the toast. He's a little prejudiced since my folks pay him a small fortune to train me."

Everyone laughed.

About midnight, Julie went to pee and never came back.

Two days later, two guys fishing found her mutilated body floating in the Trinity River. The police report said it would be a week before the cause of death could be determined.

At the request of the Warfield Police Department, Dallas PD sent fifteen-year veteran Detective Thomas Mecana to investigate.

Mecana was a tall, square-jawed, good-looking poster-type ex-Marine with brown wavy hair and penetrating gray eyes. He prided himself on staying fit and looked ten years younger than his forty-two-year-old body: A complete opposite to the Police Chief of Warfield, who looked like an eggplant.

Mecana's wife divorced him and moved to Austin ten years ago with his two daughters. For caring more about his job than his family, she claimed.

After researching a variety of recent murders, Mecana discovered that a murder in Houston had something in common with Julie. The vagina had been removed from both victims. Could be this sicko had come to Warfield, Mecana thought, and there would be more murders. Most of the information Mecana passed on to the Warfield Police was wasted. They wanted it all to go away and to get back to writing speeding tickets and working security for private businesses for extra money.

Warfield Police Chief David Orr was working on his second McDonalds Super Breakfast when the telephone rang.

"Warfield Police, Chief Orr speaking."

"Chief, my name's Rustin Kemp. I was involved in the Belmont murder case here in Houston last year. The Crawford murder sounds like the same MO."

"Yeah, you're not the only one. We got a detective here on the Crawford case that thinks it might be the same guy. I remember reading about you last year," Orr said. "He stabbed you and got away." Orr stuck a fork in a piece of sausage and jammed it in his mouth. "You still on the Houston force?"

"Doing private eye work now. I want that son of a bitch bad. I wanted to come up and take a look."

"Don't have a problem with that. I'll take all the help I can get, but you'll have to clear it with Detective Tom Mecana in Dallas. He's the lead guy on the case."

"I've heard of him. I'll call him, Chief. Thanks."

"No problem," Orr said, and went back to eating his breakfast.

2

Rustin looked up from his pancakes and saw Bill Lucas coming toward him. He wondered why Bill was at IHOP, he usually ate breakfast at home. He would always say, with a laugh, that nobody could cook instant oatmeal better than his Amy.

"Thought I would find you here," Bill said.

Rustin removed his cane from the empty chair and offered Bill a seat.

"Man, looking at those pancakes makes me hungry," Lucas said.

"I thought Amy always fixed your breakfast."

"I cheat sometimes," Bill said and sat down.

A cute, dark-haired waitress with 'Maria' on her name tag stopped at the table, poured Bill a cup of coffee and asked if he was ready to order.

"Yes. I'll have a stack of blueberry pancakes and sausage to go with my coffee, Maria."

"That oatmeal didn't go very far, huh, Bill?"

"Don't tell Amy. She's always nagging me about my weight."

"Not a word, I promise," Rustin said, grinning.

"Good. Got a call from Tom Mecana yesterday," Lucas said and took a sip of coffee. "You know who he is?"

"Yes. He's probably solved more murder cases than anyone else in Texas."

"Right. He wanted to know why you were trying to butt in on his case. I told him you didn't work for me anymore and I didn't have a clue what he was talking about. He said he didn't need any half-ass cops. I got to thinking about it this morning, figured you would be here since Debbie decided to take a powder, and find out what the hell was going on."

"I haven't talked to him," Rustin said. "The Police Chief in Warfield must have. The case he's talking about is a lot like the Belmont one. I was going to have a look but I needed his approval. I guess that's a no."

"Get you a client. Maybe the girl's folks. He may not help you but he can't stop you from earning a living."

"True. That would give me the right to be there," Rustin said, and took the last bite of his pancakes and reached for his wallet.

The waitress brought Bill his breakfast and poured him a fresh cup of coffee. He wolfed the pancakes down, pushed the empty plate away and picked up his coffee cup.

"Heard anything from Debbie?" he asked, and blew on the coffee.

"Nope, she said she needed to get away for a while to think things over. That was last Friday, haven't heard a word from her since. Her sister called for her, said she was at her folks'. Knew I would be worried. What she couldn't handle was me being a cripple."

"Well if that's her reason you're probably better off with out her. Think she would have done the same thing if you had been wounded in Iraq?"

"Don't know. Got out of there without a scratch and then this happens. You never know what cards you're going to be dealt."

"Good thing you don't have any kids to worry about."

"We tried. After three miscarriages we gave up."

"You should have called for backup that night. Maybe things would be different. You wouldn't be in this shape."

"Like they say, hindsight is 20/20. I thought I could handle it."

"Sounds like he's back in business," Bill said, holding his empty cup up for Maria to see.

"Don't know for sure what I'm going to do. Everything seems to get more complicated every day."

"Only you can decide that, partner. But it should be over for you. Let it go before you wind up getting hurt, physically and mentally."

"I know you mean well, Bill, but it's easier said than done. It won't let me go. It's chewing my insides up." The waitress passed by with the coffee pot, looked at Bill and poured him another cup. "I'll let you know what I decide to do, Bill, thanks."

Rustin picked up his cane and stood up. "My treat," he said, and dropped a twenty on the table.

"Thanks. Take care," Lucas said.

Rustin nodded and limped away.

3

Rustin arrived at the rehab center ten minutes before his appointment, took a couple of pain pills and made a call to Debbie's parents in Beaumont. They said she was there but didn't want to talk to him. She was going to file for divorce and her lawyer would be in touch. That was that.

The therapy lasted an extra hour because the doctor said he was not making enough progress with his weight lifts. He needed to strengthen his leg muscles more to compensate for the nerve damage in his back. Debbie would have agreed with that. When they had sex she had to do all the work. That wouldn't be a problem anymore.

Eight years down the drain. He thought about driving to Beaumont and begging her to come back, but it would probably be a waste of time and he wasn't sure his pride would let him do it any way.

He did ten more lifts with the leg weights, pulled himself up to a sitting position, picked up his cane, placed both hands on it and lifted himself up, leaning on the cane. The right leg was the one he supported most of his weight on, and the left with the cane. The pain got really bad sometimes; he needed his pills to keep going.

His doctor quit writing prescriptions for fear of him becoming addicted and told him to get some over-the-counter pain medicine if he needed it. That was a moot point now. With a new doctor in Dallas he should be able to get what he needed, at least for a while.

He reached in his pocket, got his phone and dialed.

He heard a voice say, "Lucas here."

"Bill, I decided to go to Dallas to find that prick. I wanted to say goodbye and thank you for everything."

"I understand where you're coming from, son, but don't you think you should quit while you're ahead and just move on? You're working with a big disadvantage."

"That has occurred to me but I don't have much of a life at the moment anyway, and those young women he mutilated never had a chance at any kind of life. A leopard can't change his spots. It has to be him. He leaves a gruesome calling card."

"That he does. Keep in touch."

"I will. See you."

Rustin limped to his Ford Explorer and drove home to an empty house. Everywhere he looked he saw reminders of Debbie. She was his high school sweetheart. He was the quarterback and she was a pretty blonde-haired, blue-eyed cheerleader. They had big dreams for their future. Everyone said they looked like the perfect couple.

He dropped his cane to the floor, sat down on the bed and tears came rolling down his cheeks. The only reason he had for living was to catch that bastard.

He wiped the tears away, packed a suitcase and decided he would wait until he got to Dallas to call his mom and dad to watch the house. He locked the front door, put the key in the mailbox, put his suitcase in the Explorer and headed up Interstate 45 to Dallas, into a setting sun and the unknown.

4

Mecana ordered a beer and looked up at the TV. Monday night football was on, something he never got into much. Griffin's was full of twenty-something college students. Some faculty members came in and he hoped he would blend in with them.

He noticed a pretty redhead wearing a revealing red dress at the end of the bar; four empty margarita glasses in front of her.

She raised a fifth salted glass to her crimson red lips, finished it off, got up and tilted to the left as she moved down the bar to where Mecana was sitting. She pushed a stool in between him and a little, skinny nerd-looking-guy. The nerd gave her a dirty look but said nothing, only slid off his stool, picked up his beer and walked away.

"Hi," she said. "Buy a lady a drink?"

At closer range Mecana could see her long red hair, cream-smooth skin and sparkling blue eyes, the cleavage of perfectly sculptured breasts and her long strong legs as she climbed up on the bar stool next to him.

"Don't you think you've had enough?" he said.

"Goodness no, I'm just getting started. My boyfriend dumped me, thought I would get drunk. You want to help me?"

"You must have a dumb boyfriend."

"You a teacher?" she asked.

"No. I stopped in to watch the game."

"You want to take me home, get in my pants?"

"You're drunk."

"I sure am. My name's Kinky, what's yours?"

"Mine's Tom. Kinky's an odd name for such a pretty girl."

"Got another one I don't like. You do want to get in my pants don't cha? Been watching you, you're a good-looking dude. You got a wife?"

"No."

"Don't matter; I fuck for the fun of it anyway."

"I think you need to call it a night, young lady. You got a friend here that could drive you home?"

"Nope. I don't know what happened to my ride. You're it."

"I'll call you a taxi, my treat. Go home and sleep it off. The world will look better tomorrow."

"Buy me another round and I'll consider it," she said and smiled, showing her perfect white teeth.

Mecana thought about his teenage daughters, and the perils of growing up. "Alright, I'll buy you one more and you go home. Deal?"

"You sure you don't want to go with me?"

"I'm sure. Margarita, right?"

"Right. I like big ones with lots of salt," she stuck her finger in her mouth, rolled it around and sucked on it.

Mecana shook his head, waved at the bartender.

A little guy with short black hair, a goatee and both arms full of tattoos walked over and leaned on the edge of the bar. He pointed to Mecana's beer bottle. "Another beer, mister?"

"Give me another beer and a large margarita for the lady."

The bartender looked at Kinky, then back to Mecana. "Don't you think you're a little old for her?"

"Just bring me the drinks," Mecana said, and dropped a twenty on the bar. "Keep the change." There was a roar from the crowd. Somebody scored a touchdown.

The bartender gave him a hard look, picked up the twenty and moved away.

Kinky looked at Mecana and laughed. "I think you're just right, Tom," she said. He couldn't help but chuckle too.

"We made a deal, Kinky. After you drink this one I'll call a taxi to take you home."

"I'd like it better if you came with me."

"I don't think so." Mecana was spending too much time with Kinky. He didn't have time to observe the clientele for anything unusual. He had good instincts for that sort of thing. That's why he came, but it wouldn't be tonight.

Kinky devoured the margarita in a few gulps and Mecana called a taxi. He walked her outside. She got in the cab with his help and mumbled her address to the driver. Mecana gave the driver thirty bucks and asked if that would cover it. The driver nodded yes. He closed the door and the cab pulled away.

He felt good about sending her home. By tomorrow she would be sober. The boyfriend a small bump in the road as she got on with her life.

He thought about his daughters again and how much he missed them, got in his Silverado and headed home. He didn't feel like playing cops and robbers anymore tonight.

5

Rustin woke up the next morning a little after eight in Warfield in Room 38 at the Sunset Inn in a king size bed. That was about the only thing the place had going for it. A look at all the ten-year-old cars parked at the orange motel doors were a reminder of his financial status. A policeman's pension was just above the poverty level, and his savings had already run out.

A more immediate problem was obtaining pills. He would have to find a doctor that didn't question him too much or insist that he provide his medical records before writing a prescription.

He stopped for some coffee at McDonalds, and went in search of a doctor. There were only four listed in Warfield. The one that ran a 'Doc in the Box' emergency clinic in a small strip center looked the best. The cane helped.

He picked up his prescription at Walgreens and headed for the Warfield police station.

The police station was a wooden building, about the size of a three car garage, painted a sea green with white trim. A police cruiser was parked out front. City Hall was across the street in a small red brick building. The mayor and four councilmen all had reserved parking spaces in front. If you didn't see the 'Population: 832' sign coming into town you wouldn't even know you had left Dallas.

Rustin opened the door of the Explorer and stepped out, made his way to the station door and went in. An obese man in his fifties wearing a police uniform was sitting at a desk at the back of the one-room building, chomping on a Big Mac. A sign on the desk said 'Chief David Orr.'

He had a bad haircut, bushy eyebrows, droopy brown eyes and fat jaws. He saw Rustin, swallowed hard and took a drink of Coke. "What can I do for you, sir?" he asked.

"Chief, my name's Rustin Kemp. I spoke with you the other day about the Julie Crawford case. My former boss said Tom Mecana called him and was less than enthusiastic about me coming."

"Yes," Orr said. "I talked to him about it. He said you'd be in the way and might get yourself hurt again and he didn't want that responsibility. I can't go against him."

"I can understand that but I'm here until this nut is caught by Mecana, me or whoever." "Don't expect any help from me. You get out of line, I'll have you arrested."

The door opened and Mecana walked in wearing a blue shirt, a half-zipped gray windbreaker, jeans and black loafers.

"There's the man now. Talk to him," Orr said and picked up his Coke.

"Talk to me about what?" Mecana asked, looking at Rustin.

"About the Crawford case," Rustin said. "I'm Rustin Kemp. I came here to find a killer."

"Oh yeah. The guy who fucked up; let the asshole get away when he murdered the Belmont girl. Best you stay out of my way. You don't, I'll put your ass in jail. "

"There are a lot of threats being thrown around," Rustin said. "I may have made some mistakes but I'm not giving up. Somebody has to catch him."

"I'll get him. You wouldn't be much help anyway, walking on a cane. Go back to Houston. When I catch him I'll let you know. You can come up for the trial, if I don't have to kill him."

"I heard you've been known to crack a few heads," Rustin said.

"When needed. That's why I'm still alive. You hesitate and they bury you," Mecana said.

"That's the damn truth," Orr said, looking at Rustin. "That's why you're in the shape you're in, boy."

"That's your opinion, not the board's," Rustin said.

"I know about that too," Mecana said. "The board cleared you but I don't think I want you watching my back."

"Me neither," Orr added.

"I know you're one of the best, Mecana," Rustin said. "I was hoping we could work together. If we can't, so be it. Sorry you feel that way. I have to do this. I'm at the Sunset Inn for now, if you want to talk."

"Don't sit by the phone, Kemp."

"See you around," Rustin said and limped toward the front door.

6

Chief Orr was munching on a chocolate donut when the phone rang. He answered with a full mouth and somehow managed to get, "Warfield Police," out without choking.

"This is Detective Winslow from the Dallas Homicide Department. Is Tom Mecana there?"

"No, but I'm expecting him any minute."

"I tried to get him at his number, but no answer. There's been another murder he needs to know about. She lived in your town. That's two. You got a real monster on your hands, Chief. They fished her out of the Trinity this morning. Have him call me at the number on your ID when he comes in. He can fill you in, after I talk to him."

"Sure," Orr said, eyeing the donut. When Mecana didn't show up by noon, and Orr couldn't get him on the phone, he sent a car to his address. He wasn't there.

At 5PM, Mecana was still missing and no one had seen him.

About 7:30 that evening there was a knock on Rustin's motel room door. There stood the last person he was expecting - Mecana.

"This is a surprise," Rustin said. "What changed your mind?"

Mecana stepped inside and plopped down on the corner of the bed like his legs wouldn't hold him up anymore. He looked at Rustin and wiped his red eyes. "The murderer has struck again, and I think I helped him."

"What do you mean you helped him?"

"I went to Griffin's bar night before last to check it out. I meet a young lady there who was very drunk. I sent her home in a taxi, alone. They found her mutilated body this morning. I heard it on the scanner on the way to work. At first it didn't register. They said her name was Barbara Jean Sadler. I took off for the crime scene. When I got there, I took a look at the body. It was the girl I put in the taxi. The examiner said she had been dead approximately twenty-four hours. That would have been the night I sent her home alone. She called herself Kinky. Should have drove her home. Been riding around all day trying to decide what to do, thought about you. Know how you feel now. What's going on in your head? I made a mistake and it cost another human being her life. I wanted to come by and apologize for the things I said to you."

"No need to apologize but I'm glad you understand. A young woman died when I fucked up too lost my wife, my job and my self-respect. I'll never be the man I was again. We both made mistakes, bad ones, and we can't undo them. I've spent the last year thinking about it. The only thing we can do is catch this monster and stop the killings. If you want to give up that's your business, but I could use your expertise. I'm not a homicide detective, but either way I'm going to find him."

Mecana dropped his head and sighed. "You're right, Kemp. I owe it to Kinky to find her murderer."

"If you mean that, Mecana, I think we can solve this case. There has to be something we haven't looked at hard enough or long enough."

"There always is," Mecana said, and sat back down on the bed. "I'll check the forensic info and the autopsy reports on Kinky and the Crawford girl, see if I can speed it up. Kinky said she broke up with her boy friend. It might be interesting to see what he has to say. It shouldn't be too hard to find him."

Rustin nodded in agreement.

7

It was about five in the afternoon the next day when Rustin Kemp and Tom Mecana found the address they were looking for. The bartender at Griffin's gave them a name and a police rap sheet gave them the address, 2410 East Fairmont. The old houses on the street had seen better days.

Two teenage boys wearing ass-hugger pants, cowboy caps turned backwards and fancy-looking Nike shoes quickly walked away. The Explorer had a plain-Jane honky look with two white dudes in it. It was like 'COPS' was written all over it. Mecana spotted the number they were looking for and motioned to Rustin to pull over. He parked and they got out.

Rustin managed to make it up the two rickety steps to the front door, and Mecana went around to the back. Rustin moved to one side of the door and knocked on it. No answer. He glanced at the big Harley Davidson sitting in the driveway. Someone was home. Nobody would leave a Harley unattended in this neighborhood.

About the time Rustin started to knock on the door again, it flew open and a young, tall, thin black man, with bushy hair and wearing jeans and a t-shirt, ran by him and headed for the Harley.

Mecana came charging around the corner from the back of the house and tackled him. He fell onto the side of the Harley and knocked it over. Mecana jumped up, drew his gun and yelled at the young man. "Police!

Stay on the ground and put your hands on your head!"

"Shit!" the young man exclaimed, and stretched his arms up on his head.

Rustin made his way down the steps and walked up beside Mecana, who still had his Glock pointed at the man on the ground. "Your name DeMax Baker?" Rustin asked.

"Yeah," he said, eyeing Rustin.

"Street name 'Stitch?'"

"Some folks call me that."

"You got some ID?"

"My back pocket."

Rustin leaned on his cane, reached down and removed DeMax's wallet and looked at his drivers license, then dropped the wallet on the ground beside him. "Okay, why you running, DeMax?"

"Didn't know you were cops. Thought you were some of them drug dealers, come to rob me."

"You got some stuff they want, DeMax?" Mecana asked.

"Ain't no dealer."

"You don't sound too convincing."

"Got nothing else to say. Can I get up?"

Mecana holstered his Glock, pulled handcuffs off his belt, stuck the wallet back in DeMax's pants, clamped the handcuffs on his wrist and lifted him to his feet.

A chubby-faced black woman in an old white Ford Taurus stopped in the middle of the street and stuck her head out the window, watching.

DeMax looked Rustin over. "Didn't know cripples could be cops."

"Shut up," Mecana said.

"You know a Barbara Sadler, DeMax?" Rustin asked.

"Might," he said.

"Did you know she's dead?"

"Yeah, saw it on TV this mornin'."

"The bartender at Griffin's said you were Kinky's boyfriend. You don't seem very broken up over the fact she's dead," Rustin said.

"Ain't nothin' I can do for you cops to find the mudderfucker who did it. Me and Kinky hooked up a few times, don't know if you could say we boyfriend-girlfriend."

"She seemed to think so. Said you broke up. Why?" Mecana said.

DeMax twisted his head, looked off into space for a moment then back to Mecana. "Met her a couple of months ago at Griffin's. Hit it off, and everything was cool until last week. Wanted me take her to a swingers party. You know, group sex, everybody fuckin' everybody. Not this dude. I do my fuckin' in private, so I split."

"I don't believe you," Mecana said.

"Why you think they call her Kinky, man? She's into that sort of thing."

"You're lying," Mecana shoved DeMax and he stumbled backwards and fell down.

DeMax rolled over and looked up at Mecana. "Check it out, man. I'm not the only one who knows."

"I will," Mecana said. "Get up." Mecana reached down, grabbed DeMax's arm and pulled him to his feet. The lady in the Ford shook her head and drove on down the street.

"Where were you last Monday night?" Rustin asked.

"My new girlfriend's place. There all night."

"What's her name and address?" Mecana asked.

"Judy Blackwell, 1342 East Cross Street. Got a roommate, too. Her name's Sara Moore. She was there from about midnight on that night. Don't know nothin' about what happened to Kinky, man, I swear."

"We'll see," Mecana said.

"You know a Julie Crawford, DeMax?"

"Not that I remember."

"You didn't know she was one of the victims?" Mecana said.

"Nope."

"We may need to talk to you again, DeMax," Rustin said. "We didn't see any open warrants on you but we could probably find one if we looked hard enough especially if you don't cooperate."

"You sure you're not dealing, DeMax?" Mecana said.

"Ain't goin' there, man."

"Let me rephrase that," Mecana said. "That Harley didn't come out of a Cracker Jack box. You've been picked up for drugs before. How you get your money?"

"I deliver pizzas for Big Top Pizza; pick up some money at Griffin's when they need an extra bartender. That how I met Kinky."

"You don't seem like the intellectual type, DeMax," Rustin said. "If you're not dealing, how come you're hanging out at a college bar?"

"Same reason any guy would - pussy. Lots of it and a lot of those rich white college chicks got money like Kinky. They like us brothers 'cause we got a little extra, if you know what I mean."

Mecana and Rustin looked at each other. There wasn't much they could say to that.

Mecana took the handcuffs off DeMax.

"Remember, DeMax, you be around if we need you. You got it?"

Rustin said.

"Yeah. Got it. Think I broke some'n on my Harley. You goin' to pay for it? Your fault."

Rustin and Mecana grinned at each other. "I don't think so," Rustin said as they walked toward the Explorer.

"What you think, Mecana?" Rustin asked.

"If I was a betting man I would say no. This guy's mostly a street crook and cock hound. I don't think he's into that sort of thing. Of course, that's just what I think. I've been wrong before; we'll have more to go on when we get the lab results. We might pay them a visit and see where they are with it."

"Good, I'm anxious to know what killed them," Rustin said.

8

Mecana and Rustin drove over to have a look at the evidence. They got off the elevator on the sixth floor, walked through double doors with 'County Medical Examiner' printed on them. A tall, thin man wearing a white coat with 'David Seymour, MD' on it stepped out into the hall from his office in front of Mecana and Rustin.

"I was going to call you," the doctor said. "Your timing's perfect."

"Naturally, Doc," Mecana said and smiled. "This is Rustin Kemp, Doctor Seymour, he's from Houston. He's the one that found the Belmont girl."

"I hope what I've got helps," Doctor Seymour said, looking at Rustin.

Doctor David Seymour was in his fifties, gray hair, ramrod straight. He walked like he had a corn cob up his ass. The veterans called him Doctor Frankenstein. Today was business as usual.

He sat down with Rustin and Mecana at the conference table, laid a large folder on a table and opened it. He placed his pencil point on a picture. "You see the incision here," he said, "the vagina was removed by someone who knew precisely what he was doing. The cut runs from the urinary bladder to the rectum. Maybe he did it to collect a grotesque trophy. I don't know what other reason he could have for doing it."

"I've heard that terrible stuff before, Doc," Rustin said.

"It could be the same person," Seymour said.

"So, we may be looking for a doctor," Rustin said.

"Possible, or someone that knows a lot about female anatomy," Seymour replied. "I looked at the evidence of the murdered girl in

Houston and the Crawford girl, also. It's not like a signature, but all three were done by skilled hands."

"That's a gruesome thought," Rustin said and cringed. "Did all of them die from the same thing?"

"They died from an overdose of tricyclic antidepressant. Better known as Ludimocson. The drug is out-dated, not prescribed anymore, but if someone had a supply. It would probably still be effective if it was sealed. I am convinced that whoever administered the drug knew its makeup. The effect is increased with the addition of alcohol. They were legally drunk when the drug was induced into their system. The Crawford girl had bicarbonate of soda in her blood. That increases the effect. She probably died quicker than the other two."

"How long did it take to kill them, Doc?" Mecana asked.

"Well, I can't say for sure, everyone's different, but they would have encountered blurred vision almost immediately. Gender has an effect. Estrogen in the female body speeds the effect. They would have had hallucinations and became disorientated shortly after the blurred vision, along with a number of other problems, before passing out. All of them probably died shortly after the drug was injected. If he wanted to keep any one of them alive longer," Seymour said, "he could have administered the drug in smaller quantities, and still have had a lethal dose if it was done in less than twenty-four hours. I think that may have been the case with the Belmont girl. They found several needle marks on her."

"Not only did this nut kill them," Mecana said, "but he knew it was the perfect drug to conceal his identity and render them helpless."

"Yes," Doctor Seymour said. "He knew what he was doing."

"I know this sounds ghoulish, Doc," Rustin said, "but do you think they could have been alive when they were mutilated?"

"No. The incision was too exact and smooth. Someone alive would have moved, the cut would have been jagged in some places. There's no sign of that here. There also wasn't any semen in any of them, and the vagina being removed left a lot of trauma to the abdominal cavities. Without semen and the other entire trauma to the body, I can't tell for sure if they were raped.

"The guy may have used a condom, or couldn't have sex. That may be part of his problem. One thing he did, though, was make sure he didn't leave any DNA."

"I know," Mecana said. "I checked out the cab driver, and the cab Kinky was in. The forensic boys also didn't find anything in the apartments of either girl. The bed was still made in both apartments; they never got home. I've talked to neighbors, friends and family. Nothing they didn't know each other, but they were beautiful, rich and liked to party. That has to tell us something, but so far I don't know what. You think the same person did all the killings, Doc?"

"I can't say with certainty; but from the evidence, I would say yes."

"This helps a lot, thanks," Mecana said.

"Where do you want me to send the lab bill, somebody has to pay for this, we can't."

"Send it to the Warfield Police Department, attention Chief David Orr," Mecana said.

"Okay. I'll let you know if I come up with anything else," Doctor Seymour said.

"Thanks, Doc, we'll see you later," Mecana said.

Doctor Seymour nodded, picked up the folder and left.

9

The sign on the door said 'Kevin E. Johnson - Hospital Administrator.' Diplomas from four different universities hung on the wall behind a large desk in a den-sized office with shiny hardwood floors. To the right of the desk - a big, closed, draped window hid a view of the hospital parking lot from the fourth floor. Seated at the desk was a neatly groomed six-foot forty-plus man with thinning blond hair. He was dressed in an expensive-looking brown suit tailored to fit his trim body. He glared intently at the two men seated on the other side of the desk for a couple of moments then spoke. "My secretary said you were policeman," he said. "What can I do for you gentleman?"

"Mr. Johnson, I'm Detective Thomas Mecana and this is my associate, Rustin Kemp. He's a former detective from Houston. We have been investigating the murders of three young women who-"

"Were they the ones they found in the river?" Johnson interrupted. "I read something about that."

"Two of them," Mecana said. "The first was in Houston. We believe they were all murdered by the same person. The evidence indicates that person could be a doctor, more specifically, a specialist like a gynecologist. We discovered a Doctor Dawson Durant took up residency here last October. He's the only GYN in the Dallas area that would have been in Houston at the time of the first murder. The murder victim in Houston was also a patient of his and was murdered on property owned by his father-in-law. We plan to spend some time checking out Doctor Durant and we wanted you to know."

"Are you saying you suspect Doctor Durant of theses crimes?"

"Let's just say he's a person of interest," Rustin said. "I am sure you have heard that before."

"Yes, I must say I am shocked. I don't know Doctor Durant well but his credentials are excellent. I know about the two frivolous lawsuits. We determined they were invalid before we let him come here. My nurses think he's extremely good-looking. I had one nurse say she would volunteer to be examined by him anytime he wanted." Johnson cut off a quick laugh and became serious again. "It seems unbelievable that he would be involved."

"He's probably not," Mecana said. "But life's full of surprises, so we have to cover all the bases. Whoever is murdering these young women does some hideous things to them. We have to stop him."

"Yes, I understand. Is there anything you would have me do?"

"No," Rustin said. "We wanted you to know when you saw us around why we were here. If it's alright with you we'll pretend to be maintenance employees. That gives us access to go anywhere."

Johnson nodded in agreement.

"Doctor Durant may not have had a thing to do with the murders, but he was in the right place at the right time. One of the murdered women was a patient of his. He was accused of sexual harassment by two of his former nurses and he is a GYN. All of that makes for an interesting combination. We'll need you to get his personal file for us."

Johnson leaned back in his chair and rubbed his chin. "The employee thing is okay but I'll need a court order to let you have his file."

"I'll get you one." Mecana said.

"Should I restrict his patient base?"

"No. We don't want to spook him," Mecana said. "Keep it business as usual. We'll have a tail on him for the next two weeks, at least. Don't do anything that might raise his suspicions."

"Is that it, Detective?" Johnson asked, and stood up from his desk. "I have a meeting I must attend."

Rustin and Mecana stood up. "That's it for now," Rustin said. "Thank you for your time. We will let you know what the outcome is."

"Good," he said and walked out from behind the desk.

"We can find our way out," Mecana said.

Johnson nodded and left the door open as he walked out of his office.

10

Chief Orr was going through speeding tickets from the night before when Mecana walked in. He stopped and gave Mecana a sour look. "What the hell are you doing having the examiner send me the lab invoice?" Orr asked. "Where do you think I am going to get the money? The budget they give me barely covers the salaries and the light bill."

"They're your murders, happened in your town. I couldn't very well send it to Dallas. There helping you out now by paying my salary. Which isn't enough, but that's another story. Write more tickets."

"I got two of the councilmen on my ass now because one of my dumbass patrolmen wrote their wives speeding tickets."

"You'll figure it out," Mecana said. "I need to set up a stakeout. Need two of your boys to help me."

"For how long?"

"Don't know."

"How am I going to write more tickets to pay for this bill if you take my guys away?"

"Write some yourself, instead of hanging out at the Beef Master."

"Who is this guy you want to watch?"

"His name's Doctor Dawson Durant."

Orr looked puzzled. "A doctor? You've got to be kidding."

"Nope. If he does anything suspicious, call me. Make sure he doesn't ID them or give them the slip. Here's a folder with his info and pictures. Be careful," Mecana dropped the folder on Orr's desk. "Me and Kemp will help you."

"I thought you didn't want Kemp on this?" Orr said.

"That was before I knew him. Brief your boys and be ready to go when I give you the word."

"I'll send Goodman home to get some sleep," Orr said. "Skinner can take first shift. He doesn't come in until 5 P.M. anyway."

"Whatever, just get it done," Mecana said.

"What makes you think it's a doctor, Mecana?"

"It's a long story. One I don't have time to tell you now."

"Alright, it's your call," Orr said.

"Good. Remember, don't try to arrest him without backup, no matter what he's done. You got me?"

"Yeah I got you," Orr said and reached for a Twinkie.

"Have you ever considered going to the gym and working a little of that fat off? You would feel better," Mecana said.

"What, and give up my standing in the Fat Man's Club?" Orr laughed and took a bite of Twinkie.

Mecana shook his head and left.

11

Mecana made contact with a real estate company to use an empty building not too far from the Durant Mansion as a lookout post. For the first three days, watching Durant was very routine. He got up, went to work and came home.

A stakeout could be one of the most boring things a cop could do. Sometime the boredom made you think too much. It was starting out that way for Rustin tonight. He couldn't get Debbie off his mind.

He parked behind Mecana's car, grabbed his flashlight and went in the 'For Lease' building to a big room with a clear view of the mansion several hundred yards away. "All quiet?"

"Not much to report," Mecana said. "He got home about six. His wife left soon after in the Lexus for somewhere. He's been in the house ever since. May have gotten lost in that place. It's as big as a hotel. Why would anyone want to live in something like that?"

"To impress. Show how rich they are," Rustin said.

Rustin bent down and took a look through the mounted binoculars on a tripod. "This guy has been a model citizen so far," he said. "We may be barking up the wrong tree."

"You never know."

Rustin's thoughts jumped back to his wife. "Mecana, you married?"

"Been divorced ten years. Spent too much time doing this sort of thing."

"I will be soon," Rustin said. "My wife left me. I think it was out of frustration more than anything. She didn't know how to deal with what happened to me. And I didn't have the patience to help her understand."

"Sometimes it's impossible to know why they do things," Mecana said. "In my case, it was easy to figure out. I took her for granted. Didn't spend enough time with my family or show them how much I loved them. The job came first. I was an asshole."

"I've been thinking about that," Rustin said. "After this is over, I think I'm going to get into another line of work. One that lets me come home at five and take the weekends off. Maybe she will take me back."

"This shit gets in your blood, buddy. You get hooked on the

adrenaline rush when you take a bad guy down or save a potential victim. You'll just wind up making you both unhappy."

"Maybe, but maybe not," Rustin said. "Why don't you call it a night, Mecana, I'll watch our boy. If anything happens I'll let you know."

"Alright. Hey, I'm sorry about what I said. If you think that will save your marriage that's what you should do. Call me if you need me."

"Will do. See you in the morning," Rustin said.

"One of Orr's boys will relieve you. I got to go to the office in the morning to brief the Chief. Call if you need me."

12

About eight-thirty that evening, Durant came out of the house wearing jeans, a pull-over red sweater and a brown suede jacket. Not the attire he generally wore when he went to the hospital. He got in his BMW and headed toward town, Rustin following. Instead of making a right turn for the hospital, he drove on by and hit the freeway toward Dallas.

The traffic was light. Durant pushed the BMW up to speeds of ninety and hundred. It was all Rustin could do to keep him in sight.

He slowed down about five miles down the freeway turned off an exit over a railroad track, into an old neighborhood with small brick and frame houses. He pulled over and stopped in front of a small brick house with a chain link fence around it; no car in the drive. He cut the BMW off, walked up on the porch to the front door, took a key out of his pocket and went in. A light came on in the house.

Rustin drove on by, turned around, cut his lights and pulled up to the curb a block away. He took his .38 out of its holster and placed his hand on the door handle. Images of the Belmont girl popped up in front of him like a billboard and he froze, dropped the gun in the floorboard and began to shake. He fumbled for his pain killers in his pocket, grabbed some pills and poked them in his mouth, swallowed and looked at the house. There wasn't time to call for backup, just like before. He pushed on the door handle again and the door swung open. A chill ran through him. He felt the knife, the pain, the blood soaking his back again. It was so real he threw up and slammed the door. He couldn't do it. He punched the re-dial on his phone and Mecana answered.

"I can't do it. I can't. I tried, but I can't," Rustin said, his hands shaking.

"What the hell are you talking about, Rustin?"

"I'm in Dallas. I think I found his killing place, but I need help."

"What's the address? I'll send a SWAT team."

"1422 South Novel," Rustin said, looking at the street sign.

"I'm on my way. If he leaves, follow, and let me know where. It's alright, we'll get him. Stay in the car."

Rustin shook uncontrollably. All he could see was Linda Belmont's eyes pleading for help.

Durant was still in the house, and he couldn't do a thing.

Five minutes later, he heard approaching sirens. Four squad cars and an armored wagon came flying down the street. Rustin slid down in the seat. Officers surrounded the house. People were running out into the streets from nearby houses in panic. Some were jumping in their cars and hauling ass. A big black guy with a hooded jacket came charging out of the house across the street firing a pump shotgun at the police, they had to take him down.

Durant appeared at the door. A spotlight hit him and someone tossed a tear gas canister on the porch. Two SWAT team members, wearing gas masks, rushed in and knocked him to the floor. One put an assault rifle to his head. The other one handcuffed him. They jerked him to his feet and rushed him to a nearby cruiser and shoved him in the back seat.

Cops ran in the house from front and back. A couple minutes later, they came out with an old white-haired man wrapped in a blanket. His hands shaking, his eyes rolling around like marbles. An ambulance showed up shortly afterward. The dead black guy was put in the ambulance, the old white-haired man in a squad car, and they all left. It was all over in less than ten minutes. Several of the locals were still roaming around the street in a daze, wondering what the hell just happened.

13

Two men were standing inside a glass-paneled office, talking and gesturing at each other. One was Tom Mecana and the other one Assistant Police Chief for Homicide Robert Verves, a five-foot-six black man with a voice like the Jolly Green Giant.

From outside the office, the only thing you could tell for sure was they were mad. From the inside all hell was breaking loose.

"What were you thinking, Mecana, letting a civilian attempt to arrest a suspect that you didn't have any reason to be after in the first place?"

Verves said, placing both hands on his desk, shaking his shaved black head like a bobblehead doll.

"He's not a civilian. He's a trained combat solider, a certified police officer for the State of Texas and a licensed private eye."

"All of which does not qualify him to be on this case," Verves said. "On top of that, you tell me he panicked and you had to rescue him!"

"It wasn't a rescue. It was providing backup like we're supposed to."

"To arrest a man that went to his grandfather's house to check on him? Come on, Mecana, let's get real."

"He was under surveillance. Rustin didn't know that. Why the hell is a doctor's grandpa living in a place like that anyway?"

"Because it's his home. He has lived there for forty years. That's why the good doctor transferred his practice to Dallas to take care of the old man until he died. Did it ever occur to you to check that out?"

"No, not really," Mecana ran his hand through his hair.

"Well I did. There was no way he could have committed the Houston murder. He was in Los Angeles for a seminar. And it looks like he was with his brother when the Crawford girl was killed. Not sure about the Sadler murder yet, but it looks like you're way off track."

"I wouldn't be too sure of that. I've seen a lot of arranged alibis."

"We could be in deep shit over this, Mecana."

"For doing our job?"

"You didn't do it right."

"You want this damn badge?" Mecana took his badge off and slammed it on the desk, then turned to walk out.

"No, hard head, I don't want your badge. I think we dodged a bullet. I told the doctor we were there to arrest the shooter from across the street and mistakenly went to the wrong house. I think he bought it. We may have got lucky and avoided a lawsuit as big as Mount Rushmore. The guy we took down was wanted for murder. He thought we were there for him. We sure as hell can't afford to have Kemp on this anymore. You understand, Mecana?"

"Rustin Kemp has been though hell," Mecana said. "I don't know if I could have handled it any better if I had been through the same."

"Mecana, I can sympathize with the boy. I want the murderer caught just as bad as he does. But we can't let Kemp continue on the case. You can let him be an advisor. Talk to him about the case, but he can't be out in the field with us. He will get us both fired, and maybe even get himself killed."

Mecana let out a big sigh and shook his head. "As much as I hate to admit it, I know you're right, Chief."

"Alright then, lets move on, enough about that," Verves said. "Do you know Darcie Connors?"

"No, should I?" Mecana asked.

"She's been working on the abused wife case we just wrapped up. Good cop."

"What are you telling me, Chief?"

"She's your new partner, like it or not."

"Well, it's not, but I know when to eat crow. Could use some help keeping an eye on Griffin's."

"What I thought. I have already talked to the owner. He knows to keep it quiet. We'll have her go to work there as a waitress. Here's her number, call her so you two can get acquainted."

"Okay, in the meantime I'll keep an eye on the doctor. There's something about that dude that's not right."

"What did I tell you, Mecana? Leave the guy alone. It's not him."

"I'll make it very indiscreet."

"You're going to give me an ulcer, Mecana. I should fire you now."

"Your call, Chief."

"Go away, let me die in peace," Verves sat down in his chair and put his head in his hands.

Mecana grinned, blew Verves a kiss, and walked out of the office.

14

Mecana had on his US Marines sweatshirt, gym shorts and running shoes, going nowhere on a treadmill. There was something calming to Mecana about working up a sweat in the gym. It energized him and cleared his head. He needed a clear head right now. He had asked Rustin Kemp to meet him at the gym. He got there early to work off his frustrations and think about what he was going to say to Rustin.

Rustin had put him back on the right path when he wanted to quit, now he was going to have to tell him to quit. Maybe he should hang it up, too, and let someone else give Verves an ulcer. The difference was Rustin may still have a shot at saving his marriage and a future if he quit. He didn't have anything but unemployment. He was nothing without his badge.

He elevated the treadmill and increased his speed. An overweight guy next to him looked at Mecana's muscular body, smiled and cranked his treadmill up.

Rustin came in and saw Mecana on the treadmill. He shuffled over to him, looked at Mecana and grinned.

Mecana cut the treadmill, got off, picked up a towel and wiped his sweaty face.

The fat guy cut his treadmill, staggered over to a chair and sat down, huffing and puffing.

"There was a time I would have kicked your butt good in a gym," Rustin said. "Was a quarterback - a damn good one. Then I quit college and got married. My old man wanted me to be a pro. But you know how it is, love conquers all, or some garbage like that. Next thing I know I'm chasing a crackhead down an alley and discover Linda Belmont about to die, and I almost did. How do you explain something like that?"

"You don't," Mecana said. "It's like when you're driving down a county road and a squirrel runs out in front of you. One second sooner, or one second later, and he lives to be an old nut-gathering squirrel. But that's not what happened. Why was it you? Why at that precise moment? Why that squirrel? There's not a reason for it, it's a thing called fate. That's what life is. We're all victims of fate, good and bad."

"Well, it sure has some lingering effects."

"That's why I asked you to come by. I have something to tell you. You deserve to hear it without the candy-coating I had planed on. The other night's events had some lingering effects. The doctor may try to sue the city. My boss is pretty upset. I'm going to have to ask you to go home and let me take care of this. We fucked up and they're making you the scapegoat. It's just as much my fault as yours, but they want you to take the fall. I offered my badge but it didn't make any difference. It's probably for the best. You said you were going get into something else. Go home, and start over with your wife."

"I can't go home. I will have to do it by myself," Rustin said. "I wasn't prepared for the emotional consequences of the other night. I am now. It won't happen again. I don't have a life until I can put this thing behind me. I have to find the killer of that young lady. It's my fault she's dead."

"I don't think you were listening, Rustin. You have no authority here. They will put your ass in jail. Then what will you do? You can stick around if you want, I'll keep you informed. But you can't get in the way of this case."

"Mecana, I know you went to bat for me. I appreciate that. But I have to do this. I know that may be hard for you to understand but I don't have a choice. I have nothing else."

"I know what you're saying, but there's nothing I can do. My hands are tied," Mecana wiped his face again; Houston tossed the towel over his shoulder. "Sorry, headed for the shower."

15

Mecana was walking toward his truck in the parking lot when his phone rang. It was Rustin.

"Mecana, I want you to find that bastard for me. You're right, I can't do it alone. I'm not able. The best thing for me to do is check out."

"Where you going?"

"To hell, probably," he said and was gone.

Mecana stared at his phone in thought. "What the hell did he mean by that?" Mecana thought. "Damn, he's going to kill himself."

He attempted to call Rustin three times, but no answer. He fired up the Silverado and took off like Silver for the Sunset Motel.

Mecana saw Rustin's Explorer parked in front of Room 38. The room was dark. He cut the Silverado off, got out and rushed to the door, knocked; no answer.

Then he yelled, "Rustin, you in there?" Still no answer. He raised his leg and kicked the door as hard as he could and it flew open. Rustin was lying on the floor beside the bed, fully clothed but unconscious. Mecana flipped the lights on and bent down and checked Rustin's pulse. He was breathing. He looked for wounds and saw none; he dialed 911. A few minutes later, an ambulance arrived, put Rustin on a ventilator, and he rode to the hospital with him.

After two hours, a tired-looking young black doctor came out and asked if anyone was with Rustin Kemp.

"I am," Mecana said.

"I'm Doctor Kelly. Mr. Kemp took an overdose of pain killers. He had an empty prescription bottle in his pocket. We pumped his stomach and put him on an IV. He had three times the amount of the drug in his system that he should have. If you had not found him when you did he would have died. We will keep him for a couple of days, make sure there's no further complications before we release him. He may need treatment if it was intentional. You can talk to him about that."

Mecana camped in Rustin's hospital room until he woke up. When he did he was drowsy and confused. "Where the hell am I?" Rustin asked, wide-eyed.

"You're in a hospital. You did a foolish thing. Let's don't do that again. It takes too much out of me."

"Oh yeah, I remember. Figured the world was better off without me."

"Hey, no skin off my ass, but you're the one that told me not to give up. You disappointed me."

"Don't have much to live for," Rustin said.

"That's a shitty answer. What about your family, your wife?"

"My wife could care less."

"I don't think so. I found her number in your wallet and called her. She should be here any time. You need to get your damn act together, buddy boy, and quit feeling sorry for yourself. There's a lot of people worse off than you are. Besides, we got a killer to catch."

"You had no right to call my wife."

"Then who does? You do this 'poor pitiful me' bit and everyone is supposed to ignore it? I don't think so. You want me to butt out, fine, but have the guts to face your problems. Let me know when you grow a backbone." Mecana got up, pushed the chair back angrily and left.

A nurse walked in and stuck a thermometer in Rustin's mouth and wrapped a blood pressure strap around his arm.

"I wish to hell everybody would leave me alone. They don't have to live in my skin,

I don't want to live any more."

"Mr. Kemp, everything is going to be alright," the nurse said.

"No, it's not. Go away," he said.

"Your blood pressure is going sky high; you're going to have to calm down," the nurse said.

"Get the hell out!"

The nurse backed off with a frightened look. "I'll go get the doctor," she said and left.

16

Debbie walked in the room, dressed in a blue sweater and jeans. Her long blonde hair resting on her shoulders, she looked like she could still be a cheerleader if she wanted to.

She looked at Rustin, then took a depth breath "Mr. Mecana said you needed me."

Rustin nervously looked at Debbie. He wanted to jump out of the bed and take her in his arms and kiss her passionately, but he wasn't sure she would want him to. "Mr. Mecana should mind his own business," he said.

"You want me here or not?"

"Only if you want to be."

"I tried to help before but you shut me out. I felt like I didn't matter, our love didn't matter. You were only interested in what was happening to you. I couldn't take it any more."

"I thought you resented me for being a cripple; didn't love me."

"Rustin, I have loved you since I was six years old. You think I could just turn that off?"

"You think I'm nuts," he said.

"I think your feelings of guilt have got the best of you. But you're just as much a victim as she was, it's not your fault she's dead."

"If I had been the cop I should have been it would have never happened. I failed her. I'll never get over that."

"No one expects you to, but you can't destroy your life and mine because of it. We all make mistakes. Sometimes the consequences are horrible, but that's life. We don't know what our fate is," Debbie said.

"That's what Mecana said. Gave me some corny analogy about a squirrel."

"He's right. It's not the end of the world. I'm sorry for the lady and her family, but I'm sorry for us too. Life goes on, if you let it."

"I don't know what to say. I'm sorry for what I put you through," Rustin said.

The door opened and Doctor Kelly walked in. "Mr. Kemp, I'll take your vitals and if everything is okay, I'll remove your IV and you can go home. We're not going to keep you against your will. I don't have the authority to do that. But I can tell you, you need treatment," he said. "I can call the rehabilitation center for you if you want an appointment to have a psychiatrist get you into rehab. It's up to you."

Rustin looked at Debbie. Debbie smiled and nodded her head yes.

"Thank you," he said. "Please do that. The sooner the better."

"Very well. I'll remove the IV. Get dressed and I'll make the call."

PART TWO
Linda Longstreet

1

Mecana stuck his Glock in the nightstand, went to bed and tossed and turned all night, thinking about Rustin, and his new partner. He was going to have to call her before Verves gave him another ass chewing.

He got up early, picked up a cup of coffee at Seven Eleven and stopped off at the hospital to check on Rustin. Before going to Psychiatrist Rupert P. Wyler's office, he went barreling into the room to discover a fat lady uncovered on the bed in a short nightgown.

The view was not a pretty sight.

He apologized as he backed out of the room then stopped at a nurse's station. They told him Rustin left with his wife and checked into the Fort Worth Addiction Clinic. Maybe the boy was going to be alright after all, he thought. A pudgy Hispanic receptionist was answering phone calls in English and Spanish in the outer office at Doctor Wyler's, as Mecana sat waiting his turn.

A reproduction of Norman Rockwell's 'Doctor/Little Boy' painting hung on one wall, a TV mounted on another had Wild Kingdom on. A lion chasing an antelope that was running for his life.

A middle-aged man in a business suit walked out of the doctor's office with a wild-eyed expression and disappeared out the front door.

The receptionist rose up from her desk and motioned for Mecana to go in.

A little man wearing a white shirt, red bowtie, blue suspenders and Einstein-looking bushy white hair with a matching mustache was engrossed in a paper he was reading. He pointed to a chair for Mecana to sit down without looking up, and kept reading. Mecana sat down and waited to be recognized like a schoolboy.

Doctor Wyler coughed and dropped the paper on his cluttered desk and looked at Mecana.

"I've been expecting you, Mecana. I was reading the examiner's report on the victims again. You've got a real dingbat this time," he made circler motions with his index finger.

"Looks like it, Doc. I–"

"Don't call me Doc. I hate that," he interrupted and shivered. "Rupert will be fine."

"Sorry, Rupert, didn't mean any disrespect."

"I just have a thing about it, gives me the willies. Now, what were you saying?" he asked, adjusting his bright blue suspenders.

"I was saying I hope you can give me some insight into what this nut's about."

Doctor Wyler leaned back in his chair and ran his hand through his bushy hair. "This one is something special. Schizophrenic most likely, and a chronic insomniac. I would suspect some kind of trauma at an early age. Perhaps a parent was murdered and mutilated, or he was the murderer. Something that blew his mind into another orbit, where the monster now lives.

"He's probably perfectly normal most of the time. Then something triggers it, and he becomes this 'Jekyll and Hyde'-type person. People like him appear to be in control but, there's a storm brewing inside of them all the time, waiting to explode. I would think he would be an average size male in his late-thirties or early-forties. The drugs and knife indicate a need for added confidence. You might look at the drug. It's outdated. Where would he get it, or did he already have a supply? I understand why he's using it, fits his crime perfectly. The potency of a drug that old, I would question, but that's not my area of expertise."

"The Medical Examiner said he thought the drug would be effective if it was sealed," Mecana said.

"He should know," Wyler said.

"Anything else, Doc? Oh, sorry, Rupert."

"He'll continue to kill. Most likely using the same MO. The time between his first and second victim is a bit confusing. He may be trying to stop killing but can't. The bottom line is I would look for a highly educated person, not necessarily a doctor, but someone who has enough knowledge of female anatomy to perform surgery. That's part of the reason for the mutilations. He's proud of his skill, maybe more than a doctor would be. That's why he does it, and the possibility, of course, that it has something to do with a warped sexual fantasy. He may not be able to have sexual intercourse, and instead gets his 'jollies' from the murder and mutilation."

Doctor Wyler dug a folder off of his cluttered desk and handed it to Mecana. "This is my official report. It has some technical jargon in it, in case we have to go to court, but basically it's what I told you. It's only a question of time before he does it again, if you don't catch him."

"You confirmed what I already knew, Rupert. The trick is catching him."

"Alright, but I am still sending my bill to the city."

Mecana grinned, stood up with the folder, shook hands with Wyler and left.

He tossed the report on the truck seat and took a few minutes to work up the courage to call his new partner.

"Hi," he said. "This Darcie Connors?"

"Your ID say's Tom Mecana. I've been waiting for your call," she said.

"Thought we better meet, get started," Mecana said. "How about the Warfield Police Station around one-thirty this afternoon?"

"Good," she said. "See you there."

2

Mecana pulled up to the Warfield Police Station at one-twenty-five in the afternoon. A new black unmarked Charger was parked next to Orr's car. It had that Government Issue look. He assumed it belonged to Darcie Connors. When he walked in he wasn't prepared for what he saw. She was thirty-something, wearing a chic black dress with short, shiny black hair. Big, soft, brown eyes, delicious-looking red lips and a body designed for a man's temptation.

She must not have been there long because David Orr was still trying to get the smile off his face.

She spotted Mecana, glided toward him with hips swaying and high heels tapping out a three-quarter-time sonata on the hardwood floor.

Not what he expected at all. He waited for the lady to extend her hand. It was soft and smooth with long red nails.

He shook hands with her. "Tom Mecana," he said, holding on to her hand. "Been hearing good things about your work."

"I hear you're one of the best," she said, retrieving her hand. "It's a privilege to meet you."

Mecana gave her that 'aw shucks' look, gestured toward a chair for her to sit down and laid the profile on the table.

After Darcie was seated, he sat down and pointed to the folder. "Why don't you take that home and read it. Have you ever worked on a case like this?"

"No, mostly domestic cases. Still fighting the stigma of being a woman. That's why I wanted this case, gives me a chance to break the mold."

"We got a real sicko here," he said.

"You're the expert. I'll follow your lead. Tell me what you want me to do."

"Our best bet is to have you go undercover at Griffin's Bar and Grill. Do you have any family here?"

"No. Divorced, no kids. My family lives in Waco. I come from a long line of educators. Mom and Dad are retired school teachers A sister and a brother, both teachers."

"I'm divorced too," Mecana said. "Have two daughters in Austin, no family here. My old man's a retired Marine Colonel. My mother's deceased. Have a brother that's a Marine Major. Not having family here takes some pressure off. Makes it less complicated. We only have to worry about each other."

"I'm ready to go," Darcie said and tapped the folder.

"Chief Verves set up a job for you at Griffin's. I'll follow you to work, and home after every shift, to make sure this nut hasn't figured out what we're doing. Keep a gun and phone handy at all times. If anything suspicious happens, let me know. Do not try to apprehend a suspect by yourself."

"When do we start?" she asked.

"How about tomorrow to give you time to read the profile and ask any questions you might have."

"Sounds good. I'm looking forward to working with you, Tom."

"Thanks. Call me Mecana, everyone does."

"Alright, Mecana," she said.

"How long you been a cop?" Mecana asked.

"A little over six years. Thought I wanted to be a lawyer. I didn't. After a couple years of practice and a divorce, I got bored, wound up being a cop."

"Okay, tomorrow. Let's meet at the McDonalds down the street, say eight-thirty. Being the big spender I am, I'll buy breakfast."

"My, you are gracious," Darcie smiled, got up and extended her soft hand again. They shook hands. She picked up the folder, waved at Chief Orr and was gone.

"Damn," Orr said. "If there had been lookers like that on the force when I was there I never would have left."

"She is pretty, isn't she," Mecana said.

"Pretty is not a strong enough word." Orr said.

Mecana had mixed emotions about his new partner, especially a woman. The last time he had a female partner she decided to break down crying right in the middle of a gun battle. This one sounded more confident. It wouldn't take long to find out.

"Orr, I want you and your men to be ready to assist us in case the killer shows up at Griffin's, and I don't want any excuses. You don't answer our call and I'll have you before the boys across the street to fire your ass," Mecana warned.

"Don't worry about us. We'll be there," Orr said.

"You damn well better be."

"Quit worrying, Mecana. I may not look the part but I know how to be a cop."

Mecana nodded and walked out the door.

3

Mecana made several suggestions on what aliases Darcie should use at Griffin's, none of which she liked. She applied some kind of female logic that Mecana didn't understand and said, "A woman has to like who she is even if that's not who she is."

"Yogi Berra would have been proud," Mecana mumbled to himself.

She finally decided on Linda Longstreet because she thought it sounded poetic.

She went to work the late shift, when the young ladies would be the most vulnerable. Mecana hung out at a nearby pool hall. He instructed Darcie to call immediately if anything suspicious happened. Nothing did for over a week. Both got red-eyed from loss of sleep.

On a Friday night the following week, at half past eleven, Mecana was about to take a shot at the eight ball, when Darcie called. She said she was watching the parking lot camera and a young woman left the bar alone and was being approached in the parking lot by a man with a knife.

"Call for back up, Darcie," Mecana said. "I'm on the way."

In less than three minutes, Mecana came speeding up in the Silverado and got out with his Glock in hand.

A big man wearing a hooded coat and jeans was trying to force a woman into an old blue Ford van at knifepoint. The man saw Mecana coming at him. The woman screamed and the man broke into a run across the parking lot, knocking a couple down as he ran by. He ran across another parking lot, into a clump of trees, and flung the knife and something else away. He tried to jump a four-foot-tall chain link fence, caught his heel and fell over to the other side. By the time he got to his knees, Mecana jumped the fence and had a gun pointed at his head.

"Police! Get on the ground, hands on your head!" Mecana jerked his coat back and showed the badge on his belt. The man hesitated. "Get down, asshole, last time before I blow your shit away!" The man looked at Mecana's cold gray eyes, got the message and lay down on the ground. Mecana squatted down, put his knee in the man's back, clamped handcuffs on him and searched him. He had an expired Nevada driver's license and some change in his pockets. His name was Luther Leroy Davidson, age thirty-four.

Two Warfield units came flying up beside him. Two officers got out, guns drawn.

Darcie came running up with her Beretta in one hand and her badge in the other. "We got him, Mecana," she said.

Mecana nodded, holstered the Glock, and worked on getting a deep breath.

The officers got Davidson to his feet and sat him down in the back of a squad car.

"He threw away the knife and something else back there," Mecana said. "Why don't you read him his rights, Darcie, I'll go look for it," Mecana said.

One of the officers overheard Mecana and pulled a Miranda Rights card out of his shirt pocket and handed it to Darcie. She walked over to the car and opened the door and looked in at Davidson.

"I'm going to read you your rights," she said.

"Fuck you, bitch!" he said, and scooted over in the seat away from her.

4

Darcie and Mecana were waiting in the conference room when Verves walked in. "Well, we got a bad guy, but not the one we were looking for. Luther Davidson served five years for attempted sexual assault. He was released from a Nevada prison last week. Didn't take him long to try it again. I turned the knife and crack over to property."

"I figured that out by the time I took him down," Mecana said. "Won't do any good to work Griffin's anymore. He will damn sure know what we're doing now."

"I agree," Verves said. "We have to widen our search. I'll try to hold off the press. The public is getting impatient. I can understand why. Go through the wrap sheets again, expand the search. There may be someone we overlooked before. Let me know if there's anything you need."

"We haven't run a check on the drug yet," Mecana said. "We need to do that. Find out if any doctors or medical personnel were being treated in Houston during the time the drug was being prescribed."

"I'll have the computer boys do that, let you know," Verves said. "Got to run. We can't leave a stone unturned. Find him."

"We'll do our best, Chief," Mecana said.

"That's all I can ask." He padded Mecana on the shoulder and left the room.

"I was reading about serial killers," Darcie said. "Most were flying under the radar before they were caught. People that appeared to be normal family men. They had their hobbies and extracurricular activities. Maybe this guy has a similar hobby to one of the known killers, that would give us a clue."

"Come on," Mecana said, mocking Darcie's comments. "Like I enjoy cutting up live chickens on the weekend to see them bleed, or roasting dogs over a camp fire, or being a clown like Gacy."

Darcie stared at Mecana, her dark brown eyes flashing. "What have you come up with besides checking drugs and a prominent doctor, Sherlock? We're no closer than when I joined this merry band."

Mecana shook his head, looked at the ceiling, then Darcie. "Sorry, Darcie. The guy is outsmarting us at every turn. I don't like that. It frustrates the living hell out of me."

"And you think it's Durant, in spite of his alibis?"

"Yep. Something about that guy's not right."

"Maybe so, but the chief said to expand our search with known sex offenders. Are you ready to do that?"

"Sure, I'm open to checking everything and everybody. Tell you what, let's start after lunch. I'll take you to someplace other than McDonalds. My treat."

Darcie smiled and shook her head at Mecana. "You are losing it."

"Not really. I thought I would take you to Brogans. They have a discount lunch special every Thursday." They both laughed.

5

After lunch, Mecana and Darcie checked files of known sex offenders, especially the ones with a history of violence.

Darcie ran the mouse on her computer down the page and something caught her eye. "I think I got something, Mecana," she said. "This guy's crime was fifteen years ago for rape and attempted murder. His name is Simon Carter. He's Caucasian, a former hospital orderly, forty-two-years-old. He was paroled a little over a year ago after serving seventeen years; that means he was on the street when the murders were committed."

"Yeah, let me see that." Mecana moved closer to Darcie and looked at the screen. "A parole board let him out for good behavior," he said. "That's like letting a rattlesnake back in the bushes. He left his victim for dead in a field after he stabbed and raped her." Mecana paused and grimaced. "My god, he stabbed her twenty times. Somehow she managed to crawl to the edge of the highway and a passing motorist saw her and called 911. She survived. Damn, that lady has guts. She even testified against him. He was given fifteen-to-life. The victim moved out of state after her testimony. His last known address was in the Dallas area. He's working at the Green Way Landscape Company as a laborer."

"How can supposedly-smart men and women let someone like that out on the street again?" Darcie asked. "It boggles my mind. Common sense would tell you no."

"You are naïve, partner, it's all about money - getting it and not getting it, depending on your agenda. Let's go have a talk with this rehabilitated citizen."

Mecana parked the Silverado in the space marked 'Visitor' and he and Darcie got out and went in a small portable building with an office sign.

A large lady with short brown hair was sitting in an oversized chair holding a phone to her ear; with a computer monitor on her desk, flashing a solitaire card game. A sign on her desk said 'SHIRLEY NEWMAN -

53

MANGER.'

"I know the tree is blocking your driveway, Mr. Owens," she said, "but I can't get anyone out there until tomorrow." She jerked the phone away and rubbed her ear. "Jerk." She put the phone down. "I hope you don't have an emergency," she said, looking up at Mecana and Darcie. "The thunderstorm yesterday has got us running our tail off."

"No, nothing like that. We're from the police. We called you earlier to verify you have an employee by the name of Simon Carter. We need to have a talk with him."

She tried to cross her legs, couldn't and dropped her leg back down. "What now? One of you guys shows up every time there's a sex crime?"

"Yes we do. Where is he?" Mecana asked.

"He's with a crew on Early Street, off LBJ Freeway. Bunch of trees down, we're trying to clean it up."

"Thanks, we'll find it," Darcie said, and they turned to leave.

"Wait, I'll call him to come in, don't want the police going to my work site."

"Okay, but don't tell him we're here," Mecana said.

The fat lady nodded, picked up her phone and dialed. "Stormy, I need Carter in here now, I'll explain later," she said. "Have him take your truck and you come in with the crew." She punched the phone off and set it back on her desk. "Okay he's on his way."

An hour-and-a-half later, Carter still hadn't arrived.

"How long should it take for Carter to get here?" Darcie asked.

"Should have been here half hour ago," Shirley said.

"Has he got a phone, or one in the truck?" Darcie said.

"No, we use cell phones. Don't think he has one."

"He must have figured out what was going on," Mecana said. "You got the number of your truck?"

"Yeah, sure." She reached in a drawer and took out a copy of the registration and handed it to Mecana.

"Thanks, we'll let you know where your truck is when we find it. If he shows up, or you hear from him, let us know." Mecana handed her a card. "To be on the safe side, don't let him see that card or hear you call. If he wants to know why you had him come in, send him over to Mr. Owens' house," Mecana smiled.

Shirley smiled back. "I'll do that."

"You may need a new employee," Mecana said.

"Hope I don't need a new truck," she replied.

"Me too," Mecana said.

6

Mecana got on the radio and gave the dispatcher the license number of the Green Way truck, with a warning it may be stolen and that the man driving is a parolee by the name of Simon Carter. "He could be armed and dangerous." Mecana requested back up to 1457 North Maple as soon as possible. He would be waiting. "No sirens. I repeat, no sirens."

"Why would he run before we talk to him?" Darcie asked.

"Fear, for whatever reason. The crimes we're investigating, another one, or going back to prison; I would think any one of the three would do it. We'll go to his house. If he's running, he may go there to get whatever he considers important before he bugs out."

The white and green Green Way pickup was sitting in the driveway. No one was in it.

Mecana parked on the street a block away. "Well, we know we got the right address," he said.

"Should we wait for back up?" Darcie asked.

"Yes, but let's get in position before he knows anyone is here. When the back up arrives, we'll go in after him."

Mecana motioned for Darcie to go around to the back. She nodded and drew her Beretta. Mecana took a position beside the door, drew his Glock and waited for Darcie to get in place.

Two cruisers came roaring up, making all kinds of noise. The cops jumped out, drew their revolvers and leaned over the hood, pointing them at the door.

Mecana held his badge up. "Must be rookies," he said to himself. He made a downward motion with his arm for the uniforms to lower their weapons and they did.

"Carter, it's the police," Mecana spoke into the speaker. "Come out with your hands in the air."

No answer.

"Come out of there, Carter. Now. We need to talk, you're not under arrest."

Still no answer.

Mecana motioned for a cop to move to the back of the house to join Darcie; the other one to stay put. He holstered his Glock, stepped back and kicked the lock off, and the door opened and swung inside the house. Mecana drew his gun again and ran in the house, the cop right behind him. Darcie and the other cop busted in the backdoor. They moved through the house room by room, still no one. Darcie saw a light under a basement door and pointed it out. Mecana tried to turn the doorknob, but it was locked. Again, he stepped back, only this time he kept the Glock in his hand and gave a big kick to the door. The wood splintered. The door came open, bullets whizzed by his head and he dropped down on the floor.

"Get back!" he yelled to Darcie and the young cops.

The windows of the room were covered with black paint. There was a single overhead light. A rugged-looking man with a shaved head had a rifle pointed at Mecana and a knife stuck in his belt. He was standing in front of a naked girl with a chain around her ankle tied to the wall. Her hands cuffed behind her back, a ball gag in her mouth tied around her head.

"Drop the gun Carter, now!" Mecana said. Darcie and the cops were crouched beside the door.

Carter raised the rifle to fire again. Mecana put three quick rounds in his left shirt pocket. He dropped the rifle and fell to all fours, blood spilling out across the floor. He looked at Mecana, reached for the rifle with a blood covered trembling hand, made a painful moan and fell to the floor with a thud.

The girl was screaming hysterically, but the sound was muffled by the gag, saliva trickling out the sides of her mouth. Her big blue eyes rolling around like a pinball machine. She looked like an attractive blonde teenager, maybe fourteen or fifteen, small cuts and bruises all over her body.

Darcie came rushing in and wrapped her coat around the girl, holding her. She stared at Darcie, her blue eyes wide with fear. Darcie started talking to her. "You're alright. You're safe, were cops."

The hysterical girl collapsed to the floor, Darcie sliding down with her, holding the coat around her. She rolled her eyes back in her head and passed out.

"Call an ambulance," Darcie said to the young cop.

Mecana checked Carter. He was dead. He holstered his Glock and moved over to Darcie and the girl. "How's she doing?"

"She needs a doctor."

"The ambulance is on the way," Mecana said.

"How did he know?" Darcie asked, her arms around the unconscious girl.

"Don't know. Being called in may have never happened before, and having the girl here made him suspicious," Mecana said.

"I think we got our killer, Mecana," Darcie said.

"Don't know. One thing's for sure, he won't do it again."

Darcie looked down at the unconscious girl. "Poor thing. Hope she's okay."

"Yeah, looks like she's been through a hell of an ordeal. Go get some cutters out of your car, officer," Mecana said to the young cop. "Let's get this damn stuff off her."

The cop nodded and left the room.

Mecana looked around the room at the mattress on the floor, two sets of shackles, and various sex toys on a table with a stack of porno magazines. An assortment of food trash was piled in the corner. The strong smell of urine filled the room.

"You know, Darcie, she's not the only one that's been in this room. No telling what he's done here. I don't know how they do it, but people like him seem to have some kind of radar for spotting troubled kids."

"Unfortunately, it's a sick world," Darcie said. "I wish that damn ambulance would get here. This kid's shaking like a leaf."

"They will be here in a minute. From the way you're mothering that kid you might reconsider having some," Mecana said.

"I don't think so. I'm doing what has to be done," she said.

7

Mecana and Darcie arrived at headquarters a little after nine. Verves was writing something on a notepad when they walked in.

"Morning. You two okay?" he asked.

"I think so," Mecana said. "What did you find out about the girl?"

"A fifteen-year-old runaway from Florida. Her name's Suzann Micelles. She's going to be okay, or at least okay physically. She said she met Carter at a hamburger joint, where she went to spend her last dollar for something to eat about two months ago. He played the fatherly bit and told her he had a room she could stay in. He's had her tied up at his house ever sense, raping her at his leisure. You found her just in time. He told her he was tired of her and would have to get rid of her; that was two days ago. She was overdue.

We searched his house from top to bottom. Unfortunately, nothing in his house or any personal effects ties him to any of the mutilator murders. According to Greenway, he was two hundred miles away on a job when the Freeman girl was killed. The only drugs were a small amount of crack. These nuts keep showing up, but it's like winning the lottery, and being disappointed at the amount. We're taking some bad guys off the street, but we haven't found the worst of all."

"Damn," Darcie said. "I was hoping there would be a connection and we had him."

"Yeah, me too," Mecana said, "but I realized his MO didn't fit."

"As they say, back to the drawing board," Verves said.

"Chief, you think we should continue to look at the wrap sheets?" Darcie asked.

"Wouldn't hurt, but I don't have too much faith in you finding anything else."

"Me neither," Mecana said. "From the way this whole thing is going down I think we're dealing with a first time criminal, a very sick one, but someone that doesn't have a criminal record."

"Like a doctor," Darcie said and looked at Mecana.

"Yes, a doctor. Like Dawson Durant. He would be smart enough to not leave any DNA because he knows how it works, and the drug is his kind of thing."

"We've been down this road before, Mecana," Verves said. "The doctor has alibis that have been checked and rechecked. It's time you moved away from that and approached this with an open mind."

"I can do that, but I want to be certain first."

Verves looked at Darcie. "Maybe you can talk some sense into him. I don't seem to be getting anywhere. Instead of an open mind, he's got a one track mind."

"I'm the junior partner here. I'm following his lead. I just hope whoever it is makes a mistake and we catch him before it happens again."

"There's some kind of plan to the murders," Mecana said. "That's why I keep coming back to Durant. Somewhere in this puzzle is the answer to who, and why, they all have a connection to Durant. I think he's the one to answer it."

"I don't think so," Verves said. "But you seem to have a sixth sense for these sorts of things, so I won't rule it out completely. Get back to work and keep me posted."

8

Shortly after Mecana and Darcie left, Lineal Crawford showed up at Verve's office unannounced. He was tall and slim, had salt and pepper hair with a salon cut, a tailored gray suit that fit his slim body perfectly, a hand painted tie and custom made shoes.

"Chief Verves, my name's Lineal Crawford. I'm an attorney. I represent the Lamonts and the Durants. I'm also the father of Julie."

"I know who you are, counselor," Verves said.

"I'm here to have you remove Thomas Mecana from the mutilator case. He's constantly harassing my clients, and there's no proof they were involved in any way."

"Mr. Crawford, are you serious? I've been on this job for almost twenty years and I have never seen anyone as cold. Your daughter was brutally murdered and you're here because of some rich folks? Let me ask you one question: What if Mecana is right? How are you going to live with that?"

"He's not. I have known the Lamonts for twenty years, they're good people."

"I don't condone everything Mecana does, Crawford, but he is one of the best homicide detectives I have ever seen. Until I am told by my boss, or a court order, he stays on the case."

"Very well, if that's what it takes. I'll see if I can accommodate you, and include you in the process," Crawford said.

"Whatever, Mr. Crawford," Verves said.

"Mr. Verves, Mecana has been abusing his authority for years; it's about time someone did something about it. He killed that kid two years ago and nobody did anything."

"The internal affairs board cleared him. It was self defense," Verves said.

"So you say," Crawford added.

"That kid, as you call him, Mr. Crawford, was twenty-three-years-old and wanted for murder. He was pointing a gun at Mecana. If Mecana had hesitated one more second he would have been dead. He was defending himself against a cold-blooded killer. People like you make me sick to my stomach. You don't even care what happened to your own flesh and blood. It's all about money. Get out of my office!"

"You'll be hearing from me, Verves," Crawford said and walked out.

Verves stood there like a statue, looking at the door Crawford went out, then mumbled, "I told you you were going to give me an ulcer, Mecana."

9

Cindy Freeman was an attractive, petite twenty-five-year-old flight attendant who shared a condo with her boyfriend ten miles from the DFW Airport. He was on a two-day flight to California and Washington.

She had just returned from a turnaround to Chicago, arriving back in Dallas at one in the morning. She drove home, punched the garage door remote, pulled into the garage, pressed the button again and watched as the door dropped down and settled on the garage floor. Her boyfriend had cautioned her about being secure. She cut the engine on her black five-year-old Corvette, got out, unlocked the kitchen door and went in, and sat her purse on the bar.

She went to the bathroom to take a quick shower before going to bed. She undressed, turned the water on and waited for the temperature to get just right, put on a shower cap and stepped into the shower. The water was warm and soothing. She soaked for about ten minutes, turned the water off and reached for a towel when she thought she heard a noise. She quickly wrapped the towel around her, pitched the shower cap on the vanity and moved slowly into the bedroom. She picked up the baseball bat her boyfriend kept by the bed. She stood in the middle of the room, listening. After three or four minutes she decided she was hearing things, put the bat down, dropped the towel, took a gown from the closet and slipped it on. She went to the kitchen, dug her phone out of her purse and walked into the living room. She sat down on the couch, pulled her legs up under her, ran her fingers through her damp, blonde hair and dialed. After four rings a voice came on the phone.

"Hello."

"Hi, Billy. You said call you when I got in. Sorry if I woke you."

"That's alright, honey. I'll see you tomorrow; should be in around noon. I'll take you to dinner and that movie you wanted to see."

"Sounds good."

"Get some rest. I'll see you tomorrow, sweetheart," he said.

"I will. Goodnight." She tossed the phone on the couch and went to the bedroom. As she walked through the bedroom doorway she felt a sharp pain in her buttocks, it stunned her and she stood motionless for a second or two. A quick dizziness came over her. She looked behind her and saw something in the hand of a blurred, shiny figure moving toward her.

She staggered and fell down. The blurred figure stuck tape over her mouth. She tried to get up but her legs wouldn't work. Everything was out of focus. The room was spinning. The image of some kind of huge animal appeared and was charging her. She tried to scream but no sound came out and the animal went right through her and disappeared. She gasped and her pulse rate skyrocketed. She fought to stay conscious; her body limp and helpless.

The blurred figure jerked her gown off, wrapped something around her wrist, placed her on the bed and tied her in a spread-eagle position on her back.

Her throat began to close, her air supply becoming less and less. Everything was getting dimmer and dimmer. She looked up toward the blurred figure with pleading blue eyes, gulped for one last breath and was gone. Cynthia Ann Freeman was dead.

10

A dozen police cars, ambulances, TV trucks and a company of reporters were in front of Cindy Freeman's condo. She had been murdered with neighbors only a wall away.

A big uniformed cop, one Mecana and Darcie knew, was standing in the door way.

"Hi, Mecana, Detective Connors," the cop said.

"Hi, Scotty," Mecana said. "Do we know how he got in?"

"No forced entry, so we don't know yet," Scotty said.

Mecana nodded. The cop handed Mecana and Darcie latex gloves. "Doc wants everybody to put these on."

Mecana and Darcie slipped on the gloves and walked in. Mecana spotted two FBI men he knew making notes. One was William Sullivan. He was about Mecana's age and size but looked a lot older. He was almost bald, with beady blue eyes and a dimpled chin. Mecana knew him from their days as street cops in Dallas ten years ago. The other guy was younger, bigger and slimmer. A transplanted Yankee from New York, with thick black hair by the name of George Kaminski. He didn't like anybody.

"What're you guys doing here?" Mecana said.

"She was crossing the state line on a federally regulated flight. That makes it federal," Sullivan said.

"What? You are reaching, Sullivan. That's bullshit."

"Take it up with your boss. I'm doing what I'm told," Sullivan said. Sullivan and Kaminski grinned at Mecana and walked away.

"Where do they get off coming on like that?" Darcie asked.

Mecana stared at Darcie for a moment. He had that Yogi feeling again.

"Makes me mad," she said.

"Happens all the time," Mecana replied. "You'd think they would have enough work with terrorists from two wars to worry about without horning in on local cases. I'll talk to the Chief. Let's have a look."

Two men in white coats, wearing gloves with plastic bags and magnifying glasses, were scanning the bedroom for clues; another man dusting for fingerprints. Doctor Seymour was standing in a corner writing something in a notebook.

Mecana and Darcie walked up to the bed to look at Cindy. Dried blood ran in all directions on the bed like a road map. Her lower body was covered in blood. Part of her missing. Smeared bloody footprints tracked from the blood by the bed disappeared at the bedroom door. Her milky-colored eyes had a fixed stare, like she was looking at someone when she died. Darcie stuck her hand over her mouth and ran to the bathroom.

Doctor Seymour noticed Darcie head for the bathroom. "Damn," he said.

Mecana give her a glance and walked over to Doctor Seymour.

"Hope your partner's not throwing up in the sink, contaminating my crime scene."

"Her first time at a homicide, Doc."

Doctor Seymour shook his head.

"How long you think it took him to do this, Doc?"

"Maybe thirty minutes, a little more."

"When?"

"Early this morning."

"Same drug?"

"Looks like it. No gunshots, stab wounds or head trauma. I'll know more when I get her back to the lab. We got footprints. May be the killer. Had something on his feet, though, can't tell if they were size eight or twelve, too smeared."

"I noticed," Mecana said. "Would you call me when the report is ready? We've got some FBI in here. Don't think they're supposed to be."

"Yeah, I saw them. I'll have to give them a report, but I'll make sure you get a head start."

"Thanks, Doc."

Darcie reappeared. "Never seen anything like this," she said.

"Me neither," Mecana replied. "We have some fingerprints and footprints. He may have made some other mistakes. We'll have a closer look at her when the lab boys get through."

Darcie gave Mecana a sideways look, frown wrinkles appeared on her forehead. She gulped, covered her mouth and headed for the bathroom again.

Mecana noticed a leather-bound notebook lying under the edge of the bed. He moved closer, bent down and flipped the book open with his pen, and turned the pages with it. Her scheduled flights, hair dresser, accountant and several other appointments were listed, and then he saw it: DOCTOR DURANT, FRIDAY, OCTOBER 12, 2 P.M., BIRTH PILLS. He picked up an evidence bag from the nightstand, put the notebook in the bag with his pen, checked to see if anyone was looking and stuck the bag in his coat. He walked over to the bathroom and leaned on the wall next to the door, and waited for Darcie to come out.

Maybe, he thought, just maybe he knew who the killer was. This Jack the Ripper won't get away.

11

Mecana poured a cup of coffee, took a sip and twisted his mouth like he had bit into a lemon.

Darcie was watching. "Now you know why I don't drink the coffee here," she said.

"Man, tastes like burned leaves." Mecana stuck his tongue out and flicked it like a snake.

Chief Verves appeared at his office door. "Mecana, you and Darcie can come in now."

Mecana dumped the cup in the trash and he and Darcie walked in and sat down.

Verves followed them in and sat down. "I just got off the phone with the FBI. They're not going away. We're going to have to deal with the situation the best we can. It's not worth the effort to fight them. The best course of action is to continue to march and try to avoid them as much as possible."

"Chief, you know that's not going to work. They're going to have priority on everything and we're going to be sucking hind tit," Mecana said, then looked at Darcie. "Sorry."

"It's not a problem," she said.

"I don't like it anymore than you do," Verves said, "but the main thing is to catch the killer. If they can do that, more power to them."

"I may have something that will change that," Mecana said. "Didn't want the FBI to get it." Mecana took the notebook out of his coat pocket and laid it on Verve's desk. "Found this at the scene. It's Cindy's appointment book. One of the appointments was with Doctor Dawson

Durant a week ago. Forensics matched Durant's prints on the headboard of her bed with a cup I picked up at the hospital when we had him under surveillance. I think we're back to Doctor Durant. There were other prints, but they haven't come up with a match yet."

"You didn't tell me about the notebook," Darcie said.

"You were too busy throwing up."

"That's interesting, Mecana," Verves said, "but I want you to get that notebook to the property room immediately. A good defense attorney would blow us out of the water for tampering with an evidence claim."

"I'll take care of it, boss, but do you think we have a suspect?"

"I think we need to know how Durant's fingerprints got on her bed and what his relationship with her was. You and Darcie go have a talk with him. Get his story before you go off half-cocked. If he doesn't have the right answers, bring him in."

"What about the footprints?" Darcie asked.

"Too smeared," Mecana said. "He probably had his shoes wrapped."

"Is Cindy a local girl?" Verves asked.

"She hasn't been in Dallas very long," Mecana said. "Transferred here last year from Chicago for a promotion."

"I'll have public relations contact her family. Anything else?" Verves asked.

"Just one," Mecana said. "Throw that damn coffee pot out the window and buy a new one, with a different brand of coffee. That's the worst tasting stuff I ever tried to drink. I still got that horrible taste in my mouth."

"You don't get that notebook to property you're going to have a worst taste than that."

"I hear you, Chief. We're going, right, Darcie?"

"Right."

"Oh," Verves said. "Almost forgot. Didn't turn up anything on the drug prescription. No medical people on it that we could find."

"Darcie, I think we better get the book to property then pay the doctor a visit. You watch his hands, I'll block the door. If he makes a run, make sure you don't shoot anybody else. Especially me."

"I may not have worked homicide before but I'm a good cop, Mecana," Darcie said.

"I'm sure you are, but when someone pulls a gun or breaks to run, a lot of people will overreact. Wanted to make sure you didn't," Mecana said.

"You do your job and I'll do mine, Mecana."

"Good enough," he said.

12

A pretty, young black nurse wearing a bright flowered smock was standing inside the nursing station, writing on a chart when Mecana and Darcie arrived. She saw them and smiled.

"Can I help you?" she asked.

"We're looking for Doctor Durant…Nadine," Mecana said, looking at her name tag. "His office said he was at the hospital." Mecana pushed his coat back and showed her his badge.

"One moment please." She walked away and went into a room down the hall.

Doctor Durant came out of the room. He looked more like a TV doctor than a real one, with his athletic physique, curly brown hair, six-foot-plus body and handsome face.

Darcie stuck her thumb in her belt, her Beretta a couple of inches away under her coat.

"You wanted to talk to me?" He said.

"Is there someplace we could talk in private, Doctor?" Mecana asked.

Durant gestured toward a room across the hall and they went in and closed the door.

"I'm Lieutenant Thomas Mecana and this is Detective Darcie Connors of the Dallas Police Department. We need to ask you some questions about a patient of yours, Miss Cindy Freeman."

"I've been expecting you," Durant said. "I saw what happened to her on the news. I recognize you, Mecana, from seeing you here before the fiasco at my grandfather's house. I can confirm she was a patient, that's all. Patient confidentiality."

"Doctor, your fingerprints were on her bed. You want to explain that? Or do we need to get a warrant?"

Durant let out a big sigh and dropped down on the edge of the bed, pushing the stirrups out of the way. "I guess I don't have a choice but to tell you the truth."

Mecana and Darcie looked at each other, their adrenaline rising.

"I made the mistake of going to her condo."

"Why?" Darcie asked.

"She came in for a physical to get a prescription for birth control pills. When I wrote out the prescription, she suggested I come by and test them, as she put it."

"Then what?" Darcie asked.

"I let it pass, but the next day she called and said she was alone and the invitation to test the birth control pills was still open, so I went. I have a weakness for beautiful women."

"What does your wife think about that?" Darcie asked.

"She doesn't know. I would like to keep it that way. She's very socially connected and this would hurt her standing on the social scene, not to mention what she might do to me."

"Where were you last Wednesday night, Doctor?" Darcie said.

"I anticipated that question, too. I checked my schedule; fortunately I was here all night. I had an emergency that required me to be with a patient."

"You have witnesses?" Mecana said.

"Yes, various staff members. I can give you their names if you need them."

The excitement in Mecana and Darcie's eyes dimmed a bit, and Darcie moved her hand away from the Beretta.

"We'll need that," Mecana said. "Linda Belmont was a patient of yours in Houston, right?"

"That's right. It was about her menstrual problems. I treated her for them."

"You were at a seminar in LA when she was found," Mecana said.

"I've already confirmed that with the Houston Police."

"You mean you confirmed you were in LA when they found her? Not when she was murdered?" Mecana said.

"Yes, that's right. They seemed satisfied with my answers."

"Did you ever see her outside of the medical visits, Doctor?" Darcie asked.

"We had lunch on a few occasions."

"According to the Houston Police report, her roommate said you showed up at their apartment the day she was murdered around one in the afternoon; said she had lunch with you."

"I explained that to the police. I thought it would be best to take her to lunch and discuss her medical condition with her in a different environment than the hospital. She was having a false pregnancy. That can be very traumatic for a young woman."

"What happened after that?" Mecana asked.

"Nothing. I left her at the restaurant and went back to the hospital."

"Did she say where she was going that evening," Mecana asked.

"No. I don't know where she went."

"You didn't see her that night?"

"No. I've already covered all this with the Houston Police."

"Yes, you have, doctor," Mecana said. "Do you know Julie Crawford or Barbara Sadler, better known as Kinky?"

"Don't know anyone named Kinky. I do know the Crawford family. Her dad is our lawyer. I've spoken to Julie a couple times at social functions. She wanted to be an actress, that's all I know about her."

"No hanky panky?"

"No. You're barking up the wrong tree, to use one of my father's favorite phrases."

"Do you recall where you were Monday night two weeks ago?" Darcie asked.

"No."

"We'll check it out," Darcie said.

"Cindy is the only one I had any kind of personal relationship with." He stood up, took the stethoscope from around his neck and laid it on a table. "Can we keep this between us?"

"I suppose so," Mecana said. "One last question. You know, or ever hear, Cindy mention a man named DeMax Baker?"

"Not that I recall," Durant said.

"If we have anymore questions we'll let you know," Mecana said.

13

Mecana and Darcie were having lunch at Brogans, discussing their meeting with Durant, when FBI Agents Sullivan and Kaminski came in and walked over to their table.

"Well, Mecana, got to give you one," Sullivan said. "We just had a talk with Doctor Durant. You beat us there. You're not one of his favorite people."

"I'm not trying to win a popularity contest."

"Too bad that weirdo Carter didn't work out for you. Got another suspect, though, and it isn't Durant. I'll let you figure out who it is."

"You're full of shit, Sullivan. If you had another suspect you wouldn't be telling me."

"Her boyfriend and Durant weren't the only ones she was sleeping with. Seems like Miss Cindy got around," Sullivan said.

"You weren't one of them, were you Mecana?" Kaminski laughed.

"How would you like me to kick your Yankee ass, Kaminski?"

"I don't think I have to worry about that."

"Go away," Darcie said. "We're having lunch."

"I bet you take good care of your pretty little partner, Mecana,"

Kaminski said, smiling.

Darcie's brown eyes took on a viper stare at Kaminski. A forked tongue could be expected to dart out of her mouth. "If he doesn't kick your ass, I will," she said.

"Oh, a real spitfire, aren't you?" Kaminski said, and began to laugh again as they walked away.

"Don't let them get to you, Darcie, that's what they want. Sullivan is trying to plant a seed, get us to spend time coming up with someone they can move in on without doing the legwork. I know him."

A waiter brought two plates of food and sat them on the table.

"Maybe Sullivan isn't that far off," Darcie said. "She either let him in or he had a key. She may have accidentally gotten hooked up with the killer. Someone we don't have a name for. We know the boyfriend didn't do it. He had his key on him. We should have a rundown on her phone soon, maybe that will give us a name."

"Wait," Mecana said. "It just occurred to me we didn't ask Durant how he got in. We just assumed she let him in. One of two things happened: what you said, or she may have given Durant a key. If she did, what happened to that key? Did he use it again when he killed her? Did someone else get the key somehow?"

"You want to call him and check?" Darcie asked.

"No, we'll do it in person. He's less likely to lie. We'll take it from there."

"Okay. I don't know about you but I lost my appetite," Darcie said.

"Yeah, me too. Sullivan has a way of doing that to people."

"Let's get out of here," Darcie said.

14

"What? You two again?" Durant said. "I thought we were done? If I see you again, you better have a warrant."

"Just one more small thing," Mecana said. "Did Cindy Freeman give you a key?"

"Didn't I tell you that?"

"No, you didn't. Where is it?"

"I think I gave it back to her."

"But you don't know for sure?" Darcie asked.

"No, not something I gave any thought too."

"Doctor, it's important that you remember," Mecana said.

"You think the murderer may have gotten the key, right, and it's my fault?"

"Possibly. We need to know what happened to the key. Call me when you remember." Mecana handed him a card. "Good day, Doctor."

They made their way to the Silverado and climbed in.

"He knows what happened to the key," Darcie said. "Two-to-one it turned up missing, that's why he doesn't want to tell us - afraid we will try to connect him as an accessory."

"If Durant doesn't call by tomorrow morning we'll try a little blackmail. It's obvious he's afraid his wife will find out about his infidelities; we'll threaten to tell her."

"You're vicious, Mecana. I love it. Makes me feel better to know another cheating man is going to suffer. You a cheating man, Mecana?"

"No, my mistress was my work. I didn't have my priorities right. Your ex must have been a fool to cheat on you."

"Why, Lieutenant Mecana, you do have a sensitive side." Darcie smiled at Mecana. "You sound like you still have feelings for your wife."

"I do, we have two beautiful daughters that will always bind us together no matter what we do. I know we both have to get on with our lives. I don't have any fantasies about a reconciliation. We're both past that."

"At least something good came out of your marriage. Mine was quite different. It was a physical attraction that burned out pretty quick for both of us. He started sleeping around; I buried myself in my studies. That was the end of it. College kids that thought they were in love. We weren't."

"We'll, I still think he was crazy for letting you get away."

Darcie gave Mecana a long look.

"What?" Mecana asked.

"Why don't you drive me home and we can discuss this 'til morning."

"I'm not very good at reading between the lines Darcie. Are you saying what I think your saying?"

"You could say that."

Mecana fired up the Silverado.

15

Darcie shook Mecana's arm and his eyes popped open.

"Coffee's ready, big guy." Darcie handed him a cup. "You can drink this."

Mecana rose up in bed, and took the coffee cup.

"It wouldn't have to be very good to be better than that tree bark Verves calls coffee."

"I can fix breakfast, or we can go out."

"Coffee's enough for me."

"Okay, I'm going to take a shower and get dressed. Maybe Durant's memory has improved."

"Sounds like a plan to me. Where's my pants?"

"On the floor where you left them."

The nurse they spoke to before met them in the hall.

"The doctor's not here."

"Where is he, Nadine?"

"Don't know, he hasn't showed up for his rounds. You're here about the Freeman girl that was murdered, aren't you?"

"You know about Doctor Durant and Miss Freeman?" Darcie asked.

"I overheard him and Miss Freeman talking, she was coming on to him something furious. He gets a lot of that from his patients. Some twice his age."

"Do you know anything about a key she gave him?"

"I saw it on his desk in the examining room after she left. I picked it up to take to the lost and found office. He saw me and took the key from me."

"You ever see it again?" Mecana asked.

"No. I was going to throw it away if I did."

"You have any idea where Doctor Durant is?" Darcie asked.

"Maybe his home. His wife is having a big party tonight."

"Why don't you call him? Don't say anything about us, just where he is. We'll wait." Mecana smiled at the nurse. She smiled back.

"Alright give me a couple of minutes. I have to take medication to a patient."

Mecana nodded, and watched Nadine's perfectly rounded derriere move back and forth as she walked away. Darcie scolded Mecana with her eyes and he gave her a sheepish grin.

Nadine returned shortly. "I paged him, called his house and his wife's cell; no answer. Don't know where they are."

"Give us the phone numbers, we'll find him," Mecana said.

"Is that legal, giving you someone's private phone numbers?" Nadine asked.

"It's okay. If you don't give them to us we can get them from the phone company."

Nadine nodded, wrote the numbers on a pad and handed them to Darcie.

Mecana and Darcie left the office.

"What do you think, Darcie, could Nadine be another Durant bed partner?"

"Speaking of bed partners," Darcie said, punching the elevator button, "think we should cool it for a while. Think it over…partner."

"Was thinking the same thing…partner," Mecana said.

PART THREE
Watermelon Head

1

Darcie was working on Cindy's phone calls at the phone company. Mecana was briefing Chief Verves in his office on the key and Durant's absence when a tall, beautiful blonde came in and walked over to one of the detectives.

Mecana recognized her as Mrs. Durant from the stakeout. She was dressed to the hilt in a green designer outfit that matched her eyes. The dress hugged her slim, curvy body like it was happy to be there. The jewelry she wore could have made a down payment on the national debt.

The detective stood up, said something to her and pointed to Verve's office.

Mecana looked at Verves. "That's Durant's wife, I'll see what she wants."

Verves took a look and nodded. Mecana walked out of Verve's office toward Mrs. Durant. She saw him coming, and struck a pose.

"You Detective Mecana?" she asked.

"Yes, I am."

"I'm Lisa Lamont Durant," she said, and looked at Mecana like he was supposed to applaud.

"Would you like to sit down, Mrs. Durant?" Mecana slid an office chair close to her. She looked at the worn, soiled chair and frowned. "No, thank you. I'll stand."

"What can I do for you, Mrs. Durant?"

"My husband had nothing to do with the murders of those young women, and yet you insist on interfering in our life and harassing him. Thought I would make one last attempt in person before we sue you and the city. Leave my husband alone, Mr. Mecana."

"Mrs. Durant, your husband has, or knows the location of, evidence we need. I'm trying to conduct a murder investigation. When he produces the evidence I'll go away. You know where he is?"

"He's at home, helping me prepare for my party. What evidence do you think he has, Mr. Mecana?"

"I'll take that up with him."

"You can discuss it with me."

"I don't think so."

"Mr. Mecana, my husband has one of the most successful practices in the country. The wealthiest women in Dallas come to him. That translates into a lot of money. More in one year than you will probably make in a lifetime. You're hurting his practice, costing us money by showing up at the hospital. That has to stop."

"Mrs. Durant, you have your priorities, I have mine. If money had anything to do with it, I wouldn't have come to work this morning. You tell your husband he can come see me, or I will meet him somewhere if he doesn't want me coming to his workplace. He has my number. He knows what I want. Now if you will excuse me, I have work to do."

"It's apparent you do not understand the seriousness of your dilemma, Mr. Mecana. I want to see your supervisor."

"That's him in the office," Mecana pointed at the glass panels. "His name is Robert Verves. He's Chief of Homicide. I'll introduce you."

She brushed her long blonde hair away from her neck, gave Mecana a snobbish glare, and followed him to Verve's office.

"This is Mrs. Durant, Chief. She wants to talk to you. She's not happy with the way I'm conducting the Freeman investigation."

"Have a seat, Mrs. Durant," Verves said.

She eyed the chair before being seated.

"What can we do for you?"

"Your detective Mecana insists on harassing my husband. Dawson has told him all he knows about Miss Freeman. She was a patient, that's it. As for the others, he knows nothing about what happened to them. Leave us alone."

"Mrs. Durant, I can appreciate your concern. I know sometimes it appears like we don't exercise the best protocol, I apologize for that. But we're trying to solve some brutal murders. We have to make sure we cover all the bases."

Mecana stood in the doorway behind Mrs. Durant.

"Would you like some coffee, Mrs. Durant?" Verves asked.

"No, nothing, Mr. Verves. I came here to give you the opportunity to avoid a lawsuit. Mr. Mecana is a public servant who has overstepped his authority. I want him taken off the case, now. If you don't, you both may be out of a job." She stood up and Verves followed.

"I can't do that, Mrs. Durant, sorry."

She batted her long eyelashes. "Mr. Verves, you will regret your decision. I know the Mayor personally," she said before stalking out.

When she was out of ear range, Verves eyed Mecana. "You better find that son of a bitch or we'll know the Mayor personally, too," Verves said.

"I will."

"What do you know about the Durants and the Lamonts, Mecana?"

Mecana reached in his inside coat pocket and pulled out a notebook.

"She has an interesting and controversial family, the typical poor little rich girl. Her father is Doctor J. Barnard Lamont, a heart surgeon in Houston, very rich. The mansion the Durants are living in has been in her family for over a hundred years. Her great-grandfather Jackson Bernard Lamont inherited a railroad from his father, got in some trouble embezzling money from the company and fled from Austin to London. The charges were dropped two years later; he returned, moved to Dallas, married a socialite and built her that mansion. They had a son. She turned up missing when the boy was four, and was never found. Her family raised the boy, who became even richer during the Industrial Revolution and World War Two before her father inherited it all.

"Lisa's sister, Shelly, two years older, died from an accidental fall when they were teenagers. Her parents couldn't get it together after that and divorced two years later. Her mother remarried and lives in Florida. Dawson Durant's family are average working people. There are two other boys. One in the Army in Iraq and one is a teacher in California at a small private school. She met Durant at Baylor. She has a genius IQ over 160, works as a freelance professional photographer for all the top magazines. Durant's kind of the male version of the trophy wife.

"That's about it."

"You do your homework, Mecana," Verves said.

"She's not going to leave us alone, Chief. Her kind thinks rules don't apply to them. I've seen it too many times," Mecana said.

"I think you're right about that," Verves said. "Her lawyer paid me a visit asking for your head. Said he was going to pursue legal means to have you removed from the case."

"That doesn't surprise me," Mecana said. "I expected her to get her lawyer on me."

"I'll stick with you as long as I can," Verves said, "but you have to crack this case or both of us may be looking for a job."

"I will. It's just a matter of time," Mecana said.

"We may not have a lot of that," Verves picked up his empty coffee cup. "Bring me some good news, Mecana."

Mecana nodded and left.

2

Dawson Durant adjusted his black bow tie and took Lisa's arm as they entered the ballroom. The magnificent room was big as a basketball court. The social elite of Dallas were waltzing on the mirror-shined marble floors to the music of a large live orchestra. Lisa had invited everyone who was anyone. The expensive crimson gown she wore complemented her beauty.

"You better behave yourself, Dawson," Lisa said. "Don't embarrass me in front of my friends."

"I didn't want to come to this damn thing anyway. I should have been at the hospital instead of helping you push the servants to get this place ready for tonight."

"You think spending a day with me is a waste?"

"Don't twist my words. You know what I mean."

"You're not a country bumpkin anymore, Dawson, you have an obligation when you're class."

"What, kissing each other's ass?"

Lisa saw the mayor coming toward them. "We will discuss this later."

The mayor looked suave in his black tuxedo. Not a gray hair out of place. He was a good-looking man, though not in Dawson Durant's league. He shook hands with Dawson and kissed Lisa's hand.

"Everything is perfect, Lisa," he said. "There's something I've wanted to discuss with you. I need a new chairman for my reelection campaign. Why don't you stop by the office next week?"

"Thank you, Mayor Pratt, I would like that," she said. "I have something I want to discuss with you, too."

"You're quiet tonight, Dawson," the Mayor said.

"Kind of tired, been a long day," he said and smiled.

The Mayor smiled. "Have to circulate," he said and walked away.

"You really want to help that jerk get reelected?" Dawson asked.

"Yes, it would be fun. He may not want me if we don't get Mecana off your back. I had a talk with him, but it didn't do any good. I'll drop a word on the Mayor when we have our meeting."

"I can handle my own problems, Lisa."

"It doesn't look like it, my dear," she said.

"I need a drink," Dawson said.

"By all means, enjoy yourself, sweetheart," Lisa said sarcastically.

Dawson looked bewildered as he walked to the bar.

The president of the social register came up to Lisa and they made small talk while Doctor Durant worked on a gin and tonic.

It wasn't long until an attractive brunette caught his eye.

3

The next morning, Mecana was on his way to the phone company when his phone rang.

"Mecana, my wife said she came to see you. Did you tell her about Cindy?"

"No, I didn't. I told her you had evidence I needed."

"I don't know what happened to the key. I really don't. I remember dropping it back in my pocket when I unlocked Cindy's door that night and it disappeared some time after that."

"Finding that key may find a killer, Doctor. I hope it's not you. May have to go to your wife, see if she can help your memory."

"No, don't do that. Lisa said she was going to the Mayor to get you fired. I'll see if I can talk her out of it."

"Doctor Durant, if the Mayor wants my job he can have it. I don't intend to back off one bit doing what I think will find a killer."

"She's a determined woman. When she sets out to get something she usually does."

"Me too. Do you have a personal relationship with Nadine?"

"She's my nurse."

"That wasn't what I asked you. I'll make it simple: Are you fucking her?"

"I don't have to answer that."

"You just did. Don't leave town, Doctor, you're still on my shit list.

I'll be in touch." Mecana hung up and pulled into a parking space at the phone company.

Darcie met him at the door. "Didn't find much, but I do have the transcripts." Darcie picked up the paper and begin running her finger across it.

"She called her boyfriend several times in the last two weeks. She made a call to the pizza place almost everyday and the pizza place called her twice. She must really like pizza. Two calls to Durant's office. All the other calls were to businesses, no individual names. That's as far as I've got."

"Any of those calls to a medical facility, besides Durant?"

"No."

"What was the name of the pizza place?

Darcie flipped a page. "Lets see. Big Top Pizza."

"Well I'll be damned. DeMax."

"What's a DeMax?" Darcie asked.

"Not a what, a who. A boyfriend of Kinky Sadler. DeMax Baker. Street name 'Stitch.' We checked him out before you came aboard. A real character. He thinks of himself as a ladies' man. Him and Durant have a lot in common. I wonder if there's anything that went on besides delivering pizzas. Let's go have a talk with him. He may know something we need to know. I'll drive."

Darcie followed Mecana to his truck. They got in and drove away.

"Did you find Durant?" Darcie asked.

"He kind of found me. His wife came by the office. She's trying to get me fired and Durant doesn't know what happened to the key. I 'm not sure I believe him."

"Have they got any kids?" Darcie asked.

"Didn't see any on the report. If they do I feel sorry for them."

"What about the nurse?"

"He didn't say he was screwing her, but he might as well have. If we solve the Freeman murder it will solve all the others. I'm convinced of that. Durant is at the top of my list."

"I don't know about Durant, but I agree it's one killer," Darcie said.

"Glad you agree, partner," Mecana smiled and winked at Darcie.

Mecana made a turn on South Freemont Street, a block from DeMax's.

The big Harley wasn't in the driveway. Mecana pulled in the drive and cut the engine.

"Looks like DeMax isn't here. I'll check to make sure. You can stay in the truck."

Mecana walked up to the door and knocked several times - no answer.

An old black woman, with a rake comb stuck in her hair and wearing a faded, flowered house coat and flip flops appeared on her porch at the house next door. "If ya lookin' for DeMax, mister, he ain't there. Bunch of men with 'FBI' on their shirts showed up this mornin' in droves, hauled 'em way."

"You know why?"

"Don't know, rough with the boy. Slammed 'em to the ground. One of 'em sit on his back. Put cuffs on him. No need, boy wasn't tryin' to resist."

"I see. They take his Harley?"

The old lady nodded. "Don't get know respect," she said, shook her head and went back in her house.

Mecana opened the truck door and got in.

"You hear that?" he asked.

"Yeah, I heard. They must think he's the killer."

"Maybe so. If it had been for something else the locals would have showed up."

"What now, Sherlock?"

"Don't know exactly. Hell, I wouldn't think DeMax could peel an apple, let alone perform precise surgery."

"I wonder if they're questioning him without a lawyer present," Darcie said.

"Let's go find out," Mecana replied.

4

Mecana and Darcie stepped off the elevator in the federal building and walked down the hall toward Sullivan's office. A small, square wooden box extended a couple of feet out into the hall beside a drinking fountain.

"That one?" Darcie asked, touching the box as they walked by.

"Yep, don't see why they don't take that damn thing out. It's like they think it's going to come back, and they can put a 'Coloreds Only' sign over it again."

Mecana knocked on a door with 'Special Agent William E. Sullivan - FBI' painted on it. A voice from the other side said, "Come in." Sullivan was seated behind his desk, holding a file. A picture of his hero, J. Edger

Hoover, hung on the wall behind him.

"Well, well, Mecana. I figured you'd show up." Sullivan dropped the folder on his desk, leaned back in his chair and propped his feet up on the desk. "We got him."

"You got who?" Mecana asked.

"The mutilator, of course. Was right under your nose and you couldn't see him."

"You talking about DeMax Baker?"

"You do know."

"DeMax is a petty crook but he's not a killer, especially this kind," Mecana said.

"That's where you're wrong, Mecana. He knew all the victims, his alibis are shaky. We found underwear of two of the victims in his house. We'll have a confession before the day's over."

"What about Houston?"

"We're still working on that one. Maybe where he got the idea."

"You think he will confess to murdering three women?"

"Yep. When we get through with him."

"You going to take a rubber hose to him?" Mecana asked.

"Look, Mecana, I don't have to take that shit from you. We're going to charge him with the murders. Did you know he's a former Army medic? His street name is Stitch because he stitches up the wounded in the neighborhood."

"Don't you think we've checked him out, and everyone else that remotely knew any of the victims?" Mecana said. "The only name that keeps making me nervous is Doctor Dawson Durant."

"Mecana, take your lady friend and get out of my office."

"Where's DeMax?" Darcie said.

"He's in interrogation. Going to take him to your jail after he gives us a confession."

"I want to see him," Darcie said.

"I don't think so," Sullivan said.

"Does he have a lawyer?"

"No, you want to get him one?"

"No, I am one. He's entitled to have an attorney present during questioning. Let us see him."

"We've done everything by the book, Missy."

"My name is Attorney Darcie Connors, or Detective Darcie Connors, not Missy. Take your pick, Mr. Sullivan. You understand?"

Sullivan's eyes took on a squinted stare at Darcie. He got up and slid his chair back. "Leave your guns on the desk and follow me. I'll take you to him, Counselor."

Mecana looked at Sullivan and grinned. They followed Sullivan down the hall to a room. Sullivan unlocked the door and they all went in.

Kaminski was sitting on one side of a long metal table and DeMax on the other, in handcuffs; a yellow notepad and pen lying in front of him. Kaminski turned to see who had entered.

"What the hell are those two doing here, Bill?" Kaminski asked.

"She's a lawyer."

"No shit?" DeMax said, looking at Darcie.

"That's right," Darcie said. "Now if you two will let us talk to the accused in private."

"Can't do that," Sullivan said.

"If you don't, you're violating his civil rights," Darcie replied.

"You can watch him through the window," Mecana said, and pointed to a big mirror on the wall.

DeMax leaned forward and looked at the mirror. "I'll be damned," he said.

"You got fifteen minutes," Sullivan said, as he and Kaminski walked out and closed the door.

DeMax looked at Mecana. "You put the feds on me, man?"

"No. You play ball with us and we may be able to get you out of here."

"Like what? Don't know who did it. Feds said I did. Tellin' me how I carved up all them pretty ladies. Make me want to throw up. Know'd them all, but didn't do nothin' but fuck 'em."

"Watch your mouth, DeMax," Mecana said. "Thought you didn't know Julie Crawford?"

"Didn't know her name 'til they showed me a picture. Seen her at Griffin's. Played a little paddy cake with her in the back room one time, that's all."

"What about Cindy Freeman?"

"Liked to fuck. Called me when she wanted a good one."

"What did I tell you about your mouth?" Mecana said.

DeMax cut his eyes up at Darcie. "Sorry, lady."

Darcie nodded.

"DeMax, if you were visiting Cindy that much how come your prints didn't show up?"

"Guess 'cause I kind of got in the habit of wearing gloves and wiping things down, you know, since you cops are always trying to take my black ass to jail."

"You're saying you deliberately removed your prints from her place?

You know how incriminating that looks? You fucked up, DeMax," Mecana said.

DeMax looked at Darcie again. "He got a bad mouth, too."

"He sure does," Darcie said, and flashed her big brown eyes at Mecana.

"Sorry, lady," Mecana grinned.

"Didn't hurt any of them ladies," DeMax said.

"We believe you," Mecana said, "but if there's anything you haven't told us, now's the time."

"Can't think of nothin' else. Everything's kind of mixed up in my head."

"Did you know Cindy was seeing a Doctor Durant, DeMax?" Darcie asked.

"Yeah, she says she fuckin' that pussy doctor, too. No never mind to me. She a nympho, or something, anyway, wore me out."

"What about her boyfriend? You know him?" Darcie asked.

"No. She always calls me when he's gone on a trip."

The door opened and Sullivan and Kaminski walked in.

"Times up, Councilor," Sullivan said.

"If you're going to charge him you better have more than circumstantial evidence, Sullivan," Darcie said.

"We got witnesses that saw him at the Freeman girl's place the day she was murdered. He just admitted he removed his prints from her place. Why would he do that if he didn't have anything to hide?"

"That was supposed to be privileged information, Mr. Sullivan. I'll make sure you never get it into court," Darcie said.

"We won't need it. I'll have a confession when I get through," Kaminski said.

"Don't sign anything, DeMax," Darcie said. "I'll see if I can get you a lawyer."

DeMax nodded, raised his cuffed hands and pushed the pen and notepad further back on the table.

Darcie and Mecana walked out. A group of reporters were waiting in the lobby when Darcie and Mecana got off the elevator.

"Hey, Mecana!" one yelled. "We hear the FBI has got the mutilator."

"You better ask them about that. We don't think they have the right man."

A young woman with 'KXTU TV' printed on her shirt, fire red hair and big breasts stuck a microphone in Mecana's face. "You sure it's not just sour grapes, Mr. Mecana, because you didn't catch him?"

"I don't have anything else to say," Mecana said, speeding up his walk. They pushed their way through the reporters outside to the Silverado.

5

At eight the next morning, Mecana was on his way to pick up Darcie when Rustin Kemp called.

"Rustin, how you doing, boy?"

"Getting ready to go home. Working on getting my shit together. How about you?"

"Ah, you know, chasing my tail, trying to solve this case."

"I saw on the news the FBI arrested DeMax. Don't seem like he would do that."

"He didn't. They're looking for a scapegoat. Won't last long, though, when the real killer strikes again."

"Yeah, what I figured. I've decided to let you have it. Just wanted to say thanks for everything. Know you'll catch him. Hope it's before he kills someone else."

"Me too. What're you going to do?"

"Got some GI Bill left. Think I'll be a lawyer with my wife's help."

"Good choice. I'm sure you will make a good one."

"Hope so. Catch that son of a bitch, Mecana."

"I will."

"There's something stuck in my head about the night I was stabbed. I can't get a handle on it yet. I know it's important, though. A lot of things I didn't remember about that night are starting to come back to me. Maybe I'll remember what it is later. I'll let you know if I do."

"Good, I can use all the help I can get."

"Watch your back, Mecana."

"You bet."

Mecana pulled into Darcie's driveway, cut the engine, got out and walked up to the door and rang the bell. The door opened and Darcie handed him a cup of coffee with one hand and ran a brush through her shiny black hair with the other.

"Have a seat and drink some coffee, I'll be ready in a few minutes. First time I've seen you in a suit. Like the red tie. You clean up good."

"So do you," he said.

Mecana sat down, took a sip of coffee and Darcie disappeared into the bedroom.

He got up and walked into the bedroom to the open bathroom door, took a drink of coffee and watched Darcie as she looked into the bathroom mirror applying her lipstick. Mecana couldn't take his eyes off her. That little black dress fit perfectly.

"You're a beautiful woman, Darcie."

Darcie looked at Mecana's reflection in the mirror and smiled. "Somebody got up horny this morning."

"Well you shouldn't look so damn good."

"Thanks. I think."

"Maybe I better change the subject," Mecana said. "We need to go or we're going to be late for the nine o'clock news conference to play nice with the FBI."

"Do we have to go?"

"Yeah. I'm walking on thin ice with the powers-that-be as it is."

"I'm ready, let's do it."

"That's not a good choice of words, Darcie."

"Mecana, I think the old adage is true."

"What's that?"

"A woman is looking for a relationship when she has sex; a man is just looking for a place." She smiled, walked by Mecana, flipped his red tie with her long red fingernail and kept walking toward the door.

6

A group of reporters was camped outside the District Attorney's office, yelling questions at anyone who went in or out of the office. When they saw Mecana, they converged on him like bees on pollen.

"What's happening, Mecana?" a young reporter asked. "You still think they got the wrong guy?"

"The District Attorney will have a statement shortly."

"That wasn't what I asked you. Answer my question."

"No comment," Mecana said.

"Is it true you're going to resign, Mecana?" she asked.

"No comment," he repeated.

"What about you, lady, you got a comment?" She thrust the microphone toward Darcie.

"Miss, you best move away and let us through before I put that microphone in a most unusual place."

The TV reporter stared at Darcie for a moment before backing off.

A little bald-headed man, holding his recorder in front of Mecana spoke up. "Have they arraigned Mr. Baker yet, Mecana?"

"Not that I know of. The District Attorney and FBI will have a statement for you. I've got nothing else to say."

Mecana and Darcie walked past a recently-installed podium in front of the District Attorney's office and went inside. The office was filled with lawyers and police, including Chief Orr.

The District Attorney was talking to FBI Agent Bill Sullivan. "We don't have a strong case here, Bill. You better come up with some more evidence or we can't get an indictment."

"Don't worry, Mr. Seville, we will," Sullivan said.

Randall Seville had been the District Attorney for almost ten years. He was a neat, well-dressed, average sized forty-something man with short gray hair. The latest gossip was he was going to run for the U.S. Senate next year. That might not be possible if the Baker case blew up. His star was hitched to a shaky wagon.

Chief Orr saw Mecana and walked over to him. "Looks like I don't have to worry about paying anymore bills, Mecana."

"I don't think you worry about anything anyway, Orr, except when your next meal is. Freeloaders like you get on my nerves."

"That was a shitty thing to say, Mecana. Fuck you," Orr said and walked away.

"Not in the best of moods, are we?" Darcie said to Mecana.

"He wouldn't make a pimple on a policeman's ass," Mecana said.

Chief Verves spotted Mecana and Darcie. "Glad to see you decided to wear a suit, Mecana, and join the rest of us. Darcie, you always look good."

"Thanks, Chief," she said.

"I expect you two to be on your best behavior. I know you don't agree with this but we have to let it play out."

"Chief, you know there's a rush to judgment here to convict somebody because it's a high-profile case," Mecana said. "It's easier when the suspect is a poor black man."

"Don't try to put me on a guilt trip, Mecana. I don't see you coming up with anything. I stuck my neck out a mile long to protect you and you're not giving me anything. I can't do it anymore. If you don't like what's happening, resign."

Frown wrinkles appeared on Mecana's forehead, he looked at Darcie. His steel gray eyes sending a message. She shook her head no. "Can we go now?" he asked.

"Yeah, get the hell out and keep your mouth shut."

Darcie took a step closer to Verves. "Just so you know, Chief, I agree with Mecana."

"Get him out of here, Darcie," Verves said.

Mecana and Darcie made their way back to the elevator.

"You had me worried for a minute there, partner," Darcie said. "I thought you were going to clock him."

"I was close. Verves is afraid of losing his job. He will have his twenty next year and still has a kid in college."

"It's understandable he's a little jittery with all the pressure on him," Darcie said.

"Maybe so, but you know as well as I do that DeMax didn't murder anyone, but he may be convicted on circumstantial evidence because they want a conviction so bad." The elevator doors opened and Mecana and Darcie got on.

7

Mecana whizzed along the highway on his way home, thinking of all the people he had spoken to and investigated. Only one kept turning up as a possible suspect, Doctor Dawson Durant, and he had some iron clad alibis. He was either missing something or he was way off base and his mind wouldn't let him turn loose of his one and only suspect. Rustin had given up, maybe it was time for him to do the same; go visit his daughters and figure out where his life was going from here.

He pulled into his driveway and cut off the Silverado. The guy next door, who he hadn't had a conversation with in five years, was watering his lawn. Mecana had quit doing yard work when his wife left. A lawn service handled it now. The inside of the house wasn't much different. He had a maid come in three days a week. He probably could have made out better if he moved to an apartment, but somehow he just couldn't let go of the house. It was nothing fancy, like most of the three bedroom bricks in the neighborhood, but it was special to him. Maybe subconsciously it was a way of holding on to a little piece of his family.

The first thing he always did when he got in the house was check his answering machine. He had pictures of his kids by the machine to look at when he talked to them. They had his gray eyes and their mother's Southern Belle beauty.

The message light was blinking. He punched the play button, and grabbed a beer out of the fridge.

"Daddy," the voice said. It was his oldest, Emily. "I know you probably won't get this until tonight so call me on my cell phone. I didn't want to bother you at work. I have to fix my car. The man at the garage said I needed new brakes."

Mecana grinned. She was using psychology to ask for money.

Mecana dialed his daughter's number.

"Hi, Daddy. You get my message?"

"Yes, I got it. How much is it going to cost?"

"Two hundred and fifty, I think."

"Doesn't your mother ever give you any money? I send her the biggest part of my paycheck."

"She said you bought it, you have to keep it up."

"That's your mother's revenge for me buying a sixteen-year-old a car."

"Are you going to give me the money, Daddy?"

"Have the garage pick it up. I don't want you driving it if the brakes are bad. Tell them to call me and I'll give them my credit card number."

"Oh thank you, Daddy, you're the greatest!"

"Naturally. Where's Morgan?"

"She's at dance practice."

"She doing okay?"

"Yes. She's a pest, though, always wanting to go with me."

"That's what little sisters do. You take care of her."

"Yes, Daddy. Thanks for fixing my car. Maybe I can come see you before long."

"That would be nice. I love you, baby. Tell Morgan I love her, too."

"I will. I got to go, Daddy."

"Bye, sweetheart."

"Bye, Daddy."

Mecana sat holding the phone after Emily hung up, his mind working overtime again. He picked up her picture and sighed. "I love you baby," he said and sat the picture down.

The doorbell rang. He hung up the phone and moved to the door and looked through the peep hole. It was Darcie, wearing jeans, a pullover red sweater and holding a sack.

He opened the door and Darcie stepped inside and gave him a big smile.

"After the ordeal today, I figured you needed some company tonight," she said. "I brought an old friend in case we need a little help."

She held up a bottle of Jim Beam and smiled again.

"Might be a good time to get reacquainted. I'll get the glasses," Mecana said.

8

It was a Saturday and Mecana and Darcie slept in. Later, Darcie was fixing breakfast and Mecana was watching the news when a bulletin came on, saying that DeMax Baker had confessed to being the mutilator and was giving the FBI the details of his gruesome crimes.

"Holy shit! Come here, Darcie. Look at this."

Darcie came into the room, wearing nothing except one of Mecana's dress shirts that barely covered the essentials, and sat down beside him on the couch.

"What the hell is DeMax doing?" Darcie said. "Why would he do that? He's not the mutilator!"

"Do you know if they have appointed him a public defender, Darcie?"

"I can make a call and find out. He damn sure needs one."

"Can you do it?"

"No, they won't let me. His attorney will have to come from the attorney pool. Whoever is up next."

"That's a piss poor way of doing it."

"Actually, it's a pretty good way to keep the system balanced."

"Maybe. Get dressed, let's go find out if he's lost his mind."

"What about breakfast? I was fixing you pancakes."

"I'll take you to McDonalds."

"Always the big spender. Let me cut the stove off and find my undies and jeans."

The short, obese jailer had a loaded key ring in his hand. He shook his head at Mecana. "I can't do it, Mecana. Unless you have something to do with his defense, I can't let you talk to him. I've got strict orders, no visitors. That means cops, too."

FBI Agent Bill Sullivan appeared in the hallway right on cue, walking toward Mecana and Darcie. "What're you two doing here?" he asked.

"Checking on that rubber hose," Mecana said. "What's this bullshit about a confession, Sullivan?"

"He decided to tell us about the Freeman murder after we found his prints in her condo and he couldn't account for his whereabouts that night."

"What did you do, have him sign a confession you typed up after he signed it?"

"He read it."

"Sullivan, you know damn well that man is not the mutilator. The only drugs he knows about are the ones you buy on the streets."

"Why do you keep taking up for this guy, Mecana? What the hell is he to you?"

"He's someone that's being used to further yours and the District Attorney's careers. You don't give a damn if he's innocent or guilty as long as you get a conviction."

"Has an attorney been assigned to him, Mr. Sullivan?" Darcie asked.

"One you know, Detective Connors. A Nicklaus Booker."

"Know him, Darcie?" Mecana asked.

"He's my ex. A lousy husband, but a good lawyer."

"You never said anything about him being in Dallas."

"You never asked. Before you ask the next question, I had the court restore my maiden name."

"Mecana, you're wasting your time. Based on his confession, the judge has refused to set bail and until someone overrules that, no visitors."

"Looks like we will have to have a talk with your ex."

"Looks that way," Darcie replied.

"Why don't you do that, Mecana, and leave my prisoner alone," Sullivan said.

"I'll call Nick," Darcie said.

"Let's go," Mecana said. "Something smells in here and it has a suit on."

"Mecana, you can't be right all the time," Sullivan said. "Did you ever stop to consider that?"

"Not where you're concerned, Sullivan. You don't give a shit about anyone but yourself."

"You're damn right. I learned a long time ago you have to take care of number one first," Sullivan said.

"Let's go, Darcie, I got a bone to pick with you, too."

"Didn't know, did you, Mecana?" Sullivan laughed.

Mecana didn't say anything and walked away.

"Why the hell are you mad at me?" Darcie asked, looking surprised.

9

Mecana was silent as he drove back to his place. For some reason he felt Darcie should have told him about her ex practicing law in Dallas. He was a bit confused over his feelings because he and Darcie were only sometime lovers. There weren't any commitments. She didn't owe him any explanations and he didn't her.

"You want to stay over for the weekend, Darcie?"

"I don't think so. I don't know if I cheered you up but I did me. Think I'll go work out and drive down to Waco to see my family. We can check in with Nick on Monday."

"Why do I have that used feeling?" Mecana said, never taking his eyes off the road.

"Maybe you were, but you got your share."

"You don't pull any punches, do you, lady?"

"Nope. Kind of a waste of time. I care about you, Mecana, but I don't want this to get out of hand. You seem to be a little jealous over Nick. That puzzles me a bit. I don't want to complicate my life. I like who I am and I like who you are. Let's keep it that way."

"Fine with me. Just drop in anytime you want to get laid and I'll take care of you."

"Now you're getting nasty. Time for me to go home."

Mecana pulled into his driveway and cut the engine.

Darcie got out and closed the door. "I'll see you Monday and we'll go have a talk with Nick. Try to get some rest. I may be back." She smiled and walked away.

Mecana couldn't help but smile, too. She had a way of putting everything into the proper perspective.

Mecana watched Darcie drive away and went in the house and turned on the TV to watch a football game, but couldn't get his mind on it. He kept thinking of Darcie and realized he was beginning to think about her too much. She had made it quite clear she was happy with the way things were.

He spotted the almost-full bottle of Jim Bean on the kitchen table. He walked over to the kitchen cabinet, got a big drinking glass and poured the liquor to the rim, put the glass to his lips and began to let the whiskey slide slowly down his throat. He blinked his eyes and continued swallowing the whisky. By the time the glass was empty he didn't care what Darcie thought, and by the time the bottle was empty he didn't care what he thought, either.

He fell asleep with the TV on, the empty whiskey bottle lying on his leg.

10

Mecana's head felt big as a watermelon as he stumbled to the bathroom the next morning. He had never tied one on like that, not even in the Marine Corps, and hadn't had a drink of anything in over a year.

He called Darcie and her phone kept ringing. Finally he heard her say, "Hello."

"I was beginning to wonder if your phone was working," he said.

"I just woke up. You made me feel guilty. I didn't go to Waco. I took a bottle of Jim Beam to bed with me and we got drunk, or at least I did. Did you know he doesn't care how you feel?"

"Sounds like you're still drunk."

"I may be."

"Fix some coffee and I'll be by to pick you up and we'll have a talk with your ex."

"If my legs work, I'll do that," Darcie said.

Mecana was going to have the last laugh. He wasn't about to tell her he did the same damn thing.

When he rang the doorbell she opened the door holding a water bottle on her head.

"Come in. You can help me get ready for my funeral."

"Damn, you're not kidding. You look like forty miles of bad road."

"Oh, shut up. The coffee should be ready, pour me a cup. I'll see if I can navigate to the bathroom and wash my face."

Mecana brought her coffee to the bathroom. She was bent over the sink washing her face, her panty-covered butt sticking out. She looked in the mirror and saw him staring at her rear end.

"Don't let it even cross your mind, Mecana."

He grinned, handed her the cup and walked back into the living room.

It was after ten when they arrived at Nick Booker's office. He had a plush office in one of the ritzy office buildings. His matronly secretary informed them it would be a few minutes, that Mr. Booker was finishing up with a client on the phone.

Mecana and Darcie sat like zombies, still reeling from the night before. After almost an hour, Booker came out of his office, Mecana and

Darcie half asleep. He was tall, good-looking with bright blue eyes and neat brown hair, dressed in a gray suit.

He walked over to Darcie to embrace her. When she didn't respond he changed his mind and shook hands with her. "How are you, Darcie?"

"Doing okay, Nick. This is my partner, Thomas Mecana. We wanted to talk to you about DeMax Baker. We think they have the wrong man." Mecana shook hands with him.

"Come in and we'll talk." He led them into his office and gestured for them to sit down; he sat down behind his big mahogany desk. What looked like a good reproduction of a Picasso hung on the wall behind him. A picture of a beautiful young blonde on the desk caught Mecana's and Darcie's eyes. They glanced at each other for recognition. The new woman in his life.

"I was assigned the case a couple days ago," he said. "Was hoping I wouldn't have to do anymore public defender work. Haven't had time to review it. Looks like it's an open and shut case with his confession. Maybe I can cut a deal, save his life."

"Mr. Booker, he's not the killer," Mecana said. "He's being railroaded by overzealous FBI agents and prosecutors."

"Like I said, I haven't had a hard look at it yet, but it looks like he's saying he did do it, Mr. Mecana."

"I'm sure his confession was under duress, not of his own free will."

"That's a serious charge. I would watch who I threw that out to."

"Nick," Darcie said. "We have a suspect we think is the killer. What we need you to do is get a postponement or a change of venue to give us time to get the evidence we need to arrest the real killer. Don't let this go to trial anytime soon."

"I'm not sure what grounds I would have to do that. As you know, Darcie, this conversation could be construed as tampering by the court."

"I told Mecana you were a good lawyer. Don't make me take it back."

Booker looked at Darcie and his eyes softened. "I'll see what I can do."

"Good. We're counting on you."

"Thank you, Mr. Booker," Mecana said.

"Call me Nick. Your name's Thomas, right?"

"That's right, but everyone calls me Mecana, kind of rolls off the tongue better. If I ever need a lawyer I'll give you a call."

"Good. You do that. Darcie, why don't I give you a call? Take you to lunch."

Darcie gave Mecana a quick look and Booker picked up on it.

"Maybe I should take both of you to lunch," he added.

Darcie ignored the comment.

"Thanks for your help, Nick."

"My pleasure," he said.

PART FOUR
Doctor Golf

1

Doctor Durant came out of his office, handed a patient a prescription and saw his wife sitting in the waiting room.

"What are you doing here, Lisa? Is something wrong?"

"We need to talk."

"As you can see, I have patients. Can't this wait until I get home?"

"No, it can't," she said and rushed past him into his office.

"Nadine, I'll be out in a minute," he said.

"Yes sir."

He followed Lisa into the office and closed the door.

"Okay, what's so damn important that you have to scare the hell out of my patients?" he asked.

"I want you to take a vacation. Get out of town for a while, until this murder investigation is over."

"Mecana doesn't have any proof of anything," he said.

"They arrested a black man for the crimes, but until they put him on trial I think you should go away."

"I can't just walk off and leave my practice."

"I would have agreed before, but now that flatfoot won't back off. Go visit your brother, play golf."

"Don't you think it would look more suspicious if I suddenly left my practice and disappeared somewhere?"

"That's what I want you to do, disappear. I'll handle the police and press. Mecana's not going along with arresting the black man. He'll have him back on the street by tomorrow. He's after you. If you're not here he will quit snooping around."

"You mean he will quit annoying you?"

"Yes, that's part of it," she replied.

"I have to get back to my patients," Dawson said.

"You know I know best, Dawson," she said.

"Not always, Lisa. You just think you do."

"I want you to fire that prissy black nurse, too. I don't like the way she looks at you."

"Go home, Lisa. Let me get back to my patients."

"Dawson, please do what I ask before Mecana puts you in jail."

"I'll think about it."

2

When Nadine finished filing paperwork, she locked the office door and walked down the long hallway to the parking garage. It had been a long day. She was getting tired of it. Durant didn't give a shit about her anyway. She was just a convenient piece of ass when he was bored.

There were only two other cars on the third level, and no one but her in the parking lot. She punched her key lock and the lights came on in her car. She had an eerie feeling someone was watching and turned around.

There stood a person wearing a plastic suit from head to toe. The plastic figure lunged at her with a syringe. She swung her purse at the syringe, knocked it to the ground and it smashed into a thousand pieces. She jumped back, screamed and began to run, dropped her purse and picked up speed as she headed for the stairs.

She could hear footsteps behind her. She grabbed her phone from her jacket pocket and tried to dial 911, but was too scared and dropped the phone. When she got to the stairs she took a quick look over her shoulder and the plastic figure was gone. She took a couple of steps down the stairs and looked back again; no one was there.

She ran inside the building and saw one of the security guards coming at her, waving a .38 pistol. He looked to be in his mid-sixties and was shaking almost as much as she was.

"Was that you screaming, Miss?"

"Yes, someone was after me!"

"Where did they go?"

"Don't know. He was wearing a plastic suit, trying to inject me with something! I broke the syringe and took off running."

"You stay here, I'm going to go look."

"No, don't leave me! Call the police. Tell them to call Detective Mecana. He knows me. My name's Nadine," she said, pointing at her name tag. "Thanks for coming to my rescue."

"What I'm here for," he said, holstering his pistol. He liked the flattery and gave her that Barney Fife twisted-mouth look.

"The police. You need to call 911," Nadine said, pointing at the phone on his belt. "He may still be in the building."

"Oh yes, of course." He grabbed his phone and dialed.

A voice on the phone said, "Emergency 911."

"This is security guard Willie Black, license number 42671 at the Liberty Office Complex on 34th street. We have had an assault. At the moment we don't know where the suspect is. The victim is okay. She's with me. She knows a Detective Mecana and has requested you notify him. Her name is Nadine."

The dispatcher's voice came on the phone again. "A unit is on its way. I'll notify Mecana."

"Thanks, we will be waiting in the downstairs lobby," he said and hung up.

3

The police were already at the scene when Mecana and Darcie arrived. Sergeant Wayne Overfield, an athletic-looking thirty-eight-year shift supervisor met Mecana and Darcie at the door. "Whoever it was is not in this office building now. We covered every floor," he said. "I haven't interviewed the victim yet, thought I would let you do that. I recovered her purse and phone. We're still looking for evidence."

"Good. There should be some cameras. Check them out and let me know if we got anything."

"I'll check," Overfield said.

Mecana walked over to where Nadine was sitting. She had calmed down some and was drinking a cup of coffee.

"How you doing, Nadine?" Mecana asked.

"Better. Whoever that was scared the crap out of me!"

"Tell me about what happened."

"I was walking to my car, alone, when this thing snuck up behind me, trying to inject something in me. He was covered head-to-toe in a plastic suit. I knocked the syringe out of his hand and ran back in the building and he ran away."

"A plastic suit?"

"Yeah, it looked like one of those radiation outfits you see the x-ray people wearing. I couldn't make out the face."

"Did he say anything?"

"Nope, just lunged at me with the needle and I took off."

"Did you hear or see him leave? What kind of car?"

"No I was too busy running. There were two cars in the parking lot when I came out but I didn't pay much attention to them. I think one was a red sedan and the other one was a black SUV. I didn't notice what kind, both were new looking."

"Was there anything else you noticed about him - how tall, fat, slim, anything?"

"He was taller than me, average size maybe."

"How much taller?" Mecana asked.

"I don't know for sure, just taller. I was so scared I don't remember."

A police officer walked up to Mecana carrying a plastic evidence bag with the pieces of the busted syringe. Some of the liquid contents were still inside the syringe pieces.

"What do you want me to do with this, Mecana?" he asked.

"Give it to me, I'll take it to the lab later. Nadine, it might be a good idea for you to spend the night at a hotel. I'll send a female officer to keep you company and we'll talk in the morning."

Nadine took another drink of coffee and tossed the cup in the trashcan. "I'm ready. I need to get away from here."

"I'll stay with her, Mecana," Darcie said. "Maybe she will remember more later."

"That's a good idea if you're up to it. I'll stick around here and make sure we go over this place with a fine tooth comb. The killer is getting careless; broke his MO. Taking chances. He may have left something for us."

"I'll see you tomorrow," Darcie said. "Let's go put you to bed, Nadine."

Darcie and Nadine walked out the remote doors of the lobby.

4

Mecana called Darcie the next morning at the hotel. "Nadine wants to leave town, Mecana, she's scared," Darcie said.

"I can understand that but we need her for a witness. I hope she will do it voluntarily. The parking lot video should show us something. They're supposed to have it here by one. See if she will come to the police station to view it with us. She may be able to add something."

"Hold on a minute." Mecana waited. "She said okay, but wants police protection until she leaves town."

"Tell her she's got it. See you at one o'clock."

"Okay," Darcie said.

Mecana and Verves were as nervous as a whore in church, waiting for the techs to set up the video. Darcie and Nadine showed up and they all sat down to take a look.

A flash of light hit the screen then went out. All that was visible were two shadowy figures too dim to make out. The film rolled and jumped as the events Nadine described took place in the dark.

"Damn, damn, damn!" Mecana said, jumping to his feet. "What kind of mess is this? I thought we were supposed to be in the electronic age. Don't those people ever check their cameras?"

"I'll have the techs take a look," Verves said. "They can do amazing things. Maybe they can enhance it to make out the details."

"Yeah do that, Chief. This has been the most difficult case I ever had. You would think we could catch a break, son of a bitch."

"Well," Nadine said, "you can see enough to know I didn't make it up. That madman is after me for some reason."

Mecana flopped down in his chair again and let out a big sigh. "Yes, I can see that much. But the man in that tape is so vague it could be Mickey Mouse for all we know. I thought we had something we could throw at Durant this time."

"Why do you keep connecting Durant?" Darcie asked. "Maybe he doesn't have anything to do with the murders. He has some good alibis. They check out."

"My gut tells me there's a hole in those alibis somewhere. I just have to find it."

"What if your gut's wrong and you're after an innocent man?"

"It's not."

"Well, I'm as disappointed as you are, Mecana," Verves said, "but after fifteen years I've learned you're right more times than you're wrong.

Pick Durant up for questioning. We'll improve this video some and show it to him; he just might break."

"I tried to call him before I left work to remind him he was scheduled at the hospital for surgery tomorrow," Nadine said. "No answer from any of his phones. He does that sometimes, even his wife won't know where he is. I know I'm damn sure not going back there."

"We'll pay him a visit at that hotel he lives in. His wife can call the Mayor," Mecana said.

"I'm sorry I was so rough on you about Baker, Mecana," Verves said. "To tell you the truth, that's what I thought, too. I was trying too hard to be politically correct."

"Get Nadine a body guard for us, Chief," Mecana said. "You coming, Darcie?"

"You're my partner," she said and picked up her purse.

5

Mecana turned on to the long drive and drove up to the front of the eighteenth-century mansion. Tall stone pillars and big hundred-year-old double front doors marked its elegance.

"You ever been in a house this big, Mecana?"

"Not unless you count the American Airlines Center."

Two Hispanic-looking men with hedge cutters were trimming hedges nearby. Mecana rapped on the door with the door knocker three times before the door opened. A small, middle-aged black-eyed woman wearing a maid uniform stood in the doorway.

"May I help you?" she asked with a strong Spanish accent.

"We're from the Dallas Police," Mecana said, showing her his badge. "We're looking for Doctor Durant."

"Mister Durant not here."

"How about his wife? May we speak with her?" Mecana asked, stepping into the doorway.

"No, no, not come in," she said. Mecana pushed past her and she ran into another room.

Lisa Durant appeared a moment later wearing a white bikini; the top barely covering her large breasts and the bottoms hanging on her shapely hips. She had a towel wrapped around her shoulders, water dripping to the floor.

The little woman returned with two helpers with mops. "I try to stop them," the woman said, as the two other women mopped up the water as fast as it hit the floor.

Lisa spoke to the woman in Spanish. ("It's okay, Maria, I will take care of it.")

"Sí," she replied, and they continued to mop up the water.

"I was informed you were leaving the police department immediately, Mecana," Lisa said.

"Don't believe everything you hear."

"What do you want?" she asked.

"We're looking for your husband. We have some questions to ask him."

"You can talk to our lawyer. He's not answering anymore questions."

"I'm afraid he doesn't have a choice this time. We have a warrant." Mecana pulled the paper out of his coat pocket, took a couple steps closer to her and held the warrant up for her to see. "Where is he?" Mecana asked again.

"He's at the club, playing golf, I think. He always plays on Wednesdays," she said.

"You don't know for sure?"

"No, I had to go out early this morning on a shoot, but I know his schedule. He plays every Wednesday. He wasn't here when I got back."

"When was that?" Mecana asked.

"Around eleven," she replied.

"Where does he play?"

"The Broadview Country Club on J. B. Lamont Road. Now leave me alone," she said, rubbed her wet hair with the towel and walked away.

Mecana stood looking at the shining spiral staircase that climbed to the second floor and disappeared, the giant paintings of the Lamont clan patriarchs, the burgundy velvet drapes and eighteenth-century hand-carved furniture. The huge crystal chandelier in the center of the magnificent room probably cost as mush as Mecana's house, he thought.

Darcie saw Mecana gazing and interrupted. "Seen enough?"

"Yes. How's your golf game?" Mecana asked.

"Never played," Darcie replied.

"I think three times for me, if I remember right."

There were golfers everywhere; it would be hard to find the doctor. Mecana's limited golf experience told him the clubhouse would know when he teed off and who he was playing with.

An elderly man with white hair, wearing knickers and a dark tan was minding the store.

"Excuse me," Mecana said. "What hole would Doctor Durant be on?"

"None. He didn't show. Was scheduled to tee off at eight with whoever was here. He doesn't care who he plays with as long as he plays. Very unusual for him to miss tee time. Golf's his passion. Likes it more than being a doctor, I think."

Darcie looked at Mecana. "What now, Sherlock? You think his wife clued him in?"

"Hell, he could be in that house and it would take a week to go through all the rooms," Mecana said. "I read about this hotel in Vegas in the eighteen hundreds that had a tunnel running from the hotel to a nearby brothel. The married men would sneak off to the brothel and their wives never knew they had left the hotel. Maybe he's got a tunnel." "Only you would think of something like that, Mecana," Darcie said.

"It's true," Mecana added.

"Maybe we should back off a little, see if he turns up."

"We can't do that. We have to find him before it happens again."

"I agree with the questioning part of what we set out to do, Mecana, but we don't have anything stronger than what they got on DeMax. If you count the confession they have more; Mrs. Durant is not completely wrong. She could get us for false arrest and a lot more."

"The difference is we're after the real killer."

"I hope you're right, but you're so locked in on Durant. It's becoming an obsession. What if you're wrong?"

"I'm not. Let's go put out an All Points Bulletin on him."

"Wish I was as sure as you are."

"You will be."

"I don't know. Has it crossed your mind that the guy on the tape is doing this alone? That he's your everyday, ordinary, run-of-the-mill serial killer, and doesn't even know Durant?"

Mecana gave Darcie a puzzled look. "Remind me to get a new partner," he said.

"Hey, I'm just trying to be helpful," she said.

"Well, you're not."

"Is this a partnership or not?" Darcie said. "I have an opinion once in a while that might just be worth listening to. Take me to my car. I don't think I want to ride with you. There's an apartment I have to go look at, anyway. I've got to move."

"Whatever," Mecana said.

6

Mecana waited in the lounge of the forensics lab while Doctor Seymour went to check on the status of the report on the drug used in Nadine's attack. After about thirty minutes he came out of the lab.

"We ran some comparison tests that we can do in our lab and there is a similarity, but I need a more sophisticated analysis to say for sure. It will take a couple of weeks for that."

"How would he get that much of the drug, Doc?"

"Easy if he's a doctor or someone that had access to it, like a pharmacist, pharmaceutical salesman or even a patient. The drugs would come in a box of six vials if it was the usual amount, and those vials would have three to five hundred units per vial. He would have enough to kill ten more women. A normal dose is ten units and he injected two hundred. The drug could have sat there for years and actually gotten stronger or have been contaminated. Either way, he didn't care."

"We haven't told anyone what drug was used, so it must be our killer," Mecana said. "I'm pretty sure it's the same drug," Seymour said.

"Doctor Durant is the only one I've come up with that fits all the prerequisites. Now we can't find him. He's scared to death of his wife. She's the one with all the money and he doesn't want to lose it. But why mutilate them if your motive is to shut them up? Seems like that's enough. Why the brutal overkill? That's the part that's confusing me. The psycho element. I'm not sure about the attack on Nadine. He could have not intended to kill her, but send a message of some kind."

"Regardless," Seymour said, "I would bet my last dime the guy who tried to kill Nadine murdered all of the others."

"Yeah, this one's kind of got me buffaloed, Doc."

"You'll figure it out, you always do."

"Thanks, Doc."

"Where's your shadow?" Seymour asked.

Mecana grinned. "Don't think she would like that comment too much, Doc. Pretty damn independent."

"Didn't mean any harm."

"I know you didn't. They're going up on her rent and her lease is up next month. She's looking for a new place for the old price."

"In this town, good luck," Doctor Seymour said.

7

The last thing Mecana needed to see when he got home that night was a red Mustang convertible sitting in his drive way, but there it was.

The door was unlocked. He heard the TV blasting when he walked in.

There sat Emily, munching on some stale chips he had opened two days ago.

"What are you doing here? Where's your mother?"

"I came by myself. Your key was where it always is. You should get a new hiding place, Daddy."

"You came by yourself?"

"Yes, I ran away. I'm going to live with you."

"Your mother doesn't know where you are?"

"Don't think so," she said, flipping through the channels.

"Cut the TV off, we need to talk."

Emily turned off the television and stood up and brushed her long brown hair from her face. Mecana stared at her. It had been a year since he last saw her. She wasn't a little girl anymore. He was looking at a full-grown woman.

"Why did you run away?"

"Mom was going to take my car! I told her you bought the car and she had no right to take it."

"Why was she going to take your car?"

"Because I made a 'C' in Algebra and a 'D' in PE."

"How do you make a 'D' in PE? Nobody makes a 'D' in PE. All you have to do is show up!"

"That's why I made a 'D'. I didn't see any reason to go to that class, running around the gym, accomplishing nothing."

"And the Algebra?"

"Who's going to use Algebra? Waste of time."

"I see. You have become an expert on life at sixteen."

"No, but it's my car. Not hers!"

"Have a seat and let me call your mother."

Mecana dialed. "Hello? That you, Tom?"

"Emily is here," Mecana said.

"Thank god! I was about to call the police. I've been worried sick."

"She's fine, Amanda. She said you were going to take her car."

"She's been ignoring her studies ever since you bought her that car. All she wants to do is run up and down the road with her friends."

"She told me. Don't you think that might be a little drastic?"

"Don't you have any sense of responsibility, Tom? You don't have to deal with the everyday situations. You can stand back and play the hero without having to make the hard choices."

"You're right, Amanda. It's your call. If you think that's the thing to do to get her back on track that's what you should do."

Emily was listening. "I'm not going back," she said.

"Go sit down, young lady. I'll deal with you in a minute," Mecana said.

Emily folded her arms, frowned and marched back to the couch and sat down.

"I'm up to my butt in alligators, Amanda. You're going to have to come get her."

"You always are. Nothing is more important to you than your job."

"Let's don't get into that now. Forget what I said, I'll drive her home and catch a flight back to Dallas. It will give me a chance to see Morgan."

"Tom, you need to make her understand that she keeps the car only if she brings her grades up and starts showing a little more respect."

"I'll talk to her. I'm going to leave now. I have to be back in Dallas tomorrow."

"I'll be expecting you."

"Bye, Amanda."

Emily jumped up from the couch and ran over to Mecana. "Don't make me go back, Daddy, I don't want to!"

"Emily, you can't stay here. I have no one to take care of you."

"I can take care of myself. I'm a big girl now."

"Yes, you are, but you still need someone around to keep everything going. I don't know when I'll be home. I work all hours. You wouldn't like it here. All your friends are in Austin and your mother is trying to do what's right for your future. She loves you very much. The same as I do."

"Is she going to take my car?"

"Probably for a little while, but get your grades up and she will give it back. Tell you what I'll do, you go home and behave yourself, and next year when you graduate, I'll buy you a new car - if you graduate with at least a 'B' average."

"A new car?"

"Yes, a new one."

"A convertible?"

"Yes, deal?"

"Okay, deal," she said and hugged his neck.

"Just one thing. Don't say anything to your mother about the new car. That will be our little secret."

"Okay," she said.

"Let's get you back to Austin. I have to work tomorrow."

"I can drive myself. I came up here by myself."

"I know, and the thought of that scares me to death. Let me make a phone call and we'll go."

Mecana punched his speed dial and Darcie answered.

"Your nickel, Mecana," Darcie said.

"My sixteen-year-old daughter showed up unexpectedly in the car I bought her. I have to drive her back to Austin. I'll catch a flight and be back tomorrow."

"What happened?" Darcie asked.

"Oh, growing pains. Trying to assert her independence. But I got it handled. I bribed her."

"You're a real diplomat, Mecana."

"I thought so. I'll call you when I get back. You can pick me up."

"Okay. I'll petition the court for the search warrants in the morning."

"Good. See you tomorrow," he hung up the phone. "You need to go to the bathroom before we go, Emily"

"I'm not five years old anymore, Daddy. But I am hungry, let's stop at McDonalds and get a hamburger."

"You got it kid. Like old times."

8

Darcie called headquarters and had them send two uniforms to Durant's Liberty Building Office to pick up his computers for analysis. When she got there it was open, and Lisa Durant was going through her husband's desk. Lisa turned to look when Darcie walked in, closing the desk drawer hurriedly.

"Mrs. Durant, you will have to leave the office. I have a search warrant and no one can take anything out of this office except the police."

"May I see the warrant please?" Lisa asked. Darcie took the warrant from her purse and handed it to Lisa. She glanced over it and handed it back to her.

"What do you expect to find, Detective Connors?"

"Don't know yet. What are you looking for?"

"Making sure he didn't leave a check book or any credit cards. Someone could rip us off big time."

"You know where your husband is?"

"No, I'm as much in the dark as you are. Filed a missing persons report. Haven't heard from him."

"Mrs. Durant, we will find your husband. Don't help him. If you know where he is you should let us know, or you will be charged with harboring a fugitive."

Her eyes got big and she stared at Darcie like she was from another planet. "Has it occurred to you, Miss Connors, that something may have happened to Dawson? Why do you think I filed the report? Your bunch is making all kinds of wild assumptions and harassing me instead of finding Dawson."

"We have an APB out on him. Every police station in the entire country is aware we're looking for him."

"I have to go," she said, picked up her pearl-inlaid purse, and hurried away.

Two young uniform cops walked up to the open door; one still trying to follow Lisa's backside down the hall with his eyes.

"Alright, guys, come in, show's over. I need you to package everything that's not nailed down. Make sure you don't damage anything, then lock up and take everything to the office. Put the keys in my desk drawer."

The officers nodded. Darcie walked out the door. Her phone rang. "You on the ground, Mecana?"

"Yeah, Love Field. I'll be waiting for you on taxi row."

"I'm not too far away. I'll be there in about fifteen minutes."

"Thanks, I'll be watching for you."

Mecana spotted Darcie's black Charger and stepped onto the curb. She stopped and he got in.

Darcie made a turn off the exit and they headed downtown.

"Get your daughter back on the right path?"

"I hope so. Big mistake buying that car, it's caused me all kinds of problems."

"Kind of glad I don't have any."

"What, cars?"

"No, kids. Smart ass."

Mecana grinned.

"Lisa Durant was at the doctor's office looking for something when I got there," Darcie said. "She said she was looking for credit cards. I think she was looking for something else. I had all the office stuff sent downtown. I don't think we're going to find anything. I'm sure she's already anticipated the search warrant for the house. You know she hates your guts. Blames you for all her problems."

"Most likely. Take me by the house, I need to shower and get my truck," Mecana said.

"You have a problem with lady drivers?"

"You want the truth or a lie?"

"Never mind. I got another apartment to look at anyway. On the other side of town but the rent's good."

"Is it safe?"

"Got a fence and security guards like the old place, but I haven't had a chance to check out the neighbors yet."

"Alright, I'll pick you up after lunch and we'll pay a visit to the Durant Mansion."

"One-thirty, my place," Darcie said.

"I'll be there," he said.

9

Mecana stepped out of the shower and his telephone rang. It was his youngest, Morgan.

"Daddy, did you tell Emily you were going to buy her a car for graduation?"

So much for secrets, Mecana thought. "Yes I did, if she made good grades and behaved herself."

"What about me? I graduate from junior high next year. Are you going to buy me a car, too?"

"Don't think so. We'll figure something out."

"It's not fair! I make good grades and I'm not going to get anything."

"I didn't say that. How about a trip to Disney World?"

"Will you go too?"

"We'll see."

"Daddy, mom wants to talk to you."

Mecana sighed and considered hanging up. "Put her on, Morgan."

"Tom, how am I going to teach these kids work ethic and responsibility when you spoil them like that?"

"Christ, Amanda, I love my kids. I'm trying to be a good father."

"Instead of buying a car, help me with her college tuition," she said.

"Amanda, you're a CPA, you make more money than I do. I send you most of my check. Why don't you tell that good-for-nothing boyfriend of yours to get off his ass and pay his own way?"

"That's none of your business, Tom. I can see this conversation is going nowhere. We'll discuss it later."

"Much later, as far as I'm concerned. Put my daughter back on the phone so I can say goodbye."

"Yes Daddy?"

"Morgan. You plan on me and you going to Disney World next spring."

"Thanks Daddy!"

"Tell Emily she's going to get the car I promised, because I promised."

"Yes, Daddy, I'll tell her."

"Bye, baby," he said.

10

Mecana was still thinking about his kids when he picked up Darcie. "Darcie, you may be right."

"Right about what?"

"Not having any kids. I love mine to death but being a parent is a hard job. Even harder when you have to do it long distance."

"Something else happen?"

"My thirteen year old thinks she's not getting her share."

"Is she?"

"She is now, got me to promise I would take her to Disney World. I may have to sell the house to pay for all I promised them."

"That's not your kids' fault."

"No it's not. You call Booker about DeMax?"

"He got the judge to set bail since there is some question of his guilt with the attack on Nadine. They released him this morning."

"Good. I bet Sullivan is fit to be tied."

"That man gives me the willies," Darcie said.

"Not exactly my favorite person, either. He's been trying to get me fired ever since I testified against him in an Internal Affairs investigation when we worked together on the Dallas PD. Had a drug dealer tell me he paid Sullivan off, so I told the investigating team. Unfortunately, the guy turned up dead before he testified and the charges were dropped. Sullivan resigned and a couple years later turned up wearing an FBI badge."

"We don't find Durant soon he might get his wish," Darcie said.

Mecana and Darcie arrived at the Durant mansion early, parked where they could see the entrance and waited to approach Lisa on neutral ground.

She came out about an hour after they got there and headed downtown in her Lexus, parked and went in a camera shop on Whitehurst.

Mecana and Darcie did the same. They walked up beside her as she was making a purchase.

"Fancy meeting you here, Mrs. Durant," Mecana said. "Did you know your husband was not at the golf course? Do you have any other suggestions?"

"I don't have anything to say to you, Mecana; or your whore."

"Well, she's not a whore, but if she was, your womanizing husband would pay big bucks for her."

"Mecana, what the hell did you just say?" Darcie asked. "You're comparing me to a whore."

"Sorry about that, Miss Connors," Lisa said. "Mecana seems to bring out the worst in me."

"He has a way of doing that," Darcie said, frowning at Mecana.

"I would think you would want to cooperate, Mrs. Durant," Mecana said.

"Are you trying to match wits with me, Mecana?"

"I wouldn't dare. Where is he?" Mecana asked.

"I don't know."

"You expect me to believe that?"

"Since you are a crude imbecile that chooses to do this in public, let's get it over with once and for all. My husband and I have been having marital difficulties, primarily for the reasons you implied, which are none of your business. Yet you continue to harass us about those brutal crimes with no evidence. You're a worn-out old cop that has lost his edge and you're grasping at straws to save your job. I don't know where Dawson is. My concern now is for myself and I will not answer anymore questions about him. Any other communication you have with me will have to go through my attorney. Leave me alone and go play cops and robbers with someone else."

She snatched up her bag and walked out of the shop.

"I think I have just been told off big time," Mecana said.

"He'd pay big bucks..." Darcie said. "Why the hell did you say something like that, Mecana?"

"Thought she would get mad, lose her cool and spill the beans."

"Well she didn't." Darcie's brown eyes were dancing as she hurried out the door.

Mecana looked at the clerk and shrugged his shoulders. The clerk gave him one back. Mecana shook his head and walked out.

11

Darcie was still sulking when they got back to headquarters. Mecana opened the office door for her, offered to get her a Coke and even complimented her on her pretty green blouse to no avail; nothing worked.

"Okay," he said, "you want me to say it. I screwed up. I'm sorry. You happy?"

"You should be. Insinuating I could be a whore."

"I didn't mean it like that."

Mecana started to pour a cup of coffee, remembered the last time and sat the cup back down.

Darcie was watching. "Contrary to what Lisa said you're not as dumb as you look."

"I eventually get it," Mecana said. Verves walked out of his office.

"You wanted to see us, Chief?" Mecana asked.

"Let me get a cup of coffee first." Verves walked over to the coffee pot, poured a cup of coffee and took a sip. "Okay, let's talk."

Mecana and Darcie shook their heads and followed him into his office.

"As you guys know, the shit rolls downhill. Things have changed again. I have been instructed to take you off the case if I want to keep my job. The boss and District Attorney want to get a fresh face, someone that's not so locked in on one suspect. Plus they're still looking at Baker."

"You agree with that, Chief?" Darcie asked.

"No, but I don't have a choice. I have been told to replace you and that's what I'm doing."

"When is this supposed to happen?" Darcie asked.

"Immediately," Verves said.

"We can solve this case if you don't pull the rug out from under us," Mecana said. "We're getting close. I can feel it in my bones."

"It's not my decision, Mecana. I have to answer to my bosses, too. The Mayor wants you to resign. I'm the only one standing between you and unemployment. Maybe it's because we're both Marines, or you talked me into believing you knew what the hell you were doing, but you keep coming up zero. The public is clamoring for heads to roll and the first one is going to be yours."

"Chief, you yourself said Mecana was right a lot more times than he was wrong," Darcie said. "I know it's frustrating. We're frustrated, too. I don't know about Mecana's bones but like he said, I know we're getting close. Something is going to break soon. The glass is half full, Chief. Give us a little more time."

Verves put his hand on his chin like 'The Thinker' and stared at Darcie.

Mecana kept quiet. He knew she had him. How could any man resist a face like that?

"Alright, Darcie, you convinced me," Verves said. "Give me something positive I can show the boss before I have to do what I don't want to do. It has to be soon." He got up, picked up his coffee cup and headed for the coffee pot, then stopped and looked back over his shoulder and smiled at Mecana. "I think you owe her ten, Marine. She saved your ass."

"Yeah, sure," Mecana said.

"Well…" Darcie said, raising her chin up in an aristocratic pose.

"Well, what? You can't be serious?" She batted her eyelashes. "You are serious. You're still ticked off." He let out a deep sigh, rolled up his sleeves and got down on the floor and did ten one-arm push ups and got up.

"Okay, you satisfied?" he said.

"I'm impressed. Now do it with the other hand."

"Let's go, Simon Léger," Mecana said.

Verves came walking back in the office with his coffee cup filled to the brim, stopped and took a big drink.

Mecana did a little wet dog shake and frowned. "How can you drink that stuff?"

"I like coffee," Verves said looking at his cup.

Darcie and Mecana looked at each other. "Won't do any good to say anything," Darcie said to Mecana.

"Yeah, you're right. It's an acquired taste."

Darcie nodded.

Verves stood there staring at them with a puzzled look.

"Thanks, Chief," Darcie said. "You won't regret this. See you later."

"Yeah, later," Mecana said as they walked away.

Verves sat back down in his chair gingerly, like he had hemorrhoids, sipped his bad coffee and looked out the window. "I already do," he said to himself. "It sure looks lonely out there."

12

Mecana was waiting in the hallway while Darcie went to the little girls' room. A slender, gray-haired man with stooped shoulders and dressed in a dark blue suit walked up beside him. Mecana glanced his way.

"Mr. Mecana, my name is Charles Durant," he said. "I recognized you from TV. I was on my way to see you."

"Yes, sir. We spoke on the phone a couple of times. I'm sorry I had to send someone to search your house. Your son is a wanted man."

"That's not why I came."

"You know where he is?"

"No. I believe something terrible has happened to my son. It's not like him to just disappear."

"I'm sorry, I disagree with you, sir. There's every reason in the world for him to disappear. He's wanted for questioning in the murder of four young women."

"Mr. Mecana, we buried his grandfather this morning. I never told my father about the trouble Dawson was in. It would have broken his heart. They had a special bond. That's why Dawson moved to Dallas. His wife wanted to move into the old mansion, and that gave him the excuse he needed to come to Dallas to watch over his grandpa. He liked women too much, but murder? Never."

"Mr. Durant, I know how you must feel but I don't know what to say to you. Sometimes the people we love the most are the ones that hurt us the most. Your son may not be who you think he is."

"My son has his faults but it's not in him to do those kinds of things to another human being. When he was ten years old he saw two teenage boys on a bridge putting kittens in a sack to throw in the river. He grabbed the sack and ran as fast as he could to get away. The boys caught up to him and beat him to a pulp, but he never let go of the sack. No, he wouldn't, and couldn't, do that. I wanted you to know my boy is innocent. You're wrong about him, Mr. Mecana." Tears began to roll down his face. He brushed them away with the back of his hand and walked away.

Mecana stood there with a lump in his throat.

Darcie came out of the restroom and saw the man walk away from

Mecana.

"Who was that?" Darcie asked.

"Doctor Durant's father. He had to get something off his chest."

"He knows where his son is?"

"No. He was coping with the situation the best way he knew how."

"Can't help feeling sorry for him, however this turns out," Darcie said.

"Yeah, you can tell he's a good man; tried to raise his kids right. I've seen it a hundred times. Some turn out wrong no matter what kind of home they come from."

13

Mecana drove away from headquarters thinking about what Charles Durant said. What if he was wrong? He was locked in on the wrong person.

"Awful quiet, Mecana," Darcie said. "You planning your next move or thinking about unemployment?"

"Both, what about you?"

"I can go back to being a lawyer. What would you do if you weren't a cop?"

"Don't know. Too damn old to go back to the Marines. Maybe pull an Orr, and find me a small town that needs a cop and doesn't care too much about his past."

"You know I was blowing smoke with Verves," Darcie said. "I don't have a clue where Durant is, but I trust you."

"Thanks. I hope I deserve it. Let's go get some lunch."

Mecana pulled in to the Brogans parking lot and they went in and found a table. They had just finished their meal when Sullivan walked in.

"Ignore him, maybe he will go away," Darcie said.

"No, Sullivan likes to goad people when he thinks he's got the upper hand. I'm sure he knows DeMax is out of jail."

Sullivan walked past Mecana and Darcie looking straight ahead, like he didn't see them, stopped and backed up to their table.

"Well, I'll be, walked right past my old buddy, Mecana. You're going to be looking for a new job soon, buddy."

"I wouldn't count on it, Sullivan. Didn't you hear about the attack on Doctor Durant's nurse? A guy with the same drug tried to kill her. Don't that sound like the real killer to you? Why do you think they let DeMax out of jail?"

"Mistake, but I'll get him back," Sullivan said. "He's the real killer. That was some copycat. Your boy is dead meat." He paused, looked at Mecana and laughed. "Hey, I made a funny; dead meat."

"There's nothing remotely funny about you, Sullivan. Why don't you move on?"

"Your days are numbered, Mecana. The Dallas Police Department will soon be telling you to hit the road."

"We'll see," Mecana said.

Sullivan laughed again and walked away.

"I don't know why you waste time talking to him, Mecana," Darcie said.

"Kind of makes me understand why some animals eat their young," Mecana replied.

Darcie smiled. "I'm not coming here anymore."

Mecana picked up the check and looked at it. "Okay this one's on me, but don't think I'm going to get them all the time just because you're a woman."

"Why, Mr. Mecana, I wouldn't dare make that assumption," she got up, looked down at Mecana, slid her hand gently down the side of his face across his lips and pushed the ticket towards him with the other hand. "You can get the tip, too."

PART FIVE
Midnight Mutilation

1

A plastic-covered figure stepped out of the dark next to a camera mounted above a door and sprayed the lens with black spray paint, opened the door with a key, picked up a bag and got on the elevator. The elevator climbed to the ninth floor. The plastic-covered figure got off and walked up the stairs to the tenth floor exit door.

A big burley cop sat outside Apartment 1028, rubbing his eyes. At three in the morning everyone gets sleepy. He didn't notice the elevator down the hall had stopped on the floor below him.

A few minutes later, he thought he heard a door open and got up to look. He walked to the corner of the hall and looked around the corner, nothing. He started to turn back when he noticed the exit door was slightly open and closing.

He took a step toward the door and a shadow appeared on the wall in front of him. He reached for his revolver and a long needle plunged into the back of his neck. He fell against the wall with a slight thump and slid down the floor to his knees, his body leaning against the wall face-first. He took two more breaths. Death was so quick his hand was still wrapped around the handle of his .357 Magnum. He didn't even lose his hat. A gloved hand inserted a key in the apartment door lock, opened the door, went in, and closed the door. Nadine was sprawled out on her king sized bed in the nude, sound asleep. A bottle of sleeping pills was sitting

114

on the bedside end table next to her. With her jet black hair across her shoulders, and her shapely body, she looked like she was in a pose for a Playboy centerfold.

The plastic figure moved beside her bed, bent down and placed a syringe against the nape of her neck. The needle sliding into her smooth skin. Her big brown eyes flew open. She let out a moan as a gloved hand covered her mouth. She tried to move but couldn't. The drug was paralyzing her. Her breath began to come in short gasps as her body fought the deadly fluid. Her eyes darted back and forth then stopped focusing and became a frozen stare, her body limp.

A shiny scalpel appeared in the gloved hand and began to cut into Nadine's lovely body like she was a side of beef. The exacting cuts sliced her vagina from her body and left a mutilated naked corpse that a few minutes ago was a beautiful young woman. The vagina was placed in a black bag and the plastic-covered figure rose from the ghastly deed with the bag, stopped at the front door, took a pair of plastic foot covers and slipped them over bloody feet from Nadine's blood running off the bed. The figure picked up the bag, slowly opened the door and looked out into the hall. No one was there.

The next morning, a young woman on her way to work found the dead cop in the hallway about 6:30 and made the 911 call. Shortly thereafter, an ambulance and a police car showed up.

2

A somber group of police and medical personnel went about their business in the apartment of Nadine Howell. Mecana and Darcie arrived at seven-fifteen and made their way through a large group of media people in the lobby, rode the elevator up to the tenth floor, stopped in the hallway and looked at the fallen cop. Two medics were preparing to put him into a body bag. Mecana looked into the cold dead eyes of the cop. He saw the small trickle of blood on the back of his neck that had run down to his blue collar. "Whatever got him did it quick."

"Yeah, his hand is still on his gun," Darcie said. Mecana pointed at the key in the lock as they entered, Darcie nodded in recognition.

Doctor Seymour and his staff were doing the usual things.

Mecana and Darcie walked over and took a quick look at Nadine.

"He didn't bother to tie her to the bed," Darcie said. "He's becoming so proficient at it; it's like pulling a tooth for him."

"I don't think he had to, looks like she was already out of it," Mecana said, gesturing toward the sleeping pills.

"Yeah, looks like it," Darcie said, eyeing the bottle.

"Darcie, I'll have a chat with the doctor. Why don't you go talk to the super and find out how this place works. What kind of security. See if Nadine had any visitors lately. If she came in with anyone. I'll join you later."

"Okay I can do that. Meet you down stairs," she said.

"Thanks," Mecana said.

Mecana walked over to Doctor Seymour. "What about the cop, Doc?"

"Looks like the drug got him, too. There's a small hole in the back of his neck," Seymour said.

"I saw it. What time did this happen, Doc?"

"Sometime after midnight."

"Anything different this time?"

"We found small amounts of blood on the doorknob, in the elevator and on the stairwell. It's probably the victims'. Looks like he put something on his feet again, the blood tracks stop at the door. He left a calling card this time. A key in the door. We'll check for prints."

"Let me have the key when you get through with it, Doc. I may be able to get some information from it, too. Where it was made, etc."

"Wonder why he left it there?" Seymour asked. "He's too thorough to forget something like that. It must have been deliberate, but why?"

"That's what I was thinking," Mecana said. "Taunting us with it. Sending a message of some kind."

Robert Verves came in and stopped at the bed and looked at Nadine. "If you're through with your work here, cover her up, damn it," he said to no one in particular and moved over to where Mecana and Doctor Seymour were.

"Well, Mecana, what am I going to tell the media and the boss? The Police Chief will have my ass now and I don't blame him. With a little push from you and Darcie we let the one suspect we had out of jail, now this. What do you think about Sullivan's suspect now?"

"Chief, if you choose to use me as the scapegoat, so be it, but I'm not going down without a fight. If you fire me, I will appeal and keep working the case, with or without the department's support. Darcie is just following my lead and there's no reason to include her in this."

"We had him," Verves said. "Get him back in jail and don't give me anymore bullshit about Durant. For all we know he's dead, too. I'll have to give the boss something to take to the Mayor and City Council, and it's going to be your head. I'm assigning someone else to the case and asking you to resign by the end of the month. I hope you do, I don't want to fire you. I'll try to save Darcie's job if I can. You've got two weeks, either way."

"Fine, whatever. Let's keep this conversation to ourselves. No need for Darcie to know." "I can do that," Verves said. "Doc, let me know what you find when you finish your investigation," Mecana said.

Seymour looked at Verves, Verves nodded yes.

"Alright," Seymour said.

Mecana took the elevator down to the lobby. The reporters came rushing over to him.

"Can't say anything right now, guys, the department will have a release for you later," he said, and kept moving toward a sign on a door across the lobby that read 'Superintendant.'

Darcie was talking to a little man with a bald head, faded blue eyes, wearing a white shirt blue tie and kaki pants. He was leaning his butt against his desk, his arms folded across his chest. He looked frightened.

"This is Mr. Mark Colton, Mecana. He's the super. He said Nadine hasn't had any visitors since the office attack and didn't go out very often. She was planning on moving out at the end of the month but, get this, Durant was a regular visitor."

"When was he here last?" Mecana asked Colton.

"Two weeks ago," Colton said.

"You remember it was two weeks?"

"It was the first of the month. The day I always collect the rent."

"How long did he stay?"

"Until the next morning, I think. Didn't see him leave."

"Did he ever bring anyone with him?"

"A young lady one time. The three of them didn't come out of the apartment until the next day. Doctor Durant's a good looking devil, quite the ladies man."

"Yeah, we know," Darcie said. "Could you identify the woman he brought to the apartment?"

"Think so. A very pretty woman with red hair. I heard Doctor Durant call her name as they were going to the elevator. It was most unusual. I didn't think I would forget it, but I can't think of it now. Too shook up."

"Was it Kinky?" Mecana asked.

"That was it," he said.

"Was that the only time he brought any one with him?" Darcie asked.

"As far as I know."

"You have any cameras in this place?" Mecana asked.

"Only at the front door. The tenants don't want them, say it's an invasion of privacy"

"You think you could find some footage of Durant and Kinky coming in or going out?" "Think so," the super said.

"Why don't you do that for us? Include what was on the disc last night. Call me and I'll pick it up."

"Okay, I'll do that."

"Thank you, Mr. Colton, we'll call you if we need to talk again," Mecana said, handing him a card.

"Yes sir," he said, rubbing his hands together like they were dirty.

Mecana and Darcie came out of the office and the reporters converged on them again. The red headed TV reporter in the lead, her cameraman close behind.

"Come on, Mecana, tell us what's going on," she said. "Was it the mutilator? What about Baker?"

"You'll have to talk to Chief Verves when he comes down. I've got nothing to say."

3

Mecana drove along in thought. Durant had lied about Kinky, which means he could have lied about a lot of other things. DeMax told him she was a swinger but he didn't believe him. She was so young and innocent looking. After all these years as a cop he could still be snookered in, especially by a pretty woman. He was pissed off at himself for it.

Darcie broke the silence. "You think Durant lied about Kinky because he didn't want his wife to know, or because he killed her?"

"I was contemplating that. Could be either one, or both."

"Why would he come back and murder Nadine? Why take that kind of chance when there's no need to shut her up now? His wife knows about all his escapades."

"Most serial killers come out of nowhere to do their killing," Mecana said. "Don't know the victims. A one-victim murderer generally knows his or her victim. In this case it appears we have someone who knew all the victims from the get go, which is a total reversal of a serial killers MO, but that is exactly why I believe the killer is Durant. There's something else going on we don't know about that connects them all."

"I hate to bring this up, but you could be wrong," Darcie said.

"You've told me."

"To use a term you men use, why would you throw away your career and marriage for a strange piece of ass?"

"Compulsive obsession. I've seen men with it before, they have to continually prove their masculinity, it becomes an absolute necessity for survival. Being married to a dominate genius like Lisa could make any man go haywire. He's taken it a step further to the macabre, gone off the deep end. Listen to me, I sound like Doctor Wyler."

"You're making good sense."

"He's out there somewhere," Mecana said.

"Whatever you say, Sherlock," Darcie said, arched an eyebrow and smiled.

"You think you're funny?"

"Trying to be."

"Kind of are," Mecana grinned.

"You need to improve your sense of humor, Mecana."

"Don't have time."

4

Mecana was backtracking Durant when he got a call from the airport police. They had seen the bulletin on Durant and found his BMW in parking lot H2C, locked.

"Leave it alone. Don't touch it," Mecana said. "I'm on my way." He hung up and redialed.

"Hi," he said, "this is Mecana. I need you to send a CSI crew out to DFW Airport to dust a car. Parking lot H2C, red BMW. I'll be there by the time you get there. Good, I'll see you there." He hurried to the Silverado.

When he arrived at the parking lot the airport police, wrecker and crime scene crew were waiting.

He pulled up in front of the BMW, shut off the Silverado, reached behind the seat and grabbed a crowbar, walked up to the BMW, stuck the crowbar in the trunk latch and gave out with a heave-ho and the lid popped open. He almost didn't want to look, but there was nothing there but a sample box of Viagra and a spare tire.

"You want to pop the door for us too, Mecana?" one of the lab guys asked.

"Yeah, stand back." Mecana jammed the crowbar in the lock on the door, grabbed the crowbar with both hands, leaned against it and pushed, letting his weight put pressure on the crowbar until the lock busted, and made a shotgun sound as the handle fell off and the door flew open.

119

"Let me have a quick look inside before you start dusting." Mecana opened the glove box. Nothing but car papers, insurance and service receipts. He ran his hands under the seats, nothing. The service sticker had a date from the day before on it and showed the car had been driven only forty-eight miles since it was serviced. He stuck the papers in his coat. "You can dust it now."

A mousey little fellow pulled on gloves and snapped the wrist bands as he crawled into the car with his equipment. Another fellow was checking the trunk.

"I need those prints as soon as you can get them," Mecana said.

"Doesn't everyone?" the little man said. "Depends on how many prints and if we got them in our database. If we don't, we have to send them to the FBI and it will take a lot longer."

Darcie appeared, walking toward Mecana. Her high heels doing a high-pitched clickity-clack across the concrete floor. "I got your message, what we got?"

"The airport police found Durant's car. He had it serviced yesterday so we know it hasn't been here for more than twenty-four hours. Why would he have his car serviced if he was leaving the next day?"

"I've seen people do stranger things," Darcie said.

"True. I got the name of the service place on the receipt, maybe he let it slip where he was going."

"Or didn't go anywhere and left the car to make us think that was what he was doing," Darcie said.

"Possibly. We need a rundown on the flights, see if his name shows up anywhere. That's going to take a day or two. Let's go have a talk with the auto service shop. See what they have to say."

5

Mecana drove up to the service sign at Super Auto Lube and a young man wearing a blue uniform with 'Sam' on his shirt walked up to the truck window.

"Can I help you sir?" he asked.

"We're from the police department, Sam. My name's Mecana and this is my partner, Darcie. We need some information about one of your customers, a Doctor Dawson Durant." Mecana cut the truck off, stepped out and showed Sam his badge.

"Doctor Durant's a regular customer. Has a red BMW, always gives us a big tip. He was in a couple of days ago, for the usual service."

"Did he say anything about going out of town, or taking a flight somewhere?"

"No. If he was going out of town he always had me take him to the airport and store the car until he came back. He was supposed to come back for tires today; hasn't shown up yet."

"How long have you been servicing the doctor's car?" Mecana asked.

"Since he bought it a couple of years ago."

"If he said he was coming back for something before, did he?"

"Yes, always. He loved that car like some men love a woman."

Darcie glanced at Mecana and grinned.

"What do you mean, Sam?" Mecana asked.

"He had it serviced like clockwork, and we picked it up once a week to wash and polish it. If it didn't sound just right he would bring it in for me to check. He was so afraid someone would hit it, he parked in two parking spaces to keep anyone from getting too close."

"Did he always bring the car in himself?" Mecana asked.

"He didn't trust anyone to drive that car except himself and me. If he couldn't bring it in he would call me and I would pick it up, and then deliver it back to him when we were through. What's this all about? Has something happen to Doctor Durant?"

"We don't know, Sam. That's why were checking. No one has seen him in the last three days."

"That's too bad, he's a nice man."

"You knew him pretty well, didn't you, Sam?" Darcie said.

"Would think so."

"You said he loved that car. Do you think he would leave it in an airport parking garage?"

"Never, he would be too afraid someone would scratch it. No, that's something he wouldn't do."

"Thanks, Sam, you've been very helpful," Mecana said.

"I have to get back to work. Hope nothing's happened to Doctor Durant."

"We do too," Mecana said.

Mecana and Darcie climbed back in the truck, Mecana fired it up.

"You thinking what I'm thinking, Darcie?"

"He didn't drive the car to the airport and he's not on a flight."

"Looks like someone may have punched his ticket," Mecana said. "We're chasing a ghost."

"Could it have been DeMax?" Darcie asked. "He was out of jail."

"The only connection between them is Cindy Freeman. Durant said he didn't know DeMax and DeMax only knew Durant by what Cindy told him"

"Could they have been lying and there was some kind of disagreement, a love triangle, that they didn't own up to?" Darcie said.

"I wouldn't think so. DeMax was there for one thing, and it wasn't for long lasting love."

"Sullivan could be right," Darcie said, "if we tie the two together."

"That's a scary thought," Mecana said.

"Even scarier than that is if it's DeMax. He has a partner."

"You know if Sullivan is right I'll have to move out of Dallas. Couldn't show my face again."

"Then let's hope he's not right. I like being your partner."

6

Lisa leaned forward in her chair and gave Lineal Crawford a cold stare.

"Lineal, I pay you a fortune to take care of my legal affairs and a six figure retainer fee, not to mention the millions my family has already paid you over the years, and you're not doing your job. I want Mecana off the case. He got the black guy out of jail and he's coming after my husband again. You're supposed to have some influence in this town but I haven't seen it."

"They revoked Baker's bail, he will be arrested again," Crawford said. "That should move him away from your husband. The department will assign him to another case and that will be the end of it."

"Mecana has a one track mind. He will pursue Dawson and harass me as long as he has the authority to do so. It doesn't matter what they do with Baker."

"Mecana has been on the Dallas police force for fifteen years, Lisa, it's going to take a little time. The Police Chief promised me he would take care of it, but it has to be done in the right way. Hopefully we can put enough pressure on Mecana that he will resign, if the arrest of Baker doesn't solve our problem."

"I've heard all that before. 'Hopefully' doesn't cut it. If Mecana is not off the force by next week you're fired," Lisa said. "I've got too much invested in Dawson - financially and emotionally - to see it all go down the drain."

"We can sue. Would you like me to do that?"

"I want him gone, Mr. Crawford, you understand? Gone," she said, angrily. "Can you get it done or not?"

"Yes, but like I told you it will take a little time. By the way, where is Dawson? I didn't see him at the golf course Wednesday."

"I convinced him to lay low for a while. Doctor Handan is going to take care of his patients."

"I'll get it handled, Lisa, but you have to understand this is a very emotional time for me, too. My daughter was murdered. Contrary to what some people think, I want justice like everyone else. It just happens to be a coincidence that a suspect was already a client."

"I know. I'm sorry for you, but Mecana is not going to solve the case. He has a vendetta against me and Dawson. He's not looking for the real killer."

"I'll push the Chief. He owes me. I know where all the bodies are buried and he knows it. He can't afford to not do what I want."

"Unless he decides to bury yours," Lisa said.

"He wouldn't dare. I've got proof put away just for this kind of thing. You can count on it. Mecana is good as gone."

Lisa batted her big green eyes and studied Crawford for a moment.

"Alright, Lineal, next week. No more excuses."

"Thank you. Sorry for the inconvenience."

"It's not inconvenient, it's degrading and annoying and I won't stand for it. I always get what I want. You know that."

"I know, Lisa. I know."

7

Mecana pulled into DeMax's driveway. The Harley wasn't there. The old black woman from next door was sweeping her porch. She had on the same housecoat and flip-flops. The only thing different was she didn't have the rake comb in her hair. Mecana walked up to the porch and she stopped sweeping. "Suppose you lookin' for DeMax again," she said.

"That's right. You seen him?"

"Saw 'em yesterday. Put a bag on his bike and left. Ain't been back, far's I know."

"Did he say where he was going?"

"Wouldn't tell if'n he did," she said and started sweeping again.

Mecana stood there looking at her for a second or two; decided she meant what she said. He took a window tour around the house, looking in the windows and went back to the truck. "He was here, but gone now," he told Darcie.

"Think he'll come back?" Darcie asked.

"Don't know. This whole thing gets more bizarre by the minute."

"What now, Sherlock?"

"Don't say that anymore!" Mecana said, and slammed his fist onto the dash of the truck. "It's beginning to really piss me off!"

"Sorry, what the hell, didn't mean to upset you!" Darcie looked at the imprint on the dash. "Won't do it again."

Mecana shook his head back and forth, gritting his teeth. "What am I doing? My fault we're where we are with this. I was so sure. Now, I'm not sure of anything."

"Hey, it's alright. I know how you feel."

"I'm sorry," Mecana said. "Didn't mean to take it out on you. I wasn't going to tell you but Verves plans to assign someone else to the case in two weeks. He gave me a choice. I can resign or be fired; either way I'm history. I think your job is safe."

"So you're giving up? Feeling sorry for yourself because you may have made a mistake? I say may have because we don't know for sure until we find Durant. In the meantime let's get DeMax back in jail, just in case. Get your ass back in gear and catch the son of a bitch, whoever he is. We've got two weeks."

Mecana looked at Darcie, placed his arms around her and gently drew her to him. "How can I refuse, Counselor?" he said as he held her.

"You better not," Darcie said.

He let go and leaned back in the seat. "Well, if we're going to do this let's start by talking to a friend of DeMax's. He may tell us where he is if we lean on him a little. Name's Tyrone Simmons. They call him Little T. Ran across him when me and Rustin Kemp was checking DeMax out."

"Some friend," Darcie said.

"Survival, my dear. Uno, number one. Called saving your own ass."

"I'm right behind you, Sherlock, lead on." She held her hands up over her face like she was expecting a blow.

Mecana smiled. "You are something special, lady."

"That's what I've been trying to tell you."

8

Tyrone Simmons' last known address was a rundown apartment

building not far from DeMax. The tenants were mostly addicts that peddled drugs. Tyrone was one of them.

The front door was open to a filthy foyer with graffiti all over the door and walls. Two skinny black men with bloodshot eyes and needle marks all over their arms were sitting on the stairs. One looked to be in his forties, the other just out of his teens.

"You two lost?" the older one asked.

"No. You seen Little T?"

"What you want to know for?" the young one said.

"We're cops. He's not under arrest. But we need to talk to him."

"No shit. Surprise, surprise, ain't seen him," the older one said.

"He's around somewhere," the young one said.

"Shut up," the older one said.

"We'll find him," Mecana said and they stepped around the two men and started up the stairs.

In the next instant a small, thin black man with a shaved head, wearing a dirty white t-shirt and ragged jeans came flying down the stairs and knocked Darcie down as he pushed past her toward the front door.

"That's him!" Mecana yelled. "Stay put, I'll get him."

Darcie was struggling to her feet when Tyrone and Mecana disappeared out the front door. She ran to the door and saw Mecana chasing Tyrone down the street. The frail young man was no match for Mecana, who caught up with him at the end of the block and shoved him to the pavement. "I'm a cop! Stay down. Put your hands on your head."

"I know who you are. Seen you enough on TV."

Mecana cuffed him and got him to his feet. Darcie came running up.

"Think you broke my arm," he said, grimacing as he rubbed his arm.

"You shouldn't have run. We're not here to arrest you. We want to know were DeMax is," Mecana said.

"Ain't seen 'em. In jail last I heard."

"Out on bail but we need to find him. Thought you would know," Mecana said.

"Ain't his keeper, how would I know, man?"

"Not even if it meant going back to jail?"

"Heard about the women. DeMax like women too much to hurt 'em. Got the wrong nigger, man."

"If we don't find him someone else will, and they may kill him," Darcie said. "You don't want that."

"Lady, won't do no good to drop that stuff on me. Ain't seen 'em."

"If you don't want to talk, lean against the wall and spread 'em, Tyrone," Mecana said. "Let's see if you've got something in your pockets we can bust you for."

"Okay, I get it. He came by, gave me a few bucks and split. Didn't say where he was going."

"Is there a place you think he would go?" Darcie asked.

"Got a half-sister, don't know where she stays."

"That's a new one on me," Mecana said. "Mother or father?"

"Hell man, we don't know who our own daddy is. Maybe the same bastard. I'm his half-brother too."

"What's her name?" Darcie asked.

"Was Tameka Brown, two years ago."

"Anything else?" Mecana said.

"Don't know no mo'."

"Okay, Tyrone, you can go. Get yourself in rehab," Mecana said and took the cuffs off.

Tyrone didn't say anything, just rubbed his arm and was gone. Mecana and Darcie went back to the truck. The two black guys they ran into on the stairs were studying the chrome wheels on Mecana's truck.

"How would you guys like to visit our jail?" Mecana asked.

"What we do?" the old guy said.

"It's not what you did, but what you were thinking about doing, and if we hadn't showed up when we did, you would have done it," Darcie said.

The young one looked at the older guy with a confused look. "What the hell she say, Beagle?"

"Damn if I know, Bobby."

"Think about it. We saved you from committing a crime," Darcie said.

Mecana smiled and climbed in the truck. "Do you know who Yogi Berra is, Darcie?"

"Sure, why?"

Mecana paused, started to speak, and thought better of it. He gave Darcie a sideways look. "Never mind," he said and started the Silverado.

9

Mecana turned on his computer and ran Tameka Brown through the database. Twenty-one names came up, four blacks in Dallas, about DeMax's age.

The first three on the list didn't work out, but the fourth one's address was an old rundown apartment building not too far from where they had found Little T. It was obvious Little T was not completely truthful. With some questioning, they found her in one of the rooms with three other women. She admitted she was DeMax's half sister. She was in her late-twenties but looked fifty. They had the same mother who died two years ago. She said she would tell them where he was for fifty dollars.

"How about for nothing," Mecana said, "before I book you for harboring a fugitive."

"Ain't here, left, don't know where he went," she said. "Just funnin' you." Her eyes were foggy from the drugs and her mind kind of came and went as she talked. She paused and went into a trance for a few seconds then came back. "There a reward for him?"

"No, other than you won't have to go to jail."

"What would I go to jail for? Didn't do nothin'."

"If you know where DeMax is and don't tell us you have. Now where is he?" Mecana asked.

She looked at Mecana with a blank stare again and batted her eyes. "Don't know." Mecana and Darcie could see it was useless talking to her anymore and left her sitting in a chair, staring at a wall.

They were getting back in the truck when DeMax came roaring up on his Harley, spotted them and took off.

Mecana spun the truck around and gave chase. DeMax cut the bike through a yard and came out on another street, the Silverado right behind him.

Mecana dodged some trashcans and bounced into the street. DeMax let the hammer down and was pulling away.

"He's headed for the freeway," Mecana said. "Call for backup."

Darcie picked up the mic. "Officer needs assistance, any unit. In pursuit of murder suspect on a Harley Davidson, Texas license number 136HFC. Headed north on Frugal 1600 Block. Intercept, may be armed."

DeMax hit the freeway doing ninety and begin weaving in and out of traffic. Three black and whites showed up in hot pursuit. DeMax jumped his Harley over a curb, made a turn off an exit into a residential neighborhood. A small boy on a bicycle appeared out of nowhere right in front of the Harley. DeMax swerved to miss him, lost control and the bike fell on its side and skidded down the street, chewing up DeMax's leg on the pavement as it went; finally coming to a stop some fifty feet later, still running.

The three units surrounded the bike, the officers got out with their weapons drawn. Mecana pulled up in the Silverado, siren going, lights flashing. He and Darcie jumped out of the truck.

"Cut the bike off, DeMax, it's over," Mecana said. DeMax reached up and turned off the ignition. "Don't move, DeMax. I'm going to get you up. You know the routine. Keep your hands on your head."

"Ain't got no gun," DeMax said. "Didn't want to go back to jail."

"Well, you played hell then because that's where you're going," Mecana said.

"My leg's broke," DeMax cried out.

"Call an ambulance, Darcie." Darcie nodded and dialed 911.

Mecana lifted the bike and DeMax slid his leg out from under it. His pants leg was torn off; his leg bloody. "Man, it's fucked up," he said. His face was showing the pain.

DeMax held his arms up and Mecana cuffed him. "We've got an ambulance coming, DeMax. Before anyone else gets here I want to ask you, did you kill Nadine or any of those other women?"

"Man, I didn't kill nobody," he said. "Somebody's settin' me up."

"Wish I could believe that," Mecana said.

"Fact, man, swear. Ain't killed nobody."

"We'll get you to a hospital, DeMax," Mecana said.

Darcie walked over to the officers. "Thanks, guys," she said. "We've got him now."

10

Mecana and Darcie put DeMax in the hospital for a broken leg with around the clock guards, and stopped off to file their reports.

Nick Booker walked in. He didn't look like a happy camper.

"I should punch you in the nose, Mecana. Just on general principal," Booker said.

"What's your problem, Nick?" Darcie asked.

"You need to find you a new partner, Darcie," Booker said. "Mecana's a bad influence on you."

"Booker, I don't know what your problem is," Mecana said, "but I'm going to solve it for you in about two seconds."

"Tough guy. That's what's turning you on. That right Darcie, tough talk. I bet that's all you are, Mecana."

"Nick, you've always have been a poor judge of people," Darcie said. "He will stomp a mud hole in your ass. Now calm down and tell us what this is all about."

"You talk me into getting bail for Baker and he murders someone as soon as he gets out of jail!"

"We're not sure of that," Mecana said.

"You made me a laughing stock!"

"So that's what this is about," Darcie said. "Your ego."

"I didn't do it for Baker. I did it for you, Darcie."

"Then you shouldn't be practicing law," Mecana said.

"Don't you know I still love you, Darcie?" Booker said.

"Me and about ten others," Darcie replied. "Go back to your office, Nick. I'll get DeMax another lawyer."

"If you want to leave here upright, Booker, you need to do it now," Mecana said. "DeMax is back in jail. You're off the hook."

"You know it wasn't all my fault, Darcie," Booker said. "You're a hard woman to live with." He noticed everyone staring at him, realized he had an audience and charged out the door.

Verves was standing in the doorway of his office, his coffee cup in hand. "Thought I was going to have to put you in jail for a minute there, Mecana," he said. "A lot of macho mojo going on. You're supposed to be able to control your emotions."

"Hey, I'm on borrowed time anyway. What the hell," Mecana said.

"Maybe less than you think. Finish that report for me, I have a briefing I have to go to," Verves said and walked away.

Darcie walked up to Mecana and put her hand on his shoulder. "Would you have really kicked his ass?" she asked.

"Just as sure as god made little green apples."

"I don't know what got into him. I haven't given him any reason to think I wanted to get back together. The meeting we had about DeMax is the first time I have talked to him in over a year."

"I think he was a little juiced, he'll get over it," Mecana said.

11

After the incident with Booker, Mecana and Darcie spent the afternoon checking Durant's computers without finding anything they didn't already know. Several of the other detectives came by to give their advice, none of which helped.

"Looks like we wasted an afternoon, Darcie," Mecana said. "You ready to call it a day? I'll take you home."

"Okay, tell you what, Mecana, I'm feeling domestic. If you want a free dinner, take me by the grocery store and I'll pick up whatever is your favorite and cook dinner for you."

"You have an ulterior motive, lady."

"No, thought I owed you one for you having to put up with Nick's behavior."

"You don't owe me anything, Darcie."

"Nevertheless, I would like to fix you dinner."

"Alright, I never turn down a free meal. Let's go."

After Darcie did her grocery shopping, Mecana drove her home and parked the Silverado in her driveway next to the Charger.

Each picked up a sack and made their way into the house. As they entered, they heard a noise in another room. Mecana drew his Glock.

"What the hell are you doing, Mecana?" Darcie asked.

"Someone's in the house," he said.

"My sister is here, flew in this morning. Put the gun away!"

"Sorry, a little jumpy," he said.

"Sis, I'm home!" Darcie yelled as they carried the groceries to the kitchen.

"I thought we we're going to have a really big meal for two with all the stuff you bought. Why didn't you tell me?" Mecana said.

"Slipped my mind."

Mecana and Darcie sat the groceries down and Darcie's sister walked into the kitchen.

"Hi," she said.

Mecana's mouth flew open. "My god there's two of you!" he exclaimed.

Darcie and Marcie both laughed.

"Mecana, this is my sister Marcie; we're twins."

"You sure are," Mecana said. "I'm Thomas Mecana, Darcie's partner. Everybody calls me Mecana."

"Glad to meet you, Mecana. Darcie has told me all about you."

"Well, she hasn't told me about you. She said she had a sister, but she didn't say anything about you being twins. You look just alike, even your hair is the same style. I'm blown away."

"Why don't you and Marcie get acquainted, Mecana, and I'll fix dinner," Darcie said.

Mecana and Marcie went to the living room to talk and Darcie prepared dinner.

"Darcie tells me you're a teacher," Mecana said.

"Yes, although I'm thinking about getting into law enforcement like Darcie. Came up to have a talk with her about it. Thought we might open up a private detective agency together at one time, but she seems to be happy here since she became your partner," Marcie said.

"The feelings mutual. She's a good cop," Mecana said. "Tell you one thing, though, if you two worked together you would confuse the hell out of the bad guys. You could be in two places at once."

Marcie laughed. "Yes, everyone is always getting us mixed up."

"I may be leaving the department," Mecana said. "Maybe the three of us should have a talk about opening an agency."

"Anytime, if it's okay with Darcie," Marcie smiled.

"Married, Marcie?" Mecana asked.

"No, still looking. Darcie said you were divorced," Marcie said.

"Got two great kids, though," he replied.

Darcie sat the table with T-bone steaks, vegetables and a salad. Before they could cut the first piece of meat someone was banging on the front door.

"Who could that be, Darcie?" Mecana asked.

"I don't know. I'm not expecting anyone else."

Mecana got up and walked to the door and looked out the peephole. Nick Booker was standing there, his hair rumpled, one half of his shirt collar turned up; a wild look in his eyes.

Mecana opened the door. "What are you doing here, Booker?"

"Might ask you the same thing, buddy," Booker said, leaning against the side of the door. "You screwing my ex-wife?"

Darcie ran to the door. "Get the hell away from here, Nick! Don't you think you have already made a big enough fool of yourself?"

"I knew you were fucking this moron," Booker said, pointing a shaking hand at Mecana.

"My sister is here, we were having dinner, but it's not any of your business who I'm going to bed with!"

"Booker, go home before I have to put your ass in jail," Mecana said.

"You and what Army, asshole?" Booker said and swung at Mecana. Mecana ducked and caught him with a right cross. He fell backwards out of the open door, off the porch into the front yard. He didn't get up.

Darcie ran out the door and fell to her knees, looking at Booker. "Mecana, I think you killed him!"

Marcie came to the door. "Is he dead?" she asked.

Mecana walked over to Booker and looked down at him. "He'll come around in a minute. I just cold-cocked him. He'll be alright." Mecana bent down and slapped him a couple of times. Booker moaned and opened his eyes. "See, I told you."

"We can't leave him here," Darcie said. "Help me get him in your truck, we'll take him home."

"I'm not putting him in my truck. You still got a thing for him or something?"

"No, I just don't want to take him to jail. He would be disbarred."

Booker rose up on his elbows, shaking his head. "What the hell happened, where am I?"

"Call him a taxi," Mecana said. "I lost my appetite, I'm going home."

"Alright, go. You would do the same thing if it was your ex-wife," Darcie said.

"No, I wouldn't. The guy's on something, you want to get arrested, too?"

"Go home, Mecana, I'll handle it," Darcie said.

Mecana looked off into space, bent down and put his hands on his knees, looking at Booker. "Ah, shit. Let's put him in the truck."

"Can I help?" Marcie asked.

"No, I'll get him," Mecana said. "Darcie, you drive his car and lead the way to his house."

"Thanks, Mecana, I knew you would understand," she said.

"I don't understand, but I can't leave you here with him."

"I'll be alright. Marcie is spending the night."

"I'd feel better if I was spending the night, too."

"You can sleep on the couch."

Mecana smiled. "Figured that."

"Thanks," Darcie said placing her hand on Mecana's. "I really appreciate your help."

"I see now why Darcie speaks so highly of you, Mecana," Marcie said.

"Get in the car, Marcie," Darcie said and nudged her towards the car.

12

The next day Mecana and Darcie didn't talk about Booker, but there were some unsaid words that needed to be said. Finally, Darcie cleared the air.

"Mecana, thanks for helping me last night. I don't think we'll have any more trouble out of him. He called this morning, apologizing, said he was moving out of town."

"That's good. I put up with his shit for you, but I'm not sure whose side you're on."

"I'm on yours," she said. "Always have been."

Mecana looked at Darcie; she held eye contact with him to validate her comment.

"Okay, let's get back to chasing the bad guys and forget Booker," Mecana said.

"I'll never mention his name again," she said.

Mecana nodded and smiled. "You still owe me a steak dinner, lady."

Mecana and Darcie were on the street headed for the Silverado when a van came by with a big sign on the side, advertising a vacation in Costa Rica.

Darcie glanced at the sign and stopped. "Mecana, that advertisement on the van reminded me of something. There was a big travel-type poster in the guest house at the Durant's with Costa Rica on it. I didn't think anything about it at the time, but why would it be there if there was not some reason? What if that's where he went?"

"A long shot, but we don't have anything else," Mecana said and made a call to DFW airport security to check for him. It didn't take long for a computer check to confirm there was Flight 1245 from New York to Costa Rica on the day Durant's car turned up at the airport, and the flight did make a stop in Dallas.

Mecana whipped the Silverado up to the curb, flipped the flashing lights switch and walked away, leaving the truck sitting in a no parking area next to the entrance of the American Airlines counter.

Mecana and Darcie walked up to the counter and approached an attractive young female attendant. Mecana showed the attendant his badge.

"Miss, we're working a homicide and would appreciate your help"

"What do you need?" she asked.

"Would you check to see if a Doctor Dawson Durant boarded Flight 1245 from New York to Costa Rica on the twenty-sixth, for a departure of one-thirty-five? We ran a check before but they didn't turn up anything, may have missed this one."

Mecana took a pen from his pocket, wrote the numbers down, and handed her the paper.

"This will take a few minutes," she said and typed the information into her computer.

"Thank you," Mecana said. "We'll wait." Mecana turned to Darcie. "Maybe we will get lucky."

"He had to have a passport," Darcie said. "If he's on that flight they won't extradite him back if we're seeking the death penalty. They've had a law since 1877 against capital punishment. The only way we can get him back is if he comes back voluntarily, which isn't likely, or we waive the death penalty, and it would still be difficult. They're not too willing to extradite anyone unless they have already been convicted, which may be why he went there, if he did."

"How do you know all that?" Mecana asked.

"Just smart, I guess."

"Sure, level with me."

"A case I worked on."

"Sir," the attendant said, and stepped in front of Mecana to get his attention. "That name does not appear on the manifest. Seven passengers boarded the flight in Dallas. Here's the list." She handed it to Mecana.

He looked at the list. Three U.S. citizens, two female, and four native Costa Rican men. No Doctor Dawson Durant. "No Durant, but we've gone this far, let's check out the ones that did get on the flight," Mecana said.

"Customs could tell us," Darcie said. "They had to have passports to get out of the country and customs would have their records."

"Alright, you're the one that knows all this stuff. Lead on, my dear. Let's have a look."

"Start looking for a customs sign," Darcie said.

13

Mecana and Darcie walked up to a door with a 'U.S. Customs' seal on it and entered. A uniformed customs agent, a little overweight with puffy checks, was sitting at a desk behind a counter on the phone. Darcie took a seat and Mecana leaned on the counter and waited for the agent to get off the phone. Mecana visually surveyed the office. Various pictures of supervisors and the President hung on the walls. He could see the customs line through a big glass window on the other side of the office. People running their things through the x-ray.

The pudgy agent hung up the phone and got up and walked over to Mecana. "What can I do for you?" he asked.

"Dallas Police," Mecana said, and showed him the badge. "We have reason to believe that a passenger or passengers on a flight to Costa Rica yesterday may have been involved in a crime. We have the names and thought you could tell us about the status of their visas: addresses, etc."

"Do you have a warrant for their arrest? I need a warrant."

"No you don't," Darcie said. "We have probable cause that a crime has been committed and when we verify fingerprints we should have what we need to make an arrest for at least Grand Theft Auto. As a law agency, we need your help in doing that. That's called due process. Now, run the names please."

The agent leaned on the counter and looked at Mecana. "Is she for real?" he asked.

"I'm afraid so. She's a lawyer."

"I hope she's right," he said. "Give me the names." He took the list from Mecana and sat down at his computer and inserted the information and waited. A few minutes later the names popped up. He printed them out and handed them to Mecana. Darcie joined Mecana at the counter and they began to scan the list. All of them had thirty-day temporary visas except one. He had an indefinite work visa. The one with the work visa jumped out at them the minute they saw it: Rubio Dominguez. His employer - Lamont Estates. Occupation - Gardner.

"Look at that," Mecana said.

"Yes I see it," Darcie said.

"Thanks for your help, sir," Mecana said.

"No problem. I think. Good luck," he said and watched Mecana and Darcie leave.

Mecana called the lab and checked on the fingerprints from the car.

"Got some back," the tech said. "The doctor's, of course, the Sadler girl, and some we sent off to the FBI we don't have back. That's it."

"You're going to come up with a Sam Little. He's okay but the one I need to know about is a Rubio Dominguez. He worked for the Durants. I need to know as soon as possible. Especially if they were on the steering wheel or gearshift. Call Washington and ask them to put a rush on it. He's on a work permit from Costa Rica. His prints should be on file from his passport. Call me," Mecana said and hung up.

"Okay," Mecana said to Darcie. "We may be able to break this log jam if Dominguez's prints are on the driver's side. He either stole it, or Lisa Durant knows more about her husband's disappearance than she's letting on."

"What if she says she was just helping him get to the airport and would pick up the car later?" Darcie asked.

"Durant didn't let anyone drive that car if he was around."

"I get you," Darcie said. "Why would she let him leave it at the airport if her husband was going to need it?"

"Exactly," Mecana said.

In less than an hour the tech called back. "It's his prints on the wheel, gearshift and dash. No criminal record, just the passport," he said.

"Thanks, that's what I needed. Lisa Durant has some explaining to do, Darcie."

"I would think so."

"It's looking more and more like one Doctor Durant is history," Mecana said, "and Lisa knows what happened to him. She's so damn smart, she hasn't left one trace of DNA or anything to help us find Durant. Maybe if I face her down she will slip up."

"Going to try the whore routine again?" Darcie said, staring at Mecana.

"Not on your life," Mecana said and shook his head. "I learned my lesson."

PART SIX
The Box

1

Across town, another kind of meeting was taking place.

Robert Verves looked at the door with 'Quinton C. - Bolden Police Chief' on it, opened it, walked in, said hello to the Police Chief's secretary and sat down.

"Chief Bolden will see you in a few minutes, he's on the phone," she said.

Verves nodded. He looked at the coffee pot and thought about getting coffee, then changed his mind; he was too nervous. He knew what the Chief wanted to talk to him about - why Mecana was still on the job.

The secretary heard the phone drop back on the hook.

"You can go in now, Chief Verves," she said.

Verves got up and walked into the office.

The Police Chief was a husky man with thin red hair and deep blue eyes. He had a body like a middle linebacker, and no sense of humor.

"Have a seat, Robert, and tell me why Mecana is still out there."

"I gave him to the first of the month to resign or be fired. I thought we owed him that much after fifteen years."

"Normally, I would not have an objection to that, but the Mayor, District Attorney and a multitude of reporters are making my life miserable. They want this guy caught and Mecana's not doing it. Before you say anything, I know someone else will probably not do any better, but making a change will show we're trying to do something."

"Are you saying I should call him in and fire him now?" Verves asked.

"Yes, I want him gone immediately. You've got until tomorrow at quitting time to get his resignation, or fire him. I would prefer his resignation, looks better for us and it will give him more benefits."

"Then you're going to have to do it, Chief. I gave him my word," Verves said.

"Robert, sometimes you really puzzle me. You're a top cop with all the tools. I was going to recommend you for this job when I left, but if you can't take orders I don't know. I don't have anything personal against Mecana, it's just business; a part of being the boss. Sometimes you have to do what you don't want to do."

"There's something going on with the Durants and Mecana has got a handle on it. Let's give him a few more days anyway," Verves said.

"Mecana has blinders on, Robert. He's not exploring any other suspects and Durant has good alibis. I've looked over all the files and I don't find anything that would make him a suspect."

"Maybe not," Verves said. "But I've learned he has a nose for finding the truth. He has a reason to think Durant did it."

The Police Chief dropped his head and rubbed his forehead. "Robert, I have a problem with changing my orders. It doesn't look good to the other supervisors when I do it for one and not the other, but I'm going to make an exception. Today's Wednesday. I want his resignation on my desk by nine o'clock next Wednesday morning," he said.

"Okay, I can do that."

"If you don't, I want yours," the Chief said.

"Is that all, Chief?"

"Yes. Remember, no later than Wednesday morning, nine o'clock."

Verves nodded, got up and walked out.

2

Lisa Durant's Lexus wasn't parked in the driveway when Mecana brought the Silverado to a sudden stop and got out. The garage door was open; a sky-blue Silver Shadow Rolls Royce was the only car in the garage.

"Looks like we missed her," Darcie said.

"I'll see if her maid knows where she is," Mecana banged on the door several times with the knocker but no one came to the door. He walked back to the Silverado and cranked it. "Cover your ears, Darcie," he said and flipped two switches. Lights started flashing in the grill of the truck, rear lights going on and off, the siren screaming a shrill, ear-piercing sound.

The front door flew open and a frightened little woman, eyes as big as saucers, stood there looking at Mecana, not knowing whether to shit or go blind.

Mecana saw her at the door, shaking, and cut the siren off.

"You know where Lisa Durant is?" he asked, walking towards her.

The frightened woman's words were stuck in her throat. She shook her head up and down trying to coax them out. Finally, the words jumped out. "Don't know. Go away."

"You sure you don't know where she is?" Mecana said. "You want me to turn that noise on again?"

"No, no, lady doing pictures," she said.

"Where?"

"She say windmill where everybody goes. Don't know where."

"Windmill? What kind of windmill."

"Old place, shoot pictures. Don't know.

"You know Rubio Dominguez?" he asked.

She nodded her head. "Uncle," she said. "Go back to Costa Rica."

"Why did he go back?"

"No more job. She buy him ticket, go home. I go soon."

"Did she tell him to drive Durant's car to the airport?"

"Don't know."

"Has Mr. Durant been home?"

"No. Lady say he gone away."

"Where?" Mecana asked.

"She don't say."

Mecana nodded and told her "Thanks."

He walked back out the door to his truck and got in.

"Well?" Darcie asked.

"Rubio Dominguez is her uncle. I think Lisa sent Dominguez to the airport in the car to get rid of it because she knew her husband wasn't going to be driving it anymore and it would look like he left in it. She didn't expect it to be found so soon. Durant's disappearance may be revenge for his infidelities."

"Or maybe worse," Darcie said. "She got even with her rivals for his affection, too. Only one catch: the surgery."

"Thought about that. Don't think that would be a problem with her. She may be a psycho, but a hundred-and-sixty-plus IQ gives her an advantage most killers don't have. She has all the medical books she needs at her disposal. She grew up in that atmosphere. A little practice and she'd be as good as any surgeon. If I was a betting man, I would bet the farm she got the drugs from her father, either as a patient or she discovered them and decided it was the way to a perfect crime. So far she's right. Her maid said she was shooting pictures at an old windmill where everybody goes. That ring a bell with you?"

"No, unless she's referring to the Old West Museum. There's a big windmill there," Darcie said.

"Let's go have a look."

When Mecana drove up, two men were setting up lights and a model was having oil applied to her body in preparation for the session. Lisa Durant was checking her cameras.

Mecana ran the Silverado up behind the Lexus, blocked her escape and got out.

Lisa walked up to the Silverado and put her hands on her hips.

"What now? You find Dawson?"

"You know we didn't, but I bet you did," Mecana said.

"What's that supposed to mean?"

"It means we think you murdered your husband, and five women," Darcie said.

"You know those kind of statements are grounds for a lawsuit," she said.

"Big on this lawsuit thing aren't you?" Mecana said.

"You've lost your mind, Mecana."

"You let the gardener drive your husband's car to the airport?" Mecana said. "He wouldn't let anyone drive that car, plus you were trying to get rid of it by hiding it in the airport."

"You came to that brilliant conclusion all by yourself because someone drove Dawson's car to the airport?" she asked. "I wasn't there, remember? How could I give him permission to drive the car? I gave you too much credit, Mecana. You're dumber than I thought."

"Unfortunately, you're right. I was after the wrong Durant. You're a horse of a different color."

"Spare me your hayseed analogies, Mecana."

"Were not done, lady. You're a clever woman, but not enough to get away with murder. You'll slip up and I'll come for you."

"Not in this lifetime," she said, her eyes narrowing with a faint smile. "If you had any evidence you wouldn't be standing there running your mouth. You better have that truck out of my way when I finish or I'll run it over."

"We'll be back," Mecana said.

She slung the camera straps over her shoulder and walked away. Mecana and Darcie got back in the truck and drove away.

"If we can get her for his murder, they can juice her for that," Mecana said. "But we don't have enough evidence to get a warrant on her. I may have to go back and take another look in that house, anyway."

"That's breaking and entering. You'd go to jail," Darcie said.

"At this point does it matter?"

"It does to me," Darcie said, rolling her eyes.

Mecana looked into those big brown eyes. "You ever find you a place to live?" he asked.

"No, not yet."

"Why don't you move in with me? It's just me rattling around in that big house, plenty of room. We could split the expenses. You could have your own bedroom and I wouldn't charge you any rent."

"What would you charge me?" she smiled.

"Whatever you wanted to pay," Mecana said and smiled, too.

"I'll think about it," she said. She leaned over and gently kissed him. "That was sweet. You're a good man, Thomas Mecana."

"Not according to Lisa Durant and Robert Verves," he said.

3

Mecana didn't tell Darcie he was going to his house.

"What are we doing here, Mecana? I thought we were going to plan our attack on Lisa Durant?"

"We are, but I thought I would give you the guided tour to help you decide what you wanted to do."

"I've seen it," she said.

"Kind of, mostly from a horizontal angle."

"That's not what you're thinking now, is it?" she asked.

"Nope." Mecana unlocked the door and he and Darcie walked in the house. "You can have the master bedroom if you like. I moved to the guest room when my ex-wife decided to leave."

"Why are you still living in a place that has so many memories?" Darcie asked.

"I guess that's just the reason. Makes missing my kids a little easier. They know where I am and this was where we had a lot of good times, as well as bad."

"You sure this is a good idea? Sounds like you're not ready for someone else in this house."

"No, it's alright. You're welcome to move in and do exactly what you want, except bring another man here. I don't think I could handle that."

"Then what you're really saying is you want me to be your partner and girlfriend?"

"Yeah, I guess you could say that. I'm not proposing marriage but I'm very fond of you, plus we make a good team."

"I don't know, I like my independence. Give me a little more time to think about it."

"Sure, take your time. Either way it's okay with me," he said. There wasn't any Jim Beam left but he had an expensive bottle of red wine he had been saving for a special occasion. And since he hadn't thought of one before today, he decided Darcie's visit would do.

"They tell me I make a mean spaghetti dinner, if you're interested. I got some good wine, too. It's about supper time."

"You cook, Mecana?" Darcie asked. "That doesn't sound right."

"There's a lot of things you don't know about me. If you move in you'll find out. I don't know if that's good or bad," he said and laughed. "You want dinner?"

"You sound serious. You apparently think you can cook. Why not, I'll live dangerously. Rattle those pots and pans. I'll get comfortable, as they say. That is, if I can borrow your bathroom."

"Help yourself. I'll start dinner."

Mecana started cooking dinner and a little later Darcie came in wearing Mecana's Marine shirt and sweat pants, carrying her clothes. "Which way to the washing machine?"

Mecana pointed at the door and she proceeded toward it. Her 38C bra fell to the floor and Mecana's eyes brightened as he gave the bra a curious look.

"Men," she said, shook her head, picked up the bra and continued to the utility room.

When she returned, Mecana had set the table. "Be ready in about ten minutes," he said.

"Tell me officer, are you trying to bribe me?"

"Crossed my mind, but I was too hungry."

"That's what I thought." She saw some pictures sitting on a dresser. "Tell me about your family," she said, pointing at the pictures.

"Well, that's my dad, my brother Ethan and me in the first one. My dad retired from the Marines, moved to Florida. I don't get to see him as much as I would like, and my brother is a career Marine officer. I tried to follow the family line but I didn't have a war, got bored with all the training and got out. That's my mom next to us, Melinda. She died of cancer ten years ago. She was a very special lady. I miss her very much. The other two pictures are my kids. Emily, who's grown into a beautiful young woman, and Morgan, who's not far behind."

"Quite a family," Darcie said.

"Thanks. Dinner's ready, let's eat," Mecana said.

Mecana fixed Darcie's plate and poured the wine.

"Hey, this is good," she said. "You can cook."

"Told you."

"It will be a while 'til my clothes get dry. Think I'll try out that bed you were telling me about after dinner."

Mecana nodded. "The bed's made. Tomorrow we'll take a drive down to Houston and have a talk with Lisa's father. He may have left something out when he was questioned by the Houston Police. We need more background on her."

"Okay, thanks for the great dinner."

"You're welcome."

"You need some help with the dishes?" she asked.

"No, I've got it."

"You're definitely earning points," she said, and gave him a peck on the cheek.

"Take your time. I know it's a big decision."

4

It didn't take twenty-twenty vision to see that Doctor Lamont was the favorite of the rich. The women, even the old ones, looked like they were going to a fashion show, and the men to the bank.

Mecana walked up to the receptionist. She looked to be in her fifties, with bottle red hair, small eyes and mouth, too much makeup and several large diamond rings on her fingers. She looked at Mecana and Darcie; they didn't meet the dress code. "Do you have an appointment, sir?" she asked in a sarcastic tone.

"My name's Mecana, we're detectives from Dallas. We need a few minutes with the doctor. It's about his daughter."

Mecana could see he got her attention. Her chest began to rise and fall. "Has something happened to Lisa?" she asked and stood up.

"Something might, if we don't talk to him. We won't take long."

"Have a seat, I'll let him know."

"That's alright, we'll stand," Mecana said, as the lady opened the office door.

"You think bravado will do it?" Darcie asked.

"We'll see."

The receptionist came out of the doctor's office, held the door open and motioned for Mecana and Darcie to enter.

The first thing you saw when you walked in was a huge painting of Lisa. The office had big tinted windows, expensive furniture and a wet bar. A tall elderly gentleman, with perfect silver hair, green eyes and a stylish goatee, wearing an expensive gray suit, was helping himself to a drink. He didn't offer Mecana or Darcie one.

"You've got ten minutes to tell me what this is about, and it better be worth my time," he said.

"I think you will find it interesting," Mecana said, showing the doctor his badge.

"I know who you are from the news. You have been harassing my daughter and son-in-law unmercifully. But I also understand you will be gone in two weeks, otherwise I would have you in court by now."

"You do have your contacts, don't you," Darcie said.

"That I do, lady. Now what is so important that you thought you had to drive to Houston to see me? Make it quick, I've got a busy schedule."

"Alright," Mecana said. "Has your daughter ever been treated for any kind of mental disorder?"

"Did you find anything in her medical records? I know you had access to them."

"No," Darcie said.

"Then why ask me?"

"Did you treat her?" Mecana asked.

"What the hell are you getting at? What's your point?"

"Our point is we think your daughter is unbalanced," Mecana said.

"You're the one with the problem, Mecana. I see now why my daughter is so frightened of you."

"She told you that," Mecana said.

"Yes, you're making her physically ill. She's letting the servants go in preparation for closing up the house and moving back to Houston."

"Doctor, your daughter isn't afraid of the devil himself. She's playing games with you. Has your daughter ever been prescribed Ludimocson or been exposed to it in any way?"

"The drug was taken off the market years ago," Lamont said.

"We know, answer my question."

"I'm not going to answer anything," he said.

"You just did, Doctor. I know my place, and I know I'm not as smart as you and your daughter. But sometimes smart people can be pretty dumb. I didn't just fall off the turnip truck. Good day."

"Yeah, Doctor, what he said. Goodbye," Darcie said.

They came out of the office and the receptionist was standing by the door. The way she reacted she gave the impression she was more than a receptionist. Possibly the doctor's girlfriend.

She turned her nose up and walked back to her desk.

"You could have come in," Mecana said. "The secrets are the doctor's, not ours."

5

Mecana cruised up Interstate 45 toward Dallas, contemplating his next move.

"Well, we didn't get anything we can use in court, but I think we know where the drug came from," Darcie said.

"Only the police and the killer knew about the Ludimocson, but I bet Doctor Lamont knows now. I'm convinced he used the drug on Lisa, and she learned what it would do if you abused it."

"We still don't have any proof, other than the car incident, and that's not going to get us very far if we don't find Durant," Darcie said.

"Not only that but we're running out of time, as the doctor pointed out," Mecana added. "We have the entire country looking for Durant and he's nowhere to be found. Everything hinges on finding the Doctor. I think we have to think outside the box as they say. What would a genius like Lisa Durant do with a body? I would think the unexpected, the last thing we would think she would do."

"Alright, what?" Darcie asked.

"I don't know, I'm thinking out loud. Maybe keep it in the house."

"Well, while you have your brain in gear you might also consider he may be very much alive and a part of the whole thing."

"That's true, but I don't think so. She's too much of a control freak," Mecana said.

"We have to get in that house again, one way or the other."

"Take me home. Let's sleep on it, maybe we will figure it out by tomorrow," Darcie said.

Mecana dropped Darcie off, stopped by the gym for a two-hour workout, picked up a salad and went home. No messages from his kids. He couldn't get his mind off the case.

6

He dressed and drove out to the mansion. Lisa's Lexus wasn't there. He sat some three blocks away, watching with his binoculars, and wondered how he was going to get back in. He knew the place was wired, and if he was caught breaking and entering Verves would throw the book at him. Only a few lights were on in the downstairs rooms. Her father said she was letting the staff go. Who was there? She may be gone for days, hours or minutes. Mecana's phone rang. It was Rustin. "Hello, Rustin?"

"Mecana, that thing I've been trying to remember came to me. Right before I was stabbed, I got a big whiff of a woman's perfume. The killer is a woman, Mecana, not a man."

"That does make a difference, doesn't it?" Mecana said.

"Yes, damn it! I wish I could have thought of it before now."

"Thanks, Rustin, I'll let you know what I find."

"Yeah, it isn't Doctor Durant after all," Rustin said.

"No, it isn't."

"Thought that would help."

"It sure does, thanks. Talk to you later." No sense raining on his parade, Mecana thought.

He cut his phone off and decided to take a closer look. He walked in the shadows to the mansion, peeked through the iron gate and didn't see anyone. No wires running on the fence. He grabbed the top of the six-foot stone fence and pulled himself up on top and jumped down on the other side. He ran to the mansion and hid in some shrubs. A few seconds later, car lights hit the driveway and he ducked down. The car pulled up to the gate and the gates opened. The car drove through and the gates closed. It was Lisa. She parked in the driveway, got out carrying a large Big Top Pizza. The Lexus was loaded with travel bags. All kinds of thoughts were going through Mecana's mind. Somehow he couldn't visualize rich people eating pizza, especially Lisa, or having an affair with DeMax.

She unlocked the door and carried the pizza inside. As she cleared the entrance, Mecana darted to the door and stuck a credit card in the doorway and it stopped the door from closing completely. He waited a few minutes and pushed the door slightly open. When he didn't see or hear anything he opened the door, left the card in the door and went in.

All the furniture was covered with sheets. She was getting ready to move out. He carefully made his way down a hall, past the spiral staircase into another hallway. As he turned the doorknob to enter a room, he heard a noise and turned to look.

Lisa Durant was standing there with an automatic pointed at him, wearing Jeans and a white shirt with her hair tied back in a pony tail. That was the first time he had seen her in what he would call 'common folks' clothes.

"Want some pizza?" she said.

"No thanks," Mecana said, eyeing the automatic.

"Hand me the Glock, butt first," she said.

Mecana did as he was told and handed her the gun. She stuck it in her belt.

"Now what?" he asked.

"You're going to love this," she smiled. "I dismissed all the staff, was going back to Houston tonight until I figured out how to deal with you, and here you are to make it easy. First, I think I'll cut off your balls, eat pizza, and watch you die a little bit at a time. I expect you to put on a good show. Dawson did. He begged me not to do it, even pledged his undying love, but that's exactly what he got."

"What if I decide to get it over with and make a play for the gun? You shoot me, I'm done for and you don't get to have your fun."

"I'll cut them off anyway, but I warn you, I'm an excellent shot. You won't die immediately, and it will give me more pleasure."

"I believe you. In that case, you can count on a good show. I won't disappoint you."

"This way," she motioned the gun toward a bookshelf.

She walked to the shelf with Mecana in the lead and removed a book titled, "Jack the Ripper."

A plunger popped out of the wall and the shelf turned to allow room to walk through into another room.

"That's appropriate," Mecana said. "You're certainly the female version."

"You don't know the half of it. Go in."

They walked through the opening into a large room with the smell of formaldehyde. The old brick had been whitewashed. A large surgical light positioned on a stand hung over a steel operating table with metal clamps for the hands and feet. Next to the operating table was an instrument table. Except for an old rusted metal door at the far end of the room, it had the appearance of a hospital operating room with some extras. A folded plastic suit lay on a table, next to a row of five sealed-glass boxes filled with fluid containing the remains of the vagina of each of her victims. The boxes were labeled with their names. An un-posed photograph of the victims, that Lisa apparently took, hung above each box. At the end of the boxes was a large jar labeled 'Dawson Durant - A Cheater.' His testicles floating inside the jar. A phone-booth-sized glass box contained what was left of Doctor Dawson Durant. He was naked. His eyes were nothing but white round balls. His mouth gaped open, with blood bubbles floating around in the tank. His testicles were gone, his penis shriveled up so much it was almost sunk into his body.

"How do you like my little sanctuary, Mecana?"

"You are a very sick woman," Mecana said.

"I would like to think of myself as unique, different in my own way. Not like that do-goodie sister of mine. She tried to take the affection that was due me, so I pushed her off the roof. I think Daddy knew. I discovered later the drug Daddy gave me was what I needed, but for a different purpose. None of my friends were really friends. They hung out with me for the money. And Dawson, I made him what he was and he couldn't keep his dick in his pants. I had to have my revenge. You can understand that, can't you, Mecana?"

"No, not like this," Mecana replied.

"Got them all," she said. "Took the one thing they were most proud of, their sexuality. They paid the ultimate price."

"That's sure as hell an understatement. Does anyone else know about this?"

"No. It's my great-grandpa Jackson Bernard Lamont's and my little secret. I accidentally found the room when I removed a book and there it was. I put the Jack the Ripper book there later, kind of a tribute to my grandpa. There's more behind that door," she said, looking at the rusted metal door. "That's where grandpa kept his sex slaves and the corpses of people who got in his way. His missing wife is chained to the wall in there. There's much more but I don't feel like talking about it anymore. Let's get back to the matter at hand. Climb up on that table, Mecana."

Mecana changed the subject. "You do the surgeries?" he asked.

"Of course, nothing to it. I read up on it and found a couple of female bodies to practice on. Although that first slut of Dawson's was a little touch-and-go, with that nosey cop showing up. Enough talk, Mecana, take your pants off and get on the table."

He knew if she ever got him on the table he was done for.

"I don't think so. If you want me on that table you're going to have to kill me. No way I'm volunteering to have my nuts cut off."

"Alright, have it your way, but I'm not going to kill you right away. I want to see you suffer for the trouble you have caused me. How about I take your balls off with a bullet?"

"You're a real monster."

"Thank you. My grandpa would be proud," she said, and aimed the automatic at Mecana's crouch.

In the next instant, Darcie was standing in the doorway, her Beretta pointed at Lisa. Lisa glanced at Darcie, and hesitated. Darcie fired. A bullet hit Lisa in the chest. She staggered back against the wall.

"Bitch!" she said, struggling to raise the automatic. Mecana grabbed the Glock from her belt, pressed the barrel between her eyes and pulled the trigger, her emerald green eyes blinked and she made a slight jerk of her head, then dropped the automatic and slid down Mecana's body to the floor. Blood running through her long blonde hair onto the floor.

"You alright?" Darcie asked.

"How did you know I was here?"

"Thought you might be here when you didn't answer your phone. Saw your truck down the street. You men have a special relationship with your transportation. Knew you wouldn't be too far from that truck. Climbed up on the top of my car and jumped over the fence, walked in with out a problem."

"I didn't know you were that athletic."

"Was captain of my high school basketball team," she said.

"Lisa finally made a mistake," Mecana said. "Left the bookshelf door open, otherwise you would have never known I was here."

"You were wrong, it wasn't Doctor Durant."

"I was half right. We got backup coming?"

"Nope. I didn't have time to call. Why didn't you? You know your supposed to call for backup. That's what you're always telling me."

"I know. Everything happened so quick. I can understand why Rustin didn't call now."

"What is this place?" Darcie asked, looking around the room.

"Where a beautiful monster lived," Mecana said.

"My god. I'm going to be sick." She bent over, put her head in her hands and threw up.

"Good thing Doc Seymour's not here to see that, he would be bitching about you contaminating the crime scene again."

"To hell with Seymour. You two may have ice water in your veins, but I don't."

"Sorry I pissed you off."

"Me too," she said.

"Lisa said there was more in that room," Mecana said, pointing to the rusted metal door.

"You look, Mecana. I'm going to sit this one out."

Mecana holstered his Glock and pulled on the door. It made a screeching sound and stuck. He pulled on it again and it came open enough that he could see it was dark inside. The smell was worse than the formaldehyde. He felt a light switch inside the door and flipped the switch. A Light came on. He looked inside. A single bulb was suspended by a wire from the ceiling.

"Wait to call until I come back," Mecana said. She nodded.

Mecana slipped through the crack and slowly moved into the room. It was dirty and sweaty, with mildew fungus growing on the walls. Several large rats ran in between the old worn brick and disappeared.

About ten feet in he saw what Lisa told him about. A skeleton chained to the wall. From the size and pelvis he knew it was female. Bones were scattered all around, he recognized some of them as being human. Hand and foot shackles were mounted on the wall next to the skeleton.

An old tattered table with deep cut marks in the top was pushed up against the wall, and what looked like an eighteenth-century black weather-cracked leather Gladstone bag sitting on it. The bag was slightly open. He pushed the top back. Underneath a load of rat droppings he saw a sharpened rusted railroad spike, with what looked like bloodstains on it. What was left of a pink handkerchief was laying next to the railroad spike with 'S.H. Austin Symphony Member' on it. A small rusted ball-peen hammer and two long steel-bladed stained knifes. In the other compartment, a small leather purse with two shillings in it and the name 'Mary Jane Kelly' engraved inside the flap. 'J.G. Beard Leather Shop – London, July 1888' was stamped in the leather inside next to the letters 'JBL.'

"Darcie, come in here!" he yelled.

A voice came back "No, come out of there."

"You have to see this."

"Oh shit," bounced around the room. She came through the crack. "What is it? I've got to get out of here. One minute you're pissed off because I don't call in, then you're telling me not to."

"Alright we'll go, but look at this. You remember me telling you about Lisa's great-grandpa that built this place?"

"Yes. He owned a railroad, right?"

"Yes, and he was in Austin when those women that William Sidney Porter, better known as O. Henry, the short story writer, called the Servant Girl Annihilator murderers.

"The what murders?"

"Several women, and a couple of men, were murdered and mutilated, some survived, from New Years Eve 1884 to Christmas Eve 1885 in Austin. They called them the Annihilator Murders. The murderer drove a railroad spike through their ear into their brain with a hammer and cut off body parts."

"A railroad spike?"

"Yes, see the connection? And he was in London when Jack the Ripper murdered those women in 1888. This bag proves he did both. His tools are in the bag along with some souvenirs he kept."

"Come on, are you telling me Lisa's grandpa was Jack the Ripper?"

"That's why he was never caught. He left Austin and they gave up the chase for the killer shortly afterwards. He goes to London, does the same thing, then comes back to Texas. Only this time he builds his horror house in Dallas and continues his mayhem until he dies an old man, without anyone except his great-granddaughter ever figuring out who the hell he was."

"And grandpa's genes caught up with his great-granddaughter and turned her into a monster, too," Darcie said.

"Exactly," Mecana said.

"If it wasn't for the horrible things she did you could almost feel sorry for her," Darcie said.

"Almost," Mecana agreed.

"Do we try to prove you're right? We could make a lot of money."

"Maybe."

"Do I detect some hesitation in your voice?"

"Yes, it occurred to me we would never see another peaceful day the rest of our lives. The press and curiosity seekers would hound us forever about one thing or the other. If we leave the bag here they're going to come to the same conclusion and we would still be in the crosshairs."

"Are you thinking what I think you're thinking? You know we could wind up in jail." "Not if we just take the bag. The rest would be speculative. Nothing for sure and we get rid of the bag. We know who the Ripper was, but no one else ever will. We solved the most famous crime of all."

"We would be the only ones who know who Jack the Ripper really was."

"That's right, Sherlock," Mecana said, grinning. "If you agree, I'll get the bag."

"You're awful trusting. How do you know I won't change my mind?"

"Alright, then. Do you, Darcie Connors, promise to never reveal what we found here today, so help you god?"

Darcie put her hands on her hips and gave Mecana a cold stare. "Get the damn bag, Mecana. I'll make the call for the crime scene gang."

"You're sure?" Mecana said.

"Yes, I agree. Our life would be hell. Not to mention the souvenir hunters that would tear this place down brick by brick and dig up the old man. That's something I don't want to be a part of."

Mecana took the bag to his truck and hid it in his tool box. By the time he got back to the mansion, the police and ambulances were arriving.

7

The expression on everyone's faces defied description as they wandered through the carnage, looking at something they found very hard to believe.

Mecana and Darcie by now just felt numb.

Verves arrived and stared at the boxes, mesmerized for several minutes without saying a word.

The medics put Lisa in a body bag and were collecting the vagina boxes. No one seemed to know what to do with Dawson Durant. Doctor Seymour decided they would remove him from the box. Poor bastard, all because he liked women too much.

The press had gotten wind of what was going on by some big mouth cop and were coming to the scene by the dozens.

Verves leaned up against the wall, his knees weak. He finally found his voice. "Unbelievable. How the hell did you find this, Mecana?"

"I would like to tell you through my shrewd detective work. But the truth is, as a last resort, I came to the mansion looking for I-didn't-know-what. Then Lisa showed up. Darcie saved my ass and I whacked Lisa when I got the chance."

"Well, you were on the right trail," Verve said. "Forget the letter. No way am I going to let you resign. Come by in the morning and we'll talk about your next assignment. I have to go deal with the press now. You want to help me?"

"I don't think so, Chief. Not exactly my cup of tea."

Verves frowned, took a deep breath, rolled his tongue around in his mouth like he had a bad taste in it. "How do you describe or explain something like this? It's so inhumane. It's like a nightmare you can't wake up from."

"Lisa didn't think so," Mecana said. "She thought she was getting even for being betrayed and that they deserved what they got."

"Sick woman. Maybe too smart," Verves said.

"Maybe so," Mecana said.

"I think you and Darcie are due a commendation for valor. See you in the morning." Verves left to face the media mob.

Darcie was listening, and walked over to Mecana. "My, how the worm has turned," she said to Mecana. "Yesterday he couldn't wait to get rid of you, now you're his fair-haired boy."

"It's kind of disgusting, isn't it?" Mecana said.

"Right now, I think you could run for Mayor and beat Pratt."

8

A large crowd of reporters and spectators had gathered outside police headquarters, waiting for Mecana and Darcie to arrive. Someone had spilled the beans and they knew they were coming.

He parked the Silverado at a parking meter across the street and got out, took a taped-up cardboard box out of the truck tool box and put it under his arm.

"What's that?" Darcie asked, puzzled.

Mecana turned the box so she could see the writing on it. It read 'POLICE PROPERTY - CASE 16385. FILE UNTIL NEEDED.'

"You're kidding," Darcie said.

"No, it may be there forever. No one's going to call for something they don't know about. But if it is ever found, I say I took it to the property room and forgot to tell them."

"Mecana, you may have come close to losing them, but you do have balls. You're going to just walk through the crowd with that box under your arm?"

"Yep," he said.

"What the hell, lets do it," Darcie said and smiled.

The reporters rushed them as they crossed the street, almost knocking the box out of Mecana's hand. The red headed TV reporter looked at the box. "What's in there, Mecana?" she asked, the camera focusing in on the box.

"Evidence," Mecana said.

"Can we see it?"

"No, sorry."

Someone yelled from the back of the crowd, "You going to give us a statement?"

"After I meet with Chief Verves, I'll talk to you."

"What about you, Miss Connors?" the TV reporter asked.

"It's over, time to move on," she said and Mecana nodded in agreement.

"That's it?" the reporter asked.

"That's it," Darcie said and glanced at Mecana.

Mecana smiled and tightened his grip on the cardboard box.

A young, athletic-looking man with a notepad and pen stepped in front of Mecana. "What are you going to do next, Mecana?"

"That's up to the department," Mecana said. "Let us through, please."

"What about you, Miss Connors?" the young man asked.

"I'm with him. Whatever they tell us to do," Darcie replied.

Mecana dropped the box off in the property room, and he and Darcie took the elevator up to Chief Verve's office.

9

Mecana and Darcie were surprised to see the Police Chief, Mayor and District Attorney there. They all began to applaud. Chief Verves was the first to reach them. He shook hands with Mecana and hugged Darcie.

"Mecana, thanks to you and Darcie, the case is closed," Verves said. "We found Cindy Freeman's house key in that horror chamber, along with personal items from the other victims.

"That's what Lisa was looking for in the office," Darcie said. "The keys to Nadine's apartment. That's why she left the key in the door; it was a message for me, for catching her snooping around in the office."

"Lisa said she practiced on two bodies," Mecana said. "It probably happened in Houston."

"We may never know," Verves said. "But there is something I know you will like. The FBI transferred Sullivan and his partner to Los Angles." Verves patted Mecana and Darcie on the back and laughed.

Mecana looked around the room at all the people that wanted his head yesterday but were praising him today. They all looked away when he made eye contact with them.

The Mayor walked over and stuck out his hand for Mecana to shake. Mecana looked at it and turned away.

"What are you doing, Mecana?" Verves asked, embarrassed. "Let bygones be bygones. It's over. Everyone is here to show their appreciation."

"That's right," the District Attorney said. "We don't hold a grudge. You shouldn't. It all worked out okay."

"That's right," Police Chief Bolden echoed.

"What about DeMax?" Mecana said.

"We dropped the charges this morning, he's a free man," the District Attorney said.

"Let's celebrate, Mecana," Verves said.

"Thanks, but no thanks, Chief. You're all a bunch of damn hypocrites." He took off his badge and Glock and dropped them on a nearby table before walking away.

Everyone was stunned in silence, including Darcie. She looked at the badge and gun on the table, studying them for a moment. She sat her Coke down, removed her Beretta and badge from her purse and laid them on the table beside Mecana's.

"Wait up, Mecana." She followed him out of the room. "You've got to help me move."

THE END

WHEN THE NIGHT BIRD SINGS

For
Joe and Karen

"You do what's right because it's right.
You don't have to have a reason."
Bud Lansdale

1

I was standing inside my new office, admiring the freshly-painted sign on the open glass door, when she walked up and smiled.

"You open?"

"Yes ma'am," I said.

She had sparkling blue eyes and long, shiny blonde hair with red ruby earrings matching her sinuous lips. She was wearing a tight fire-red dress that showed all her dangerous curves. The big diamond on her left hand told me someone had staked a claim.

I invited her in with a gentlemanly gesture and closed the door. She walked in, stopped and tilted her head slightly and looked at me.

"You're Thomas Mecana, right?"

"Yes ma'am," I said.

"The one who solved The Mutilator case?"

"Along with my partner and a lot of others."

"I used to see Doctor Durant and Lisa at social functions from time to time but never met them."

"Lucky you."

"My name's Candy Kane," she said. "I saw the ad in the paper announcing your new private investigation business. I want to hire you, Mr. Mecana."

"Really," I said, contemplating her unusual name. "Have a seat, Mrs. Kane. Most people drop the mister and call me Mecana," I said. "You're our first client."

She sat down, crossed her long legs and looked at me.

I sat down in my new swivel chair behind the desk, but didn't cross my legs.

"I have a problem," she said. "It has to be kept hush-hush."

"I can be so quiet you could hear the proverbial pin drop."

"And what I tell you will be in confidence, right; it goes no further?" she said.

"Maybe my partner, that's it."

"Who's Connors?" she asked, pointing to the sign on the door.

"She was my partner on The Mutilator case. Darcie Connors, you can trust her. She will be here soon."

"How come you quit the police?"

"A long story," I said. "What can I do for you?"

"My husband and I need protection. I have reason to believe someone is trying to kill us."

"Why?"

"My husband is Ashton Kane, a psychotherapist M.D.," she began. "A stock broker he was treating has accused him of hypnotizing him and planting a plot in his mind to acquire a million dollars of his money. He filed a lawsuit three years ago against my husband but it was thrown out of court for lack of evidence. And now he's trying to kill us. I think he shot a hole in the window of my car yesterday, missing my head by about two inches."

"What's his name?" I asked.

"Edward G. Fillmore. He's insane. I need someone to protect us."

"Your husband know about the window?"

"No. He's in New York to meet with Landon Fritz, a professor at the medical school Ashton attended where they became friends. I didn't want it to upset him."

"So you're whistling in the dark?" I said.

"What's that mean?" she asked.

"Means it could be anyone. Maybe an accident. Something my daddy used to say."

"It was no accident," she said.

"Then you should go to the cops."

"No cops, that's why I came to you."

"Could I see some ID please?"

"You don't believe me?"

"I don't trust myself."

She reached into a small purse she was holding and took out a Texas driver's license and laid it on the desk. The name she gave me was the one on the driver's license. I recognized her address as one in the upper crust sections of suburbia Dallas. And she was 28, still in the youthful splendor phase of life.

"Thank you," I said.

She picked the license up and put it back in her purse.

"I'm willing to pay you a hundred thousand dollars to silence this nut in whatever way you see fit as long as it's permanent and soon. Do we have a deal?" She held out her hand.

"You've got the wrong man. You're looking for a hitman, not a private investigator."

"I'll double that," she said. "Two hundred thousand."

"Not even for that."

"Very well," she said. "I'm sure someone will see it my way."

She stood up and I did too. She reached for the pen my daughter Emily had given me and wrote down a phone number. She shoved the notepad toward me.

"If you change your mind call me."

"Tempting, but no cigar," I said.

"You talk in riddles, Mecana."

"It's my daddy's fault."

She looked even more perplexed. "Think about it. Half up front," she said.

"You know I have to call the cops?" I said.

"For what? I thought our discussion was in confidence."

"It was, until you got around to discussing murder," I said.

"I don't know what you're talking about," she said. "I was asking you to persuade him to leave us alone."

"That's not what I heard," I said.

She laid the pen back on my desk and walked to the door and opened it. She stopped in the open doorway and looked at me over her shoulder. "There could be other rewards," she said and ran her tongue over her bright red lips.

"Some days are harder than others to navigate," I said. "I think this is one of them."

"Your daddy?" she asked.

"Nope, me," I said.

She smiled again and walked out, leaving the door open.

I stood at the open door and watched her hips sway back and forth as her red high heels clicked on the shiny tile floor to the elevator. It was a tempting sight.

I closed the door and sat back down at my desk, picked up Emily's pen and looked at the phone number she wrote down on the pad. A voice

in my head that sounded like my daddy said, "Don't even think about it."
I wadded the paper up and threw it in the trash can.

About ten minutes after Mrs. Kane left, Darcie showed up with two sacks of paper, folders, pens and other office supplies, looking beautiful as usual with a black dress to match her short black hair and dark brown eyes.

I usually didn't wear a suit but I was glad I did today. Jeans and a pullover would have clashed with her little black dress ensemble she had on for our first day.

She sat the sacks on her new desk. "Where's the coffee?" she said, looking at an empty coffee pot on a table next to the wall.

"I've been busy," I said. "I can make some."

"No, I'm good," she said. "You left early this morning. I'm no Sara Lee but I would have fixed you breakfast if you had waited."

"That would have been nice but I had to be here to unlock the office for the painter so we would be ready for our first day. What do you think?" I said, pointing at the door.

"Alright, except I think it would have had a better ring to it if it was 'Connors and Mecana Private Investigators.'"

"Never thought about it."

"I know. Men don't like women on top unless it's their idea."

"I'll have them change the damn thing."

"Forget it, its fine," she said.

"Then why are we talking about it?"

"I smell perfume," she said, changing the subject.

"A Mrs. Candy Kane was here."

"You're kidding," she said.

"No, that's her name. She had the driver's license to prove it. She thinks a former psych patient of her husband is trying to murder them. She wants me to snuff him before he does the same to her."

"She give you a name?" Darcie asked.

"A stock broker named Edward G. Fillmore who thinks Mr. Kane hypnotized him out of a million dollars."

"Gets right to it, doesn't she?" Darcie said.

"She offered me a hundred thousand and when I refused it she raised the price to two hundred thousand. Her husband doesn't know about the offer."

"He's better off not knowing, he would be an accomplice," Darcie said. "You know her?"

"Never saw her before. She said she saw our ad in the paper."

"You know she will find someone that will probably do it for less. You going to make the call, or do I?"

"I'll do it," I said. "Verves will be surprised to hear from me so soon. I told her our conversation was in confidence but that was before we got around to discussing murder."

"You record the conversation?"

"I forgot the recorder. She left her phone number but I threw it in the trash."

"Verves might want it," she said.

"Yeah." I reached in the trash can and picked up the paper with Kane's number on it. "You sure you're alright with the sign?" I said.

"Yes its fine," she said, smiled and batted her big brown eyes.

Beautiful women know they have a hypnotic effect over a man whatever their profession is while working their charms to get whatever it is they want. She knew damn well I'd have the sign changed because I don't want to sleep alone for however long the punishment is for a crime I didn't know I committed until I was verbally convicted.

She sat down at her desk and looked around the office. "This place looks a little drab. I think I'll get some pictures for the walls, and maybe a plant or two."

"Fine with me," I said and propped my feet up on my desk and gazed out the sixth floor window at the interstate. The morning traffic had slowed to a trickle before lunch time. I couldn't get Mrs. Kane off my mind.

"First rule, no feet on the desk," Darcie said.

"That's my thinking position," I said.

"Find another one," she said.

I dropped my feet back on the floor. "I don't think it's going to work, I've been doing it too long."

"You'll get over it. Maybe we should put a partition between the desks to create an illusion of privacy when we're talking to clients."

"Whatever," I said.

"You going to call Verves?" she said.

"Yes." I fished my phone out of my pocket and dialed his number.

Robert Verves was a small black man who used his intuition, intelligence and Hercules-like strength to rise from recruit to Navy SEAL to Chief of Homicide in record time.

"Hello, Mecana. The new name is showing up on Caller ID," he said.

"Darcie and I opened our PI office today."

"What about her twin, is she in with you?"

"No, she decided she would rather face the dangers of teaching."

"Good for her. I received some forms a while back the state sent me to verify your employment for your PI licenses. I gave you good marks."

"Thanks," I said. "I had a visit from a pretty lady this morning before the paint could dry on my door, asking me to cancel a guy. I think she was serious. Thought you should know."

"What do you have on her?" Verves asked.

"Her name is Candy Kane, believe it or not. Kane with a 'K.' I verified it with her driver's license. The address on her license was a penthouse at the Ellison Plaza hotel."

"The uptown crowd," Verves said.

"Yep."

"Who's her intended victim?" Verves asked.

"Edward G. Fillmore," I said. "Fillmore is a stock broker and a former patient of Dr. Ashton Kane, Mrs. Kane's husband. Dr. Kane is a psychotherapist - hypnotizes his patients - he's in New York now."

"What was Fillmore's problem," Verves said.

"She said he was insane."

"Not very descriptive," Verves said.

"He sued the doctor for hypnotizing him to get his money but it was thrown out for lack of evidence. She said someone shot a hole in the driver's window of her car yesterday, just missing her, and she thinks it was Fillmore. I haven't seen the car."

"I'll put somebody on it and let you know," Verves said.

"Good, when I told her I would have to call the police she tried to change her story.

She's in a hurry so you should be, too. I got her phone number."

"Give it to me," Verves said. "Seems like I've heard that story before but we couldn't find any proof on the doctor. I'll check it out again."

As I talked to Verves I watched Darcie bend over her desk using her arms as measuring sticks for the length of her desk, weird fantasies ran through my warped brain.

"You can have your old job back anytime you want," he said.

"Thanks but I'll try this for a while. Talk to you later," I said and hung up.

"Is he going to get on it?" Darcie asked.

"Yes, he said he'll get back to me."

"I'm going to look for some picture and plants," she said. "You want to meet me at Brogans for lunch? I know men don't like shopping for anything that doesn't fire bullets or have an engine so I won't ask you to go with me."

"That's very considerate of you. I'll find something to keep me busy until lunch."

"Okay, see you at noon." She opened the door and looked at the sign for a long moment, stepped outside, closed the door and was gone.

I looked around the office at the blank white walls and the slow turning white ceiling fans with little designer bulbs in the light fixtures. Darcie was right, it did need something but it wasn't changing the sign.

I took off my tie and propped my feet back on the desk. What she doesn't know won't hurt me. I picked up the pen Emily gave me and thought about the promises I made to my two daughters that I couldn't afford to keep. A new convertible for Emily's high school graduation was going to cost thirty thousand dollars and Morgan's trip to Disneyland for graduating to high school was probably another five thousand, with no idea where the money was coming from unless I drained my savings.

My ex sure wasn't going to help. She said it was my promises and my problem.

Maybe I would have to kill someone.

Taking Darcie's comment to heart, I decided to go kick some tires on a new truck to pass the time until lunch. I wasn't sure I wanted another truck. Even if I had the money to buy one, the one I had was like an old friend I would hate to say goodbye to.

I would never tell anyone that because they would think I was kind of weird and I already had too many weird things going for me.

The weirdest one was the box I took to the crime locker evidence room from The Mutilator case. If anyone ever opened that up I might be in more trouble than I could handle.

2

It had been a while since I was at Brogans Restaurant. It wasn't fancy but it was clean and the food was good. It was where most of the locals went for lunch or dinner when they wanted to take a step up from a fast food place. They had a semi-maître d' who watched you come in and said hello but let you seat yourself.

Darcie was sitting in a booth sipping red wine when I got there. I sat down, she smiled and pointed at her wine glass.

"No, I think I'll have a salad," I said. "I haven't been to the gym this week and I feel it."

"I'll have a salad, too," she said. "Want to go to the gym after work today?"

"That would be now. We don't have any work," I said.

"Well you could have made two hundred thousand if you didn't have a conscience," Darcie said.

"Yeah, I know, but mostly I didn't want a boyfriend named Bubba. Let's see if we can snag a waiter."

"You're going to be surprised," she said.

"About what?" I asked.

"You'll see," she said.

I looked up and it took me a minute to realize it was DeMax Baker walking to the table. DeMax was wearing black pants, a white shirt with a name tag and a bowtie. He had cut his bushy hair short and put on weight. He didn't look much like I remembered.

"Mecana. What it is?"

"Man, do you look different," I said.

"Only on the outside," he said, and smiled.

"What are you doing here?"

"I'm a working man now. A bonifide server."

"You look the part," I said.

"Yep, what can I get you?"

"Okay, Mr. Server, could we have two house salads with ranch, and I'll have a Coke," I said.

"I got it," DeMax said and wrote in his pad. "Would you like more wine, Miss Darcie?"

"No, I'm good, DeMax," she said.

"That's two house salads with ranch dressing and a Coke for Mecana, right?"

"Right," I said.

"Coming up," he said, stuck his notepad in his pocket and walked away.

"You're right," I said. "I am surprised. DeMax and work don't seem to fit in the same sentence."

"Looks like he's changed his ways," Darcie said.

"I don't know, I think I'll wait a while to pass judgment. DeMax is pretty shrewd.

He may be working an angle of some kind here. If he is I would bet a woman is involved."

"You are a Doubting Thomas aren't you," Darcie said.

"Oh…That was cute," I said.

"I thought so," she said, smiled and took a sip of wine.

"You find some stuff for the office?" I asked.

"Yes, I'll drop if off at the office after lunch and meet you at the gym," she said. "You think that sweet-smelling Candy lady will drop in again?"

"I don't think so."

"She might not, but she may send someone. I don't think it would be a social call. Some people can't handle rejection"

"I'll make a note of that, partner," I said.

DeMax came back to the table carrying a tray. "Here you are," he said. He placed the salads and Coke on the table, picked up the tray and looked at Darcie. "Miss Darcie, thanks again for getting me out of that mess with the police. You sure are a good lawyer."

"You're welcome, DeMax. They needed a suspect and were willing to do whatever they could to get one, including railroading an innocent man."

"I sure was that. I wouldn't kill all those pretty ladies."

"With your fondness for women," I said, "we had already come to that conclusion."

"Hope I didn't have anything to do with ya'll quitting the police," DeMax said.

"You didn't, it was mostly politics," Darcie said.

"We just didn't fit there anymore," I said. "We opened a Private Investigation office," I said, handing him a business card.

"That's what Miss Darcie said. You need anything, all you have to do is ask. I owe you," he said and stuck the card in his pocket.

"You don't owe us anything, DeMax," Darcie said. "The legal system owes you."

"Well, just the same. If you need me you know where I am," he said.

"We'll remember that," I said.

DeMax nodded and walked away.

"How long you think he'll be here?" Darcie asked.

"Good question," I said. "DeMax marches to his own drum."

"I think I'll go," she said. "I'll see you at the gym."

"You barely touched your salad," I said.

"I'm not very hungry," she said, finished off the wine and stood up. "Watch your back. I have a bad feeling about Candy Kane."

"I'll be okay. See you at the gym," I said.

"You can get the check," she smiled. "And give DeMax a big tip."

3

The lunch crowd was leaving the gym when I pulled in. I saw Darcie's SUV and parked my Silverado beside it. When I went in I saw Darcie's trainer Mindy showing an overweight young lady how to use a treadmill. Two gym rats were lifting weights.

Mindy saw me, we waved at each other.

When I came out of the locker room in my gym shorts and Marine t-shirt Mindy was talking to Darcie. As I walked up to them she smiled.

"Hi Mecana haven't seen you for a while," she said.

"I know, been busy getting our office open."

"Anything I can get you?" she asked.

"No, I think I'm good."

"Okay, have a good workout. I've got a class to teach. See you."

"Yeah, see you," I said as she walked away. I turned to Darcie. "What were you two talking about?"

"You," Darcie said. "About what a good-looking dude you are with those sexy gray eyes and that bod. I think she wants to play nice-nice with you."

"What do you think about that?" I said and grinned.

"Fine, I'll go home and pack since it's your house," she said.

"Not to worry. Not my type."

"Then I won't pack. For now."

"Good. I would be lonesome."

"Not for long if she knew I was gone."

"I don't know, I suspect she may have more interest in you."

"Not into that sort of thing. I have enough trouble with you."

"You know the house can be yours, too. We can go to a Justice of the Peace or do the whole ball of wax wedding thing."

"That's a subject for another day," she said, pushed the treadmill button and started running.

After a good two-hour workout I had had enough. "Think I'll call it good and take a shower. Want to take one with me?" I said.

"I think management frowns on coed showering," she said.

"Party poopers," I said.

"That doesn't mean we can't take another one when we get home," she said, and

winked.

"Time to go," I said, picked up my towel and headed for the locker room.

We stopped by the office to look at the new things Darcie bought. The place looked a lot more alive with reprints of dead painters' art on the walls and a couple of artificial plants. She even got us nameplates to set on our desk.

"It's looks great," I said. "Can we go now?"

"What's your hurry," she said.

"We were going to take a shower together?"

"Maybe," she said and stopped at the door, looked at the sign again and sighed.

"I'll take care of it," I said, locked the door and headed home.

I got a call from Chief Verves two days later.

"Mecana, they found Mr. Kane dead this morning in a New York City hotel with four 9mm slugs in him, all in his heart," Verves said. "I got someone on the way to see Mrs. Kane. His buddy Landon Fritz said he had dinner with him at the hotel and went home around ten that night."

"Fritz have any family?" I asked.

"Said he didn't but we're still checking him out," Verves said.

"She wasn't whistling Dixie," I said. "Sounds like the hitman beat her to the punch."

"Yeah, I'll let you know," he said and hung up.

Darcie walked in the room with a towel wrapped around her head and another around her body. "Who was that?" she asked.

"Verves. They found Candy's husband full of holes in a New York hotel very dead.

Maybe I should have been more sympathetic about her situation before I turned her away."

"You did the right thing," she said. "But she may not think so."

"Why didn't you wait for me?" I said. "I kinda liked the coed showering the other day."

"Go take a cold shower by yourself," she said.

"Won't change anything," I said.

"Well switch gears, we've got an insurance company man coming. He has some work for us."

"Do you know you're naked?"

"Knock it off and get ready," she threw the towel wrapped around her waist at me and walked back to the bedroom buck naked.

4

We arrived at the office at ten the next morning. Darcie made coffee and a Mister Summers from the insurance company showed up a short time later. He was middle-aged, trim with thin gray hair and glasses, wearing a light gray suit and a red tie.

"Congratulations on your new business," he said. "I saw your ad."

"Looks like that ad was money well spent," I said. "Have a seat, Mr. Summers."

He sat down and placed his briefcase beside the chair.

"Would you like some coffee?" Darcie asked.

"No thank you," he picked up his briefcase, opened it and took some papers out. He looked at Darcie like he was inhaling her, placed the papers on my desk and sat the briefcase back beside the chair.

"I think we have some claim adjusters taking kickbacks. That's the information you will need to check out," he said, motioning toward the papers on my desk. "We had a client tell us he paid off one of our claim adjusters to get the figure he wanted. There may be more. We don't want to handle this in-house, they might catch on."

I picked up the papers, took a quick look, nodded and handed them to Darcie.

She looked at them and leaned against my desk facing the man. "Mr. Summers, this may take a day or it may take a month, depending on what we have to do. We charge five hundred a day plus expenses. You only pay for the days we are working on your case."

"That will be fine. Let me know when you finish your investigation," he said.

I thought it would be. She could have sold him the Brooklyn Bridge.

"The first five hundred is up front, Mr. Summers," I said. "We'll bill you for the rest."

"I came prepared," he said. "I have a signed check. I'll fill it out."

"Make it out to Conner's and Mecana Private Investigators," I said, looked at Darcie and grinned. She didn't show any expression, I didn't think she heard me. He made out the check and handed it to me, picked up his briefcase and stood up.

"Thank you," I said and shook his hand.

"We'll keep in touch with you, Mr. Summers," Darcie said.

"Thank you," he said and walked to the door. I opened it and he walked out.

I held the check up and looked at it before handing it to Darcie. "Our first money," I said. "You want to make the deposit?"

"I can't until you change the name at the bank to Conner's and Mecana."

"You did hear me," I said. "It was a joke, you're trying to rattle my cage."

"I don't think they will take it," she said.

"Quit rubbing it in and take the check to the bank," I said. "I'll see if I can come up with some information on the claims adjuster."

"Alright, we'll see," she waved the check at me and left.

I stared at the sign on the door and poured myself a cup of Darcie's coffee and sat back down at my desk, propped my feet up and took a sip. It felt like my eyes were going to cross. It was worse than the stuff Verves made at the station. I was glad she didn't give it to Mr. Summers or we might not have a client.

I was still gagging when my phone rang. It was Candy Kane.

"Mecana, Ashton is dead," she said.

"I heard, I'm very sorry. Have you talked to the police?"

"A cop showed up to tell me about Ashton, asked some questions and left."

"Why did you call me?" I said.

"I need your protection," she said.

"Not interested," I said.

"Mecana you're the only one I can turn to."

"We've already discussed your situation; the cops are your best bet."

"You don't have to do anything you don't want to," she said. "Just keep me alive. Someone took another shot at me when I pulled into the hotel parking lot last night. Just missed me, it went over my head as I got out of the car."

"Where had you been?" I said.

"Shopping. I was lonesome, please."

I knew it wasn't a good idea but the please part got to me. "Did the bullet hit anything? A post, a trash can, anything?"

"Not that I know of," she said.

"We can talk but I'm not promising anything," I said.

"There's a 'K' on the door, top floor of the Ellison hotel," she said and was gone.

I considered calling Verves, but decided to hear her out first. I stuck the insurance folder in my desk and dumped the bad coffee in the trash can.

On my way to the hotel, I called Darcie and told her to meet me to check out this Candy lady.

"Wait for me before you go up," Darcie said.

"Meet you in the lobby," I said. I wasn't sure if she was conscientious, cautious, jealous or all three.

I had just walked in the hotel when Darcie showed up.

"You deposit the check?" I said.

"They took it with some reluctance," she said and smiled.

"Never give up do you?"

"Nope. What have we got here?"

"I told her we would talk," I said. "I didn't make any promises."

"You go on up. I'll make sure no one is following you," Darcie said.

"Okay, it's a penthouse on the top floor, room K." I got on the elevator alone while Darcie waited for the next one.

I got off on the top floor and walked down a long hall with Ansel Adams photographs hanging on the walls. I rang the buzzer and stood to one side of the door with the "K" on it, waiting.

A voice from the other side asked, "Who is it?"

"Mecana," I said and she opened the door. I walked in and she closed it quickly.

"Am I glad to see you," she said.

"You should let the cops handle this," I said.

"I was afraid they would arrest me."

"Should they? Did you have anything to do with your husband's murder?"

"Of course not. How could I? I was in Dallas."

I looked around the massive room. I always thought of motels and hotels as a place for two things, and the only thing that was required for both was a bed and privacy. This place had large windows with a view of jets taking off and landing at DFW. Wall-to-wall folding doors stood at one end of the room, opening to a bedroom where I could see a king-sized bed that had not been slept in for several days.

The doorbell rang.

"Oh no," she said, and gasped.

"I think that's my partner Darcie, she was covering my back." I walked over and stood beside the door. "Darcie?"

"Yes," she said. I unlocked the door and let her in.

"This is Mrs. Candy Kane, Darcie."

Darcie acknowledged her by looking her up and down. "You want a private investigator or a hitman, Mrs. Kane?"

"I need you to find a hitman before he finds me."

"Your husband have any family?" I said.

"Ashton's parents were killed in a plane crash when he was ten. He grew up in his aunt's home. She helped pay his way through medical school. He doesn't have any siblings, kids or ex-wives that I'm aware of."

"What about the sister? Where is she now?" I asked.

"She died last year from cancer," Candy said.

"Anyone else?" I said.

"Not that I know of."

"The cops won't cost you anything," I said. "But we will."

"No cops," she reiterated. "I don't want our lives plastered all over the news."

"You may not have a choice," Darcie said. "We'll have to call the cops and let them know we're working for you. If we decide to."

"Then you'll do it?" she asked.

I looked at Darcie and she nodded yes.

"As long as you understand that we're getting paid to solve the case. The two hundred thousand you offered, plus five hundred a day for expenses - with half the fee in cash now," I said.

I checked Darcie's reaction to my proposal and she nodded her head.

"Okay with me," Candy said.

Darcie and I looked at each other surprised. She went for the deal.

"We've got to get you to a safer place," I said.

"I'll pack some things," she said. "I have to handle Ashton's funeral when they ship his body back to Dallas."

"We'll help you take care of it. Where's your car?" I said.

"In my parking spot in the parking garage. Same as my age, spot twenty-eight."

"We'll leave it there. Give me the keys," I said. "I'll check for a bullet in the parking lot."

"Can't that wait? I'm afraid. I want to get out of here."

She did look very frightened. "Okay, I'll come back later."

"Darcie, why don't you get us a rental and I'll have a talk with Novel and let you know where we're going to stay. May be someone on our trail already."

"Could be, call me," Darcie said and walked out.

"Where are we going?" Candy asked.

"I have to make a call to a friend of mine and find us a safe place at one of his real estate listings."

"That's kind of odd," she said.

"It works," I said. "Done it before."

"What's your daddy do?" she asked.

"Retired Marine Colonel. Unfortunately, he's dead."

"I'm sorry to hear that." After a short pause she changed the subject. "Are you as good as they say you are, Mecana?"

"Depends on what you mean," I said.

"Whatever I want it to be," she said and smiled.

"Maybe," I said.

"You better be."

5

I called my fat friend Novel who said he had a place on Lake Tawakoni that would be available for a month. The occupants were on vacation in France. He gave me the code for the front gate. We both knew we weren't supposed to do it but we did. He said there was a key in the fork of a tree on the front lawn and he would pick up a sneaky five-thousand-dollar check for a month tomorrow. I told him to give me an address and I would mail it to him. We were on a case where visitors weren't welcome. He said he would do that if I would feed the fish, so I agreed.

I drove to the lake with Candy. The place was for high-rollers judging by the size of it. Candy should feel right at home. I drove on by, looking for a tail but didn't see one; made the block and waited for fifteen minutes before going into the lake property.

"What're you doing?" Candy asked.

"Checking for a tail, we'll use the car Darcie is picking up when we go out again," I said. Took one last look – still no traffic – drove up to the gate, punched the code and we drove through the drive and down to a large bungalow on the waterfront.

I grabbed her bags, found the key in the tree, and we made our way to the back of the house. Out on the lake, sailboats were whizzing along in a strong breeze while ski boats were pulling happy skiers. A bunch of white ducks saw us on the lawn and hurried to us. When they realized we didn't have anything to give them they waddled away.

When I turned the key a dark, tinted glass door disappeared into the wall and we walked in the room. Inside there was a large round bed, a Jacuzzi tub, multi-colored lights built into the walls and an electric star light ceiling with a white bear skin rug lying on the thick carpet by the bed.

"If it's alright with you," I said, "I don't want you in a bedroom that leads outside. Let's find another one."

"Okay with me. I have to take a bath, if you hear me scream come running," she said.

"You'll think it's Superman," I said.

We walked down a hall and came to a bedroom bigger than my den and I put her suitcases on the bed. "Don't let anyone know where you are and don't order food."

"I'm not going to like this," she said.

"I'm not either, but if someone is out to kill you…"

"There is," she said. "I'm going to take a bath."

I nodded and walked back out to the massive living room, sat on a twenty-foot-long white couch and looked at a wall-to-wall stone fireplace.

A large aquarium was built into another wall. Bigger fish than I've ever caught were swimming around in it. I got up and walked over to the aquarium and picked up the fish food and shook a large amount into the tank. A feeding frenzy began. I went back to the couch and called Darcie.

"I think I can find it," she said. "Where's Candy?"

"Taking a bath."

"No coed bathing Mecana," she said.

"Of course not," I said.

"I'm going to buy some TV dinners, we may have to eat in for a while. I rented a blue van," she said.

"Good." I hung up and called Verves.

"Mecana?" he said. "Are you in trouble?"

"Candy Kane is with me," I said.

"That's a surprise," he said. "Figured you'd pissed her off."

"May have but she's hired us. I promised her you wouldn't arrest her when I called you. Did I lie?"

"No, I don't have any evidence to arrest her," Verves said. "I checked out the stock broker Fillmore, he was in London when Mr. Kane was murdered. He said Candy was an evil woman. We woke Mrs. Kane up this morning to tell her. New York gave the investigation back to us. I would like to talk to Mrs. Kane, for the record. We didn't find anything that would have put her in New York when her husband was murdered."

"She would have had to make a round-trip flight in one night. Possible, but not probable," I said.

"Time of death was early this morning according to New York. Think I agree with you for now, but I still have to talk to her."

"I'm keeping her under wraps for now while I find out who the players are. Have someone meet me at Bleaker's Bowling Alley on 34th at three this afternoon."

"I'll send Benny Modele," he said.

"Is that the guy who always dresses to the hilt and looks like he lost his best friend?"

"Yeah, that's him."

"Have him come alone. No one else. Do I have your word?"

"You got it," he said.

"Tell him he may not see me when he comes in but I'll see him."

"What little we know so far looks like it was a professional hit. The only fingerprints in the room were Kane's," Verves said.

"That's what I was thinking. Three o'clock at the bowling alley," I said again and hung up.

"How long do we have to stay here," Candy asked as she walked in the room.

"I don't know," I said. "Maybe until we find the killer."

"I made plans to move to France after I bury Ashton," she said.

"Did you make those plans before or after he was murdered?"

"After," she said. "Keep me alive until I leave and I'll pay you."

"If that's what you want," I said.

"I heard you talking to someone," she said.

"The cops. We have to meet a detective this afternoon. They want to ask you some questions. You don't have to go to the police station. I arranged for it to be on our terms."

"No, I won't go."

"They just want to talk to you. There's nothing to worry about."

"No," she flatly said.

"I give you my word. That's it. They're not going to arrest you. Why are you so worried?"

"I don't trust them. I don't want the cops to put me through hell for nothing."

"I'm not sure I trust them, either, but I do trust my former boss. He's always been true to his word."

"He better be or I won't trust you anymore," she said and disappeared back in the bathroom.

I sat down and waited.

6

Darcie showed up at the house about an hour later with a stack of frozen TV dinners.

Darcie and I ate chicken but Candy almost threw up looking at hers. Funny how money can change your appetite. She refused to eat so we headed for the bowling alley.

We pulled up to a restaurant across the street from the bowling alley about five minutes early.

"I'm not eating here, either," Candy said.

"We not going here, it's the bowling alley across the street. I'll go check it out. Darcie, drive around the block. Anyone shows up who shouldn't, haul ass."

I got out on the passenger side between the car and the restaurant and hurried inside the restaurant. Darcie drove away with Candy while I cased the bowling alley from the restaurant. It usually wasn't hard to spot an unmarked police car. They drove solid white or black big-engine Ford or Dodges most of the time.

A black Challenger drove up in front of the bowling alley and Detective Bennie Modele got out of the car and went inside alone. I watched for about ten minutes for another car to show up but it didn't. I called Darcie and told her to pull into the alleyway beside the bowling alley.

The owner Henry usually left the back door unlocked during working hours so his employees could come and go from the back when they took smoking breaks. I hung out here when I was a kid and even did some pin work before they were automated.

Henry Bleaker had owned Bleaker's Bowling Alley since he came back from the Korean War with a chest full of medals, a Korean wife and a gimpy leg. He never had any kids, said he didn't think he would be a good father, but he was always good to me.

He was past eighty now, and slumped over when he walked. His hair was white and thin and his face showed the marks of time, but he showed up for work every day, rain or shine.

About a year ago I had stopped in to see how he was doing. The place looked a step away from the wrecking ball and was mostly a watering hole for the wrong kind of people these days. Addicts shooting up in the bathrooms, whores working the bar and the street outside. I knew he didn't have any other place to go so I put in a word for him with the street cops to cut him some slack.

I crossed the street and walked in the front door. Modele was standing at the end of the bar with a beer. An old man was trying to bowl but could barely lift the bowling ball. Two painted-up young women with very little on were sitting at the bar, drinking what looked like water. I saw one of them nudge the other and they looked my way. I gave them a look back, shook my head no and the message was delivered.

Henry was sitting behind the bar working his obsolete cash register as usual.

He saw me and smiled as I walked up to the bar. "Tommy," he said. "Where in the hell have you been? I haven't seen you for ages."

"Playing cop, Henry, how're you doing?"

"Still here, want a beer?"

"Maybe later, got a little business to conduct with that fellow at the end of the bar," I said.

"Man has to take care of his business. Good to see you, Tommy."

"You too," I said. He was the only one in the world that called me Tommy.

Modele looked up, sat his beer down and walked over to me.

"You Mecana?" he asked.

"Yeah. Modele?"

"Yes, knew you by your reputation. Don't mention the beer to anyone, okay?" he said. "I normally don't drink unless I want to look like someone else."

I wasn't sure what that meant and didn't want to find out.

Bennie Modele was in his forties, a confirmed bachelor, over six-feet-tall, with short black hair and brown eyes. He spent a lot of money on clothes and looked more like a banker than a cop. The lines on his forehead showed most of the time and the corners of his mouth drooped slightly at the edges like he was always expecting his worse day ever.

"She here?" he asked, his dead-pan expression never changing.

"She's here," I said.

"Let's get this over with," he said. "I've got other appointments."

"Follow me," I said and headed for the back of the bowling alley.

As we stepped out the backdoor, a black Mercedes turned into the alley and rammed the back of our rental, slamming it into a dumpster. A big man dressed in black jumped out of the passenger seat carrying an AK-47. He took aim at Candy through the back glass.

Darcie saw him in the rearview mirror, pushed Candy to the floor, opened the driver's door and rolled out under the car with her Beretta in hand.

I grabbed the shooter from behind and we fell to the ground, wrestling for the gun. Out of the corner of my eye I saw the driver make his exit from the car, wearing the same type of clothing as the other man, and firing an Uzi at Modele. Several bullets from the Uzi hit Modele in the arm and leg and he fell to the ground, blood spilling out of his tailor-made gray suit. Everything was happening at micro-second speed.

Darcie rolled out from under the car and emptied her Beretta into the driver. He fell down beside Modele, their blood running together as it traveled across the dirty concrete alley.

I was hanging on the AK-47, trying to pull it from the shooter's grasp while Darcie was scrambling to reload. He jerked free and stood up. I drew my Glock and put three bullets in his head as fast as I could pull the trigger. He fell forward, bounced off the car, dropped his gun and collapsed to the concrete in a puddle of blood.

Darcie had the Beretta reloaded with no one to shoot.

I bent down and checked the pulse of the men. The shooters were both dead. Modele was unconscious but alive. He was having that worse day ever.

Henry and three other people were peeking out the open backdoor. When they realized the shooting had stopped they ventured out to take a closer look.

"I called 911, Tommy," Henry said.

"Thanks, Henry."

Darcie holstered her Beretta, walked over to Modele and kneeled down beside him. The arm was just grazed but blood was pouring out of his leg. She unbuckled Modele's belt and pulled it free of his pants, ejected the clip from his pistol, extracted the round in the chamber and wrapped the belt around his leg, ran it through the trigger guard and twisted it into a tourniquet and tied it to his leg with his red silk necktie.

We could hear the sounds of the sirens getting closer.

I walked over to the bullet-riddled car and looked at Candy. She was crouched down in the front floorboard in a fetal position, her hands covering her head.

"Are you hit," I asked.

"No," she said. "Did you kill them?"

"Yes. I need you to take a look, see if you know them."

"No, get me outta here," she said.

"Get out of the car," I said.

She slowly slid back up on the seat and looked at me. I opened what remained of the door. She got out of the car, slipped off her high heels, held them in her hand and walked over to the dead men.

"I don't know them," she said, cringing at their bodies.

"Would your husband have known them?"

"I don't think so," she said.

"Henry, you still got that restored '58 pickup?"

"I do," he said.

"Can I borrow it?" I asked.

"Sure, Tommy," he said. "I don't need it anyway, my licenses has expired." He fished the keys out of his pocket and handed them to me.

"You know how to drive a stick shift, Darcie?" I said.

"Better than you. What do you want to do?"

"Take Candy back to the lake. I'll take a taxi when I think it's safe to go, if I don't wind up in jail."

"I think we just stepped in a world of shit, Mecana," Darcie said.

"Yeah, we're going to earn that money," I said.

"The cops aren't going to like us leaving."

"We have to find out what the truth is but we can't do that if Candy's in the slammer."

"Okay," she said, holding out her hand for the keys. "I see the truck."

"Candy, go with Darcie, she's going to get you out of here."

"Thank goodness," she said and followed Darcie to the truck, still holding her shoes in her hand. I followed behind them.

The engine started and Darcie looked at me. "I'm glad it wasn't your truck that got shot up. I would hate to see a grown man cry."

"Me too," I said. "You buy insurance on the car?"

"Of course," she said.

"We're going to need it," I said.

Darcie smiled and drove away.

I checked Modele. The tourniquet was holding. He was unconscious but alive. The two hitmen didn't have a wallet or any papers on them. Before I could check the Mercedes, a police cruiser came to a squeaking halt in the alley. Two uniformed cops got out, weapons drawn. I knew one of them.

"Sergeant Nelson," I said. "I thought you retired?"

He shook his head no. "I didn't expect to see you here, Mecana. You go back to work?"

"No, working as a private eye now."

"Is Modele alive?" he asked.

"For now," I said.

"What happened here?"

"The two dead ones tried to blow us away."

"They must not have known who they were messing with," he grinned and holstered his weapon. The younger cop did the same.

"They weren't rabbit hunting, not with those guns," Nelson said.

Sergeant Nelson was a small man with big brown puppy-dog-eyes, a beer belly and a whiskey nose.

"This is my partner, Officer Sid Gilliam," Nelson said. "I'm teaching him the ropes until I retire."

Sid was an athletic-looking young man with bright blue eyes and blonde hair. He looked like he was born about the time Nelson became a cop.

He stuck out his hand. "I've heard of you, Mecana, you're one of the best. Nice to meet you," he said as we shook hands.

"Thanks," I said. "I don't feel very competent right now, almost got my client killed."

An ambulance made a quick turn into the alley with the deafening sound of the siren shaking the walls. The ambulance stopped, the siren stopped and two well-built paramedics jumped out with a gurney.

"Any of them alive?" one of the medics yelled, to anyone listening.

"Detective Modele, the one with the tourniquet on his leg," I said.

One medic hurried to him and checked his vitals, inserted an IV into Modele's arm, strapped him on the gurney and headed for the ambulance.

The other medic verified the two gunmen were dead then stopped in front of Nelson.

"We'll call the coroner's ambulance to pick the dead ones up," he said.

"I've got the crime team coming," Nelson said. "They'll have to wait until they're done."

"You can take that up with them when they get here," the medic said and moved on toward his ambulance.

A crowd was gathering in front of the alley. "What's going on in there?" someone yelled from the crowd.

"Call for back up, Sid," Nelson said. "We may need them to get out of here."

"Okay, I'll see what I can do in the meantime." Sid walked to the street, cautioning everyone to stay out of the alley.

"He's going to be a good cop," Nelson said.

"Yeah, I think so, too," I said.

Henry, the whores and the little bowling man were standing beside the backdoor, staring.

Sergeant Nelson looked their way and said, "You see what happened here?"

"Those two," Henry said, pointing at the two dead men, "were trying to kill everybody, but Tommy mowed them down."

"Who's Tommy?" Nelson asked.

"He's talking about me, but that's not exactly what happened," I said.

"I see. Well, all of you go back inside but don't leave, someone will be in to ask you questions," Nelson said.

They all started nodding like bobblehead dolls and walked back inside.

"I'll have to ask you to stick around, Tommy, I need a statement for the crime team," Nelson said, grinning.

"Don't let that Tommy thing get out," I said.

"You and Modele the only ones involved?" he asked.

"No, Darcie and my client, who was apparently the target, were also here."

"Were they hit?"

"No, I had to get them out of here before some more bad guys showed up."

"The crime team boys aren't going to like that, Mecana. You know better," he said.

"It was what I had to do."

Nelson told Sid to mark off where Modele fell and around the dead guys.

Sid nodded and did as he was told.

My phone rang and I quickly took it out of my pocket, thinking something may have happened to Darcie. It was Emily.

"Who's that?" Nelson asked.

"It's my daughter Emily. Excuse me a minute." I walked a few steps and answered the phone. "Emily, you picked a bad time. I can't talk now. I'll have to call you later."

"Are you going to get my car?" she asked.

"Yes, we'll talk about it when I have time."

"When will that be?"

"As soon as I can. I have to go." I hung up. "Sorry about that," I told Nelson.

"It's okay, got kids myself."

I expected my phone to ring again any minute, Morgan always followed her sister's lead.

Instead, I heard another siren on the way.

7

To my surprise I didn't get a phone call from Morgan, but something much worse.

Chandler and Blount arrived. They thought they were the old TV team Starsky and Hutch, when in reality they were more like Peter Sellers' Inspector Clouseau. They had good intentions, but they could screw up a train wreck. You never knew what they would do. Usually it was something off the wall they probably saw in a movie.

Robert Chandler was a tall, thin white guy with a moustache and pointed chin. He had a wife and four kids. It took him twenty years to make it to a plainclothes detective, and he was barely hanging on to that.

Kimber Blount, on the other hand, was the smarter of the two and the one that kept Chandler out of trouble. He was younger than Chandler, single, black, with a gym rat body.

They walked up and looked at the two dead guys. "You do that Mecana?" Chandler asked.

"I had some help. You two assigned or just happen to answer a call?"

"I think you better give me your piece," Blount said and held out his hand, working his fingers back and forth.

I reluctantly handed him my Glock. "My client was the target. The dead guys were pros," I said.

"Both of those guys were shot in the back, Mecana," Chandler said. "There's blood running out of holes in their backs. How could they shoot you with their backs to you?"

"You see the weapons they were carrying, detective?" Nelson said.

"Nelson, you stay out of this. We're in charge here," Blount said.

"Take me downtown and let me talk to Verves," I said.

"You're in no position to be giving orders, Mecana. You quit, remember," Blount said. "We'll decide what to do, not you."

"And what's that?" I said.

"We wait for the forensic guys to get here and you tell us how all this went down," Chandler said. "Where's your client now?"

"I can't tell you that," I said.

"Then we we'll have to arrest you for obstructing justice," Blount said.

"Then do it." I was like Brer Rabbit; throw me in the briar patch. Plus, I knew I would get to talk to Verves.

Chandler took his handcuffs off his belt and motioned for me to turn around. He cuffed me and pulled out his Miranda card.

"That's not necessary," I said. "I know my rights."

"You never were very good at following police procedure, Mecana. I am," he said and continued reading from the Miranda card.

A police van pulled up to the alley and three men got out wearing white coats over their uniforms and nylon gloves, carrying plastic bags and blood syringes. The crime team had arrived.

The coroner's ambulance stopped behind them and two men dressed in blue scrubs got out and wheeled two gurneys with body bags over to the dead men.

"Hey you, coroner guy," one of the crime team men yelled. "Wait up. We have to do our job before you move them."

"Then do it," the medic said. "We want to get out of here."

Chandler escorted me to the cruiser and sat me down in the back seat. "Stay put," he said and went back to talk to the crime team. A few minutes later he returned with Blount.

Chandler motioned the cruiser through the crowd, waved at Sergeant Nelson as he passed and hauled ass for the police station.

Morgan still hadn't called. I was getting worried.

8

Chandler, true to his word, followed procedure to the letter; with everything from taking my mugshot to emptying my pockets. I asked to keep my phone but he wouldn't let me. They locked me in a holding cell and walked away. Obscenities were written all over the walls, some in blood. I noticed four different colors of paint where the wall touched the concrete floor.

It was a weekly task to cover the filth with any kind of paint that was available. The inmates would carve their trash with anything that would scratch the surface.

When Verves showed up I was still reading the wall.

"Unlock the cell," Verves said and handed the jailer a paper. The jailer looked at the paper, nodded and complied. "I heard Modele is in bad shape, and you had Darcie and Mrs. Kane leave the crime scene. Not good."

"I had to get them out of harm's way," I said. "You tell anyone besides Modele what we were doing?"

"No," Verves said.

"It was self-defense," I said.

"Did you tell Chandler and Blount you were there to have your client talk to Modele?"

"I never got the chance."

"You're putting me in a bind, Mecana."

"Sorry," I said, "but this was like a mob hit."

"Maybe they were," Verves said.

"No IDs, maybe fingerprints will tell us who they were," I said.

"I'll start with that," Verves said. "I convinced a judge you contacted me and was there to see Modele when the shit hit the fan; and that you acted in self-defense. You'll have to appear in court later to clear the record but you're free to go for now, as long as you promise me you will bring Mrs. Kane in for a talk."

"Deal," I said. "I'd like to get a bio on the Kanes and a copy of the autopsy, if you'll arrange it."

"Don't have time?" Verves said.

"I can pick it up," I said.

Verves looked at me and sighed. "I'll see what I can do. You have twenty-four hours to bring in Mrs. Kane."

"Thanks," I said and walked away.

I stopped by the claims room and picked up my Glock and other items.

One thing I didn't see in the room was the box from The Mutilator case.

I caught a taxi and had him do some double-backs before it felt like we were clear. When we finally headed for the lake house I called Morgan. I explained it would be a while but we would go to Disneyland as soon as I could get the time. She was always inclined to take me at my word whereas Emily wasn't. I suspected it was her mother's fault.

Henry's refurbished Ford and my truck were sitting in the driveway. I wondered what kind of reaction the rental company was going to have when they saw their car.

The taxi stopped. I got out and paid him. It was time to have a come-to-Jesus meeting with Miss Candy.

I called Darcie when I got to the door. "I'm here," I said.

Darcie opened the door, Beretta in her hand.

"Where's Candy?" I asked.

"In the kitchen, trying to force down a TV dinner," she said.

We walked into the kitchen and Candy was sitting at a long dining table with a glass of wine and a napkin thrown over her microwave meal.

"Mecana, I can't eat this slop. Let me order us some food from Frailer."

"At two hundred dollars a plate?" I said.

"Whatever, I'll pay for it. I'm hungry," she said.

"We have to talk first," I said. "And you're going to have to talk to the cops again."

She stood up, picked up her wine glass and drank what was left.

"Anything else you should tell us?" I said.

"I figured if I told you the truth you wouldn't help me. But I guess I have to."

"That would help," I said.

She picked up the bottle of wine, poured her glass full and drank half of it before sitting it back on the table.

"You'll find out sooner or later. Might as well tell you the whole thing," she said.

"We're listening," Darcie said.

"I was a runaway at sixteen."

"From where?" Darcie asked.

"Atlanta, Georgia. My mother was a drug addict and prostitute. I never knew who my father was. I don't think she did, either. I got tired of fighting off her pimp, so I made my way to Dallas and took up my mother's profession as a freelancer to survive. She died from an overdose three months later."

"You have any more family?" Darcie asked.

"Not that I know of," she said.

"What's your mother's married and maiden names?" Darcie said. "I'll check it out."

"Adele Parnell," she said. "She was never married.

"A couple years after she died I met Ashton. His chauffer was cruising around one night, looking for a girl for Ashton and he saw me. He asked if I would like to make a thousand dollars. I said yes and that's how it all started.

"Ashton was amused by our names together. We had sex in a hotel suite that night. Afterwards, he asked if he could hypnotize me; told me he was a medical hypnotist and would give me another thousand dollars to let him. I thought what the hell and the next thing I knew, I woke up hours later naked in the bedroom."

"You don't remember what you did while you were hypnotized?" Darcie said.

"No."

"What happened after that?" Darcie said.

"He said he would like for me to stay with him; that he could help me overcome some problems he discovered while I was under hypnosis."

"Like what," I said.

"While I was under, he said I revealed my mother's psychotic abuse. He also said he could change my perception of who I was for the better, with more treatments."

"Did he?" Darcie said.

"Yes. He freed my mind through hypnosis to experience insight into my problems and a state of mind to understand how I could change my life.

"We were married that year. He's twenty years older than I am."

"Did he tell you what you did while hypnotized," Darcie said.

"No. He explained he conditioned me to have spontaneous amnesia after each session; thought it best I didn't know."

"You need to tell the cops what you just told us," I said.

"No. I'm not sure I should have even told you," she said.

"It won't go any further," Darcie said. "If that's what you want."

"No one," Candy said.

"Anything else you want to tell us?" Darcie said.

"Nothing I can think of," she said.

"That's an incredible story," Darcie said.

"I promised Verves I would bring you in for questioning," I said. "We'll get you something to eat on the way."

"I thought I didn't have to go in."

"The bowling alley incident changed all that."

"What will they do to me?" she said.

"Darcie's a lawyer, she can represent you. I don't think it's the cops you have to worry about, anyway. I'm beginning to think there's more to this than money. When you have that kind of firepower involved, it's something besides revenge."

"I wouldn't know. By the way, Ashton's body is coming home tomorrow morning," Candy said. "The funeral will be at Memorial Gardens at three-thirty tomorrow afternoon."

"We'll be there to protect you," I said. "Who's coming?"

"I didn't invite anyone," she said.

"Landon Fritz won't be there?"

No," she said. "He may be the one who's trying to kill me."

"You don't think it's Fillmore anymore?"

"Landon is next in line on Ashton's will to inherit his fortune. If I'm gone he would get the billons Ashton left."

"Why didn't you tell us this before?" Darcie said.

"I don't know," she said.

"I think you do, you just didn't want us to know. Why?"

"I forgot," she said. "That's all."

"You're too smart to forget something like that," I said.

"I did, that's the only reason," she said.

"Doubt that. We'll talk again. Let's go talk to Verves now," I said.

When we walked in the homicide department, Officers Chandler and Blount gave us a fixed stare as we made our way to Verves' glass office. When he saw us, he stood up and we walked in.

"This is Candy Kane, Chief," I said. Candy nodded and Verves did the same.

We sat and I noticed Chandler and Blount were still staring at us. "Chief, you got something for them to do? I feel like we're in a zoo in this glass office."

Verves looked up at them and waved his hand toward the outside door. They gave us a smirk, stood up from their desks and walked out.

Verves walked around his desk and looked at Candy. "I'm sorry about your husband, Mrs. Kane. We have to ask you some questions, for the record. Darcie, are you her attorney?"

"Yes," Darcie said.

"Mecana, why don't you get you a cup of coffee and mingle with your old comrades while we do this," Verves said.

Thinking of the coffee made me sick, but I nodded and stood up.

"Okay, ladies, if you will follow me," Verves said, "we'll get this over with."

Candy and Darcie stood up. Verves picked up a folder and a large manila envelope from his desk. He handed me the envelope and placed the folder under his arm.

"I think that's what you wanted, Mecana," he said.

Candy and Darcie followed Verves out of his office down the hall to the interrogation room. I sat down to wait and opened the envelope.

9

The first thing I noticed when I pulled the contents out of the envelope was one of the crime scene pictures of Ashton Kane. It showed him lying on the bed face-down, a sheet pulled over the lower part of his body with his legs and feet sticking out. He was naked when he was killed by four 9mm slugs that could have been from a small hand gun. It was also the preferred choice of pistol for many women.

Candy was licensed to carry a handgun but she wasn't there to do it; unless we could prove otherwise. Verves and his bunch couldn't.

A five-by-seven-inch picture was clipped to the page; showing Mr. Kane in a white coat with a nametag and a stethoscope around his neck. He was a good-looking man with blue eyes, a full head of combed-back black hair with a touch of gray that gave him a distinguished look. A note on the bottom of the picture listed him as six-two, two-hundred pounds and forty-eight years old.

According to the files, his parents were killed in a plane crash on their way to a business trip in Florida for the bank where they both worked. Luckily for Ashton, he was being taken care of by his aunt so he could play a little league game that day. He was ten years old when it happened, and spent the rest of his childhood in the care of his aunt.

He was turned down for a full academic scholarship to medical school because he was not active in any extra-curricular activities benefiting the country or community required for the scholarship, even though he was a straight-A student.

He had been arrested for assault and battery for beating up a kid in college after a hazing attempt and was then considered an undesirable by all the other fraternities he attempted to join.

He was also arrested three times for soliciting prostitution after the women filed complaints because of his unusual behavior.

One of the women claimed he hypnotized her to do weird sex things and another one said she was locked in a dark room where he made her watch a video of people having sex for hours and later "tested" her on it. Since no evidence was found, the school only suspended him for a year before he returned to graduate at the top of his class.

A federal charge of fraud was filed three years ago by an Edward Fillmore but Kane had been acquitted of all charges. There was no mention of any lasting relationships with any women other than Candy. Not exactly an all-American boy, but a huge success with an eye for the oldest profession.

Candy was listed as the wife of a doctor and a socialite charity fundraiser.

Her name and her mother's name were as she said. A marriage license to Ashton Kane revealed her maiden name and a rap sheet on her mother's prostitution and drug charges, but Candy had never been booked on any charges.

I heard a door close, looked up and saw Verves and the ladies coming my way. I stuffed the contents back in the envelope and followed them back into Verve's office.

"Have a seat," Verves said.

We sat down and waited for him to speak.

"Mrs. Kane, you said you were in Dallas when your husband was murdered and we have nothing to prove otherwise. But that doesn't mean we can dismiss all interest in you until we confirm other people had the motive and opportunity to kill your husband. We will also have to explore your past in more detail before we can conclude our investigation."

"Chief," Darcie said, "you have personal information and will certainly obtain more in your investigation that we don't want in the press. I want to request you give us the opportunity to prevent private matters from going public."

"That depends," Verves said. "I may be able to do that, but if my boss says they have to be made public there's not much I can do."

"I understand that, but I also know we can sue for invasion of privacy if the information is not relative to the case."

"I'll keep that in mind. We can talk first," Verves said. "Mrs. Kane, again, let me express my sympathy for the loss of your husband. We will keep you posted on any developments in the case."

"Thank you," Candy said. "Chief Verves, I've come a long way from my old life. My background would damage my status now if it is made public. Please consider that for me."

"I'll do what I can," he said.

"May we go now?" Candy asked.

"Yes. Here's a parking pass so you won't have to pay," he said and handed me the pass.

I stood up and shook hands with Verves. "Thanks, Chief," I said, gesturing toward the envelope. "If you find out who was trying to kill us, let me know please."

Verves nodded. Darcie and Candy said goodbye and we left.

We stopped at Brogans on the way home. The chef was familiar with Tibetan Highland Asian Chicken and prepared Candy a gourmet dinner to go. He said DeMax was fired for trying to seduce the manager's wife.

We headed back to the lake house. Candy poured some wine, ate about half of the dinner and retreated to the bedroom with a fresh bottle, saying she was going to get drunk and not to bother her.

Darcie and I found a steak TV dinner. We finished it off and sat down in the living room after feeding the fish.

"Well, Sherlock, what do we do now?" Darcie asked.

"Verves gave me a bio and autopsy of Ashton Kane," I said. "The crime scene picture looked like there may have been some sex going on when Kane was murdered. He had a record of arrests when he was in college for sexual perversions; and one prostitute claimed she was hypnotized by Kane. Sound familiar?" I opened the envelope and handed Darcie the picture.

"Yeah, it does look like he was in a compromising position. The spots on the bed could be semen." She shuffled through the other files. "He wasn't allowed into any fraternities, either. Looks like he worked his way through college. Must have been a loner; maybe some mental problems himself."

"They don't have a normal husband/wife relationship, that's for sure."

"Check the airlines for a round-trip ticket to New York in Candy's name the same night her husband was murdered. I'll have a look at the car. It's supposed to have a bullet hole in the window."

"I'll check the phone calls," Darcie said.

"We need something. We keep running into blank walls."

I picked up the keys to Candy's car but I gave Darcie back the keys to the Kanes' penthouse and his office. "I'd hate to break in."

"I'll go check," Darcie said.

"I'll call DeMax and get him to stay with you while I'm gone," I said. "I'm sure he could use the money. Just make sure he stays away from Candy."

"I'll tell him something like, 'You bother her and I'll shoot your balls off,'" she said.

"That should do it," I grinned. "I'm going by the house to clean up and check my machine to see if the kids called. Run a bio on Fillmore for me and send it to the house."

"You got it, Sherlock," she said.

"We'll have to go to the funeral with Candy tomorrow. It's the perfect place for an ambush."

10

After taking a shower by myself I put on a blue pullover sweater and a pair of Dockers Darcie bought me. I was buckling my Glock holster when I noticed something off...my roll of quarters was gone from the dresser. Darcie may have stuck them away somewhere and deprived me of a legal weapon.

I checked the machine. No messages from Emily or Morgan. I called my daughters to let them know I was tied up for a while but had the money to get them what they wanted as soon as I finished my case.

Emily suggested I send the money to her mother and let her help buy the car and then they would take Morgan to Disneyland. I told her I would think about it, although I knew I had no intentions of letting my ex-wife's new boyfriend play daddy.

Darcie called before I could call her. She told me to check my computer; she had sent me the bio on Edward Fillmore.

Looking over it, I read he resided in one of the more upscale buildings and was the CEO of a financial firm. He was forty years old and a Harvard grad with a PhD in Economics. Fillmore also had two kids but was divorced because he was unfaithful to his wife with Candy Kane, according to the divorce papers.

The only note listed on his medical treatment was, "Patient escapes into numbness to forget unpleasant events he has no solution for, and is best served by medical hypnotism to prevent further mind-altering thoughts."

So that explained why he was being hypnotized.

He had filed a lawsuit against Ashton Kane for ten million dollars, claiming Kane hypnotized him to transfer ten million dollars from his account. The case was thrown out of court due to lack of evidence.

I checked the marquee outside the building, this was the right place.

Inside, I stepped into the elevator with a group of well-dressed white-haired men who were probably executives of companies in the building. I got off on the tenth floor and saw a brass sign across the hall with an arrow pointing to my left.

When I walked in, a redheaded secretary was sitting at the desk next to a door labeled 'CEO Edward G Fillmore.'

"May I help you?" she asked.

"Yes, I need to talk to Mr. Fillmore," I said and handed her my newly-printed business card.

"Is Mr. Fillmore expecting you?"

"No ma'am, but I think he will want to see me. It's about the murder of Ashton Kane."

"I don't think so, Mr. Mecana. He gave me instructions not to let anyone in if it concerned Mr. Kane."

"I'm not leaving until I do."

She stood up and stepped in front of the door to his office. "I'll call the police. You're trespassing."

"I could also push you out of the way and go in before they get here."

She stared at me and didn't move.

"Wait here," she finally said, quickly opening and closing the door as she went in.

Seconds later, Fillmore burst out of his office looking at my card, jumpy as a bullfrog.

He was a tall, good-looking man wearing an expensive blue suit and red tie. He had thick black hair, dark brown eyes and a mustache.

"Mr. Mecana, take your ass outta here," he said. "I know about Kane's murder. I have an iron-clad alibi. He accused me of trying to fuck his wife and used his profession to take advantage of me. The emotional problems I have could never lead to murdering anyone. Now get out of my office before I have Miss Wingate call the cops."

"She's already threatened to do that," I said. "We can do this the easy way or the hard way, Mr. Fillmore. I have no desire to cause you further trouble, but I need the truth.

You better make damn sure that's what you're telling me."

He rubbed his hands together and grimaced like he was in pain. "Okay. Come in my office."

He motioned for me to go through the open door. I walked in and he followed and sat behind his desk. I sat down in a chair in front of his desk.

"I was in London attending a business meeting when he was murdered," Fillmore said. "Lots of witnesses. I may be glad someone killed him but it wasn't me. His wife tried to recruit me to obtain information on several of my clients for market deals, using herself as the reward. I admit I thought it over but changed my mind. Nothing happened. He's an evil mental case and she's an evil whore. I think they're the perfect pair for the devil. That's the truth as I see it. Now get out."

He got to his feet, hurried to the door and opened it, waiting for me to leave. He had been so blunt it seemed to be the truth. I got up and walked out the door.

"Another time," I said to the secretary as I left the office.

I still had the keys Darcie gave me so I decided to check out Kane's office for another look.

When I arrived and opened the door the alarm didn't go off this time. The office was in a state of disarray. It had been ransacked after I went through it the first time.

I noticed some of the things I remembered had been moved; like the replica Maltese Falcon from one of Bogart's movies was sitting on a table now instead of the marble desk, and a bottom desk drawer now open that I didn't leave that way, and a painting that looked like an original Picasso was gone from the wall behind his desk. Vandals, murderers, or both. Maybe someone who knew what they were looking for found it.

All the files were gone and either the sneaks or the police had them. I had been through the files before they disappeared but didn't remember anything suspicious, except for the fact there wasn't a file on Fillmore. Probably destroyed by Kane to keep it from the courts. Fillmore had denied any involvement with Candy but seemed too nervous for it not to have happened.

The only interesting tidbit I found was an index file card file on Kane's desk with the words 'Song for Pons, Turkey soon.' Turkey was capitalized; did he mean the country?

I was getting a headache and decided after I checked the car I would skip the penthouse until tomorrow. I stuck the index card in my pocket, locked the office and left.

I remembered the parking space number because she said it was the same as her age - 28. But it wasn't there. Someone must have towed it away. Or, on second thought, maybe she drove it away. Most people have two sets of keys. But she'd been with us since we took her case.

I scouted the hotel for info about the car. No one knew anything about it. Called all the local towing companies but none of them knew anything, either.

Would need to have another talk with Candy about the damn car. My headache was getting worse.

As I drove back to the lake house I thought about the index card, Fillmore, the doctor's funeral, Candy, and her car for a while; then decided I needed a thought break and switched to my girls.

I was most worried about what Emily said. I wondered if that was what she really thought or if it was her mother putting thoughts in her head so she could take her scumbag of a boyfriend with them to Disneyland in Emily's new car.

I thought about calling Emily but decided it wouldn't help and called Darcie instead.

She said, "DeMax was there but said he didn't make a pass at the manager's wife, she was just mad at him because he didn't."

"Not sure I believe that," I said.

"Lots of calls between Kane and a Landon Fritz about everything from golf to Candy," Darcie said. "Sounded like they're buddies. In the Candy discussion they were talking about her mental and hypnosis status and about a song for an Alonza Pons from Turkey. No idea what they meant by that. Only info I found on Pons is he is the head of an executive committee to the UN from Turkey."

"That's interesting," I said. "I found an index card in Kane's office with the words song, Pons and Turkey on it. That's a match. You got an address on Fritz?"

"Yes," she said.

"I'm beginning to think Kane was using his profession to take advantage of people and Candy was using her former profession to help make it happen."

"I'll ask Candy about Fritz," Darcie said. "She said the three of them had spent a lot of time together visiting foreign countries."

"I don't think Candy is telling us everything. And Fillmore had a good alibi but it really doesn't matter," I said. "He could have hired the goons who came after us. He's a pretty sick puppy. I'm on my way back to the lake house now. I'll be there in about thirty minutes."

DeMax met me at the door.

"Hey Mecana," he said. "They're in the bedroom. The pretty lady drank herself to sleep so Miss Darcie is watching over her."

"How long has she been out?" I said.

"About two hours," DeMax said. "I offered to stay with her, but Miss Darcie said she would."

I walked into the bedroom. Candy was lying on the bed in silk pajamas, her legs drawn up into the fetal position, her closed eyelids flickering rapidly; must be having a bad dream.

"Hope you didn't hypnotize her," I said and grinned.

"You're not as funny as you think you are," Darcie said. "She's been making gurgling noises in her sleep."

I glanced at two large empty wine bottles on the bedside table. I picked up one of the bottles and looked at the label.

"Just paying for two bottles of this would make me drunk," I said. "I'm having to deal with my two daughters. They're being brainwashed by their mother with the help of her dumbass boyfriend. Might have to go kick his ass."

I didn't realize DeMax was standing behind me in the doorway until he spoke.

"Just give me a name and I'll make the motherfucker wish he was somebody else, Mecana."

"I appreciate the offer but I need you here," I told him.

DeMax nodded and walked away.

"Never thinks about his language," Darcie said.

"Hope I didn't hurt his feelings," I said.

"DeMax is a martial arts expert," Darcie said. "Saw it in his records."

"No shit? Maybe I'll change my mind."

"Kind of sneaky," Darcie said.

"I don't care," I said and sat down on the corner of the bed. Candy moaned, turned over and flipped her hand on my crotch.

"She better be asleep," Darcie said.

"She is…I think," I said and moved her hand.

"You resent the boyfriend because he replaced you, don't you?" Darcie said.

"I resent him because he's an asshole."

"You still care for her?"

"I thought you were a lawyer, not a psychologist."

"Just trying to help."

"Well, you're not. What kind of martial arts expert is DeMax?"

"I don't know, Mecana, it just said martial arts. Once you get your mind on something it never leaves until you're satisfied with it, does it?"

"Nope."

"The insurance guy called me," she said. "I told him we would send his money back, we didn't have time to work on his case. He was pretty pissed."

"Changing the subject?" I said.

"I am," she said. "I like the clothes you have on."

"An inquisitive lady bought them for me." I stood up and struck a pose. "Did you see my roll of quarters on the dresser?"

She smiled. "No. I think it's time to wake up Candy and escort her to the shower," she said. "You can't come."

"Party pooper. I'll go talk to DeMax," I said.

DeMax was watching reruns of Hap and Leonard in the living room when I walked in. I sat down on the couch beside him.

"Thanks for offering to take care of the boyfriend but I think I'll let it go for now. Darcie told me you were a martial arts expert. I never knew."

"Maybe not an expert, but I have a black belt."

"I don't remember you using any martial arts stuff when we arrested you as a suspect in The Mutilator case."

"Would have got me in more trouble for kickin' your ass," DeMax said.

"Not to mention my broken bones. The guy's a jerk but I'm going to need you for a lot of other things, if you want to stick around."

"Fine with me," he said. "Got nothing else to do."

"Okay, you can help us solve this case."

He smiled. "You mean that?"

"I do," I said. "I'll even pay you."

"How much?" he asked.

"Two thousand a week," I said. "Until we solve the case. Won't be long I hope."

"Room and board, too?"

"I can do that, plus a bonus when we solve the case."

"Sounds fair."

"Good," I said. "We agree then?"

"We do." DeMax stretched out on the couch and went back to watching TV.

The name Landon Fritz kept popping up in my head. Maybe he could shed some light on what the hell was going on with the 'song' shit.

I glanced at the TV. "Two good ol' Texas boys getting their due."

11

The next morning I was waiting for Candy to wake up so I could get more information on Landon Fritz. I had also been trying to learn as much as possible about hypnotism on the internet. It all kind of ran together for me. I always thought of it as entertainment, and never took it seriously until I found out doctors had been studying hypnotism for over two hundred years to treat emotional, physical and mental illnesses. Some even claimed they could improve intelligence with hypnotism.

DeMax walked in wearing a #4 Dallas Cowboys jersey.

I was eating cereal. "Get you something to eat, DeMax."

"Too early for me. I'll run down to McDonalds later," he said. "Miss Darcie said I can't have a gun when you go to New York."

"Well, not legally, but if someone breaks in you can use one in self-defense."

"You going to leave one?" DeMax said.

"I'll leave a .45 over there by the aquarium," I said.

"How long are you going to be gone?"

"We have to go to the doctor's funeral today and then I need you to hold down the fort for a day or two while I'm in New York. Call the cops if someone comes around who shouldn't."

"I will," he said.

"Hopefully, all you'll have to do is watch television and feed the fish for me."

"Big job," DeMax said and turned on the TV.

We left the lake house around two that afternoon and headed for Memorial Gardens.

When the hearse arrived, two men reeled out the coffin, sat it on a stand beside the grave and backed off. I didn't see a preacher.

"Is anyone going to give him a send off, Candy?"

"No. I just have to certify he's buried and go by the bank to have his money signed over to me. You can be witnesses."

A man on a backhoe showed up. Three men lowered his coffin into the grave and the man on the backhoe covered it up. The shortest and coldest funeral I ever saw.

"Take me to the bank." Candy pitched a single flower on the grave and we left without another word.

Darcie and I parked outside the bank with Candy and went inside. We sat outside the bank president's office with the door open so we could keep an eye out.

She conducted her business. We heard bits and pieces of their conversation. She was asking him to close the accounts and give her the cash. The president looked at her like he was totally surprised at what she wanted him to do and shook his head no. She stood up and shook a finger at him and he sat back down, wrote something on a paper handed it to her. She signed it, pitched it back to him and walked out of the office.

"Don't ask, let's go," Candy said. "You don't have to sign anything."

On the way back to the lake house, we stopped by Brogans and picked up another special meal for Candy. When we got to the bungalow she poured a glass of wine and ate most of her meal.

"I'm going to get my stuff shipped to France and make arrangements to leave the day after tomorrow," she said. "I'll put another hundred grand in your account and you'll be done with your job."

"For whatever reason, people are still looking for you. We'll have to let the cops know what you're doing," I said.

"Since you put it that way, forget the hundred grand. I'll take care of myself from here on out." She drained her wine glass.

"You can do what you want, but you're not getting killed on our time. We'll keep a watch until you're gone. Unless the cops want you," I said.

"Suit yourself," she said and walked away with her glass and a fresh bottle of wine; Darcie following with a TV dinner.

DeMax and I took ours into the living room to watch television; Dallas Football was coming on in the next thirty minutes. We sat down and devoured our TV dinner just in time for football.

A roaring airplane-like sound shook the walls of the house. We thought it was the TV for a second. I looked out the window and saw a monster truck with huge Caterpillar-size tires bouncing down the driveway at an incredible speed, headed straight for the house.

A man in the passenger seat leaned out the window and started firing an automatic weapon at the house.

We hit the floor.

I yelled "Stay down!" as loud as I could and crawled faster than a snake toward the hallway. DeMax was right behind me following suit.

We barely made it to the hallway before the monster truck crashed through the wall, sending debris flying everywhere. The driver and another man jumped out, spraying the room with bullets.

I heard a woman scream and knew it was Candy. I jumped up in the hallway and ran as fast as I could toward the bedroom, DeMax in hot pursuit.

Darcie came running out of the bedroom holding her Berretta, Candy right behind her naked and wet.

"Go back," I told them.

They turned around and I saw a black bird sitting on a limb tattooed on Candy's butt. We all ran into the bedroom. I grabbed a suitcase on the bed, smashed a window with it and we climbed out with the burglar alarm screaming at us. We ran to my truck, me hoping the suitcase I was carrying held some clothes for Candy.

I opened a back door, threw in the suitcase and Darcie and Candy got in and hugged the floorboard. I started the truck, peeled out and headed for the gate.

DeMax jumped on his bike and slung dirt everywhere as he took off.

The two killers ran out the door firing at us, bullets ripping holes in Henry's parked truck and mine as I drove through the open gate to the street. All those holes in my truck were going to end my love affair with it. And I would have to find Henry a new one now, too.

DeMax wheeled his bike up beside the truck. "Everybody okay?" he asked.

Both women answered yes and I nodded at him.

"Let me borrow your bike," I told DeMax. "I have to get them before they come after us."

"You want me to go with you?" DeMax said.

"No, stay with them and take off if you see anyone besides me coming."

DeMax jumped off the bike. I jumped on, made a circle and headed back to the house.

As I wheeled through the hole in the wall, I saw the two men walking back toward the monster truck. I went full-throttle and jerked the front wheel up; it deflected some bullets and caught one man on top of his head, crushing his skull. He dropped his weapon and fell to the floor, blood streaming down the side of his head.

I brought the wheel down and dove off the bike, letting it slide across the floor to the other man, cutting his feet out from under him. He hit the floor and lost his machine pistol. I fired as quickly as I could. He yelled and crawled toward the gun. I emptied my Glock in him and blood surrounded him like a red rug.

A patrol car shot through the gate, lights flashing and siren screaming, and spun to a stop in front of the hole in the wall. I tossed the empty Glock to the floor and sat down with my hands behind my head. Two cops jumped out with their weapons drawn and ran inside.

"Don't move," one of them said.

"Don't shoot," I replied. "My weapon's on the floor in front of you. I'm unarmed."

"Stretch out on the floor, put your hands behind your back," the other said.

I did what I was told and a cop with sergeant stripes and 'Knowles' on his nametag handcuffed me. The other one was named Sawyer. He picked up my Glock and the other weapons while Knowles checked the dead men.

"You know them?" Knowles asked.

"No, I'm an ex-cop. Chief Verves knows me. Call him," I said.

"Stay where you are," Sergeant Knowles said.

From a worm's-eye view, I saw another patrol car appear, then another; lights flashing and sirens blasting from all of them. My truck roared up behind them.

"That's my people in the truck, Sergeant, don't shoot."

They all exited the truck with their hands up. Candy was now wearing pajamas, the bird tattoo now out of sight.

The cops shoved them to the ground and handcuffed them as a small crowd gathered at the gate.

The cops helped me up and led me out of the house to a cruiser.

"Are you alright?" Darcie called out.

"Yeah, you?" I yelled back, competing with the sirens.

"We're okay," she shouted back.

They put us in the cruisers. A crime scene patrol and coroner's ambulance drove up as we left the property.

12

They put me and DeMax in a cell together and took Darcie and Candy to the women's jail across the street to sort out everything.

Verves showed up two hours later wearing jeans and a police t-shirt.

"Mecana, you're beginning to be a real pain in the ass."

"Seems like somebody up there don't like us," I said.

"I stopped by the morgue," Verves said. "They look like Swiss cheese. You know them?"

"Let me guess, they didn't have any ID, either," I said.

"Nothing. I'll see if I can get bail set and get the info over to Darcie, too."

"Thanks," I said.

"Behave yourself, Mecana." He walked away, a guard following him out.

"He likes you," DeMax said. "Are we gonna get out?"

"Maybe," I said.

"I need a gun," DeMax said. "I never got a chance to shoot back."

"You don't have a license," I said.

"Won't make any difference when I'm dead."

"Good point. I'll see what I can do."

The next day, Darcie walked in with a paper in her hand; a gray-haired overweight turnkey with a keychain attached to his belt following her. He stuck a key in the lock and opened our cell, and motioned for us to come out without a word.

"Where's Candy?" I asked.

"I'll tell you later," Darcie said. "Let's just get out of here."

When we walked outside Darcie led us to a new truck and handed me the keys. It was the same make and model as the one that got shot up.

"You bought a new truck," Darcie said.

"I did?" I said.

"Yeah the other one had too many bullet holes to fix. I got you another like the one you were in love with."

"Cool," DeMax said.

"Good and bad," I said. "My damn insurance premiums are going to go through the roof. And I have to get Henry a truck."

"Never promised you a rose garden," Darcie said.

"I always smell flowers when you speak," I said.

"Well isn't that sweet. You must be glad to get out of jail," Darcie said.

"Where's Candy?"

"Deposit your butt in the truck," she said. "DeMax, you can ride up front."

I got in and there was Candy, sitting in the back seat.

"Here I am," she said. "As you can see, the cops don't want me. Find me a place to pee then take me back to my place to pack, I'm leaving today."

"There's a station across the street," DeMax said. "I got to go, too."

"Make it quick," I said and pulled into the station's parking lot. "Looks like the restrooms are inside. What about you, Darcie?"

"I'm good," she said.

"Go with Candy," I said.

"You think I need a chaperone to pee?" Candy said.

"I don't want anyone to kill you on our watch," I said. We got out and headed to the restrooms.

When DeMax and I walked in the men's room, two big men wearing suits followed in behind us. I could see them in the mirrors. They stopped in the middle of the floor and drew automatics out of their coats.

"Don't move," the older-looking man said and motioned for us to move against the wall. He placed his revolver against my head and removed the Glock from my shoulder holster while the younger one patted us down.

"Stay put you two," the older one said. "You poke your head out that door and we'll blow it clean off." They bolted from the room in a run.

We stopped at the door but it wouldn't open; they had pushed a vending machine against it. We heard a woman screaming outside. We could see through a crack in the door they were carrying Candy to their car. We shoved the door open but they were already gone. We ran into the ladies restroom where Darcie was crawling out from under a locked stall.

"They took Candy," she said.

"What did they look like?" I said.

"Two white men in suits. One had a shaved head and the other one was smaller and thinner with a beard."

"Same ones who came after us."

"Damn, they're fast," DeMax said.

"Let's go," I said. "Maybe we can catch up."

We started for the door when a little man with shaggy blonde hair ran in with a .38 in his hand. According to the nametag on his black fast food shirt, his name was George and he was the manager at the fast food place inside the station.

"I called the police," George said, waving the .38 at us. "The other ones got away but you and Sambo ain't."

DeMax looked at me with a fire in his eyes.

"Go ahead," I said.

DeMax jumped toward the little man, kicking the gun out of his hand. He spun around and laid a right cross on his chin so hard he staggered across the restroom, his arms flying around like a windmill. He banged his head on the wall and fell to the floor, out cold.

I picked up his .38 and stuck it in my pocket.

"What's he doing that for?" Darcie asked, staring at DeMax.

"The little man was insulting him," I said.

"Holy shit," she said.

"They take your Berretta?"

"Yes," she said.

"We fucked up, didn't we," DeMax said.

"Yes we did," I said.

We hurried out of the restrooms and into the station.

"Anyone see the car the men put that lady in?" I asked aloud.

Four or five people in the store stopped shopping for a moment and stared at us, but said nothing and went back to shopping.

A young woman behind the counter wearing the same black fast food shirt as George held her hand up like a schoolgirl in class.

"Are you a cop?" she said, looking at me.

"Was at one time, Sally," I said, looking at the name on her shirt.

"Two guys came out of the ladies room carrying a blonde lady, kicking and screaming, with her panties hanging around one ankle about to fall off," she said. "They put her in a white van and took off north down Reilly Street. A big black car followed."

"Do you remember any plate numbers from either one?"

"First two on the van were 16," she said. "That's all I remember."

I reached in my pocket and pulled a hundred dollar bill off my money clip and handed it to her. "You've been a lot of help, Sally. Thanks."

Sergeant Nelson and his young partner drove up beside us in the parking lot as we were headed to the truck.

"Just received a disturbance call," Nelson said. "You have anything to do with it, Mecana?"

I stopped beside my driver-side door for a second as DeMax and Darcie were getting in. "Can't explain now, Nelson. Have to run. My client was kidnapped."

I got in the truck and started the engine. I waved at Nelson and floorboarded the gas pedal.

13

The sun dropped out of sight over the next few minutes, making it harder to chase the perpetrators in the dark. If they intended to kill Candy it was done by now. I stopped at a red light and a white van roared by, heading the other direction.

"That was a sixteen on the plate, wasn't it," I said. "He's doubling back"

"I saw it," DeMax said.

"I did too," Darcie said. "But we don't know if it's the right one."

I whipped the truck around and followed the van for several miles but didn't see the big black car. The van turned off I-20 onto Highway 49 toward Houston and the black Mercedes appeared almost out of nowhere, following it.

"It's the right van," I said. "When I find a place I can block the van, I will. Darcie, you and DeMax get out of the truck and haul ass when I stop."

"You can't do that," Darcie said. "They probably have all kinds of weapons."

"May be our only chance," I said. "Plus, I've still got that manager's gun."

The van changed lanes to the right, headed towards the next exit. I waited for cars to come around me and dropped back a ways. The van made a right at the first street and the Mercedes followed.

"They must still have her. Somebody may want her alive," I said.

The van and the Mercedes made a right turn on Mable Street and headed north. I stayed back a ways, keeping the two vehicles in sight. The van moved over to the right again and, the Mercedes still following, pulled into a lit-up driveway with a big iron gate topped with 1924 SOUTH HALL ST; a rock fence surrounding a two-story brick building.

I drove past the gate and stopped under the shadow of a tree two blocks away and cut the lights and engine.

"What we do now?" DeMax asked.

"We call the FBI. We've got a kidnapping," Darcie said.

In the next instance, a whishing sound crash-busted out both front windows, glass flying all over. The two men we encountered at the station appeared on each side of my truck with AK-47s pointed at us.

"Throw out your weapons or we'll kill you," the bearded one said.

I tossed the .38 out the busted window. "That's all we've got."

"Come on, the rest of it."

"You already have it."

"Get out of the truck," the bearded guy said.

We opened the door and stepped out of the truck. I saw the baseball bat he used to bust the glass laying on the ground. Must be another one on the other side, I thought.

"Give me the keys," the bearded one said.

"They're in the truck," I said.

The shaved-headed one pushed Darcie and DeMax toward the front of the truck with the barrel of his AK-47 and motioned for them to keep walking.

"Go to the gate," he said.

The other one drove the truck up through the gate and cut the engine got off. He threw the keys as far as he could and picked up his AK-47 off the seat.

They opened the front door and walked us into a big room with a long table and eight straight-backed chairs.

"Sit down," the younger one said.

No sooner had we deposited our butts on the chairs than an old white-haired man with a matching white beard walked in smiling.

"Well, if it's not the famous mutilation detective," he said.

"And you look like Landon Fritz. I was going to come see you," I said.

"For a supposedly good cop you're not very good at tailing. We had to double back just so you wouldn't lose us."

"You bastard. Where's Candy?" Darcie said.

"I put her to sleep," Fritz said.

"For good?" I said.

"Heavens, no. I stuck a needle in her. But the night bird will be dead soon."

"Candy's got one tattooed on her butt," Darcie said.

I nodded affirmative.

"Ashton said she had it when they met. She called herself a night bird because of her profession. It conveniently gave him a code name for her."

"A code name for what?" I said.

"Since I'm going to kill you anyway," Fritz said, "what the hell.

"Candy killed whoever Ashton told her to kill; under suggested programming installed over a long period of time from hypnosis. She could blow anyone's brains out without the slightest remorse and wouldn't remember anything after. And with her looks, she never had any trouble getting men alone.

"A perfect assassin."

"That's crazy," I said. "Nobody could do that."

"Ashton ruined it all when he discovered she was having an affair with his private pilot," Fritz told them. "Kane told her what she had been doing for him and that he was going to turn her in to the cops. So she killed him.

"We were paid a million and a half by a terrorist group for a hit that never happened and now they're after us. I told them I would do away with Candy and give them her settlement money from Kane to make things even. I kept her alive to catch you morons."

"Your hit was Pons?" I said.

"How did you know?" Fritz said.

"Found the name on a card."

"She should have done what she was told. I had something else prepared for her if she got away."

"What was that," I said.

"Won't need it now," Fritz said and turned to the two hitmen. "Take them to the Melrose Mine Pit and bury them. I'll take care of our night bird."

Both men nodded and Fritz hurried out the door.

They were going to bury us alive.

The men were standing on each side of us a couple of feet away.

"Let's go," the younger one said, waving his AK-47.

"The three finger plan," I told DeMax.

"But we only did that once," he said.

"Now it'll be twice. Left."

"Right, on three," he said and held up three fingers.

"Under," Darcie said. We nodded.

Both men looked at each other, puzzled by what were doing.

DeMax raised his right arm and held out three fingers. "One," he said and dropped the first finger.

"Stop that," shaved head said and slapped DeMax's hand down. "Get out or we'll kill you right here."

DeMax raised his arm again. "Two," he said and dropped a second finger.

Shaved head swung his weapon at DeMax. He ducked.

"Three," he said and we all charged; myself to the left, DeMax to the right, and Darcie sliding across the floor, hitting their feet and making them lose balance.

DeMax kicked one in the face, knocking his gun out of his hands, and grabbed it on the way to the floor.

I tackled the other one and snatched his weapon as we were going down, then rolled over on top of him and pounded him with the stock several times.

We scrambled to our feet and opened fire. Their bodies looked like a screen door when we stopped. The entire fight lasted less than a minute.

Fritz ran in the doorway, saw what happened and ran out.

We hurried out the door after Fritz. I saw a small statue rocking on a table beside the first door on the right. We pushed up against the wall beside the door and I grabbed the statue off the table and threw it as hard as I could against the door. Three bullets zipped through the door, making holes big enough to see Fritz holding an automatic to Candy's head.

I busted through the door and Fritz grabbed Candy around the neck, stood her up and pushed the automatic tighter against her head.

"Don't shoot, we'll make a deal," I said. "Back out the door without shooting her and we'll let you go. Shoot her and you won't leave the room."

Fritz began to twitch his hand and mock-pulling the trigger on the automatic.

"Candy!" Darcie yelled.

Candy was blurry-eyed and in a daze. She moaned and Fritz tightened his grip on her.

"Wake up," Darcie said while DeMax and I shouted her name.

She groggily shook her head and saw Fritz was holding on to her. She started clawing at him, pulling him to the floor. Fritz let go of her and dropped his automatic. She picked up his gun and fired four quick bullets into his chest, tearing his heart apart. He fell over on his back with a thud beside her.

Darcie dropped down beside Candy, snatched the gun from her and threw it across the room.

"DeMax, go check the rest of this place," I said.

He nodded and hurried out the door, carrying an AK-47.

"Candy, do you know what happened?" Darcie asked.

"I killed him," Candy said. "Good riddance."

"Is that what you do, kill people?" Darcie said.

"You think I would be dumb enough to answer that," she said.

I heard footsteps and raised the gun, pointed it at the door.

"Nobody else here," DeMax said as he ran in.

"I'll call the FBI," Darcie said. "Mecana, you call Verves. He should know too."

"Yeah, I will. DeMax, lay that AK down. We did all the shooting, you got me?"

"I got you." He wiped the stock with his shirt, laid it on the floor and sat down beside Darcie and Candy.

Darcie patted him on the shoulder. "Thanks, partner. You were great," she said and dialed her phone.

"You too," he said.

"The FBI is on their way," Darcie said a few minutes later. "I told them to call before they drove in so we wouldn't shoot them. They said they would be here in less than an hour."

"I had to leave a message for Verves," I said. "Told him to call the FBI, too."

DeMax and I sat down with our eyes on Candy.

Something about Fritz was still bothering me but I couldn't put my finger on it. I stared at him lying on his back. The four bullet holes were in a tight grouping that tore a hole in his heart, all in one place.

The light bulb turned on.

That's what was bothering me. It was the same number of bullets and the same pattern as Kane.

***

About forty minutes later, I was making sure Candy stayed in one place.

Darcie's phone rang. "They're coming in," she said.

"I'll go outside and greet them," I said.

"I'll give you a million dollars to let me go," Candy said.

"Thought you weren't going to give us anymore money," I said.

"For the right reasons I will," she said. "Just say I got away."

"Can't do that. My daddy would turn over in his grave," I said.

"You're a simpleton, Mecana," Candy said.

"Maybe so. We misjudged you," I said. "You set Fillmore up as a scapegoat, murdered your husband, double-crossed Fritz and were using us to eliminate your adversaries."

"Because I'm smarter than you," Candy said.

"Not anymore."

14

I heard a car drive up to the gate and walked outside with an AK-47 and stood in the shadows by the door. A black Mercedes like the one Fritz had been driving pulled up and a man leaned out the driver's-side window and shot the lock off the gate.

Hope that's the FBI, I thought.

He saw me and yelled, "FBI coming in."

"Come on," I yelled. "We're expecting you."

They drove through the gate with a SWAT van behind and stopped inside, behind my truck. The back door of the van swung open and ten men ran out, fully combat dressed, three taking positions on me. The others ran past me into the building.

I stepped out of the shadow. "I'm Thomas Mecana. I'm the one who called you."

I showed the rifle over my head and slowly sat it down.

The man driving the Mercedes got out and walked up to me holding a Glock. He seemed to be the one in charge. He was tall and fit-looking with trimmed wavy black hair and wearing the traditional FBI attire: white shirt, black suit and tie, with a careful walk.

The one in the passenger side opened his door and stood behind it; looking at me, his bald head shining.

The tall one kicked the AK-47 away and said, "Turn around and lean against the wall," and patted me down. "Let's see some ID. Move slow."

I carefully removed my wallet and showed him my driver's license and PI license.

"Everybody in there friendlies?" he asked.

"The live ones are," I said. "Except for maybe Candy Kane."

He stuck his Glock back in his coat. We shook hands and went inside, the others following our lead.

Two were in the room with the dead guys and the others were in the room with my people and the dead Fritz.

"I'm Special Agent Bradford," he said and looked at Candy Kane. "Mrs. Kane, you'll have to come with us, the CIA wants you."

"Are you arresting me?" Candy asked.

"Yes, for the CIA."

"And do you have a warrant?" Darcie said. "I'm an attorney. We don't want her to walk."

"We picked one up from Judge Davis before we got here. Here's the one for her." He handed it to Darcie. She read the warrant and looked at

Candy.

"The cops want you now," Darcie said.

The bald-headed man walked up to Agent Bradford. "I'm Agent Franks," he said, looking at us. "The crime scene and coroner squads are on the way. I've made a security check on everyone, and Mrs. Kane, you are only one we will have to hold. Unless we find causes here to change that."

A few seconds later, Chief Verves poked his head in the door, hesitated for a moment and walked in. "Bodies up to your ass again, Mecana," he said.

"All necessary, Chief," I said. "Agent Bradford, this is Chief Verves of Homicide in Dallas."

"Know of you, Chief," Bradford said, shaking hands. "He's right, these were some bad dudes with murder in mind."

"I heard," Verves said. "I see you have Mrs. Kane?"

"We have a warrant for her arrest," Bradford said.

"We have some more questions for her when we can," Verves said.

"Probably be a while; we've got priority on her," Bradford said. "Franks and I will take her in tonight."

"Looks like you're not going to need us now," Verves said. "Mecana, we need to talk when you get through here."

"Sure, Chief," I said.

"They can go," Bradford said.

We walked out behind Verves and stopped him on the veranda.

"Chief, we need a ride downtown," I said. "They threw my keys away. You can drop us off at the rental agency so we can pick up Darcie's car. They're open all night. We can talk about Candy on the way."

"Get in," he said.

We loaded up with Sergeant Edward Maddox at the wheel, a twenty-year police veteran. Mattox backed out and we got back on the freeway.

"Mecana," Verves said. "Mrs. Kane has a carrying permit for a 9mm pistol. She said someone stole it when I called her yesterday. The only place we can think of that we haven't looked is her car, it's disappeared. She said you have the keys and she doesn't know where it is."

"I have the keys but I couldn't find the car, either," I said.

"If the gun checks out, she probably did it," Verves said.

"She killed Fritz during our fight with his own gun. Four tight shots to the heart, same as Kane. That was no accident. That was shooting."

"Talk to the FBI Chief, you don't know the half of it. It's unbelievable," Darcie said.

"Learned a lot in the last few hours," Verves said. "The FBI and CIA are investigating Kane, Fritz and Mrs. Kane together. They found more associates that were involved with them in some sort of terrorist group."

Verves phone rang and he answered it.

"My god," he said. "We're on the way." He turned to his driver, "Head for 4th and Berryville, Maddox."

"Got it." Maddox wheeled around, turned the siren on and flew down the street, headed for Berryville.

"Mrs. Kane escaped in her car with some young man who shot the agents," Verves said.

Ten minutes later we could see flashing lights across the street at an intersection. Cruisers and ambulances were blocking the street both ways at 4th and Berryville. We weaved our way through and stopped next to an FBI Mercedes with all four doors open.

They had Agent Bradford on a gurney, carrying him to an ambulance, and Franks lying on a stretcher on the sidewalk with a blanket over his head.

Maddox cut everything off and we jumped out and ran to Agent Bradford.

"What happened," Verves said, looking at Bradford. "You get hit?"

"Shoulder," Bradford said.

"Can you talk?" Verves said.

"Yes. A young man rammed us at a stoplight and shot Franks in the head. I ducked but he shot me in the shoulder and grabbed Mrs. Kane out of the car. She called him Cactus, I think. I saw the tag number when they sped off. It was her car. They headed west on Berryville."

"She called him Cactus?" Verves said.

"Yes. Pretty sure," Bradford said and grimaced as they hit a crack in the concrete with the gurney.

"What did he look like?" Verves said.

"That's the pilot who worked for Kane," I said.

"Stay out of this, Mecana," Verves said and turned back to Bradford. "What did he look like?"

"Maybe in his twenties, about six feet, muscular," Bradford said. "Black hair and dark eyes. Carrying what looked like a 9mm."

"Okay, guys, get him in the ambulance," Verves said as two medics wheeled the agent away. "That must have been her gun."

"Fillmore is right, she's a devil of a woman," I said. "She's headed to France and that may have been her lover Cactus who shot them. And he's going to fly her to France in Kane's private jet."

"Why haven't you told me this before," Verves said.

"We just found out a few hours ago," I said.

"Stay here, you're not going to the airport," Verves said.

"We've got to go, chief," I said. "This is our ass, too."

"Well, shit. Head to DFW, Maddox," Verves said. "If they're going to France then that's probably where they're going to leave."

We all piled in, slammed the doors and headed to the airport.

"Maddox, open up the net and put out what we know," Verves said.

"I got it," Maddox said, "opening things up right now."

He punched in Candy's boyfriend's alias 'Cactus.' The descriptions and plate numbers matched.

Less than five minutes later, a call from a cruiser came back saying the car had been spotted on Mockingbird Lane. They were going to Love Field.

Another call came in saying they turned on a side street and cut through a fence outside Love Field, jumped out of the car and ran to gate fifteen to a Lear jet sitting outside a hanger.

"They'll have to cut them off on the runway," Darcie said.

More than thirty police cars had arrived, along with SWAT teams at the fence, and directed their lights at the jet to blind them; but it didn't seem to slow them down. The jet made its way out on the runway, spun around and revved up the engines.

"Now we know how she got to New York and back in one night," I said.

"Make sure the control tower doesn't give them permission to take off," Verves said, while Maddox put out the word.

A SWAT trooper ran up to the gate, pulled a rocket launcher off his back, and readied it for firing.

"Are they going after the cockpit or the engines," I said.

"Doesn't matter at this point," Verves said.

"It does if we want to find out the whole story."

"Damn, Mecana, you always want the whole enchilada," Verves said. "This may be it."

"No, there's a lot more," I said.

Just as the trooper fired, the jet turned and the rocket cruised by, missing and blowing up a fence on the other side of the runway.

The jet took off down the runway. It picked up speed, lifted off at the end of the runway, banked to the right and began climbing.

Four or five seconds later, an explosion like a war zone blast blew the engines completely off the wings. Two big burning boxes shot out the side of the aircraft; money spilling out, floating and twisting and turning as it fell to the ground, a few bills catching fire on the way down through burning pieces of the aircraft.

The jet was burned to a crisp by the time it hit the ground, long before a firetruck was in sight. Later, no human remains would be found. At least none large enough to recognize.

Spectators started running out on the runway grabbing money.

Police cars drove out on the runway, chasing everyone off and picking up the money and stuffing it in bags.

When several firetrucks arrived, there was nothing left to save. They joined the rest in picking up money.

"I'm goin' to get me some money," DeMax said, reaching for the door handle.

"You do and I'll arrest you," Verves said.

"What about all of them," DeMax said, pointing at the runway.

"They're gathering up the money for evidence," Verves said.

"Bullshit," DeMax said. "You ain't going to see any of that damn money again."

"Cool it, I'll get it back," Verves said. "The media's going to call this a terrorist attack and be all over it by morning."

"Kane, Fritz and Candy were dealing with terrorists," I said.

A report started coming in on the car's computer screen. It stated Cactus was the alias of a former convicted drug pilot. Born in Mexico, real name Jose Eduardo Gomez, 29 years-old. No flight plan filed to New York or to France.

"Bet you that was Fritz's doing," I said.

"Just be thankful the one's who you shot were in self-defense," Verves said.

"They all were. The game's over, we win. Drop us off at the Rental Right Car Company, Chief," I said. "I'll touch base with you tomorrow after I retrieve my truck."

"Okay," Verves said. "You hear him, Maddox?"

"Yeah," Maddox said.

A big glob of foul-smelling black smoke drifted overhead and disappeared into the night, leaving flames flickering from small scattered pieces of the airplane on the runway—Candy and Cactus on their way to hell.

15

My bed at the house felt great and Darcie even better next to me. I sat up, slipped on my pants, left my Glock on the nightstand and walked into the other bedroom to check on DeMax; he was asleep. I went back in the living room and turned on the TV.

Every channel kept repeating the spectacular crash of the jet, raining money as it burned to the ground. There was very little about the participants involved and even less left to find.

After four or five minutes of television, Darcie and DeMax came in and sat down on the couch with me. We were amazed as the scenes kelp unfolding over and over.

"I ain't flying anymore," I said.

"Me either," Darcie said.

"I never did," DeMax said.

My phone rang, it was Verves.

"Morning, Chief," I said.

"I guess you've seen the crash on TV," Verves said.

"Yeah, like what we saw," I said.

"The FBI and CIA have arrested another ten people, including a terrorist by the name of Ali Juror Mohamed, who rigged the explosives on the jet for Landon Fritz."

"Figured that," I said. "Birds of a feather flock together. Fritz knew she would run with Cactus in Kane's jet."

"She had as much of Kane's money converted to cash as she could and put it on the plane," Verves said. "Maybe two or three billion. They found video that showed her closing the door to his room at 1:30 the morning he was murdered. And she may have murdered over a dozen around the world when she was hypnotized, according to info from the CIA. Personally, I think the hypnotizing thing is a lot of bullshit."

"Not necessarily," I said. "Doesn't matter now, though, unless she wasn't the only one."

"That's a horrible thought," Verves said. "Don't want to think about it anymore. Come in and give your statement today and go. They said they dropped all the charges against you three."

"The right thing to do," I said.

"What are you going to do now," Verves said.

"I have to go to Austin and give my daughters their graduation presents pretty soon."

"Think I'm going to retire," Verves said. "Wore down to a nub."

"And who's going to take care of me?"

"Simon Necessary will take over. He'll also be bringing my daughter Sunday with him from robbery to homicide."

"You and Simon go back a long ways, don't you," I said.

"We broke in together. All his kids are grown and married except for

Angela; she has a gourmet restaurant for the rich."

"I heard about it but never been there," I said.

"Nice place," Verves said. "Sunday and Angela are good friends. We raised them together. Might be best to talk to Sunday if you need anything when I retire."

"Sunday's a good cop. I'll do that. Thanks for everything," I said.

"You bet. I'll let you know when I retire so you can buy me something," he said and was gone.

I laid the phone on the couch and watched Darcie and DeMax as they stared at the TV.

"You guys ready to make a statement to the cops so we can move on," I said. "I'm flabbergasted. Can't quite figure out how I feel about what happened to Candy."

"No words for it," Darcie said.

"I thought I had already seen the unbelievable and the impossible with Lisa," I said. "But Candy took it a step beyond. Her ashes are probably blowing in the wind somewhere."

"Yeah, too weird for me," DeMax said. "Won't ever let anyone hypnotize me."

"You going to Austin with me, Darcie?" I said.

"No, I'm going house hunting," she said.

"House hunting? Are you moving out?" I said.

"No, I want us to move out of this house and into our house."

"Ours?"

"Yeah and plan a wedding," she said and smiled.

"Really?" I said.

"When you get back from Austin," she said.

"Let me get this straight. You don't care if I spend money on the kids, and we're going to get married when I get back from Austin?"

"That's right, if you still want me," Darcie said.

I jumped up, whisked her off the couch and rolled around with her on the floor, groping and kissing her passionately.

"Stop, you're embarrassing me in front of DeMax," Darcie said.

"Don't bother me," DeMax said. "Seen a lot more than that."

"You want to go to Austin with me and be my best man DeMax?" I said.

"You want me to kick that boyfriend's ass?" DeMax said and grinned.

"Only if he wants to drive Emily's new car."

"He will," Darcie said.

"Maybe I was wrong. Somebody up there does like me."   THE END

TWISTED JUSTICE

*For Keith and Kasey,
and, of course, always Mary*

*Day before yesterday comes the day
After tomorrow every day.*
Author

PRESENT DAY

As a parade of speakers put in their two cents at Robert Verves' retirement ceremony, he watched his daughter and wife glancing at him as every speaker from the Mayor on down gave him praise for his long career and all his heroic accomplishments. When they called his daughter for her turn he thought about her as a little girl, when she was the furthest thing from his mind that one Sunday morning—

THIRTY YEARS AGO

--when two men dressed in black entered the dark kitchen of a small house in a suburb of Dallas, Texas. Both men were holding automatics with silencers at the ready. Three rows of cut cocaine with straws and a razor blade lay on the kitchen table. One of the men stopped and took a quick snort of cocaine, shook his head, and followed the other man to a staircase. They tiptoed up the stairs to a partially open bedroom door where a thirty-something Mexican man and woman lay sleeping. Without a word the men pointed pistols at them. The bullets made a whiffing sound as several rounds found their mark in each body. A little girl sleeping at the foot of the bed never woke up and was spared for whatever reason. One of the men picked up a briefcase from a night table, snapped it open, nodded to the other man, closed it, and they retreated down the stairs and left the way they entered.

An insomniac from the next door saw the two strangers running from the house and called the police. The little toddler was still sleeping early Sunday morning when detectives Robert Verves and his partner Simon Necessary from the Dallas Police Department entered the bedroom with guns drawn.

The two cops had been partners for three years and were considered the odd couple of the department. Both were in their early thirties. Robert Verves was black a former navy seal. His wife ran a mail order business from their home. They had no kids. Simon on the other hand was white, thin and balding with big blue eyes. He had never served in the military and was considered a bit of a nerd with a master's degree in criminal justice. His wife was a practicing attorney who some how found time to have four kids.

"Looks like they're Mexican," Robert said.

"No shit," Simon said. "You could tell that right away?"

"One of these days… wham! boom! right in the kisser," Robert said.

"You wouldn't hit a superior officer would you," Simon said and put his finger on his badge.

"Just because you've got a lower number don't mean nothing. I might enjoy it. I'm going to get the girl out of here before I decide to do that."

"Good idea" Simon said.

Robert picked up the little girl and carried her downstairs. Simon remained in the room waiting for the crime lab guys.

The little girl opened her eyes, saw Robert, made a horrible face and began to scream.

"What's your name honey?" he asked.

The little girl continued to cry and struggled to pull free of his grasp.

"It's okay, sweetheart, I'm not going to hurt you. You can't see mommy and daddy."

Simon thundered down the stairs. "What the hell are you doing, you're scaring her to death."

"Nothing, I can't let her go up there. I was trying to find out her name."

"She's barely big enough to walk. She sure isn't going to outrun you. See if there's a bottle in the fridge."

"What kind of bottle?"

"A baby bottle, dumbass. Surely they have one."

"I don't know anything about babies. You're the one with all the kids," Verves said.

"I'll loan you some," Simon said.

"No thanks, they look too much like you."

"Never mind", Simon said. "Watch her, I'll go get it."

Simon returned with a bottle of milk with a nipple on it. She looked at it but didn't move.

"Leche, it's leche," Simon said, thrusting the bottle toward her.

The little girl looked at Simon for a second, took the bottle and stuck the nipple in her mouth.

"Como te llama?" Simon asked.

"Sunda," the little girl said.

"Your name is Sunday?" Robert said.

"I think she's trying to say Sandra," Simon said.

"I don't know," Robert said. "Sounds more like Sunday."

"Who would name their baby Sunday?"

"I would," Robert said. "It's pretty cool."

"Some people shouldn't have kids," Simon said. "The child services lady will be here soon, let her figure it out. I'm going back upstairs to look for evidence. With that coke in the house, most likely something they did or didn't do over drugs."

"You could tell that right away?" Robert said, eyeing Simon.

"Okay, we're even," Simon said and hurried back up the stairs.

"I'll call the narcs."

Later that afternoon, detectives Verves and Necessary were sitting at a desk gulping down coffee, trying to piece together the case when the telephone rang.

Robert answered it and switched on the speaker phone.

"This is Cummings at the lab. I hope you appreciate us coming in on a Sunday."

"What do you think we're doing, having a party?" Robert said.

"Probably," Cummings said. "We got some prints we matched up. The border patrol had a make on them. It looks like they were here illegally. Border Patrol sent them back to Mexico about six months ago. The man is Jose Ramirez and the woman Maria Estella. No one has claimed the bodies, probably afraid of being arrested."

"What about the baby?" Robert asked.

"Far as we know she's their kid. She has the same O blood type as both of them."

"Who's got the baby?" Robert said.

"She's at the hospital being checked out."

"Thanks," Robert said. "Do some leg work for us and see what you come up with."

"I'll send you a report."

"Thanks," Robert said and hung up.

"We might as well go home, get some rest and start checking the neighborhood in the morning," Simon said.

"Sounds good to me," Robert said.

When Robert told his wife Valisa about the toddler she asked what was going to happen to her.

"I don't know, they're checking for relatives. Seems her parents were drug mules for the cartel and must've made the wrong people mad. She's being taken care of by Child Protective Services. The assumption right now is she's a Mexican national."

"Why didn't you ask if we could keep her until they find a place for her?" Valisa said.

"It never occurred to me. I should have guessed. You take in every stray in town."

"You think they will find any relatives?" she said.

"I don't know, but I do know what's running through your head. I know we've been talking about adopting a baby but it's not likely they would let us have her, even if they can't find any kin. She's Mexican, we're black and we don't speak Spanish."

"How much Spanish could she know? You said a toddler - that means she doesn't know many words. I wouldn't think that would be a problem."

"You're really thinking about checking this out, aren't you?" Robert said.

Valisa nodded and smiled. She was pretty with big sparkling brown eyes, a good figure and a sense of humor. She and Robert had been married since they were teenagers. Unfortunately she couldn't have kids as a result of a battle with cancer.

"Won't hurt to check it out," Valisa said. "She needs a home and you know people at CPS."

"Yes I do, but I don't think I have any influence. We'll probably have to stay on the adoption list until it's our time."

"Maybe not if you use your connections. Get Simon to help you, he knows everybody."

"That he does. I'll see what I can do, but you haven't even seen this baby."

"Is she healthy, bright?"

"Yes, very."

"Then I want to help her."

With some help from Simon's connections, and a little bit of cheating the system, Robert and his wife were granted temporary custody of the baby.

A year later, the only thing the police came up with was a midwife named Juanita Gonzales who said she delivered the baby in Brownsville, Texas on Christmas Eve 1984, and signed a notarized affidavit that would make the baby a U.S. citizen. The midwife said Maria told her the child's father was a very important rich American she was a nanny for, but didn't give a name. No one bothered to change the records to show that the man Maria was killed with was not the child's father.

A year later, when the case had gone cold and no one had showed to claim her, the Verves were given permanent custody of the girl.

The adoption clerk asked her name and Robert replied, "Mostly just baby girl. We didn't know we would get to keep her. I think she said her name was Sunday or Sandra."

"Okay Sandra," the clerk said. "What's the middle name?"

"No wait, how about Sunday Morning? That's when I found her. It has a good ring to it".

The clerk shook his head. "Heaven help her," he said and filled in the name.

She was officially Sunday Morning Verves—

PRESENT DAY

--and now she was all grown up, standing at the podium wearing her police uniform, telling everyone about her dad and nothing about how she became Sunday Morning Verves.

1

It was official – Robert Verves was retired.

He even left a daughter on the force to carry on for him.

His comrades were congratulating him when he noticed Thomas Mecana standing with his new bride Darcie Connors, just back from their honeymoon. Mecana's friend and best man DeMax was also standing with the newlyweds.

"Well, what're you going to do now, Chief?" Mecana said as they shook hands.

"Guess me and Valisa will travel. Maybe I'll build some things for the house."

DeMax walked up to the chief and shook his hand. "Never thought I would be around so many policemen who weren't after me."

"Never thought you would be a detective with Mecana either," Verves said.

"Me neither," DeMax said.

Darcie hugged Robert's neck. "Congratulations. You need us, call anytime," she said.

"Thanks. I will," he said.

Sunday Morning Verves had grown into a beautiful woman with sparkling brown eyes, shiny midnight hair and curves like a mountain road. She was a Spanish beauty with a very limited Spanish vocabulary. She sat her coffee cup down on her desk and picked up a homicide report.

The primary suspect listed Simon Necessary's daughter Angela as his employer. Angela owned one of the best restaurants in town and was on a well-deserved vacation to Cancun with her boyfriend.

Sunday picked up the report and took it to Simon Necessary, the new Chief of Homicide and only a step away from retiring, who was opening a bottle of antacids. The short, once-thin-framed thirty-five-year-old of twenty-five years ago was now a two hundred pound fat guy with a bald head.

Simon took a couple of tablets from the bottle, tossed them in his mouth and started chewing. "What you got, Sunday?"

"I was looking through this drug dealer's murder file and saw Angela's name listed as the suspect's employer," Sunday said.

"Yeah I know. She told me about it. She hired him a couple of months ago. She was desperate for a cook and didn't check him out. He must have had a falling out with his supplier and they put a bullet in his head."

"You know I have to talk to Angela about this when she gets back."

"I know. Do your job. I'm sure she doesn't know anything about it other than what she told me, but you got to do what you got to do. Call her if you think you should."

"No, that's not necessary," she said, paused and looked at Simon. "I think I just made a joke."

"Get that kind of thing all the time." Simon said.

"I'll make sure she doesn't have to answer questions from anyone else when she gets back."

"Thanks. How's your dad handling his retirement?"

"Not too good. He's driving Mom crazy hanging around the house all the time. Doesn't know what to do with himself."

"That's why I keep putting it off. The only life I know is this and raising kids, and all the kids are gone. Angela's the only one who isn't married. Although that might change while she and Doug are in Mexico."

Sunday smiled "She and I had a bet when we were in college about who was going to be the first to get married and have babies. Look's like it's a Mexican standoff, if you will pardon my pun. I'm full of them today."

"Kind of. You know don't you?" Simon said.

"Yes, Mom told me years ago. We just didn't tell Dad I knew until I was in college. Afraid he was the one who couldn't handle it. Then he told me the full story. I'm a lucky woman."

"They love you very much," Simon said. "You need to find you a steady boyfriend."

"Too busy," she said.

"All work and no play will make Sunday a dull girl."

"I think I'm already there. Maybe I'll get around to it if I find someone I have a special interest in."

"I hope it's soon so I can be the godfather."

"Don't hold your breath," she said. "I've got to get back to work."

"Yeah, me too. I'm never going to eat pizza again," Simon said, reaching for more Tums.

"Famous last words," Sunday said.

2

After work, Sunday stopped by her parents' house to check on them. No one knew except Valisa and Sunday that Robert had retired because of heart problems, not because he wanted to.

She parked, unlocked the front door, walked in and called out for someone to let them know she was in the house. Robert was a little jumpy when he heard a noise he couldn't see or recognize.

Valisa walked in the room. "Hi sugar," she said. "I haven't seen you in a week."

"I've been real busy, Mom. Where's Dad?"

"He's in his workshop. He thinks he's building a table I want. I don't, but I won't tell him. It gives him something to do."

"He doing alright, taking his medicine?"

"Yes, he's just bored. Building a table is not as exciting as chasing a bad guy."

"How about you?" Sunday asked.

"I'm fine. You want to stay for dinner?"

"No, I think I'll go home, put a TV dinner in the microwave, take me a hot bath and watch Law and Order."

"You sound like your dad. You live and breathe that job. You need to find you a boyfriend"

"That's what Simon said."

"He's right. You should get a roommate or move back home."

"I thought you didn't approve of living together before marriage."

"You know what I meant; a female roommate."

"Nowadays you don't know, Mom." Sunday batted her eyes and gave her mom a hug. "I'll say hello to Dad then go."

Robert was measuring the tabletop when she walked in. He set his tape measure down and hugged her. "Baby girl, I miss you," he said.

"I do you too, Dad. Mom said you were building her a table?"

"Trying to."

"Dad, I need to ask you something."

"Shoot," he said.

"I've been working on a case you probably heard about. It's the guy that supposedly killed a drug dealer last week?"

"Yeah, I heard. Are you getting anywhere?"

"Angela is listed in the report as the suspect's employer. Simon knows that. What I didn't tell him was the guy told his lawyer Angela was supplying him with the drugs. You know how I feel about drug dealers."

"You should forget it. Have you talked to her?"

"No, not yet. I was waiting for her to get back from vacation. I thought I should give her the benefit of the doubt."

"That's the right thing to do. He's just running his mouth, trying to blame someone else for his problems. I can't imagine Angela being mixed up in anything like that."

"Me neither, but I talked to one of her employees and she said some guy she didn't know dropped off Brad's car at the restaurant and said he wanted it serviced before they went on vacation. Big Dog Lopez was with him, too."

"It could have been loaded with money going to Mexico," Robert said.

"The question is: if it was, did Angela know?" Sunday said. "I'm wondering how I should handle it."

"You know much about the boyfriend?" Robert asked.

"No, I only met him once. I know he's a lawyer."

"Might be something you should check out."

"I'm waiting on a report," she said.

"Follow your nose and work the case the way you would any investigation. Find the truth. Lopez is a lowlife but until you have the facts do like you said. Don't jump to conclusions."

"I've got a bad feeling about this," Sunday said. "The truth might be something none of us want to hear."

"You can't help that. The facts won't change and you have no other recourse. Work the case and don't worry about the fallout. You're a good detective. Do your job."

"That's what Simon said."

"He means it, whatever the circumstances. I just hope there's nothing that will hurt him."

"Me too," Sunday said. "I have to go. I'll say goodbye to mom. Thanks for the advice, it helps. Take care of yourself."

"I'll do that baby girl."

When Sunday got home she did exactly what she said she would do, but the episode of Law and Order was a rerun. She couldn't help worrying about Angela. She knew she was having money problems. The restaurant wasn't doing the business it had been doing and she was having trouble making payroll and keeping the restaurant afloat. Surely she wouldn't resort to getting involved with drug dealers. Or would she?

She lay down on the couch and tried to watch Law and Order to get her mind off Angela and went to sleep. She woke up at three in the morning, turned the TV off and went to bed. She had difficulty going back to sleep, thinking about Angela and their college days together and knew she wouldn't rest until she found out what Angela was doing. Was it right or wrong?

3

On the way to work the next morning, Sunday was wondering how she was going to tell Simon she thought Angela may be involved with drug dealers. There was no good way to do it.

When she walked in the building there was a TV crew and several reporters in Simon's office. Eddy Hanson, Sunday's partner on the occasional assignment, was sitting at his desk, looking at all the fuss going on.

"What's all this about?" she asked him.

"Mexican police found Angela's boyfriend Doug dead in a Juarez alleyway last night. Angela and the car are missing. They didn't even make it five miles into Mexico before it happened."

"Oh no," Sunday said.

Simon came storming out of his office with people following.

"Get the hell out of here and leave me alone! Don't you have any respect for my family? I'll give you a statement when I'm ready, now leave me alone." He turned and retreated back into his office and slammed the door.

Sunday walked to the closed door and tapped on it. "Can I come in? It's Sunday."

"Yeah, come on in." Simon was sitting at his desk, head in hands, tears streaming down his face.

She closed the door and stood there in silence for a few moments while he tried to get himself together. "I'm so sorry, Simon. What can I

228

do?"

"Nothing. We don't have any jurisdiction down there," Simon said. "They asked me to stay here for now. They'll ship Doug's body to his family. All I can do is wait. I don't understand why they were driving to Mexico They were supposed to fly. Juarez police found Doug sometime after three this morning dead. They said he still had his wallet and his Rolex on his wrist. Angela's purse was laying next to him with all its contents, money, cards, everything. That's how they knew she was missing and called the El Paso police. Whoever killed him left the things so everyone would know it was just about a killing, nothing else."

"Simon, I was having a hard time trying to tell you Angela may be involved with drug dealers to save her restaurant and this is what it's all about. I'm having a report run on Doug. I'll let you know what I come up with."

"Something I should have done. I have to go home and be with my family and decide what to do now."

"Of course, I understand. I'm so sorry. I had to tell you about the drugs."

"You had to tell the truth as you saw it." Simon got up gave Sunday a hug.

"I'm here if you need me," she said.

Simon nodded, and walked out.

Sunday stood there looking at all the awards he had on the wall. He deserved better than this, she thought. She walked back out of his office to Hanson's desk.

"Eddy, I'm going to pay a visit to Big Dog. Call Juarez PD and see if they know anything about Angela."

"I don't think they'll tell us anything," Eddy said. "I'll go with you."

"No, I'll call if I need back up. Make the call. If they don't know, I know someone who can find out."

"Who's that?" Eddy asked.

"Thomas Mecana."

"He's probably all out of favors," Eddie said.

"His new wife Darcie is a good friend of mine. We worked together in the civil department a few years back. She was a good lawyer and I grew up with Mecana around. I'll call him, you call Mexico."

4

Sunday pulled up to the curb in front of Shooters Pool Hall. Two young muscled-up guys with dreadlocks walked up beside her car. The bigger of the two stuck his leg between the door and the car before she could close the door.

"Hey pretty mama," he said. "Want to party?"

"I'm looking for Big Dog," she said and pulled her jacket back to show them her badge. "I hear he hangs out here."

The big guy pulled his leg back and they both stepped up on the sidewalk.

"Man, man, what a waste," the smaller one said.

"Get out of my way," Sunday said.

"Don't get your panties in a bunch, lady," the little one said and stepped out of her way.

"Might be in there," the big one said, pointing at the pool hall door. "No guarantee you'll come out if you go in, though."

"You two go first," Sunday said.

The two walked in with Sunday following. Big Dog Lopez was shooting pool and drinking a beer, his long hair flopping on his head, wearing a gold chain with links the size of a bicycle chain around his neck.

"This cop says she needs to have a talk with you," the tall one said. "Don't think it's about where you go to church."

"You know Angela Necessary?" Sunday asked.

"You're kidding. Her name's Necessary?"

"Got a witness that saw you with the guy who brought her fiancé's car to her restaurant. Somebody murdered her boyfriend down in Mexico, and now she and the car are missing."

"I don't know what you're talking about," Big Dog said.

"I think you do. Why were you in the car?"

"I got nothing to say to you, cop."

"Don't play games with me, asshole. Do you know her?" Sunday said.

"No," Big Dog said and shot the eight ball in a side pocket.

The pool hall door swung open and Mecana and DeMax walked in.

"Mecana," Sunday said. "What a surprise. I was going to call you."

"Eddy called, said Angela was missing and you went to see Big Dog. I hauled this scumbag in several times when I was a cop," Mecana said and turned to Big Dog. "You know anything about the missing woman, shitface?"

"You think I'm psychic?" Big Dog said.

"I think you're going to be dog meat if you don't tell her," DeMax said. He picked the cue stick up off the table and slammed it into the back of Big Dog's legs. He fell to the floor with a yell, shook his head and looked at DeMax.

"What'd you do that for, you sonofabitch?" Big Dog said, rubbing his legs. "I'm goin' to get you for that."

"Don't fuck with us," DeMax said. "Biggen, you and Squirt stay out of it."

Big Dog looked at Sunday. "We got rights too."

"Stay where you are, Big Dog," Mecana said. "And you two, put your hands on the pool table where I can see them."

"Why are you doing this, Mecana, you're not a cop," Big Dog said.

"I just don't like you," Mecana said.

"Tell me why you were with the driver or I'll turn DeMax loose on you again," Sunday told Big Dog.

"Just riding with my buddy."

"You're admitting you were there," Sunday said.

"Yeah, so what," Big Dog said.

DeMax kicked Big Dog's leg sideways and stepped on his knee. He yelled again and rolled over on the floor.

"What happened to you, dickhead, you get religion?" Big Dog said.

"Tell her what she wants to know," DeMax said. "Or I'm going to break both your legs."

"I don't know what happened to her. I was just helping a friend."

"You have any names?" Mecana said.

"My friend Miguel was the driver. That's all I know."

"What's his last name," Mecana said.

"We don't ever give each other last names," Big Dog said, rubbing his knee.

"I think you should go ahead and break his legs, DeMax," Mecana said.

"Okay," DeMax said and moved toward Big Dog.

"I don't know her," Big Dog said.

"But you knew what was going to happen."

"No."

"Bullshit," Mecana said.

"What about you two?" Sunday asked.

"Nah, we don't know nothing," Squirt said.

"Put your hands behind your back, Big Dog, you're under arrest," Sunday said.

"What for?"

"You're a murder suspect," Sunday said. "I'll have someone pick up your buddy. Maybe he knows something useful."

DeMax stood Big Dog up and grabbed his arms behind his back as Sunday put the cuffs on.

Sunday walked Big Dog out to her car and slammed the door.

"Where's Darcie at?" she asked Mecana.

"Waiting on furniture to be delivered to our new house," Mecana said. "We sold the old place and found a nice one in a good neighborhood. Anything you need me to do?"

"If I go to Mexico the department will drown me in red tape, and if Angela's not dead by now she definitely will be by the time we get approval to go."

"It could be a year," Mecana said. "Eddy told us what happened. Me and DeMax can take a ride down to Mexico."

"I can get you expense money but that's about it," Sunday said.

"I don't need it. I owe your dad for what he's done for me. Where's the last place she was seen alive?"

"On the Mexican side of El Paso in Juarez," Sunday said.

Biggen and Squirt opened the pool hall door and stepped out onto the street next to Sunday's car. "We'll get you out," Biggen yelled at Big Dog.

"I don't think so," Sunday said. "Go on before I take you in, too."

Biggen and Squirt waved at Big Dog as two more of his friends came out of the pool hall and stood in front of Sunday's car.

"Get you ass away from the car," DeMax said to the two guys and they slowly walked away. "Let's get out of here."

"I'll lock up Big Dog and buy you lunch at Brogans before you go," Sunday said. "Call Darcie and ask her to join us at high noon."

"I will," Mecana said. They got in their cars and drove away.

5

A day and a half later, Mecana showed a border patrol trooper his old police badge and he and DeMax crossed the border.

Mecana asked DeMax to look under the seat. He reached under and pulled out a machine pistol.

"There are three clips in the glove box," Mecana said. "You know how to use it."

"Simple enough," DeMax said. He got the clips and stuck one in the pistol. "Why didn't you use this when we were chasing Candy Kane?"

"I just put it there for that reason," Mecana said.

"Maybe it will save our ass," DeMax said.

"It's not only the bad guys we have to worry about. If the police show up we might be in trouble with them, too," Mecana said. He took his Glock out of his shoulder holster, checked it, and put it back. "There's a cantina up the road. I'm hungry, let's get some tacos. I think better when I'm not hungry."

"You got any pesos?" DeMax asked.

"Nah, they'll take American money," Mecana said and drove up to the curb and cut the engine off. DeMax stuck the pistol back under the seat and they both got out and walked up to the taco stand.

Mecana pointed at the menu, raised four fingers and mimed a drinking motion then handed the guy a twenty. A few minutes later the man handed back eight tacos, two bottles of water and no change.

"Didn't you mean four tacos," DeMax said.

"Yeah, but what the hell," he said and climbed back in the truck.

"Eat your tacos," Mecana said. "I got to piss first."

"Where? They don't have a restroom," DeMax said.

"I don't know, I'll find a place." Mecana opened the door and walked around the corner of the taco stand behind a tree and unzipped his pants. He heard a hammer click and felt a pistol hard against the back of his head.

"Your money, señor-" a voice began, but in the next instant, the man fell against him and the forty-five to the ground beside his leg. He turned around and DeMax was standing over a scrawny man on the ground out cold. His hair was combed and waxed into a peak over his head, wearing a dirty Hawaiian shirt and khaki pants. One of his flip flops had fallen off his foot. DeMax picked up his forty-five.

"Didn't take you long to get in trouble," DeMax said.

"I was concentrating on peeing," Mecana said and zipped up his pants.

"Could have been your last time," DeMax said.

"Yeah," Mecana said.

"Guy's waking up," DeMax grabbed the hombre on the ground by the pants and picked him up.

"Hang on to him and put him in the truck," Mecana said.

DeMax held his belt and pushed the man into the truck. He was trying to focus his eyes. He blinked, blinked again, and stared at DeMax in a daze in front of the open truck door.

"Let me go," he said. Mecana got in the driver side and DeMax stuck the forty-five in his belt, pushed the man in the truck and closed the door.

"What's your name, amigo?" Mecana asked.

"El Gallo," he said.

"What's that mean?"

"The Rooster," he said.

"You got any hens?" DeMax said.

"When I want one," he said.

"You're not much bigger than a rooster. You know anything about a guy from Texas named Douglas Bradford being found dead in an alley here recently?"

"I heard about it."

"You know who did it?" Mecana said.

"Don't know. Let me go," Rooster said.

"You do anything besides rob people?" Mecana said.

"None of your business," Rooster said.

"I don't think you understand your predicament Rooster," Mecana said. "I can kill you in self-defense for trying to rob me."

"Not here," Rooster said.

"I won't ask anybody," Mecana said.

"You want to kill him or should I," DeMax said and stuck Rooster's .45 against his head.

"Rooster, you know who murdered Douglas. Tell me and we won't kill you," Mecana said.

DeMax cocked the hammer. "Just say when."

"Anytime you want," Mecana said.

Rooster rolled his eyes back and forth between DeMax and Mecana, his breathing labored. "Chavez," he finally said. "Bad hombre. Let me go now."

"You see him do it," Mecana said.

"No, heard about it,' Rooster said.

"He the one who's got the car and the girl?" Mecana said.

"Don't know," Rooster said. "Maybe the car, he has a wrecker service."

"Well isn't that convenient," Mecana said.

"Everybody knows, even police," Rooster said.

"Where is he?" Mecana said.

"I tell you and I'll get out?" Rooster said.

"No. Show me," he said and pulled back out on the street.

Rooster pointed to the front. "Go to Roselle Street and turn left."

Mecana turned left and drove down the street. There was somebody selling something every few feet on both sides of the street. Some running out to the truck when traffic slowed down.

"There," Rooster said. "That big building on the left. If they see me they'll kill me for bringing you here."

"They know you?" Mecana asked.

"Yes."

"Then you're one of them," DeMax said.

"No. Everybody knows them."

"What do you do besides rob people?" Mecana said.

"A tourist guide," Rooster said.

"You got to be kidding," DeMax said.

"No, I speak good English and show people around."

"And rob them," Mecana said.

"Sometimes."

"You got family?" DeMax asked.

"Alfaro, mi tío, my mama's brother. She's dead now. Don't know who my papa is."

"I've heard enough," Mecana said and pulled over.

"Okay, tourist guide, what's that sign say on that shitty-looking building?" Mecana asked.

"Chavez Wrecker Service," Rooster said.

"They got the car," Mecana said. "Bet money on it."

"Don't know. Let me go," Rooster said.

"Hush," DeMax said.

A young tall man with long black hair walked out of the building and looked at the truck. He could see the Texas plates. He fished his phone out of his pocket and a few minutes later another man walked out of the building. He was older, shorter, wearing a black Stetson, a blue western shirt, and jeans with a big brass belt buckle and cowboy boots. He had his phone in his hand. The young one took a pistol from his back and let it down to the side of his leg and they started walking toward the truck. Three more men came out of the building and stopped in front of the truck.

"Rooster, get out," Mecana said.

"No, I stay with you. They'll kill me for sure," he said. "We leave now."

"They can outgun us," DeMax said. "I think he's right."

"Yeah, we'll have to have a better plan when we come back," Mecana said.

"Go home," Rooster said.

"Can't do that but a retreat is in order now." Mecana started the truck, threw it in reverse, turned the wheels and spun around. He floor-boarded it and hauled ass.

A van ran out in front of the truck, blocking it, as a jeep sped up behind them.

"Oh shit," Mecana said and stopped.

While Mecana and DeMax were watching the Mexicans, Rooster jumped out of the truck and took off running. Two of the men in the jeep opened fire with machine guns and Rooster hit the ground and crawled behind a parked car. Mecana and DeMax followed him out the same door and dove over a road barrier into a ditch, bullets flying all around them and peppering Mecana's new truck.

Rooster scooted over to the door of a shop and ran inside and out the back door. Mecana and DeMax jumped up and followed Rooster with their weapons in their hands. Rooster motioned them down an alley, ran through an old dilapidated building and out the other side.

He stopped and looked back but there was no one there. He lifted a manhole cover and dropped down into the sewer. Mecana and DeMax did the same and slid the cover back over the hole. They heard voices rattling in Spanish and two of them stepped on the manhole cover as they ran by. After about thirty minutes, Rooster raised the manhole cover slightly and peeked out both ways. No one was there. He slid the manhole cover off the hole. "Follow me," he said and climbed out.

"Where you goin'?" DeMax said.

"They'll be back. Come with me," Rooster said as they climbed out. He slid the cover back over the hole. "I have a place we can go, hurry." He broke into a run and Mecana and Demax did the same to keep up.

"You're not taking us back to them, are you?" Mecana said.

"No," Rooster said. "Sorry I tried to rob you."

"You wouldn't be if you had got my money," Mecana said. "You're just saying that because you need us now."

"Helping you too," he said.

"You are," Mecana agreed.

"Come on, let's go," Rooster said and took off running again.

"Damn, I just lost another truck," Mecana said in pursuit of Rooster.

"We could have lost our ass," DeMax said running along side Mecana.

"True, I'll claim it was stolen and buy another one."

"Come on," Rooster said, looking back over his shoulder as he slowed down.

Mecana and DeMax caught up and followed Rooster through a maze of people on the streets as the evening sun was disappearing on the horizon. They ran down a rock road several hundred yards and came to a six-foot chain link fence surrounding an electric tower. Rooster walked up to the gate, stuck his hand in his pocket and came out with a key and unlocked a padlock. They went in and Rooster reached through the gate and re-locked it.

"Man, we could get fried in here," DeMax said.

"We'll be alright now," Rooster said.

They made their way to a small wooden building with no windows, sitting in the corner of the compound.

"Come in," Rooster said and when they went in Rooster turned on a light. There were beds, a water bowl, a small refrigerator and a two-burner hot plate.

"Anyone else know about this?" DeMax said.

"No one except mi tío Alfaro. He works here," Rooster said.

"What's he do?" Mecana said.

"Checks the power output," Rooster said.

"They don't have anyone at night?" Mecana said.

"Police patrol comes by every once in a while, but the gate's locked, they don't have a key."

"What the hell good does it do for them to come by then?" DeMax said.

"They see anyone in here they'll shoot them."

"Now you tell us," Mecana said.

"Find a place to sleep and I'll turn off the light," Rooster said. "We'll borrow Alfaro's car in the morning and head for the border. His boy will pick him up here when he gets off. If you have to go to the baño watch out for headlights. We rest now."

"I'll call Darcie and let her know we're okay," Mecana said and started dialing. "Don't think I'll tell her about the truck just yet."

6

Darcie called Sunday after speaking to Mecana.

"Mecana said he hasn't found Angela yet and that he and DeMax are hiding from the guys who have the car. I'm going to Mexico."

"I'll call Simon and go with you," Sunday said.

"Nothing you can do as a cop," Darcie said.

"No, but I can help you. I don't want anything to happen to them," Sunday said. "It would be my fault."

"Okay, we'll catch a flight to El Paso and rent a car. Mecana would just tell me to stay here if he knew I was coming so I'm not calling him until we get there."

"I'll meet you at the airport," Sunday said.

Darcie booked a redeye for 12:25 a.m. Four hours later, they touched down in El Paso. After renting a car, Darcie called Mecana.

"I told you not to come," Mecana said.

"That's why I didn't call you before I got here," Darcie said, "Sunday came with me. Where can I find you?"

"Wait a minute." Mecana took the phone from his ear. "Rooster, turn the light on." Rooster crawled over to the wall and flipped on the light switch.

"My wife's at the airport, where's a place she can meet us?"

"We'll meet her at the border at eight in the morning. Gate fifteen."

Mecana put the phone back to his ear. "Hang out at the airport and meet us at eight at border gate fifteen."

"We'll be there, Sherlock," Darcie said.

Mecana repeated "Eight AM…gate fifteen."

"Got it. Oh, and I rented a black Honda van," Darcie said. "Don't be mad. You know you need me."

"I can never be mad at you for too long. I always need you."

"See you in the morning," she said.

"Goodbye," Mecana said and stuck the phone back in his pocket.

"Darcie's coming here?" DeMax asked.

"Yeah, and bringing Sunday with her."

"Not good," DeMax said.

"I don't know, they're tough," Mecana said.

"So are the hombres we're facing," DeMax said. "Might be best to call this off. I think Angela's dead anyway."

"Maybe, but I have to make sure," Mecana said.

"Go home," Rooster said. "They will kill you. Too many to fight."

"He's right," DeMax said.

"You can go home if you want to, DeMax ," Mecana said. "You don't owe me any favors."

"Not leaving unless you do, and I don't think you are. Let's get on with it."

"Rooster, if they kept her alive where would they take her?" Mecana asked.

"May not," Rooster said.

"Let's say they did?"

"Sell her in the sex slave market," Rooster said.

"Where?" Mecana asked.

"Many places, even in other countries," Rooster said. "She young and pretty?"

"Yes," Mecana said.

"Might keep her a while before selling her."

"Who? Chavez?"

"Yes, and pass her around as a reward to his men."

"Where would she be?" DeMax said.

"Maybe at Palamar."

"What's that?"

"Juan Chavez's ranchero."

"Was that Chavez who came out of the building dressed like a cowboy?" Mecana asked.

"Yes, he dresses like that all the time," Rooster said.

"He the main man?

"She's probably dead. You'll die for nothing."

"Did you have anything to do with it?" Mecana said.

"No," Rooster said.

"You think Darcie and Sunday should be here for this?" De Max said.

"No, but they are," Mecana said.

"Police on Chavez's side. No way you win," Rooster said. "Rest now." Rooster turned off the light.

The next morning, a 1988 Chevrolet Caprice was stirring up dust, headed toward the compound.

Mecana peeked out the door and saw the car. "That your uncle?"

Rooster peeked out. "Yes, that's Alfaro. We go as soon a he gets here." He opened the door and they walked out.

"It's got Texas plates on it," Mecana said. "He must have stole it."

"Borrowed it," Rooster said.

"From who?" DeMax said.

"He don't know," Rooster said.

Mecana and DeMax couldn't help but grin.

Alfaro unlocked the gate, walked up to Rooster and handed him the keys and walked away as if Mecana and DeMax weren't there.

"Get in," Rooster said. Mecana got up front and DeMax in the back and they headed for the border.

Rooster pulled into a parking spot next to a market facing the check points and they waited for Darcie to drive through. At three minutes to eight, she drove up to gate fifteen and the guard waved her through.

"That's her, pull out in the road so she can see me," Mecana said. Rooster drove out in front of the van and stopped.

"We should get away from here," Rooster said. "Bad place to be."

"Okay, I'll get in with her and follow you," Mecana said.

Rooster nodded and waited for Mecana to get out and drove away.

Mecana jumped in the van. "Hi babe, follow that Caprice."

Darcie accelerated to get behind it. "Where are we going?"

"I don't know but don't lose him," Mecana said, leaned over and kissed Darcie on the cheek.

"Glad I'm here," Darcie said.

"Me too," Mecana said and turned to the back. "Thanks for coming, Sunday. We still don't know what happened to Angela yet. It's not looking good. Slim possibility she's still alive."

"That's what I was afraid of," Sunday said.

Rooster slowed down and turned off onto a dirt road with Darcie close behind.

After running down the road for a mile or two, he stopped under a tree and got out with DeMax. Darcie stopped next to his car and she, Sunday and Mecana got out.

"This is Rooster, ladies. Saved our ass when we ran into who I think are the ones who have Angela. Rooster, this is my wife Darcie," Mecana said, placing his hand on Darcie's shoulder, "and our lifelong friend Sunday."

"Buenos días señoritas," Rooster said.

"What're we doing here?" Mecana asked.

"This road winds through the brush to the border, and we can drive right on into the US."

"Done it before, haven't you," Mecana said.

"Many times, but I'm not coming back this time. Here's your map. Everything I remember about Palamar. I'm going home now." He turned around and opened the Caprice.

Mecana pushed him back from the door and closed it. "Not yet," he said. Rooster walked around to the other side of the car and leaned against the fender, staring off into space and sulking.

"Why does he want to be a rooster," Sunday asked.

"Maybe he thinks he is one," DeMax said.

"He looks like one with that hair," Sunday said.

"He's a few bricks short of a load," DeMax said.

"We've got more important things to do than analyze Rooster," Mecana said. "Tonight, DeMax and I will see if we can get a look at the car at the wrecker service. Might tell us something we need to know."

"Before you head out we'll go get something to eat," Darcie said. "Nobody knows me and Sunday."

"Make sure no one follows you two coming back."

Darcie and Sunday got in the van and took off.

"Anyone at the wrecker place late at night, Rooster?" Mecana asked.

"Someone's there all the time."

"How many," DeMax said.

"Don't know," Rooster said. "How ever many it takes to kill you."

"They have a skylight?" Mecana said.

"Yes, I think so," Rooster said.

"You think or you know?" Mecana said.

"They do."

"If you know what happened to Angela, tell us now before it's too late."

"I don't know," Rooster said. "I swear."

7

Darcie and Sunday returned and they all ate tacos and drank warm Cokes.

"Rooster, do they make anything besides tacos around here?" DeMax said.

"Anything you want," Rooster said.

"We were trying to be quick," Darcie said.

"They're good," DeMax said. "Not complaining. How're we going to get on the roof, Mecana?"

"They may have a fire escape ladder. If not, I don't know 'til I look at it. May have to go in on the ground."

"You think seeing the car is necessary?" Darcie said.

"Yes, it may tell us what they wanted the car for and if Angela is alive," Mecana said.

"If there's bullet holes in both seats she's not," Sunday said.

"I would think that too," Mecana said. "Everybody find you a resting place, we're going to need it. DeMax, stand guard for a while."

"Did I volunteer?" DeMax said.

"Yep," Mecana said and stretched out beside Darcie in the van. By the time he was comfortable, Sunday turned around in the van seat.

"Mecana, Doug Bradford never represented Big Dog, but he got Biggen off for burglary three months ago."

"What!" Mecana said and sat up. "If he knew Biggen then Big Dog knew him. Angela may not have known what was going on but Bradford did and Angela was caught in the crossfire."

"I hope she's alive and wasn't part of it," Sunday said.

"You're all loco," Rooster said.

"That might include you, too, Rooster," DeMax said.

"There's more," Sunday said. "Juan Chavez was born in Mexico, served five years for drug dealing and deported back to Mexico. Later tried for murder and got off. Wanted for murder and smuggling now.

"I think we're connecting some of the dots now," Mecana said. "Bradford must have been set up for a hit. He has something to do with all this besides being an attorney for a bad guy. You know why they wanted to kill him, Rooster?"

"No," he said.

"You wouldn't lie to us, would you, Rooster," DeMax said.

Rooster shook his head no.

"You do and I'll make you a hen," DeMax said.

"Chavez will come after you," Rooster said.

"Won't have to, we're going after him," Mecana said. "Girls, you stay here and keep an eye on Rooster in the van. We'll borrow his car and DeMax and I will check out the building later tonight. Give us about three hours after we leave. If we're not back by then, call me. If no answer, head for the border and go home."

"I'll decide that, Sherlock," Darcie said.

"Was afraid of that," Mecana said.

"You don't come back, I'll come after you," Darcie said.

"I'll be with her," Sunday said.

"Don't worry, I'll be back," Mecana said.

"You better be," Darcie said.

"Give me the keys to your car, Rooster," Mecana said.

Rooster dropped the keys into his hand. "Bring it back, it's not mine."

"It's not your uncle's either."

The distant sound of an engine roaring suddenly grabbed everyone's attention.

"Someone's coming hell-bent for leather. Everyone get in the van, I'll drive," Mecana said.

"I can't leave Alfaro's car."

"Get in the van before I throw you in," DeMax said.

"You tell anyone you were coming here, Rooster?" Mecana said.

"Only Alfaro," he said.

"Well someone must have gotten to your uncle, willingly or

unwillingly," Mecana said.

"If they did he's dead now," Rooster said.

A truck appeared speeding down the dirt road with two in the cab and three men in the back carrying automatic weapons.

"You were right, Rooster," DeMax said. "It's Chavez."

"We're getting out of here," Mecana said and opened the van door. "Get in and hang on."

DeMax picked up his machine pistol and got in the van. Darcie and Sunday pulled out their guns and jumped in. Rooster sunk down to the floor of the van and curled up like a cat.

Mecana stomped the gas pedal to the floor and the van peeled out, throwing up dirt.

A thick cloud of dust rose up from the speeding vehicles as they approached each other. The truck spun around, headlights cutting through the dust, and picked up the back of the van as it weaved down the dirt road. The dust bellowed out and streaks of gunfire hit the van in several places, busting out a rear window and sinking into the backseat foam, inches short of DeMax and Sunday. Rooster was curled up in a tighter ball on the floorboard.

"Stay down," Mecana yelled. They reached the highway and Mecana darted in front of a car to block their view, pieces of glass still falling from the busted back window of the van.

The truck was catching up, bullets whizzing by without regard for innocent people on the highway. A police car showed up behind the truck. The men in the back of the truck turned their fire on the police car. The windshield busted out and the police car came to an abrupt stop in the middle of the road and caught fire. Cars were turning off the highway wherever they could from both directions, leaving the van and truck as the only ones on the highway.

Mecana used his Marine voice to yell at everyone. "I'm going to turn off behind that building on the right. Get out and follow me as soon as I stop," he said. Everyone nodded except Rooster under the seat.

Mecana left the highway and ran the van behind a big brick two-story building and stopped. "Let's go," he said. They all piled out except Rooster. Mecana stood at the open van door looking at him curled up underneath the seat. "Come on, Rooster, get out."

"No. Staying here."

"They'll kill you, come on, damn it."

"No," he repeated.

"I can't wait," Mecana said and ran to the others and motioned for them to follow. He ran around the corner of the building to the front as the truck disappeared behind the back. He raised his hand and made a shooting motion with his hand and they continued around the building. He peeked around the corner – all of the men were out of the truck approaching the van, firing at it with Rooster still inside. People were running out of the building in all directions in a foot race to get away.

Mecana motioned again, pointing his finger at the truck. Everyone nodded and readied their weapons. "Now," he yelled and they stepped out from the corner, dropping two of the men instantly in a barrage of fire and ducked back behind the wall. A man left standing turned running at them, firing. Chavez and his driver got back in the truck. Mecana and everyone ran to the other side of the building and stopped around the corner. They heard the truck engine.

The man chasing them flew around the corner and DeMax blasted him before he knew what was happening. Mecana ran back to the other corner. The truck came into view. The driver stopped and Chavez and the driver jumped out of the truck firing at him and he hit the ground. Darcie, Sunday and DeMax all showed up from behind Chavez and the driver from the other side of the building. Chavez jerked the driver in front of him and they shot the driver. Chavez's black cowboy hat blew off. He held the dead driver up then pulled him down with him as he hit the ground. The sound of screaming sirens was not far away.

"We're in a pickle again," Darcie said.

DeMax ran to Chavez, pushed the dead driver off him, kicked him in the face and grabbed the gun out of his hands.

"Everybody get in the truck," Mecana said. "The van's done for. DeMax, give me his phone." DeMax rammed his hand in Chavez's pocket and pitched the phone to Mecana.

"Soon as the police check the van they'll know who they're looking for," Darcie said.

"Probably do already," Mecana said. "DeMax, bring Chavez."

DeMax threw Chavez over his shoulder and dropped him in the bed of the truck, unconscious, and climbed in beside him. "Guess Rooster's dead," DeMax said.

"Would have to be," Mecana said behind the wheel, looking over at the bullet-ridden van. "He wouldn't come with me."

Just then, Rooster's head bobbed up from inside the van like a cork and went down again.

"You see that, Mecana," Sunday said.

"What?"

"Rooster's alive, I just saw him in the van," Sunday said.

"I think I did too," Darcie said.

"Can't be," Mecana said.

Rooster staggered out of the van holding his left shoulder, a trickle of blood running down his arm and a bullet hole through his waxed rooster peak hair.

Darcie and Sunday ran to him and helped him back to the truck, squeezing him into the cab.

"My uncle is going to kill me for losing his car," Rooster said.

Darcie and Sunday looked at each other and shook their heads. Sunday pulled a scarf out of her pocket and wrapped it around Rooster's arm. "He's just nicked," she said.

"You've got to be the luckiest man alive," Darcie said.

"For now anyway," Mecana said. "Let's get the hell out of here."

Mecana wheeled the truck out in the road and headed down the highway. Four police cars came by going the other way.

"They think we're still there," Sunday said.

"Not for long," Rooster said. "You see that side street turning off to the left? Take it, it goes to an old empty building."

"On my way, little man," Mecana said.

Mecana made a turn on the side road and ran up and over a hill.

"There's the building, park the truck inside," Rooster said.

Mecana whipped the truck inside and came to a stop.

"Everybody out, have a look," Mecana said.

They all got out of the truck. DeMax carried Chavez on his shoulder to a corner and dropped him on the floor. He moaned and opened his eyes. DeMax pulled Chavez's belt off, tied his hands behind his back and sat him up against the wall. Blood was splattered across his face from DeMax's shoe. "Rooster, come here," DeMax said.

"What you want?" Rooster said.

"May need you if he don't speak English," DeMax said.

"He does," Rooster said.

Chavez recognized Rooster. "El Gallo," Chavez said and started speaking to Rooster in Spanish.

"What'd he say?" Mecana asked.

"He said he's going to cut off my—" Rooster began but trailed off, looking at Darcie and Sunday. "He said he's going to kill me."

"It's Chavez who needs to worry about that if he doesn't tell me what happened to Angela," Mecana said and squatted down in front of Chavez. "What happened to the woman who was with the man you killed?"

Chavez stared at Mecana and didn't answer.

"Rooster says you understand English." Mecana reached down and drew a ten-inch knife from a scabbard strapped to the inside of his leg.

"You think I was shittin' you? DeMax, pull his pants off."

"I didn't know you had that," DeMax said.

"Added it to my arsenal after what we went through with Candy," Mecana said.

"Grab a boot, Rooster," DeMax said. "I'll get the other one."

DeMax and Rooster each picked up a leg, got a grip on a boot and pulled them off. Then Demax yanked the pants off Chavez. He was wearing black silk shorts.

"Ladies, why don't you stand guard over there," Mecana said, pointing to the entrance. "This may get nauseating."

Chavez kept wiping his bloody face on his cowboy shirt as he talked. "No," he said. "Not me. I business man."

"He's lying," Rooster said. "Earlier he was bragging about killing the gringo because he double-crossed the cartel. Never say what he did with the girl. I didn't tell you earlier because he would have killed me, too."

"We're going to find out one way or another," Mecana said.

"You kill my uncle?" Rooster said.

"He try to kill me," Chavez said.

"So you did kill him."

"Sí," Chavez said and spit on Rooster.

Rooster slapped him across the face several times before DeMax pulled him off.

"Back off, Rooster, we'll take care of him," DeMax said.

"Give me a gun," Rooster said.

"No," Mecana said. "Where is she, Chavez?"

"She dead with the double-crossing gringo," Chavez said.

"What did you do with the body," Mecana said.

"Throw it away," Chavez said.

Sunday ran over to Chavez. "Is this her?" She showed him a picture of Angela.

"Sí," Chavez said.

Sunday raised her gun to Chavez's head.

"No, no, I lie. She alive at my ranchero," Chavez said.

Sunday lowered the gun and stared at Chavez.

Mecana reached over to Sunday and placed the barrel of her gun back to Chavez's forehead. "If you don't take us to the girl she'll blow your brains out. After I castrate you for the fun of it and send a picture to your men."

Chavez's eyes were glued to Mecana's knife as he rolled it around in his hand.

Mecana stuck his knife against Chavez's silk shorts and his heart began to pound fast enough to see under the purple cowboy shirt.

"No, wait, I go. You get girl, you let me go. Deal?" Chavez said.

"If anyone fires one shot at us we'll kill you," Mecana said.

"Put his pants on," Darcie said. "Can't stand to look at him anymore."

Rooster and DeMax stood him up and made him step into his jeans.

"Boots," Chavez said.

Sunday reached down and threw one of Chavez's fancy boots out an open window, followed by the other one. "You won't need them if Angela's dead, you will be too."

Sunday's phone rang. "It's Simon," she said and answered. "We don't know yet. We may soon. I'll call you as soon as we know." She dropped the phone to her side. "He hung up. He was crying."

"Let's go find out," Mecana said. "Get in the cab, asshole. Rooster, get in the back with DeMax. No gun, he'll cover you."

"Before you try to protect us, forget it," Darcie said. "We're going with you."

"You better believe it," Sunday said.

8

Mecana pulled the truck over a couple of miles down the road. "There's a grocery store with a restroom. I'll stay with Chavez. DeMax, go keep an eye on Rooster and the girls. Someone's going to recognize this truck if we hang around here for very long. Bring me a big orange and a package of peanut butter crackers. Oh, and some duct tape if they have it, for Chavez."

"I'm afraid to let you go pee by your self," DeMax said and grinned.

"Get," Mecana said.

"What happened?" Darcie said.

"Nothing, go."

Darcie slid off the seat to the ground and looked back at Mecana. "I'll make you tell me later," she said and gave him a sly grin.

"Chavez, I don't really give a damn what happens to you but if we get Angela out alive I'll let you go. Whatever else you've done is somebody else's problem. You got me?"

"Sí señor," Chavez said.

"I hope to hell you do," Mecana said. "Lay down in the seat and keep your mouth shut."

Ten minutes later everyone was back. Darcie and Sunday got in. "Here's your orange and crackers, didn't have the tape," Darcie said.

"Rooster, you said this was the road to Chavez's place, right?"

"Yeah, four miles ahead, but I don't want to go."

"Fine with me but I'll keep the keys. We may need the car later."

"If I can't have the car might as well go with you and kill Chavez when I get the chance."

"Suit yourself. Get in." DeMax and Rooster climbed in the bed of the truck. "Let's go," Mecana said.

"DeMax told me what happened," Darcie said. "Want me to go with you to pee?"

"I'll wait," he said, giving Darcie a sideways look. He started the truck engine and took off out into the bare land with no trees or buildings.

"I can see why he's out here," Mecana said. "You can see for miles."

"Yeah, they probably already know we're coming," Darcie said.

"When we get there, you and Sunday stay in the truck," Mecana said. "I'm going to show Chavez. If they shoot me, haul ass before they kill you too. Won't do me any good for you to die. That goes for you too, Sunday. I'll bring him down with me."

"They'll have to kill me too," Darcie said.

"I think that goes for all of us," Sunday said.

Mecana shook his head. "Wasted breath."

On the other side of the next hill Chavez's ranchero came into view – a large two-story tiled-roof mansion with a tall rock fence and guards walking a catwalk behind the fence, heads sticking up over it.

Mecana drove a little closer and stopped the truck. "We'll wait here," he said.

"You think he's important enough for them not to kill you on sight," Darcie said.

"I big man. They do what I say," Chavez said.

"You better tell them to bring Angela to us." Mecana opened the door and got out, pulling Chavez with him, and left the engine running. "Rooster, if you want to get even with Chavez help us now. I'm going to give him his phone to tell them to bring her to us. Let me know what he's saying."

"He lies all the time," Rooster said. "Can I kill him if she don't come out?"

"Sure, why not," Mecana said. "Here's your phone, Chavez. Make the call, you said we had a deal."

"You wait and see, Rooster lie too," Chavez said.

"Call them," Mecana repeated.

Rooster moved closer to Chavez. "Turn the speaker on," he said. Chavez punched the speaker button and starting speaking Spanish.

A few moments later, Chavez stopped talking and handed the phone back to Mecana.

"What did he say?" Mecana asked.

"He said 'Bring her out quick I'm being held captive' but he didn't say what she looked like or if she was alive," Rooster said.

"She alive," Chavez said.

"That doesn't sound quite right," Mecana said and pushed Chavez back in the truck. "I didn't come all this way to leave without her. Here's the phone again, Chavez, now tell them to bring her to us or I'll throw your dead body out this truck."

"We make swap," Chavez said.

"I can go for that. Tell them."

Chavez dialed again and spoke quickly in Spanish.

"He do what I said?" Mecana asked Rooster.

"Yes," he said. The gate opened and two men came out carrying someone on a stretcher, walking toward the truck.

"I've got to go to her," Sunday said. Darcie got out of the truck and stood behind the open door.

"Wait, Sunday, let them get closer," Mecana said and grabbed her by the arm. "DeMax, when they get here put her in the back."

The two men carrying the stretcher walked up beside the truck carrying a woman. She wasn't moving. Sunday ran to her. "It's Angela," she said.

Chavez turned and kicked Darcie with both feet and jumped out of the seat. He tried to run but his hands were tied behind him.

The two men dropped the stretcher and took off running. DeMax picked Angela off the stretcher and put her in the truck bed, Sunday jumping in with her. Rooster grabbed the gun off of DeMax's shoulder and let loose on Chavez. He staggered a few feet forward and fell dead, face down. His men ran past him and Rooster killed them before they could reach the gate.

Darcie got in the truck and DeMax in the back. Mecana slid behind the wheel.

Two trucks came through the open gate carrying men with automatic weapons.

"Come on, Rooster," Mecana said. "Let's go."

"No, go ahead. I'll get them."

The two trucks were almost on them. Rooster blasted the windshields out, killing the drivers of the trucks which came to a sudden stop when they collided into each other. Several men hit the ground from the back of the trucks, firing at Rooster. Their bullets ripped him apart.

"Oh no, little guy, damn it!" Mecana said and spun the truck around. Chavez's men were taking the dead drivers out of the trucks.

Mecana glanced into the rearview mirror as they were speeding away and saw Rooster and Chavez lying on the ground dead, and Darcie looking at him through the back glass. Sunday was shaking her head, tears rolling down her cheeks.

"Angela is dead," Darcie said.

Mecana nodded and drove on in silence.

A few minutes later, Darcie spotted the trucks again. "They're gaining on us."

"Have to get to Rooster's trail to the border and get his car, we're almost out of gas."

Mecana dodged cars and trucks and turned onto the cutoff road, trucks in his rearview mirror. They turned onto the dirt road behind him. He let off the gas then accelerated and stirred up lots of dust between them and the trucks. He pulled up beside the Caprice. "Everybody in the car."

DeMax and Mecana were removing Angela from the truck. Sunday got in the Caprice and said, "Give her to me."

They sat the dead woman on Sunday's lap. Her face was severely bruised and her left arm twisted out of her shoulder socket. The only thing she had on were her panties and an unbuttoned red blouse. It was clear she had only been dead an hour or so.

Darcie got in the front of the car, DeMax and Sunday were in the back with the dead Angela.

Mecana fished the keys out of his pocket and stuck them in the ignition. "Hope this thing starts." He turned the key and it fired up. He jerked it into gear and took off down the dirt road. Washtub-size holes in the road made the car bounce up and down like a pogo stick. They came to a big overhanging tree limb. "Oh shit," Mecana said. "Have to go under it." The car cleared the limb by no more than a few inches. Thick brush dotted both sides of the dirt road.

"They can't get a truck under that," DeMax said.

In another two or thee miles they came to a fallen border fence and crossed into the USA.

"We're here," Mecana said. Two border patrol SUVs were coming towards them. The trucks had disappeared.

Mecana stopped the Caprice and cut the engine off. "Leave your weapons in the car and get out," he said.

They opened the doors, letting the foul smell of death out, and kept their hands up waiting for the border patrol.

"Thanks Rooster," Darcie said, looking back at the car and Mexico. "We won't forget you."

"Yeah, we wouldn't have made it without him," Mecana said.

"He was more of a man than I thought," DeMax said.

"We wouldn't have gotten Angela back without him," Sunday said. "Now I've got to make the hardest call I've ever made."

9

Angela's family gathered around her grave to say their goodbyes. Simon looked like he had aged ten years in the last week, and his wife clung to him every step of the way to keep from going down.

Robert and Valisa were trying to comfort them but there was nothing anyone could say that would help. A parent never expects to lose a child before they go. It's the hardest thing these parents would ever endure in their life.

Simon and his wife walked over to Mecana and Darcie. "Thank you," Simon said, "for bringing my daughter back. It would've been even harder not knowing what happened to her."

"I'm just sorry we couldn't bring her back alive," Mecana said.

"Sunday warned me," Simon said, "but I wouldn't believe it. It's partly my fault for not checking Bradford out more before they became engaged. She was so happy."

"It's not your fault," Darcie said, hugging him.

"Thank you," his wife said. "We have to go now."

"Yes ma'am," Mecana said.

Sunday walked over to Mecana and Darcie, DeMax following. "It's such a shame," she said. "We came so close but couldn't get there soon enough."

"That will always stay with us," Darcie said.

"Always," Sunday agreed. "I'll keep you posted on what's happening. Haven't found anything that makes me think Angela knew what her boyfriend was up to. I'm going to keep after it until I know the whole story. It's good to know Chavez paid for what he did, but there's others to find before this can be put to rest. Going to start with Big Dog."

"If you need us again let me know," Mecana said.

"I will," Sunday said.

251

"I feel so sorry for Angela and her family," Darcie said.

"That's why I'm going to find out who was behind Bradford's set up and if Angela was innocent in all this. May not be something we want to know now. I mean, what if she wasn't?"

10

Two days after the funeral, Mecana was sitting at his office desk watching a painter switch the name on the glass door from Mecana & Connors to Connors & Mecana.

He started thinking about Darcie and his upcoming trip to Austin to see the kids and confront Amanda's new boyfriend. He was supposed to be a rich businessman that wanted her and the kids to move into his mansion, sell their house and let him put the money into the stock market for them. The kids didn't want any part of it. Another dilemma he would have to deal with.

"It's done," the painter said, bringing Mecana out of his daydream. "Total is five hundred."

"For just switching the names?"

"Yep."

Mecana wrote a check handed it to him. He stuck it in his white overalls pocket, picked up his paint and brushes and closed the door on his way out.

Mecana's phone rang. It was Verves.

"How you doing, Chief," Mecana said.

"Been having some problems with my ticker. They got me wired up like a hot rod in my bed. Need to talk to you before Valisa comes back in here."

"What is it?" Mecana said.

"Sunday just left, said she was going to do some research on Chavez to find out who he worked for and go after them. I'm worried about her."

"Why is that?" Mecana said.

"She's determined to solve Angela's case. She doesn't know Chavez goes all the way back to when I found her as a baby and we took him to trial for murder. I was afraid to tell her. We never found the other guy with Chavez that night. Chavez got off on a technicality. If she digs that up she may find out things she would be better off not knowing."

"Like what?" Mecana asked.

"Like who her biological father is."

"Holy shit, you don't mean Chavez? That's hard to imagine."

"No, it wasn't Chavez. Read the file so you know what she's up against and keep an eye on her for me. No telling what could happen," Verves said. "I'll have Simon pull it for you."

"I'll take a look," Mecana said.

"Here comes Valisa. Thanks, bye," Verves said and hung up.

Mecana sat down behind the desk, looked at the newly-painted door and dialed Darcie.

"The door painted?" Darcie asked.

"Yeah, you owe me big time," Mecana said.

"We'll set up an installment plan," Darcie said and laughed.

"I like that," Mecana said. "I'll hold you to it. Got something I need to tell you. I got a call from the chief. He's in bad shape and wants us to keep an eye on Sunday for him. She may need us. I told him we would. I'll tell you about it when I get home to collect my payment. I think I'm going to cancel my trip to Austin. Probably better anyway for now. Amanda is breaking in a new boyfriend."

"Sunday is coming over this afternoon," Darcie said. "I thought you would be leaving for Austin."

"I'll call the kids and postpone the trip," Mecana said.

"If you want to come on home I'll make a payment on my account before Sunday gets here, but it better be soon."

"Might get a speeding ticket."

"You go too fast anyway," Darcie said.

"We'll see about that." Mecana dropped the phone in his pocket, stood up, pushed his chair back and headed out. He looked at the Connors & Mecana on the door one more time and switched off the lights.

"May turn out to be my ace in the hole," he thought to himself and grinned.

The next morning, Mecana made his way to police headquarters to pick up the file.

When he walked into Simon's office an old manila file folder was waiting on the desk, Simon behind it pouring a cup of coffee.

"Hey Mecana," Simon said. "There's the file Robert wanted you to look at. It went cold years ago and may have been a good thing for Sunday. I understand why he's concerned. I tried to take Sunday off the case but she threatened to quit if I did. That's why Robert called you."

"He told me what he was afraid off," Mecana said.

"I want to get to the bottom of this but I agree with Robert," Simon said. "I think it would be better for her not to take this trip down memory lane."

"The way I see it, I think it's her call," Mecana said. "I'm not going to take that away from her. But I'm not going to go out of my way to make sure she knows, either."

"Take a look at the file and you may want to rethink that."

"I know this has to be hard on you Simon."

"With a furious anger, I want any and everyone that had anything to do with Angela's murder to pay for it. But I would hope Sunday doesn't."

"I spent some time with her in Mexico," Mecana said. "She's tough. I think her biological father is just a name. Robert Verves is her real daddy in her heart. And I think it's even stronger now because of you and Angela."

"Whoever he is is not the problem. It's what happens if he is still alive." Simon picked up the file and handed it to Mecana. "Take a look."

"Where's Sunday," Mecana said, opening the folder.

"Already working on the case," Simon said. "Robert puts a lot of trust in you, remember that."

"I will," Mecana said.

11

Sunday didn't go to the office. She stopped by her parent's house to check on her dad and headed for Shooters Pool Hall.

Turns out Big Dog was bailed out on a half-million-dollar cash retainer put up by the law firm Bradford worked at. And no one there was talking without a subpoena.

So she went to find Big Dog.

When she drove up to the pool hall she heard the sound of pool balls hitting each other and went inside. Four guys she didn't know were playing pool and drinking beer.

Biggen was sitting in a corner fondling a Mexican girl on his lap. He saw Sunday, pushed the girl off and stood up. The girl moved away from him and stood against the wall.

"Hey everybody, a lady cop just walked in," Biggen said. "Everybody grab your balls before she steals 'em."

"Where's Big Dog?"

"He ain't been here since he got out of jail. He knew you would be coming around."

"When you see him, tell him I'll cut him a deal for the right information," Sunday said.

"He ain't no stool pigeon, he knows the same thing would happen to him that happened to those white birds in Mexico," Biggen said.

"If there's anyone else here who knows why Doug Bradford and Angela Necessary were murdered there's a ten-thousand-dollar reward," Sunday said. "You can call any precinct with information. We won't reveal anyone's identity, either."

"Thanks, but no thanks," Biggen said, with the others nodding approval.

"What happened to Squirt," Sunday said.

"He met an unfortunate accident." Biggen and everyone else laughed except the girl.

"In your business, everybody's time runs out," Sunday said.

"Yours too," Biggen said.

The girl standing against the wall like a statue was trying to disappear.

"Young lady, I don't think you're old enough to be in here. Get out." The girl darted past Sunday and out the door. Everyone got quiet and stared at Sunday. She back stepped to the door and went outside to her car.

Sunday pulled away from the curb and stopped in the next block at a red light. The girl from Shooters ran out from a side street and pulled on the locked door handle, gibbering in a mix of English and Spanish. She had both hands on the window. Sunday could see there was nothing in them so she unlocked the door. The girl jumped in and fell to the floorboard.

"I don't speak much Spanish. What do you want?" Sunday said.

The girl raised her head up, looking surprised. "I know something about the murders."

"Stay there until I tell you to get up," Sunday said. The light changed and she kicked the horses watching the rear view mirror. Nothing unusual happened.

Sunday drove across town to her house and cut the engine off inside the garage. The girl started to get up.

"Wait until I make sure no one followed us," Sunday said. She drew her gun and waited for a few minutes. Nothing.

"Okay, let's go in. Stay close to me." They walked through the kitchen into the living room. Sunday closed the blinds and they sat down on the couch, Sunday still holding her gun. She laid it beside her and took a pen and pad out of her pocket. "Okay, I have to take some notes," she said.

"Will I get the reward?" the girl asked.

"Depends on what you know. What's your name?"

"Margarita Perez." Sunday wrote it on the note pad.

"How old are you," Sunday asked and continued taking notes.

"Sixteen," she said.

"Then you didn't belong in there. What do you know about the murders?"

"Biggen makes me do whatever he wants. He said he would kill my mother and little brother if I didn't."

"He may be just telling you that," Sunday said.

"No! I saw him shoot a man for not giving him money for a fix."

"You on any drugs?"

"Heroin."

"You pay for drugs the way I think you do?"

"Yes," Margarita said.

"Go on," Sunday said.

"I had to go with Biggen and Big Dog to meet with a group of Mexicans who didn't speak English. They were setting up a trip to Mexico for the lawyer and his girlfriend because he was skimming money from the cash he took to Mexico."

"You know anyone from this group?"

"No. They work for Chavez. He wanted the lawyer to think he was making his regular trip."

"Did the woman know why he was going to Mexico?"

"They say she thought they were going on a vacation, but they intended to sell her to a brothel."

"She didn't know any of that?"

"Don't think so."

"Did they say what her name was?"

"No."

"Did you know Chavez?" Sunday said.

"I know he will kill you if you don't do what he says."

"Chavez is dead. You don't have to be afraid of him anymore," Sunday said.

"Are you sure?" Margarita asked.

"Yes," Sunday said. "I was there when he was killed in Mexico. What else do you know?"

"A limo drove up when we were talking to the Mexicans and Big Dog walked over to it," Margarita said. "A man in the back opened the door but he didn't get out. Big Dog stood by the door talking to him. They were speaking in English. The man in the limo sounded American. Big Dog called him Mr. Money."

"Mr. Money? Did you see him?"

"He stayed in the car but I could see his hands. He was white and old."

"Anything else?"

"No. Will that get me the reward?"

"That's a step in the right direction," Sunday said. "I have to make a call to find a safe house for you and your family until we sort this out. You have an address?"

"In the basement at 4237 Riesman Street. It's about five blocks from the pool hall. You sure have a lot of questions."

"It's necessary," Sunday said.

"That reminds me," Margarita said. "Big Dog said he was going to kill necessary. I didn't know what he meant."

"I do," Sunday said. "If Mr. Money is the one we're after, you will have to be a witness before you can get the reward. If you do, it will come with a stipulation that you are put in a rehabilitation program."

"That's what I want. They will sell me to a brothel when Biggen gets tired of me," Margarita said. "How come someone like you doesn't speak Spanish?"

"It's a long story I don't have time for," Sunday said. "You've given me some very valuable information. I'll make sure you get credit for it."

"Now what?"

"We wait for the unit to pick you up," Sunday said.

"Will the cops protect me and my family?" Margarita asked.

"Yes, and they'll give you a new start somewhere when this is all over."

12

Mecana and Darcie sat down on the couch and opened the file and started reading, passing pages from one to the other until they finished.

"What a horrible thing to happen to her," Darcie said. "She was lucky it was Robert and Simon who found her."

"Could have been a wasted life if she had been put through the system," Mecana said. "I think the woman who delivered her knew who her father was, but was too afraid to say."

"Yeah, that's what I was thinking," Darcie said. "He was probably involved with drugs, too."

"I can see now why Robert and Simon didn't want her to have to relive it."

"What do you think we should do now?"

"I don't know," Mecana said.

"You think her father is still alive?"

"Good question. I wonder if the midwife is still alive. We have her name, may be able to get his from her. Think I'll find out."

"Might be as simple as running a net check on her."

"We can start there."

"I'll see if I can find Juanita What's-her-face," Darcie said.

"Juanita Gonzales," Mecana said. "She said Sunday's mother Maria worked as a nanny for someone but wouldn't say who. Probably the married father. There should be documents in Maria's name for salary and other things. Even the place they were killed at. If we can find out who, maybe we can prevent the inevitable from happening to her. I think I'll call her and see what she's doing."

"It's her case, don't try and take it over," Darcie said.

"I won't."

Mecana called Sunday. "Hey kid," he said. "What are you doing?"

"I found a witness that knows what happened. Bradford was killed for skimming off money. My witness is a sixteen-year-old heroin addict but I think she's telling the truth. Even better, she remembered the name of a main man in the deal who's calling all the shots. They call him The Cleaner. I'm running a check on him now."

"Well you've had a hell of a day," Mecana said. "You need any help?"

"Not now, but I may if I have to go get the boss. I can't think of anyone I'd rather have with me than you two."

"That puts me in a position where I need to be better than I've ever been," Mecana said.

"You will be," Sunday said. "I'm waiting for a unit to pick up my witness. Her name is Margarita Perez. I'm running a check on her too. I'm at my house."

"How long you been there?" Mecana asked.

"About an hour."

"You should leave now. They figure things out pretty quickly. May be missing the girl already and are putting two and two together."

"Yeah, you're right. I'll head to police headquarters downtown."

"I'll meet you there," Mecana said.

Before Sunday could reply, the front door came crashing down with

Big Dog and Biggen running in armed to the teeth. Sunday pointed her gun at them, put the phone on speaker, and dropped it behind her. Mecana could hear every word.

"Put your gun down," Big Dog said. "The boss wants you." Sunday dropped her gun.

Margarita broke to run to the kitchen door but Biggen put at least ten rounds in her body before she could take three steps. She wobbled against the wall and slid down to the floor, her head leaning against the baseboard, her big brown eyes in an open stare with blood running across the floor like a river.

"Figured that little tramp would turn me in," Biggen said.

"She was just sixteen, you bastard," Sunday said, staring at Margarita's dead eyes.

"She was a piece of shit," Big Dog said. "Tie the cop's hands, Biggen."

"I warned you not to come back, bitch," Biggen said.

Mecana cut the phone off. "You hear that," he asked Darcie.

"Yeah, let's go," she said.

They jumped in the truck and smoked the street as Mecana let the hammer down like a racecar.

"She's not that far from here if we don't catch a train at Smyth," Mecana said. "I'll cut across the pasture at Corinth."

There was gun fire. People in nearby houses were coming out to look, then ran back inside when they saw Sunday's front door knocked down.

"Get in the truck," Big Dog said. Biggen pushed Sunday out the door, her hands tied behind her back and her gun stuck inside his belt, to a black truck painted with gold skulls. Biggen opened a door and lifted her in.

"I might have a surprise for you before I kill you," Biggen said and ran his hand up between Sunday's legs.

"You'll have to kill me first, shithead."

Big Dog backed the truck out and roared down the street.

"Where are you taking me?" Sunday asked.

"Shut up," Big Dog said. "You're lucky the boss wants to see you or I would've already killed you."

Mecana and Darcie stopped and pulled out their guns and ran into the open doorway, Mecana going one way and Darcie another. She saw the girl she thought to be Margarita lying dead on the floor.

"Nobody else here," Mecana said. They ran back outside to get in the truck. A man was peeking out of the house next door. Mecana yelled at him. "You see which way they went? Detective Sunday is a friend of ours."

The man opened the door a little wider, stuck his arm out and pointed.

"Thanks," Mecana said. "What kind of car?"

"A big black truck with skulls on it," the man said.

"Ok. Call 911, there's a body in the house."

They got in the truck and took off in the direction the man had pointed.

"Darcie, will you call DeMax and tell him what the truck looks like. We're going to need him to join us in this chase."

Darcie dialed. "What you need, Darcie?" DeMax asked.

"Sunday has been kidnapped and they killed a young girl at her place. Not sure why they haven't killed Sunday yet, but they will soon. They took off north from her house in a black truck."

"With skulls? That's Big Dog's truck," DeMax said. "Don't sound like they're going to his place, though, it's the other way. I have my Harley. I'll catch up."

13

Big Dog wheeled up to a big iron gate and punched the entry numbers. The gate opened, he drove through and it closed behind him. He stopped in front of a three-story mansion. Two men carrying automatic weapons rounded the corner then slowed down when they saw it was Big Dog and Biggen.

"Bring her along," Big Dog said. "Let get this over with."

Big Dog rang the doorbell and a tall elderly man in a tuxedo opened the huge metal door. Inside, a spiral staircase ran up to the third floor. Paintings by famous artists adorned the walls and a maid placed fresh flowers on a table in the foyer.

They walked over to double ten-foot mahogany doors with guards standing in front. Big Dog tapped on the door. A voice from inside said "Come in."

A gray-haired man wearing a purple robe was sitting at a desk with his back to them, watching a game show on a wall TV. He was in his seventies with thin gray hair, a ruddy-looking and wrinkled face with a short gray beard. He turned around and stared at Sunday.

"So, you're Detective Sunday?" he said.

"Yeah, and who the hell are you?"

"Your real father," he said.

"Not to me," Sunday said.

"When you and Necessary started giving me trouble, I found out you were adopted by Robert Verves in '89 and that your mother was Maria Estella," he began. "She was taking care of my children then and I was poking her every day. Ramirez talked your mother into stealing a million dollars from me when you were two years old. Maria told the midwife I was your father and then she told me. I gave you life, now I have to take it away like I did your mother. I wanted to see you in person before I got rid of you for good."

"I'd kill you if I could," Sunday said, trying to jerk free from Big Dog and Biggen.

He laughed. "I see you have the same fire in you as I do. Untie her, Biggen, and let her sit down."

"She'll run," Big Dog warned.

"Then shoot her," he said.

Biggen untied and sat her down, keeping a hand on the back of her chair.

"Would you like some wine or cheese?"

Sunday only stared at him.

"Might as well have some, it will be your last meal."

She continued to sit in silence.

"I can see you're not having any thoughts of living past today. So be it. Big Dog, when you dispose of her, drop her body off at police headquarters. I want them to see it."

"Be a pleasure, boss," Big Dog said. Biggen stood her up.

"They'll get you," Sunday said. "You wouldn't make a pimple on my daddy's ass."

"Take her away." He swung his chair back around to watch TV.

As Sunday was being marched out, gunfire burst through the mahogany doors and the two guards fell on the floor dead.

Mecana rushed in and put a bullet between Big Dog's eyes before he could fire a single shot. Darcie cut Biggen down as the SWAT team mowed down four more guards running into the mansion, then took a defensive position in case anyone else entered.

Sunday picked up Big Dog's gun and pointed it at the old man as he was reaching into a desk drawer.

Mecana pushed her away and emptied his Glock into the man. He fell facedown onto his desk, his hand still in the drawer.

Sunday ran to the desk and kicked him out of the chair. He fell to the floor with a chrome-plated .45 in his dead hand, blood oozing out from under him. She kicked him again and again, cussing and crying.

Darcie came to her and put an arm around her. "It's over, Sunday. He's dead."

"Why did you do that Mecana?" Sunday asked. "I wanted to kill him."

"I know, but it would have been something you had to live with forever."

"That's why I wanted to do it."

"Right now, sure, but maybe not later," Mecana said.

"Where did all the cops come from?" Sunday said.

"We called Simon for a SWAT team," Darcie said.

"How did you find me?" Sunday said.

"We'll talk about it later. We're going to take you home with us for now." Mecana said.

14

After hours of coming back down to the reality of things, Sunday regained her composure. DeMax explained to her that he saw Big Dog's truck sitting in the driveway of the mansion when they were searching for her and he knew it was the only one like that. It had real gold flakes in the paint and was worth over three hundred thousand dollars. He said Big Dog drove it to flaunt his money, but it ended up costing him his life and saving hers.

"Maybe I'm alive for a reason I don't know about yet," Sunday said. "I wanted him dead but I think you may be right, Mecana, it was better you killed him than me."

Mecana's phone rang – it was Verves calling. "I knew I could count on you," he told Mecana. "You saved my daughter's life."

"I had a lot of help, Chief, and Sunday was the main one who figured it out. We got lucky in finding her. If you have any doubts about what she thinks of you, don't. She was ready to die for you and Valisa."

"Simon told me what happened. I know what a bulldog you are and that you never give up. She might have died like Angela without you and Darcie."

"She's past all that now," Mecana said. "She knows it's time to move on."

"Yeah it is, isn't it," Verves said.

"She's making arrangements to have the murdered teenage girl buried in the local cemetery and see to it that her family gets the reward."

"I'm so proud of her," Verves said.
"We all are," Mecana said.
"Thanks again," he said. "See you soon."
"Yeah take care of yourself," Mecana said.

Mecana and Darcie decided to go to Austin together. Darcie wanted to meet Amanda and get to know his kids. They invited DeMax along but he was getting ready to pop the question to his new girlfriend Mabre.

Sunday never spoke again about her biological father, a man known only as Mr. Money. Detectives were still searching for information on the man.

Simon Necessary finally retired as Chief of Homicide and took over Angela's restaurant. He changed the name to Angela's House.

Verves' health improved and Sunday started dating Eddy Hanson. They had worked together on several cases and plus, his desk was next to hers at the police station.

Twisted justice was the answer to the past and the present.

THE END

For hardcore horror fans.

Some books are to be tasted, others to be swallowed,
and some few to be chewed and digested.
Francis Bacon, English Philosopher

PART ONE
"What the hell is going on?"

1

On a dead-end street, a man barricaded himself in his house, holding his wife and two children hostage. Outside the house, Thomas Mecana and Darcie Connors are hunkered down in the street, on the other side of Mecana's truck, guns in their hands.

"How long did the police say it would take to get here?" Mecana asked Darcie.

"They didn't say," she said.

"This needs someone better trained for it than we are," Mecana said. "You did tell the cops who and where we are, didn't you?"

"Yes, one of the cops is Nelson."

"Just in case, when they get here, let them see us lay the guns down."

The barricaded man bolted out the front door, wild-eyed and carrying an automatic rifle, blowing even more holes in Mecana's truck. Ammo magazines were sticking out of both front pockets of his black pinstriped suit, his coat sleeves ripped under his arms and a purple tie pulled down on his white shirt. The tie and his bushy black hair were blowing in the wind as he ran across the street. He looked like a spider with his long legs churning and waving his arms around in all directions.

"Shit, I got to go get him," Mecana said.

"Let the cops get him," Darcie said.

"He might kill someone if I don't."

"Yeah it could be you."

"Check on the hostages." Mecana jumped up, cut across the street and began a foot race.

The man stopped and turned to fire at Mecana as he ducked behind a nearby car. The man peppered the car with bullets and took off again, running across a lawn, headed for the front door of a neighbor's house. Mecana turned on the speed and caught the man as he reached for the doorknob, knocking him down, his weapon flying out of his hands, sliding across the porch and falling off the edge to the ground.

Mecana reached to the back of his belt, drew his Glock and pointed it at him. "Stay down," he said. "I don't want to kill you."

"But that's what I want you to do."

The man jumped to his feet. Mecana pitched his Glock out on the lawn. He tackled the man and wrestled him down, rolling him on his stomach. He grabbed the man's arms and pulled them behind his back. Cops came running up.

"Who's who?" one of the cops asked.

"That's Mecana holding the suspect, don't shoot," Nelson said. He yanked the handcuffs off his belt and snapped them on the man.

Mecana leaned up against the front door huffing and puffing as Nelson pulled the shooter to his feet and another cop grabbed the cuffs on the man's wrist and walked him to the patrol car. Suddenly, the front door came open and Mecana fell down with it. A big, bearded man wearing a Dallas Cowboys shirt and cap stepped out pointing a double-barrel shotgun under Mecana's chin.

"What the hell is going on?"

"I had to bring down a shooter," Mecana said. "Everything's alright now."

"You a cop?"

"No, but he is." Mecana pointed at the uniformed Sergeant Nelson.

"Put that shotgun down," Nelson said.

The homeowner looked out on his lawn at all the cops and laid the shotgun down on the porch. Another cop picked it up.

"Are the woman and kids alright?" Mecana asked, standing up.

"Yeah, Darcie's with them now," Nelson said. "An ambulance is going to take them to the hospital just to make sure."

"You got here just in time," Mecana said. "I'm getting too old for this kind of shit."

"I noticed that."

Mecana eyed Nelson's stern look, retrieved his Glock and holstered it.

A television news van pulled up across the street. A reporter holding her microphone and a cameraman began setting up outside it. They filmed the cop putting the shooter away in the car and some other footage from the street.

Nelson told the big guy to go back inside his house – without the shotgun – and he did.

Nelson walked across the street and confronted the TV crew.

"It's all over," he said. "You can get more info at the station than here."

The reporter nodded and they got back in the van and left.

Nelson walked back across the street to Mecana.

"Man, they sure come out of the woodwork." he said, shaking his head. "How the hell did you and Darcie even get into this mess, Mecana?"

"Bad timing, I guess," Mecana said. "Got a call from a woman wanting to talk to us about a divorce, said her husband was running around on her. Asked us to come to her house. We pulled up in the drive and that nut drove up behind us. Had us blocked in when he started to open fire and ran in the house."

"Trouble follows you around," Nelson said.

"Looks that way."

"Anyways, thanks for your help," Nelson said with a grin. They were shaking hands when Darcie walked up. "You may be a widow if Mecana keeps chasing bad guys."

"Yeah, looks like I'm going to have to take out a bigger life insurance policy on him," she said.

"Good thinking. Take care, you two," Nelson said and headed for his cruiser.

Darcie turned to Mecana, "Want to see if your truck will start?"

"It just might." Mecana brushed himself off and they walked toward the truck. "It should at least get us home."

"And if it doesn't?"

"We'll do what we always do: call DeMax."

"The insurance company may not insure another of these," Darcie said as they got into the truck.

"We'll talk about that later."

The truck cranked on the third try and Mecana and Darcie drove off.

A few minutes later, Darcie broke the silence. "That was Cindy's husband Chris Summerfield they hauled in," she said. "They've been married fifteen years. He owned an apparel business that was doing pretty well. At least his wife and kids weren't harmed. Well, physically, at least. Emotionally...that'll take a while. It all started when he called her and she told him everything. That we were on our way to the house, that she was leaving him and going to get everything he had because he had been cheating on her. That's what set him off."

"I can see why," Mecana said. "The house alone is worth a million, easy. He's apparently got a lot of money at stake in a divorce."

"He should have kept his dick in his pants."

"We don't know for sure he was cheating on her," Mecana said. "We were still looking into it."

"Yeah, probably nothing serious," Darcie rolled her eyes. "I bet he just wanted a little strange, some of that recreational pussy."

Mecana twisted his head like a bulldog, trying to figure out where that came from.

"Whatever," he said. "She doesn't need us anymore now. Besides, I could use a little recreation myself, relieve some of that tension from wrestling with numb-nuts."

"When you get you another truck, check on a new car for me," Darcie said, ignoring the last comment. "Got almost a hundred-thousand miles on mine."

Mecana didn't say anything, just turned his truck onto a side street as smoke bellowed out from under the hood.

"You need an interpreter?" Darcie said.

"No, I get your message. Loud and clear."

Darcie smiled and leaned back in her seat. Mecana turned to her with a grin and she looked at him, still smiling. They both broke into a laugh.

"What kind of ride do you want?" Mecana said, a slight chuckle jumping out.

"What kind do you want?" Darcie said and winked.

The truck's engine kept coughing black smoke out as they drove.

"We may have to call DeMax," Darcie said.

"Hope not."

But, after barely making it home in the limping truck, Mecana called DeMax after all.

"Wanted to give you the news before it comes on TV," Mecana said. "Me and Darcie are okay but some nutso tried to kill us. I got my truck shot up...again. I need you to take me to look for another one."

"Again?" DeMax said. "That's, what, three? What the hell happened?"

"I just told you," Mecana said.

"You're sure going to have a hell of a time getting insurance now."

"I know. Already heard about that, too. So, can you take me to the lot?"

"Sure," DeMax said. "No problem."

Darcie was standing by Mecana, listening in.

"Tell him to bring Mabre, too. She can keep me company while you two go look for your new truck and my tricked out red Bullitt Mustang."

"I'll tell her to get ready," DeMax said. "See you two in about an hour."

Mecana hung up the phone. "Damn, I may have to buy a used truck."

"You don't have to buy me anything if we can't afford it," Darcie said.

"Yes I do. I know when to say calf rope."

"What's that mean?"

"What my daddy used to say. Means you're hog tied."

"And…what's that mean?"

Mecana shook his head. "Means I've got to buy you a new car. First, I need to call Emily and see when she's coming for her visit."

"Can't wait for her to visit, I've got some great plans for us," Darcie said. "We're going to have a really good time."

"That sounds like it's going to cost me too."

"Oh, it definitely will," Darcie said and smiled. "I can keep the car I've got and —"

"No, no," Mecana said, interrupting. "Let's not talk about it anymore. I'll just have the insurance company send a claims adjuster to look at the truck."

"They'll go berserk once they get the report," Darcie said.

"Not my fault."

"They're going to think so. You kind of have a history with this kind of stuff."

"Just goes with the territory. We're in a dangerous business, after all."

"They won't care."

"Hey! Whose side are you on, anyways?"

"The side with reality."

"Can't argue with that," Mecana said.

2

Mecana paid cash for a used truck with a basic liability insurance policy. He financed Darcie's tricked-out red Mustang with a full coverage policy. Mecana and DeMax drove the vehicles back to Mecana's house.

That night, they all went out to Brogans for dinner. DeMax was kind enough to let Darcie drive him in her new Mustang. The owner of Brogans wasn't too happy to see DeMax. He didn't say anything, just kept eyeing DeMax and putting his hand in his pocket, like he might have a gun and could blow DeMax's head off at any minute.

DeMax just smiled at him and only opened his mouth to eat. It was obvious he didn't want his new bride to know about his past encounters with the restaurant owner's wife.

While they ate, Mabre and Darcie planned a get-together to entertain Mecana's daughter Emily when she arrived, and Demax and Mecana watched a baseball game on the wall TV.

After parting ways in the parking lot, Darcie took a long drive across town to break in her new Mustang, telling Mecana how much she liked the old Bullitt movie with Steve McQueen, and about how all the chase scenes with the Mustang is why she's always wanted one.

Mecana was planning on how she would pay for it, one way or another. It would probably be another, he figured, as she gunned the Mustang like McQueen did in the movie.

The next morning, after a late night and an early breakfast, Mecana got a call from Dallas Homicide Detective Sunday Verves.

"I saw what happened yesterday," Sunday said. "Are you and Darcie okay?"

"Yeah, we're fine."

"Good. Got a question for you"

"What is it?"

"Something is missing from the property room. Thought maybe you could help us with it."

"Not sure if I could help you," Mecana said. "I've been retired for several years now. What are you looking for, drugs?"

"That and evidence box 16385. The one you left in the property room from the Durant case – 'The Mutilator' case. You know anything about the box we don't?"

"I doubt it," Mecana said. "Scene pictures, coroner and autopsy report, and all that was left in a folder in the chief's office. The only items in the box were what we found in Lisa's mansion. Mostly stuff from the nineteenth century. An old Gladstone bag and some gruesome murder paraphernalia from that time period, I think."

"That's interesting," Sunday said. "We discovered the drugs and evidence box missing when one of the officers noticed a glob of wet toilet paper on the property room camera lens. Had to be that day or the toilet paper wouldn't have still been wet."

"That was a good observation," Mecana said.

"Whoever it was stole the Mutilator evidence and over two hundred grand worth of cocaine. Our evidence officer Dewey Flanagan was off that day. Said he lost his key the day before. But if he did, and someone found it, how would anyone know what it unlocked? And what did the evidence box have to do with the cocaine?"

"Might have just put the drugs in the box to make it easier to carry. Taking the bag was probably coincidental. Unless it was someone who knew what that particular box was."

"We felt kind of stupid for letting it happen," Sunday said. "I need you to fill out some forms for our records, in case any of the evidence shows back up. I can drop them off at your office today. I'll be in that area anyway."

"We closed the office down after Knight-Bird-Candy Kane fiasco went down. We're working out of the house now," Mecana said. "We put an ad in the newspaper and on the net. Doing better with that for less money and save a lot more gas and time. Only thing I have left from the office is the front door. Had 'Connors and Mecana – Private Investigators' painted on it. I hung it in the bathroom as a joke, but Darcie liked it so much we kept it."

"That's amusing. I bet Darcie was surprised."

"To say the least. I'll come by the station and get the form."

"Okay, tell Darcie I said hi and bye."

Mecana hung up the phone as Darcie walked in the room.

"Who was that? I heard you say something about a box."

"It was Sunday," Mecana said. "That evidence box from the Durant case is missing from the property room. Sunday wants me to fill out a form describing all the contents."

"The Mutilator case? But that would defeat the whole reason we didn't tell anyone what was in there in the first place."

"Maybe we overreacted," Mecana said. "Looking back, I don't think anyone would catch on to what we think we know, or link it to where we found the bag. It's disassociated from all that."

"What could have happened?"

"No telling."

"If someone took it, why would they want it?" Darcie said. "You think they're looking to harm someone?"

"You never know."

"You remember what was in the bag?" Darcie said. "I didn't even get a good look."

"I don't think I'll ever forget it."

3

Mecana drove to the station, memories of the Durant case rushing through his mind. He hoped to hell something like that never happened again. He parked in the parking lot that had doubled the price since he had last been there. He shook his head. "One of these days, we're going to have to pay for the air we breathe," he said to the blinking ticket vending machine.

Across the street and up in the Homicide Department, a tall, good-looking officer by the name of Eddy Hanson was pouring himself a cup of coffee when Mecana walked through the door.

Eddy offered Mecana a cup but he shook his head no, thinking of Verve's bad coffee.

"What are you doing here, Mecana?"

"I need to speak with Sunday. Speaking of, you two married yet?"

"We've been dating. Nothing serious yet. I'm trying to make it that way."

"I can understand why," Mecana said. "She's a beautiful, smart woman."

"Yeah, I'm a lucky man."

Sunday walked in the office and saw Mecana and Eddy talking. She was wearing jeans on her curvy body, a dark forest-green shirt with rhinestone buttons, her police badge pinned on her belt beside her automatic. Her black eyes sparkling, long black hair bouncing on her shoulders with every step.

"Hey Mecana," she said. "You caught me at a bad time."

"Anytime with you is a good time," Mecana said and smiled. Sunday hugged his neck.

"I'll have to remember that one, Mecana," Eddy said.

"I'll get the paperwork for you." Sunday walked over to her desk and picked up the form, handing it to Mecana. "You can fill it out and I'll put it on file."

"What was Dewey's story?" Mecana asked.

"Dewey was off that day, and since we're understaffed, there was no one in the property room."

"He said he lost his key. That's a little hard to believe."

"We questioned everyone on the property log that signed in and out for evidence but no luck," Sunday said. "People are always taking a short cut out the exit in there. Just not sure who did on that day."

"I noticed it was there several times before I left the department,"

Mecana said. "The Durant case was the most horrific case I have ever worked, and that box had a bag full of murder tools."

"If you want to help find it, I can appoint you as a temporary investigator for lost police property, if the chief will let me," Sunday said. "You know Walt, don't you?"

"Yeah, good cop, deserves his promotion," Mecana said. "Doubt we need to take it that far, though."

"Not a big deal since we wont have a trial," Sunday said. "We don't need it anymore, except for accountability purposes. Unless it's connected to another murder."

"Darcie and I have a meeting with a client this afternoon. Let me think on it and I'll get the form back to you."

"No problem. Nice to see you again," Sunday said. "Tell Darcie we need to get together soon."

"I will, say hi to your mom and dad for me."

They both walked away. Mecana took a quick look around the office for old time's sake. He saw the new homicide chief Walter Harris on the phone in his glassed-in office. He was always watching his weight and still looked fit. He had a little less hair than when he was working the street and picked up some wrinkles over the last twenty years. He had a pretty wife in the medical field, Mecana remembered, and his two girls had to be almost grown. It looked like Sunday might be in line for chief when Harris retired. Mecana thought that would make Sunday's dad proud, having his daughter hold the same position he once did.

Mecana could still see Robert Verves sitting in the office, and remembered the difficult times they had with the Durant case. How pressured everyone was to solve it or get fired.

Mecana called Darcie on the way home and filled her in on what happened at the station.

"Are we going to look for it?" Darcie said.

"I don't know. Emily is going to come to see us soon I want to be with her. May run down to Austin one weekend to see Morgan, too."

"Me and Mabre are going to keep Emily busy."

"That's a sweet thing to do. I have to figure out what I'm going to do to make her happy with me."

"Just be yourself and she'll be happy," Darcie said. "Worked on me."

"You're sure being nice."

"I plan on being the same way when you get home."

Mecana perked up. Finding the box was suddenly not as important as it was five minutes ago. Darcie and the kids were much more important than whatever happened to the box. It was probably all insignificant, anyway, he thought, and picked up speed.

4

Friday evening at the Eagle's Nest apartment building, seventh floor, a middle-aged man with a rugged-looking face was standing at the door of apartment 709. He was clean-shaven, wearing a red cap and a lightweight tan jacket, holding a nondescript package under his left arm. His right hand was in his jacket pocket and his gloved left index finger under the package was pushing the doorbell. His face was partly covered by his upturned jacket collar.

A woman's voice could be heard from behind the door. "Who is it?"

"Are you Mary Nichols?" the man said through the door.

"Yes. What do you want?"

"I have a package for you."

"From who?"

"Baytown Pharmaceutical."

"That's my employer," she said. "What on earth could it be."

"You have to sign for it," the man said. "It's Friday night, lady, and I don't work on weekends. Open the door."

"No. Go away."

"I'll hand a pen and the form to you, sign it and hand it back to me. I'll leave the package at the door and go away."

He shifted his weight, took another grip on the package and looked around the empty hallway again.

The woman cracked open the door and noticed the package under his arm. She reached through the gap for the pen.

He took another quick glance at the empty hall and threw his weight against the door, knocking it open and causing her to stumble backwards and fall to the floor. He pitched the package inside and slammed the door behind him. Dropping to the floor, he cupped his hand over her mouth and rolled her over on her stomach, Out of his jacket pocket came a rope which he looped around her neck, pulling the rope as tight as he could, cutting off her air until she was limp on the floor. He turned the rope loose, stood up and opened the package on the floor. Inside sat an old, black leather Gladstone bag.

He took off his jacket and swiped a hand across the dining room table, knocking off a candle holder and dishes, and placed the young woman on the table with her legs hanging off. He opened the bag, removed a long knife and cut her throat from ear to ear. Blood gushed out, matting in her long brown hair as it ran across the table down to the floor.

He removed a railroad spike and a tack hammer from the bag and drove the spike into her ear with the hammer, deep into her brain.

He wiped the blood of his knife blade across the laced collar of Mary's blue dress and placed the knife back on the table beside the hammer, leaving the spike in her ear.

He rolled up her dress to her waist and ripped off her silk panties, put on a rubber and spread her legs. He shot his wad in less than a minute. He left the condom on and zipped his pants

He took sneakers and pants out of the bag and put the knife and hammer back in. He then spent several minutes taking off his bloody clothes and shoes and putting on fresh ones from the bag, which he replaced with the bloody clothes. He sat the bag back in the package and picked it up, holding it snug against his side to prevent it from falling apart. He opened the door and peeked out. Still empty. He stepped out into the hallway and closed the door behind him.

He stepped into the elevator, turned up the collar of his jacket and rode down to the bottom floor. Twelve minutes after his arrival, the man was exiting the building through revolving doors.

He walked half a block down the street to a bus stop, sat down on a bench with the package under his arm, watching people walk by, smiling at the ones who looked his way every now and then.

The bus drove on for miles. When he finally stepped off, he walked over to a Cadillac Escalade parked across the street, unlocked the door, got in and sat the package in the passenger seat. He started the car and drove away.

Twenty minutes later, he arrived at his three-bedroom house, sitting on a hill separated from his neighbors by three acres. He parked in the garage and went inside the house, package under his arm.

A big yellow cat ran up to him. He sat the package down in the kitchen and fed the cat, grabbing a beer from the refrigerator for himself and drank it down. He unrolled a trash bag, dropped the bottle in, and carried the trash bag and package to the bathroom, sitting them on the floor. He took the leather Gladstone bag out of the package and sat it on the sink. Then he unzipped his pants, took the rubber off, pitched it in the commode and flushed.

He looked at himself in the mirror.

"I didn't pick you...your name picked me." He said to the Dallas/Fort Worth phone book lying by the sink.

The man removed his clothes and shoes and tossed them in with the other clothes. He reached up to his face and began peeling off a plastic-looking film. When it was gone, he looked years younger. His complexion was smoother and younger, even his nose appeared smaller.

He turned the shower on, stepped in and began scrubbing his body with a hard bristled brush until his skin began to bleed. He turned the water off and stepped out to dry himself off, leaving streaks of blood behind on the towel. He pulled on the sink and the entire fixture separated from the wall, showing a small hole in the wall. He placed the leather bag in the opening and pushed the sink back in place.

He picked up the trash bag and his phone and carried them to his bedroom naked. He put the trash bag under the bed then sat down to check his voicemail.

"I'll be back in town tomorrow," a woman's voice said. "I'll call you when I get home."

That was it.

He laid his phone on an end table, turned the lamp off and pulled a sheet over the lower part of his naked body. The cat jumped on the bed and curled up at his feet.

5

It was Monday morning before Mary was found. Her friend and coworker Judy came by to take her to work. When she didn't answer, Judy opened the door with her key and went inside. She saw Mary on the dining room table, covered in blood with her dress pulled up, showing her naked body from the waist down. Her legs were hanging off the table. Judy screamed and ran out of the apartment, tripping over her own feet and falling to her knees in the hallway.

Several of Mary's neighbors appeared at their doors and saw Judy on the floor. A middle-aged lady wearing a pink robe with curlers in her hair ran out of her apartment to Judy.

"What happened?" the lady asked.

Judy pointed toward the open door with a shaky hand. "My friend is in there covered in blood!"

A man in pajamas was standing in his doorway, watching, and said, "I'll call the police."

The elderly lady nodded and put her arms around Judy, still on the floor with tears and mascara streaming down her face, dotting her bright red dress.

Two other men appeared from their apartments and went in Mary's apartment for a look. They were both back out in a flash.

"She's dead," one of them said. "It's horrible. She's been mutilated."

"I think I'm going to throw up," the other man said.

The man who called the police came back to the door and told Judy they were on the way. Judy was still on the floor, leaning against the wall.

Once the security guard arrived he closed Mary's apartment door and stood guard, waiting for the police.

Thirty minutes later the police arrived. Sunday and Eddy showed up. The forensic squad took pictures and searched for evidence. Medics gave Judy tranquilizers, bandaged her knees and Sunday let her go home with a request to have another talk after she had time to recuperate from the horrible experience. Sunday notified Mary's family and asked them to meet her at the morgue to identify the body.

No details of the murder were released to the press but reporters still gathered in a restricted area for details. Sunday promised them more information once the coroner released his report.

Eddy walked up to Sunday, shaking his head. "The coroner said she's been dead for two or three days."

"We'll know if we got a suspect when we get the camera footage from the Eagle's Nest," Sunday said. "Don't answer any questions from the press."

"I won't. This looks like what Mecana and Darcie were dealing with on the Durant case."

"Now we've got our own," Sunday said. "Put Mary Nichols' and Judy Weller's info in the database and see what we have."

Eddy nodded and walked away.

Forensic Detective Barry Cannon walked up to Sunday.

"Barry, take a good look at the spike. It looks like there might be some numbers under all that rust."

"That's chilling. Glad the coroner has to remove it."

"Yeah the horror of it is devastating."

"I'll look in to it and get back to you as soon as I can," Barry said and walked away.

Sunday was still searching the apartment for evidence when the new Homicide Chief – Walter Harris, a man who had waited his turn for twenty years – phoned her from his office.

"Did you know your case is on TV already?"

"No. I barred the press from coming in until we got everything done," Sunday said. "I told them there would be a press conference later."

"Well they didn't listen."

"What made it on?"

"First they had video of the victim being wheeled out of the building in a bag," Harris said, "then they interviewed some residents from the building. A reporter even said the victim had been mutilated and raped. How did they know that?"

"I don't know," Sunday said. "We damn sure didn't tell them. She was mutilated, though, and raped."

"Shut it down, now. Lock the apartment and put a guard on it. I'll go with you to see her family at the morgue. Call and tell them."

"Already have," Sunday said. "Meet you there at two."

"We'll crank it up again tomorrow without the press knowing," Harris said and hung up.

6

Mecana was putting his Marine Corps shirt and basketball shorts in his workout bag when Darcie came in and turned on the bedroom TV.

"Look at this," she said. "Somebody murdered a woman at the Eagle's Nest. They're saying she was mutilated and raped. Her name was Mary Nichols and she's been dead for several days."

"Something about that name sounds familiar to me but I don't know why," Mecana said.

"You claim everything sounds familiar to you."

"That's because I have a memory like a steel trap."

"Or one who thinks he does."

Mecana rolled his eyes. "You ready to go to the gym?"

"I don't know, are you going to yell 'Gung Ho' when we start working out as usual?"

"Of course."

"Figured you would," Darcie said.

They picked up their gym bags and walked out of the house and into the Mustang.

"Think I'll call Sunday," Mecana said. "See what she can tell us." He dialed her number as Darcie drove away.

Sunday answered. "Hey Mecana. Don't tell me, you saw what happened on TV."

"Yep," Mecana said, putting her on speakerphone. "Is it true what they were saying?"

"Yes, and a whole lot more."

"Who gave your case away?" Mecana asked.

"No idea," Sunday said. "Walt told us to shut it down until we met with the family and the press backs off. We'll probably get going again tomorrow. Looks like a sex killing. Nothing missing from her purse or apartment and no signs of a struggle, other than a few scratches on the floor. Signs point to a surprise attack. Could've been someone she knew. Found some bloody footprints that may help. Not supposed to tell you this, but I know I can trust you: She was strangled. Her throat was slit. She was raped. And a railroad spike was driven through her ear into her brain."

Mecana and Darcie gasped.

"That is horrible," Darcie said.

"Familiar, too," Mecana said.

"How so?" Sunday asked.

"A railroad spike went missing with the stolen evidence box. It was in the leather bag," Mecana said. "That very spike was used the same way a long time ago in Austin. I never told anyone about it being in the bag, except Darcie."

"I'm having Barry take a good look at it now," Sunday said.

"If it's the same as the one in the box, there should be blood stains and UP1436 imprinted on it, for Union Pacific Railroad," Mecana said. "A number that's been embedded into my brain."

"I thought it was rust," Sunday said, trailing off.

"Sounds like it might be the same one from the bag," Mecana said. "There's a lot more we need to speak about, in person."

"Think it is. I'll get back to you soon," Sunday said.

Mecana hung up and looked at Darcie.

"The killer must have found out how the spike was used and did a copycat murder."

"Heaven forbid," Darcie said. "It's coming back to haunt us."

PART TWO
"It's coming back to haunt us."

1

It was a little after midnight on Ranch Street, four days after Mary Nichols was murdered. Under flashing neon lights advertising an adult movie theater, a skinny young kid was sitting on the sidewalk beside the theater door, playing saxophone, an upturned cap on the pavement to collect coins and the occasional dollar bill.

A half block down the street, a blonde white girl and a black girl were standing on the corner, applying their trade, watching cars pull up and making deals.

A gray sedan pulled up to the curb beside the black girl and let the window down. She walked to the car and leaned in the passenger window. "Want to party?"

"Don't that seem obvious," the man in the car said, staring at her breasts resting on the car windowsill.

The man tugged the bill of his black cap tighter on his head and started moving his gloved hands loosely around on the steering wheel, like he might speed away at any moment. He leaned over toward the window and held up five hundred-dollar bills.

The blonde saw the money and walked up to the car, too. She could see part of his face behind the other girl.

"How about two?" the blonde said.

"Nope, three's a crowd," he said.

The blonde flipped him off and walked back to the corner.

He held up the money again and waved it at the remaining girl. She snatched at the money and he drew it away from her.

"Get in and I'll give it to you," he said.

She opened the door and got inside when she noticed a black leather bag in the back seat, sitting on folded coveralls, and decided to keep her hand on the door handle.

"No rough stuff," she said. "If you got something weird in that bag, deal's off."

"Just want a good fucking, Annie."

She froze for a moment. "How do you know my name?" she asked. "Are you a cop or something?"

"Could be," he said. "They call you Annie Sweets, but it's really Annie Chapman, right?"

"You must be a cop," she said. "What, you going to arrest me now?"

"Nope. I'll still give you the five hundred for the rest of the night. We got a deal or not?"

Annie scooted over on the seat and closed the door. "Give me the cash."

He handed her the money, put the car in gear and drove away.

"Go to the Ritz hotel," Annie said, counting the money.

"No need to do that, we'll use the back seat. I'll find a place to park."

"Cheapskate."

"You got paid, what's it matter?" He turned into an alley next to Suzy's Cafe and drove to a dark spot shaded from the moon by buildings.

"Okay, over you go. I'll get this out of your way." He reached over his seat for the bag and coveralls.

She reached over to his crotch and rubbed his pants. "Get that thing up," she said and rubbed again. "I don't feel nothing."

"You will."

"I'll let you know when you get your five hundred worth." Annie dropped her shorts and panties as she climbed over the front seat into the back seat. "Let's get this over with."

He opened the bag and reached his hand in.

The car rocked and a muffled scream jumped out of the car with no one to hear it. Less than ten minutes later, he stepped out of the front passenger door wearing city sanitation coveralls, carrying the black bag, and hurriedly walked away to the opposite street.

Three women walked past the restaurant without so much as a glance at the car in the alley, windows fogged up from the early morning air.

2

The next morning, as daylight crept into the alley over the tall buildings, a frail young man wearing an usher uniform and carrying a lunchbox was walking through the alley to work when he saw the parked sedan.

He walked up to the car and yelled, "Anyone in there!?"

He tapped on the window. No answer.

"Going to be garbage trucks coming through here in the next hour or so," he said to whoever was in the car. "They'll run right over you."

Still no answer.

He pulled on all the locked doors with larceny in mind, cupped his hands over his eyes and stuck his face against a back door window. He squinted his eyes and looked in. He jumped back and dropped his lunch box, then stepped back up to the window and looked in again.

"Oh my god." He left his lunchbox on the ground and limped to Suzy's Café around the corner.

He found a stool inside. Two stools nearby were occupied by skinny young prostitutes – one with purple hair, the other, a blonde butch cut and a tattooed portrait of a woman on her left upper arm. Both smelled of cheap perfume.

A fat lady with bulging eyes and straggly brown hair was standing behind the counter by the cash register and a brawly black cook, his arms covered in tattoos, was looking out from the kitchen customer window at the frail man on the stool.

"Call the cops, Sue," the young man said to the fat lady. "There's a butchered dead woman in a locked car in the alley."

"Did I hear you right, Travis?" Sue said and leaned over the counter, eyeing him.

"Yeah, call the cops."

"You looked inside the car?" the cook said.

"Through a window. The car was locked, Clint, but I'm telling you, she was butchered."

"Maybe I can open a door," Clint said.

"Leave it alone, it's bad. Let the cops unlock it," Travis said. "Give me a cup of coffee, Sue. They'll be looking for me to give my statement. I'll wait here."

"Maybe she's still alive," Clint said.

"No way," Travis said, shaking his head.

Sue dialed the police and told them what Travis had said.

"They're coming," she said after hanging up. "They said we should stay here. Especially you, Travis."

"Figured that." Travis took a sip of his coffee and frowned. "Probably a whore."

"We ain't going to wait around on no police," the purple-haired prostitute said. "Don't give the cops our names, either."

"Not like we know your real ones anyway," Travis said.

"Keep your mouth shut, creep," purple hair said. The other one nodded in agreement. They both slid off their stools and hurried out.

The sound of sirens filled the street a few minutes later, as a police cruiser turned the corner. Several young women ran past the café, trying to avoid what they thought must be a raid.

The cruiser stopped abruptly in front of the café. Two uniformed cops got out and walked in the front door. One was wearing sergeant stripes on his shirt, with a name tag that read ROLLIE. The other one was younger, taller and twenty pounds lighter than the sergeant. The name on his name tag was WEBSTER.

"Is there a man named Travis in here?" the sergeant asked.

Travis sat his cup down. "That's me."

"The caller said you saw a dead woman in a car," Webster said.

"Yeah, in the alley," Travis said. "The car's locked, looked in the window."

"What's your full name," Rollie said.

"Travis Howard Harlan."

"What were you doing in the alley?" Webster said.

"I work the night shift at the adult movie house across the street. After work I was cutting through the alley to the Ritz Hotel for some shut eye. Must've been about six-thirty this morning."

"Do you know the woman?" Rollie said.

"Couldn't make her out, looks like she's been cut from ass to chest."

"You saw all that, huh?" Webster said. "You took a good look?"

"She was right in front of my eyes. Made me sick."

"This better not be a hoax, Mr. Harlan," Webster said.

"Go see for yourself!" Travis said.

"You two see her?" Rollie asked Sue and Clint.

"No," Sue said. "We've both been right here all night."

"Stay here while we go look," Rollie said. "We'll send someone to talk to you about your customers."

Another police cruiser pulled up behind the first and cut the siren and lights off. Two uniformed cops got out. Sergeant Rollie walked out of the café and met them on the street.

"You two keep a watch on the people in there," he said.

"Will do, Sarge," one of the officers said. "Another call at Suzy's, huh?"

"Always something happening here," Rollie said. "That string bean you see in the window said he found a dead woman in a locked car down that alley over there. We're going to unlock it and have a look. If she's there, I'll call homicide and the coroner. You two make sure no one leaves the scene until I say so. And keep an eye out for anyone suspicious."

The two cops nodded and they all walked in the café.

"Come with us, Travis," Rollie said.

Travis got up and headed for the door.

"Hey!" Sue yelled. "Pay me for the coffee."

Travis started fumbling for money in his pocket, brought out six quarters and laid them on the counter.

"It wasn't fit to drink," Travis said, pushing the quarters toward Sue. "Tastes like you: cold, weak and old."

Sue gave him a dirty look and flipped the bird.

"Stick those quarters up your dirty ass," he said.

"Don't come in here again, dickhead," Sue said to Travis as he walked out.

People were stopping on the street, watching the cops set up in the alley.

Rollie walked up to the car window and looked in.

"Damn. He's right. Tape off the alley, Webster."

"Told you." Travis stepped up to the car and looked in the window again. "That's pitiful."

"Move back from the car," Rollie said. "You ever been arrested?"

"Yeah, a couple of times," Travis said.

"What for?"

"Burglary."

"Then you know the drill," Rollie said. "Turn around and put your hands behind your back."

"You don't think I would be stupid enough to call you if I actually did this, do you?"

"Do what I told you," Rollie said.

Travis turned around. Sergeant Rollie cuffed him and pushed him to the ground.

"Stay put," Rollie said.

"Alright if I go to sleep then?" Travis said.

"Be quiet."

"Exactly what I had in mind."

More curious people were arriving to look at the scene. The sanitation trucks were blocked from entering the alley. The longer the cops stayed, the larger the crowd grew.

3

By mid-morning, cops were moving around everywhere in the alley between the adult theater and Suzy's Café. Annie's body had been put in a coroner's bag and carried away.

As soon as Sunday and Eddy arrived on the scene, reporters began yelling questions at them from the other side of the yellow police tape.

Eddy turned to Sunday. "The car belongs to a teacher in Frisco, twenty-five miles from here," he said. "She discovered it was missing last night and called it in. It's being dusted for prints. Ran a check on her, too, just in case. She's divorced, has two kids. She said she didn't go anywhere in the car last night. Her story checks out so far. No sign of anyone parked in the area that she or the neighbors didn't know, either. Could have dropped someone off and kept going, I guess. There's a bus stop about a block away that runs all night. Someone could have got off the bus and walked back to her house. Had to be someone who knew how to start it without a key. Fingerprints may help. That's where we are so far."

Sunday raised her notepad. "My turn," she said. "Spoke to the man who found our victim. Don't think he knows anything. A crowd of witnesses saw him at the movie theater all night last night. We'll let him go for now. No witnesses on the car in the alley. Victim had a driver's license but no money in her pockets. She's nineteen but, if I had to guess, a lot older street-wise. Witnesses say she's been working here for two or three years. Her name is Annie Chapman. They called her Annie Sweets on the street. Been arrested several times for prostitution and drug use since she was fifteen. Our other victim, Mary Nichols, was college educated, never been in any trouble. As different as you can get. But it looks like it's the same killer. No one here could identify our suspect from the Eagle's Nest murder, either."

"Was afraid of that," Eddy said.

"Something about our suspect's picture looks odd," Sunday said. "Guess it's just the poor quality of surveillance cameras. His features don't seem to match. The black hair sticking out the back of his cap doesn't match the rest of his old face. I'm going to call Mecana. He knows more about these type of M.O's, maybe he can help us prevent another one."

"The new chief may not like that," Eddy said.

"Maybe we don't tell him."

"Probably for the best," Eddy said. "We may not have a job if he finds out."

"You could play dumb, you know."

"Can't let you go it alone."

Sunday smiled. "Ask Barry when he's going to have some prints for us. I'll ask the chief if we can put a few units on patrol around here for the time being. Perp may come back."

"I'll show the night bus drivers in Frisco our suspect's picture," Eddy said and walked towards Eddy and his crew. A wrecker was pulling up to the car to take it to the forensic compound for further investigation.

Sunday stepped away from the crime scene and phoned Mecana.

"H-h-h-hi," Mecana said, breathing hard.

"I didn't interrupt something did I?" Sunday said, ready to hang up.

"No, no. Me and Darcie. Working out. Gym," Mecana said in between breaths.

"Got a minute?" Sunday said. "I wanted to get some advice from you."

"Shoot." He turned on the speakerphone as he and Darcie stepped away from the bikes. "It's Sunday," he said to Darcie in a whisper.

"The monster struck again," Sunday said. "Butchered a prostitute in an alley off Ranch Street last night."

"We saw it on the news this morning, was wondering how you were doing," Darcie said.

"Like to get with you for a talk about it," Sunday said.

"Don't know if we can be of any help," Darcie said, "but we'll be glad to talk with you."

"Have you found the box yet?" Mecana asked.

"No."

"The bag that was in the box is from a time when the same types of murders were happening," Mecana said.

"Let's set up a meeting," Sunday said.

"This would have to be a private meeting between friends," Mecana said. "Don't want to cause any trouble between you and your superiors. Meet us at Brogans for dinner at six tonight."

"I'll be there," Sunday said. "And I'm buying."

4

Around noon the next day, a tall muscular man was deleting a police report from his email. The police department sent them automatically to local attorneys. This latest one was about an Annie Chapman. She had been arrested for prostitution and released on bail the day before he murdered her.

He walked in the living room in front of a blazing stone fireplace. Framed pictures of himself and his mother adorned the mantle along with empty candle holders on each end. A large painting of his sad-looking mother with a Mona Lisa smile and empty brown eyes hung over the fire place.

He removed city sanitation coveralls and blood-covered clothing shoes, cap and a plastic human face. He tossed it all in the fire and watched it burn to ashes, wiping the perspiration from his face with his shirt sleeve. He stirred the ashes with a poker. His cat Truffles was lying on a shag rug near the fireplace and ran away from the heat. He looked up at his mother's painting.

"You didn't even want me to talk to a woman for fear one would replace you. I took care of that. I know what to do with them now."

His phone rang. It was his legal assistant Margi Fletcher.

"Hi Margi," he said. "Glad you're back."

"Can we meet at Brogans for lunch," Margi said. "I have the Winmont report ready."

"I'll be there in about thirty minutes." he said and hung up.

He went to his bedroom and slipped on a fresh shirt, then stopped in front of the fireplace on his way out of the house and again looked at the painting of his mother.

"Margi's just a business acquaintance, mother, nothing personal is going to happen between us."

Half an hour later, he walked into Brogans and saw Margi sitting in a booth.

"Hey Gipson. You hungry?" she said.

"Not really." He sat down opposite her. "When did you get back in town?"

"Came in on a redeye last night." She brushed her long auburn hair back from her big blue eyes. "Saw on the news two women were horribly murdered. It was kind of scary going home alone."

"Don't watch TV much anymore. Too busy."

"You should have a hobby."

"Working on that idea," he said.

A waiter took their drink orders and walked off.

"What did you find out at Winmont?" Gipson asked.

"The same thing is going on in Ashville as here," Margi said. "Employees are being overworked and underpaid, and there have been complaints of sexual harassment. A total mess."

"You talk to Berman about this yet?"

"No. Thought you should know first."

"We'll run it by him Monday and see where we go from here," Gipson said. "It's his law firm, after all."

"Yeah, we're just birds in the nest. This is the best case we had all year. Surely he will turn us loose on it. I can get a dozen witnesses on our side and I have never seen any one better in a courtroom than you."

"Well, you're the best snooping paralegal an attorney ever had."

Margi opened her purse and took out folded sheets of stapled papers.

"Here's a list of names, addresses and phone numbers of women in Ashville who we can call as witnesses. That alone should do it for us."

"Good." Gipson took the paper from Margie and put it in his pants pocket.

"How about I come over this evening and cook a home dinner for your birthday," Margi said.

"How did you know?"

"I know more about you than you do yourself, remember? Happy thirty-sixth. You had to overcome a lot to be where you are today. I'm proud of you."

"That's not helping," Gipson said and smiled at her.

"Oh, I'm so sorry. I wasn't thinking," Margi said. "I'll really have to cook dinner for you now."

"Only if it's not too much trouble."

"It's not. Jerry's been gone six months and mother is going to Vegas with her boyfriend. I'll be by myself."

"I don't ever cook anymore," he said. "All I've got are pots and pans."

"That's okay," she said. "I'll cook and we can spend a pleasant evening together celebrating your birthday. Then we can set up our plan to convince that old grouch Berman to sue for both the wages and the sexual harassment."

"I guess we can do that."

"What's your favorite meal?"

"Whatever you want to fix."

"I'll surprise you," she said. "You know, I haven't been to your house since Berman and I came over last year to celebrate you winning that labor case for the city sanitation employees. That was so cool, them giving you those coveralls and a free parking spot. Made you an 'honorary garbage man.' Every time I think about it I get tickled."

"Me too, but I appreciated it," he said. "That entire case was a lucky win for me. The city ended up giving them a ten percent pay raise."

"Here comes the waiter. You ready to order?"

"Think I'll just have another beer," he said. "Don't want to get too full before our dinner."

"I'll be there around six," she said. "You can pour the wine when dinner's ready."

<h1 style="text-align:center">5</h1>

Darcie drove her Mustang into Brogans packed parking lot, circled it twice to find what she thought was a safe place for her car, parked and got out. She and Mecana walked to the back of the long line of people waiting to get in. A sign on an easel near the door featured a chalk drawing of a barrel-belly chef wearing a white chef's hat. 'Chef Lorenzo Nadirs, Esquire – One Night Only!' it proclaimed.

Darcie pointed the sign out to Mecana. "I heard he cooked for the Queen of England, too," she said.

"I was wondering why there was a crowd so early."

"We should have met Sunday for lunch, instead."

"If I had known this I wouldn't have offered to pay."

"I think I'll tell Sunday what you said."

Darcie smiled. "You better not!"

They were slowly moving up in the line when Sunday appeared beside them.

"What in the world is happening?" Sunday said.

"Hey you're here," Darcie said, surprised to see her. "Some fancy chef is cooking tonight."

"Explains the crowd," Sunday said. "Eddy's here too, he's trying to find a parking spot."

"You look ravishing in your little black dress," Darcie said.

"You always do in whatever you're wearing. I like you in red," Sunday said. "Want to go somewhere else?"

"Since we're here let's stick it out," Darcie said "May be an experience we'll never have again."

"I know I won't," Mecana said.

Eddy walked up and Mecana shook his hand. They all said hello as they inched forward in line.

"We'll sit up on the veranda for our private talk while we eat some of this royal food," Mecana said. "Does Walt know you're here?"

"No, this is between us," Sunday said.

Once they finally reached the door, the four of them walked up to the veranda, sitting down at a table next to a small tree with drinks in hand, away from the crowd.

"That clerk Dewey said he doesn't have any idea where or when he lost his key," Eddy said. "The lock was hanging on the open gate with no key in it. Forensics is running all kinds of tests in the property room and at Dewey's house. Nothing yet."

"You find anything out about the spike?" Mecana asked.

"It had the markings you described," Sunday said. "Same numbers, too."

"I hoped otherwise but thought it might be," Mecana said. "We never made it known in our report, but that means the killer is using the same bag that once belonged to a suspect in the 1888 Austin Massacres. The same that O. Henry wrote about."

"That's a strange story," Eddy said.

"It is but it's true," Darcie said. "We found it in a secret room at Lisa Durant's mansion but thought it was better to leave out some of the details when we turned it in to the property room."

"So someone who may know the history of that bag could be our murder suspect," Sunday said. "What's worse, we may be employing the person who handed over the box it was in."

"Could be," Mecana said. "Both murders have the same M.O. but we may be dealing with different killers. If just one of them has the bag then it would be the one who murdered Mary Nichols."

"Why? Would he want us to know?" Sunday said.

"That may be as strange as the story I told you," Mecana said. "Dewey may know who, though."

"We've got a century-old puzzle we can't put together," Eddy said.

"Finding the bag will find the killer of the young lady at the Eagle's Nest. Don't know about the prostitute." Mecana said.

"We've already had over ten bogus confessions." Sunday reached in her purse and took out a security camera photo of the man at the Eagle's Nest. "Here's our suspect, but no DNA or ID. You know him?" She handed the picture to Mecana.

He looked at it closely. "No." Mecana passed it to Darcie. She looked at it, then shook her head no and handed it back to Sunday.

"Keep it," Sunday said and Darcie put it in her purse.

"We have to find the bag. That's why I need you," Sunday said. "Thought what you did for me in Mexico would be the last time we worked together, but, here we are again. I think about it often. Something I still have trouble believing is the loss of Angela and Rooster. We wouldn't have made it out without him."

"We think about it too," Darcie said. "I feel so sorry for Rooster. Angela and her family, too. Rooster proved to be a lot more than I think any of us thought he was. He gave his life to give us a chance to escape. We'll always be grateful."

"It's hard to believe Rooster tried to rob me when we met then wound up saving our lives," Mecana said. "We have another dilemma now. The spike came from the bag. Get Walt to sign off on it and we'll take you up on finding the box. We can learn why he's the murderer after we catch him."

"Once I explain this to Walt I'm sure he'll go along with it," Sunday said. "You will be a consultant, officially, and get paid."

Servers came to the table with their food, placing it on the table and pouring more drinks.

"Two conditions," Mecana said once the waiters were gone.

"Name it. Anything," Sunday said.

"Add Darcie and DeMax to the consultant list."

"Done. What else?"

Mecana leaned in closer and lowered his voice.

"Don't let anyone find out we're looking for the box."

PART THREE
"Don't let anyone find out we're looking for the box."

1

Gipson poured wine for Margi and himself. Dinner was ready.

"I hope you like it," Margi said. "It's a combination of several types of Italian food so take your pick or eat some of it all."

"You sure went to a lot of trouble. I do like Italian food and it looks delicious."

"Well dig in. I have a desert for you too," Margi said. "Oh, I almost forgot." She went to the kitchen and retuned with Truffles' bowl and sat it on the floor at the corner of the dining table. "Italian for us, ocean fish for him."

Gipson looked down at Truffles he was eating.

"He likes it," Gipson said. "Now me."

"Bon appétit," she said and smiled.

After dinner, they moved to the couch in front of the fireplace with another glass of wine.

"That was the best dinner I have ever had."

"I could do it again sometime," Margi said.

"I'll give you a break for a while," Gipson said. "I feel guilty for you going to so much trouble. I owe you one. Don't worry, I won't cook it. You pick where you want to go."

"I'll think about it."

Truffles jumped up on the couch and sat down in Gipson's lap.

"He loves you," Margi said.

"Not me, the special food."

Margi laughed. "We can all be bribed if the price is right."

"I've been thinking... I might go out on my own," Gipson said. "Would you be interested in working for me?"

"You should have done that a long time ago," she said. "You do all the work on a case and Berman gets the big bucks because his name is on the sign."

"I was thinking we might take over the Winmont case if you come with me. I'd give you a raise, too."

"They know you're the one who's going to handle it. I don't think they give a damn what name is on the door."

"Okay then," Gipson said. "Send a message to Winmont and I'll turn in my resignation to Berman."

"When will you leave Berman?" Margi said.

"The Rosona drug case is scheduled to go to court next week. I'll resign after that. Should be a cake walk. I spoke to the detectives at homicide, trying to cut a deal with them before I knew the cocaine stolen from their property room was the same the prosecution was going to present as evidence. They don't have any hard evidence now, just heresy. Couldn't be better if I had planned it myself."

Margi slid over on the couch against Gipson, pushing her breasts tight against his chest. Gipson eased back a little from her touch. She reached over and gave Gipson a lingering kiss on the lips.

He didn't know what to do.

Business was one thing, but this was something he wasn't prepared for. She was opening up emotions and memories that haunted him.

It was really all his first girlfriend's fault, back when they were seventeen. His mother forbade him to see girls, but he sneaked off with one in his car and she asked him to make love to her. He tried to have intercourse with her but his mother's voice kept coming to him, repeating what she constantly said all his life. "Stay away from girls, they will ruin your life." He couldn't get an erection. The girl made fun of him and wouldn't stop laughing. He grabbed her by the throat and strangled her. Once she stopped breathing she was his, to do whatever he wanted to now. He could enjoy her without a problem. And he did.

He had grabbed his Boy Scout camping equipment from the trunk of his car and put her in a sleeping bag, then drove to a graveyard. After finding a fresh grave, he dug deep and placed his dead girlfriend on top of the casket and covered everything up with dirt. The shovel he threw in the lake before daylight, then spent the morning vacuuming out his car at a car wash. No one knew she was ever with him, and her body was never found.

Margi broke his train of thought. "I'll clean up the kitchen," she said.

"No, no, you've done enough," Gipson said.

"Being useful makes you feel better."

"Yeah it does."

"I can stay tonight and fix you breakfast in the morning," she said.

Perspiration popped out on his forehead. He fumbled for words. He knew what she was really saying. His heart began to race and he could hear his dead mother's voice. The mere thought of having sex with a live woman was something he had quit thinking about a long time ago. He was trapped. He would have to answer.

"Sure, I've got a spare bedroom."

"That wasn't exactly what I had in mind," Margi said and rubbed his leg.

Gipson looked at her hand. He was wondering if he would have to kill her before, after, or not at all. When he didn't reply she stood up and picked up her purse.

"I'm embarrassed. I made a fool of myself," she said. "I'll leave."

"No, please stay." He couldn't believe what he had just said. He continued, "We're a team. I need you."

"You mean that?"

"Yes. From now on, as long as I'm practicing, I know I can always depend on you."

"Okay, I'll stay."

Gipson forced a smile.

2

When Mecana, Darcie and DeMax arrived for their meeting with Walt, Sunday and Eddy were already in his office. Walt looked up and motioned for them to come in. Hand shakes took place and they all sat down.

"So, Sunday tells me you three will help us find the box," Walt said. "And the spike used in the Nichols murder was from the bag, correct?"

"That's right," Mecana said. "They identified it as coming from the Gladstone bag I had left in the box."

"So then, most likely whoever has the bag is our murderer," Walt said.

"I would think so," Mecana said. "I thought the name Mary Nichols sounded familiar to me. And then when Annie Chapman was murdered it hit me: they have the same names as two of Jack the Ripper's victims."

"I'll be damned," Walt said. "Repeating Jack the Ripper…"

"There's some disagreement on who the later victims were, but most believed it was a woman named Mary Kelly," Mecana said. "If we don't find him soon, a woman by that name may be next."

"I'll put out an APB around the entire DFW area." Walt picked up the phone and called in the details to the information officer. He hung up and continued, "In the meantime, I've asked Doctor Seymour to come by and brief us on what the coroner's office has learned. He should be here anytime."

"He's one of the best," Mecana said. "I don't think we would have solved the Durant case without him."

"Once Sunday filled me in on the details, I got the district attorney's office to approve a special consultant contract for the duration of the case for each of you." Walt handed paperwork to Mecana, Darcie and DeMax. "Remember, the only official activity you can pursue is finding police property. You can not make arrests or interrogate suspects without an officer present. Leave that to us."

"You got a deal," Mecana said. The others also nodded in agreement.

Doctor Seymour walked in carrying a manila folder. He looked the part of a doctor, the only thing missing was a white coat and stethoscope. It hadn't been that long since Mecana saw him last. He still looked about the same – a tall, fifty year old with gray hair, wearing a nice blue suit. He always had a slight frown on his face, probably because of the gruesome work he did, Mecana thought. He defied that image by being a friendly, competent coroner.

Everyone stood up as the doctor entered the room. He shook hands with everyone, holding on to Mecana's for an extra moment, then sat down on the brown leather couch, still holding on to the folder.

"Thanks for coming," Walt said. "Mecana's crew is going to hunt for the box I told you about. For the next thirty days we'll be chasing any and all clues you have for us."

"First, let me say this is strictly unofficial. So nothing I say can be put on record," Doctor Seymour said. "You will have an official report from the coroner's office sent to you soon."

"We understand that, Doc, no problem," Mecana said. "I know how thorough you are and what you say is the way it is."

"Mind if we take notes for our own use?" Walt asked.

Doctor Seymour nodded and opened his folder. "That's fine, but keep your notes to yourself," he said. "First, I'd like to start with the spike. From what Sunday told me, it's at least a century old and was hidden in a leather bag inside an evidence box that was placed in the property room by Mecana, correct?"

Mecana nodded.

"The autopsies have been completed and both victims were strangled before being raped and mutilated," Doctor Seymour said. "The knife wounds are from left to right on the throat, with deep cuts in the body, indicating he was right-handed and strong enough to overpower his victims. The bloody size-eleven footprints tell us he's around six feet tall, two hundred pounds. We're running a check on shoe manufacturers now, find out who sells them and trace them to a buyer we think fits the M.O. That'll take some time. We found a lot of different DNA samples on Annie but not too much on Mary. We matched it with three suspects who might fit the description, but all three are in prison. Annie's pimp Tanner Rosana had the most DNA matches and prints. That was expected but he isn't as big a man as what the evidence implies the murderer is, and none of Tanner's DNA or prints were on Mary. Not ruling him out but the facts don't put him in our top suspect category. We're still looking for more DNA. The victims must have known the killer or were completely surprised by the attack. There were no drugs in Mary Nichols' system. Annie Chapman had traces of heroin in her body. The knife wounds were from a broad-base, eight- to ten-inch blade mostly used to butcher animals. Although, this style hasn't been manufactured for at least a hundred years."

"There was that kind of knife in the bag," Mecana said. "The victims also have the same names as Jack the Ripper's first two victims."

"I didn't know that but it doesn't surprise me," Doctor Seymour said. "The same kind of M.O. as the Ripper. Means our killer must know the bag's history."

"What's happening is why we kept it a secret," Darcie said. "But some nut discovered it anyway."

"The profile suggests he probably has a high degree of warped intelligence. He'll be in his late twenties or early thirties, with precise plans to continue murdering women. He has a lot of confidence in himself and left the spike to let us know. What else was in the bag, Mecana?"

"Several things." Mecana began listing them off. "You already know about the spike. There was an eight-inch knife like you just mentioned, an old handkerchief with the initials of one of the Austin victims and a diary from the same woman, documenting her life in Texas. Stamped inside were the owner's initials, the London manufacturer's name, and a date of

1880. Which means it could have been used during the same time period the Ripper committed his murders."

"He didn't leave any DNA or clues except the footprints and the camera shots," Doctor Seymour said. "That may have been on purpose to show us he thinks he's too smart to catch."

"This has echoes of the Durant case," Darcie said.

"It sure does," DeMax said. "If it hadn't been for you, Doc, I would be dead or in prison by now."

"Glad to see you're doing well." Doctor Seymour smiled at DeMax and closed his folder. "That's all I've got for now."

"Thank you very much for coming," Sunday said.

"Yeah thanks," Eddy said. "Now we know more about who we're looking for."

"Good luck," Doctor Seymour said and stood up. "Take care, we have an evil psychopath on the loose."

They all shook hands again and Doctor Seymour walked out of the office with Walt.

"Scary as hell, ain't it," Eddy said.

"Sure is," DeMax said.

"Eddy, can you get me a list of everyone who signed off on anything in the property room over the past six months?" Mecana asked.

"Sure," Eddy said. "We checked them once but maybe you'll see something we missed. I have a report on Mary Nichols and Annie Chapman, too, I can give you. Maybe someone they knew has the box."

"Thanks, email it to us. Anything's possible." Mecana walked over to Darcie and Sunday, who was telling Darcie how much she appreciated her help.

"This guy is totally insane," Sunday said.

"That might be what a shrink would tell you but that doesn't mean he's not normal in other ways," Mecana said. "He could be the last person you'd ever think it was."

"A chilling thought," Sunday said.

"It is," Mecana said. "Follow us to the house, DeMax and we'll make a plan on who does what to find the box."

"Okay," DeMax said. "I have to pick up Mabre from work at the pizza shop first and take her home."

"Bring her with you," Darcie said.

DeMax nodded and they all walked out of the office.

Darcie's phone rang when they walked into the house. It was

Amanda.

"Your ex is calling me," Darcie said.

"See what she wants," Mecana said

"Hello." Darcie turned on the speakerphone.

"Tell Mecana Emily can't come now," Amanda said.

"You're on speaker," Darcie said.

"I don't want to talk to him. Just tell him Emily has to enroll in college and find a place to live. Classes start next week. She'll try to come during the holidays."

Mecana snatched the phone out of Darcie's hand. "I can hear you," he said. "You just don't want her to come here. I'll call her."

"It's not my idea. She asked me to call you," Amanda said. "She was afraid you would get upset. Now I see why."

"I'll believe it when I talk to her," Mecana said. "You probably don't want Morgan to visit me either."

"You call her then, smartass," Amada said and hung up.

"She hung up," Mecana said and handed the phone back to Darcie.

"I would have too. You're too upset."

"Disappointed," Mecana said.

"Wait to call her when you calm down," Darcie said. "You don't want to upset her too."

"You're right," Mecana said. "I'll call her tomorrow and tell her I understand."

"That's better," Darcie said. "DeMax will be here soon. Get your mind on a plan to find the box."

"We should have just destroyed it, then we wouldn't have this problem."

"That's hindsight for you. Won't do us any good now."

"Nope." Mecana paused for a moment. "I am a smartass, huh?"

"You said it. I didn't."

Mecana heard DeMax's bike pull in the driveway.

"Back to business."

3

Gipson and Margi were sitting at the defender's table in the courtroom when the jury returned with their verdict on Rosona's drug charges. The jury sat down in the jury box and the foreman handed the bailiff a slip of paper, which he handed to the judge.

The judge opened the verdict paper. "Not guilty," he said and slammed down the gavel. "Court dismissed."

Mario Rosona hugged Margi and high-fived Gipson, a big grin on his face.

"You're the best," Rosona said, looking at Gipson.

Gipson shrugged and stuffed papers in his briefcase. "Stay out of trouble, Mario," he said. "I won't be here for you next time."

Assistant DA Bruce Albert walked over to Gipson.

"We're going to file for a retrial, Hayes."

"You lost, forget it," Gipson said. "You had no hard evidence and your witnesses weren't credible. Let's go, Margi."

The two walked out of the courthouse and got in Gipson's Caddy. He didn't start the car, just sat gazing out the windshield like he was somewhere else.

"What's on your mind?" Margi asked.

"Nothing. You need to go home."

"Is everything alright?"

He lied. "Yes. I was thinking about how that would be my last case for Berman."

"You'll get over it once we're on our own," she said.

"Yeah, you're probably right." He started the car and pulled out into the street and went back to his thoughts.

He was wondering what her reaction would be if she found out he was a necrophile. Run? Go to the police? Try to kill him? Maybe she'd think he was joking. He could have a good life with the only live woman he was ever able to have sex with, but the urges to kill were coming again. As a lawyer, he knew if he just fucked the dead and didn't kill them it was legal in many states.

"I have to take my mom to the doctor," Margi said, bringing Gipson back to reality. "She's not breathing well and has been running a temp. Her boyfriend was going to help me but he bugged out."

"I can help."

"Thanks, but I can handle it."

"Do you need any money for the visit?"

"No, we're okay, thank you."

Gipson made a turn on Margi's street and his thoughts of murder returned. Having complete control of a woman like a rag doll was what he wanted right now. Watching her fear and surprise before killing her was the excitement he needed to have sex when she was dead.

"Stop, you're going to pass my house," Margi said.

Gipson slammed on the brakes and stopped a few feet past her driveway.

"Sorry," he said. "I was thinking about evidence research for Winmont."

"You're a workaholic."

"Keeps me out of trouble. Take the week off to stay with your mom. I should have it handled at the office."

"Thanks, Gipson." Margi opened the car door and got out. "Call if you need me," she said. Gipson nodded. She closed the door and walked away.

He drove away but couldn't get the pleasure of murder off his mind. It would be another one in line with his counterparts of the nineteenth century to make it more fun. He would have never thought of it had he not discovered the Gladstone bag. How anyone could be stupid enough to let it out of the property room in such a careless way was unbelievable, he thought. There were some disagreements on the other victims, but he knew he had it close enough the cops would catch on to what he was doing, exactly what he planned.

Instead of turning off to his house, he took the freeway to the little town of Reesville, twenty miles from Dallas, where he grew up. He pulled up in front of the house. His great-grandfather built it long before Gipson was born, at a time when builders still made their houses in an art form, with special carvings and a wrap-around porch to stay cool in the summertime and two fireplaces to stay warm in the winter. Modern A/C units were added once it became available, and the fireplaces hadn't been fired up in years. The windows were boarded up on both floors. The old white paint was peeling off from the second story down. The chain link fence around the house needed repair and the grass was knee-high in the yard. The man he hired to keep it mowed was obviously collecting his fee but not doing his job.

It had been six months since he was here to look for his mother. He thought he got a glimpse of her in her bedroom after she died, but she never reappeared. And she never responded to him going to every room yelling for her.

Growing up he was an only child. Just him and his mother living in the house together. He didn't know who his father was, but there were always men coming and going. His pretty mother claimed she was a princess from some country no one ever heard of, everyone knowing she was making it up. Even Gipson didn't believe her, but he humored her from time to time and would bow when she entered a room. The entire population of Reesville called her a tramp and avoided them both. She was the only friend he had. She died from a stroke when he was twenty, after her doctor and the state had her committed to an insane asylum. He should have sold the house years ago but he always thought she might come back from the dead and still be there, waiting for him.

She left him with a fear of women but he discovered a way to control them. They couldn't hurt him if they were dead, and then he could have his way with them.

He inherited over a million dollars from the estate of his mother's father, a wealthy oilman who passed away from old age when Gipson was a baby. His grandmother ran away with another man and was never heard from again.

He thought he wanted to be an actor in college and enjoyed becoming monsters with special effects makeup like the Hunchback of Notre Dame and the Phantom of the Opera, but he abandoned the make believe world to murder in the real one.

Now things have changed again, he thought. There's a woman he cares for, one who treats him well, maybe even loves him like his mother did, but the urge to kill won't go away. He didn't know how much longer he could hold off.

He turned his car around and headed back to Dallas. He turned off on his street, into his driveway, and went in the house. Truffles ran to him. He reached down and stroked him a couple of times before walking in the kitchen, engrossed with thoughts of who would be his next victim.

He took a sack of dry cat food out of the cabinet and poured some in a bowl. Truffles smelled the dry food, gave Gipson a dirty look and walked away.

"That's all there is," he said and walked back in the den, murder still on his mind.

He noticed the phone book on the coffee table, the same one he used to pick his first two victims. He picked up the book and thumbed through it to the K section. He found four Mary Kelly's, one with a rural address. She would be the easiest if she didn't have a big family. He laid the phone book back on the table.

Truffles jumped on the table, looking at the open phone book, licking his mouth.

"You don't always get what you want, cat, but sometimes it's all you got. I may have to move to another name for my next victim, Truffles. London police had some doubt about Mary Kelly being the third victim, anyway."

Truffles was pawing at the phone book.

Gipson took a beer from the refrigerator, went to his desk, sat down and took a sip. He knew the thoughts of murder would always be his companion. Controlling them was what he hoped to do, or sooner than later he would murder Margi.

Truffles poked his head in the room from the corner of the door, thought better of coming in, and disappeared.

As Gipson went through the evidence Margi accumulated for him, he let the name Mary Kelly slip into his subconscious. He tried to organize a trial plan for Winmont but he always came back to murder when his mother's voice would pop into his head without warning.

4

The hunt for the killer was on. Mecana was at the police station with Eddy, DeMax was on Ranch Street, and Darcie was at her home office, searching for similar murders over the last year in the same area.

Mecana and Eddy walked down a flight of stairs to the property room. It had a 'DO NOT ENTER' sign on a locked chain link gate and a fence that ran all the way to the ceiling, blocking off entry to the items stacked on shelves. A camera mounted in the corner recorded the room.

"Sunday said a glob of wet toilet paper was covering the lens," Mecana said. "Did you check the tapes anyway?"

"Yes, a shadow or two, but nothing we could make out," Eddy said. "The camera wasn't where it is now. Before, it was too close to the stairwell, and anyone tall enough could reach it before coming into view. We changed the lock and camera the same day we discovered the box and drugs were missing."

"Does Dewey have a new key?" Mecana said.

"No, just Sunday and Walt now. I've been handling the property room. Walt put Dewey on administrative leave until we find out what happened to his key."

Mecana nodded and waited for him to open the gate.

"Okay, take a look," Eddy said.

Mecana walked in and strolled down the rows of shelves, eyeing them for something out of place or unusual, seeing nothing and walked back out.

"Was this place damaged in any way when the box and cocaine turned up missing?"

"No," Eddy said. "Just the wet toilet paper and a chance they went out the exit door."

Mecana walked over to the exit door and pushed the bar handle down and the door opened. He looked on the outside of the door and there was no handle or door knob. It couldn't be opened from the outside.

"You did run a fingerprint test on the door?"

"We did, but no matches except Dewey and three cops, including me."

"Did you know who had what key?"

"Yeah. Each one had a number. Walt was 34303, Sunday was 34304 and Dewey was 34305."

Mecana wrote the numbers down on a small notepad.

"Sounds suspicious as hell that Dewey would give his key to someone for any reason."

"Yeah, that's our thinking too, but we haven't been able to prove it yet," Eddy said. "He must have been desperate. We find who stole the box and we'll know for sure."

Mecana's phone rang. "Hey Darcie," he said.

"I have the report Eddy sent on Annie and Mary," Darcie said. "Mary and her boyfriend broke up three days before she was murdered, but he was in another state at the time of the murder. Judy didn't hang out with Mary much, she picked Mary up for work and Mary paid her for it. She was well thought of by her employer. No close friends or enemies, only the boyfriend and family. Never been arrested or in any legal trouble. I'm going to run a check on people she or her boyfriend might have come in contact with who could be put in the suspect category. That's going to be a pain in the ass."

"I'll see if Sunday can get the database people to help."

"I'm running a check on murders in the area similar to this one and the Durant case," Darcie said. "Came up with three matches so far from this year. The sickos are always out there. How are you doing?"

"There was no damage. Three people had keys and two of them were Walt and Sunday. Dewey said he lost his key but that's got to be bullshit. But they can't prove it until they find out who has it. Catch-22."

"His key was involved with a crime," Darcie said. "Ask Sunday to get the DA to arrest him as a suspect in the murders. It's probably a long shot but being in jail brings a lot of people to the truth. How's DeMax doing?"

"Oh, you know, he's trying to blend in with the locals, see what happens."

"Bet he's having a ball. I love you," she said.

"Where did that come from?"

"From my heart."

"Made my day," Mecana said. "I'm going to check on DeMax later to see if he's come up with anything. See you tonight. I love you too. You're always in my heart." Mecana put the phone back in his pocket.

"Wasn't trying to eavesdrop, but I heard you say I love you," Eddy said. "I'm working on getting Sunday to say that to me. I spoke to my dad about her. He's encouraging me."

"That's a good start," Mecana said. "What's your dad do?"

"He's a cop in Houston. I was too before I got this job, never dreaming I would find someone like Sunday."

They climbed the stairs headed for Walt's office.

"Sunday here?" Mecana asked as they walked down the hall.

"No, she's out on the trail checking up on the crew," Eddy said. "Walt has patrols staked outside the residences of each Mary Kelly we found."

"This is a game for him and he decided it would be the names of the Ripper's victims," Mecana said. "He made sure we knew he had the bag by leaving the spike. There could even be another Mary Kelly we don't know about. All maniacs like this have one thing in common. They won't stop until we lock them up or they die."

Mecana and Eddy walked into the homicide office but Walt was already gone. He had left a note for them.

"Looks like Walt had a meeting with the police commissioner," Eddy said, reading the note. "The powers-that-be are really starting to put pressure on him to solve the case."

"I know all about that," Mecana said.

5

DeMax was sitting at the bar in the Suzy café when Travis walked in. Sue spotted Travis and came out from behind the bar.

"I told you not to come in here again, shit face."

"Oh, come on, Sue." Travis said. "Are you really going to hold a grudge? I was stressed out over finding that dead whore in the alley."

DeMax turned around on his stool and looked at Travis. "You talking about Annie Chapman? Annie Sweets?"

"Maybe. You a cop?"

"Not a cop. Just a PI. I'd like to talk to you. You may have forgotten something when you spoke to the cops that you could tell me."

"Doubt it."

"Was there anyone Annie was fucking that looked like this?" DeMax showed Travis the suspect's picture.

"The cops showed me that. I've never seen him."

"You two get out of here," Sue said.

DeMax laid a hundred dollar bill on the bar. "Will that change your mind?"

"As long as he don't talk to me." Sue pointed at Travis and grabbed the bill.

"That's what I want, too," Travis said, "or you won't get nothin' from me." He walked up to the bar and held out his hand, palm-up.

"You better have an answer to every question I ask," DeMax said. "Or I'll break your scrawny chicken neck."

"Forget the money, then, I'll go."

"Not now, we made a deal. Talk to me and I just might give you the money," DeMax said. "Sit down."

Travis looked at the door like he might run, gave DeMax a frightened look and sat down on the stool.

"Did you know Sweets?" DeMax asked.

"Yeah. I'd seen her around peddling pussy. Was really sorry to hear it was her. Couldn't make her out in the car she was so cut up."

"You see Tanner the night Annie was killed?"

"I ain't talking about him. He'll kill me."

"You hear anything about who might have murdered Annie?"

"I'm not going to talk about that either." Travis gazed off and took a deep breath. "Ask someone else. Leave me alone."

"You tell me what you saw that night or I'm going to stomp your ass."

"I'm going to call the cops."

"Go ahead," DeMax said. "You'll regret it."

Travis grimaced and stared at DeMax.

"I saw him earlier that night from inside the movie house. He was with some new blood he was turning out on the street," Travis said. "The girls looked like teenagers. They didn't know what they were getting in to. I saw him leaving in his ride later with Shelly."

Travis looked up and noticed Sue was listening.

"She's going to tell him I was talking to you. If he kills me, it's your fault."

"Did you see Tanner again that night?" DeMax asked.

"No, man, now I got to go."

"How about you, Sue?" DeMax said.

"I don't know who you're talking about," she said.

"I can get some health inspectors out here. Hate to see what they find.

Or you could just tell me what you know about Tanner."

"That's blackmail," she said.

"Sure is. Now, save me some time and tell me."

"I didn't see him at all that night, just this punk," Sue said, motioning towards Travis. "You two get out of my place."

"He still hanging out at the Ritz?" DeMax asked.

"Far as I know," Sue said.

DeMax slapped a hundred into Travis' hand. "Thanks, you can go."

"You're a bad dude," Travis said, looking at DeMax.

"Depends on who you ask."

6

Gipson took his phone out of his pocket and dialed Margi.

"Hi," she said.

"Margi, I wanted you to know I've been going through the Winmont files. It looks like a couple of things that happened to a lady named Roberta Sallow is strong enough to make a valid accusation. There's more, too. I'll file it with the court. Might be six months or so before we get a trial date. Why don't you take off some more time to take care of your mother? I'll continue to pay you while we're waiting and get a couple of public defender cases like Rosona's."

"I want to earn my money," Margi said, "but my mother is getting worse. I may not can come back to work for awhile."

"You have earned a fair share of the Winmont case even if you don't do anything else. If we win, we may be looking at several million. You can have half."

"Oh, that's not fair," she said. "You're doing all the work."

"I wouldn't have it if it hadn't been for you coming up with the evidence. That's the way I want it."

"We'll see," she said. "When I can get a break I'll fix you one of those fancy dinners again."

"That would be nice. I'll get the case to court. You need anything, call."

"Thanks I will," she said and hung up.

Truffles jumped up in Gipson's lap.

"Well, looks like we're on our own again," he said to the cat. "I can get back to my hobby."

Gipson grabbed a pen and wrote the address of the rural Mary Kelly in the palm of his hand. He walked back in his bedroom, opened the closet and removed a bright blue cosmetic case and carried it into the bathroom and sat it on the sink cabinet.

He moved the sink cabinet out from the wall, the flex lines uncoiling, and took the Gladstone bag along with a trash bag out of the wall and sat them on the floor. He unlatched the bag and removed the thick knife and his choke rope, looked at them, ran his hand over them slowly like they were pets, and put them back in the bag and closed it. He sat down in front of the bathroom mirror and opened the cosmetic case.

After an hour of applying his mask, he looked up in the mirror. There was an old man staring back at him.

Truffles had been watching all of this. When Gipson looked at him with the old face covering his own, the cat ran away.

"Guess I'll feed you when I get back and look like me again."

He put on clothes over his own and retrieved license plates from the bag he stole. He picked up the Gladstone bag and went to the garage to put the stolen plates on his car.

Forty minutes later, Gipson pulled up outside Mary Kelly's property on the farm road. There was one car parked in the driveway and another sitting across the street. Cops, of course the fucking cops were here, he thought. His anger spilled over and he banged on the steering wheel. He pulled off on a side street, made a u-turn and parked in an empty parking lot. From there, he had a better vantage point of the street.

He waited and watched until she left, cops following close behind her, then followed them to a veterans hospital. Mary Kelly turned into the parking lot, got out of her car and the cops pulled up beside her and watched as she walked toward the entrance of the hospital.

Gipson parked on the street. He walked down the sidewalk and entered the building through another entrance. He made a left turn and walked toward the next door and saw her coming down the hall to an elevator. He turned toward a wall, pretending he was looking at the emergency exit sign on the wall. She stepped in the elevator and punched the fourth floor button. He walked back to where he came in, went back to his car and drove away, rapidly connecting the dots in his head.

She works on the fourth floor, he thought. I'll show them that's where I'll kill her but not tonight.

Most of the way home, he was so upset he kept shaking his head back and forth, like it was on a swivel, and banging on the steering wheel.

"Fucking cops," he said out loud. He almost ran over another car as he sped across lanes to turn off the freeway to his street.

Once he was home, he undressed, removed the old man face and clothes, took a cold shower and put the trash bag and the Gladstone bag back in the wall hideout. He walked into his bedroom naked, laid down on the bed and masturbated.

PART FOUR
"Got good news."

1

Mecana got a call from Sunday.

"Got good news," she said. "Doctor Seymour called. He discovered hair on both victims that he first missed. We've got the new evidence we needed."

"How long will it take to get the results?"

"Not sure but we put a rush on the results."

"That's good news," Mecana said. "DeMax said he may have found evidence that incriminates Tanner the pimp. Wants to meet on Ranch Street. He's been hanging out there for the last three days, watching. I'm on my way there now."

"Let me know. Nothing's happened to any Mary Kellys so far, still keeping watch."

"Stay with them. He's playing a game with us, trying to prove his expertise at murder."

"We'll stay on it."

"By the way," Mecana said, "Darcie mentioned you might try arresting Dewey as an accessory to murder. Scare the hell out of him. Threat of jail time might make him remember who he gave the key to. But check with the DA first."

"Good idea," Sunday said. "Darcie's a brilliant attorney."

Mecana parked on the street and went in the Suzy Café. Two girls jumped up from their table and ran out. Mecana was clean-shave, dressed in expensive jeans and a black polo shirt, the demeanor of a cop in their eyes.

DeMax was sitting at the bar, drinking a beer, the fat lady behind the bar eyeing him. Mecana walked up to DeMax and sat down beside him at the bar.

"Hey Mecana, let's go talk in your truck. Don't seem like I'm welcome here."

He pitched a ten on the bar. They left the café and sat inside Mecana's truck.

"Wanted to see what you thought about what I learned," DeMax said.

"Fire away."

"The guy I called you about is Annie Chapman's pimp," DeMax said. "Tanner something, never got a last name. He beats up his girls when they don't work enough. Has a natural cruel streak and enjoys it. He wasn't at the hotel yesterday, day or night, and his favorite, Shelly, wasn't on the street last night, either. I knew him from back before you and Darcie saved my ass. Haven't seen him today. Shelly said the guy who picked up Annie flashed five hundred bucks at her and she got in the car. I showed Shelly the photo of the suspect, she said the cops already showed it to her. She didn't get a good look and wasn't sure. Annie didn't have any money on her. He must have taken it back. She's been getting Tanner in trouble with drugs lately. He's been out a lot of money because of her. She's been spending her earnings on drugs and Tanner hasn't been getting his cut. Could be a set up, I know Doc said Tanner didn't fit the profile. But he does fit the place, have a motive, and has spent time with Annie after getting her out of jail the day before she was murdered. Maybe he heard about Mary and wanted to get rid of Annie, too, make people think it was the same guy."

"I see where you're coming from," Mecana said. "Makes sense. It could have been him, which means Mary was murdered by someone else. If so, there's more than one sicko out there."

"That's what I was thinking."

"Sunday mentioned Doc found some DNA on both victims. He's testing it now."

"The fat lady in the café keeps Tanner informed about what his girls are doing," DeMax said. "She knows I'm looking for him."

"He might run," Mecana said. "I'll call Sunday and have her arrest him. Shouldn't be any problem getting a warrant. They can hang on to him for a week, at least, give us time to find out more about this."

"I'm going to go home to Mabre," DeMax said. "This place has too many bad memories for me. I was on a path to nowhere before you and Darcie came along."

"You would have figured it out on your own," Mecana said.

"Maybe." DeMax patted Mecana on the shoulder and walked to his motorcycle. "You need anything, I'm just a phone call away."

2

A police cruiser pulled up to the curb at the Ritz Hotel, three working girls on the corner scattered.

Two uniformed officers walked up to the front desk. One was named Brown and the other one Thomas. Brown had a fat face and bulging eyes to go with an overweight body. He kept pulling his pants up. Thomas was slim, a little taller, with blonde hair sticking out from his cap. Both appeared to be veterans with the full swagger of a cop.

"What's your name?" Brown asked the clerk behind the counter.

"Rubin, most days."

"Well it better be the same tomorrow," Thomas said.

"You here for pussy or..." Rubin motioned to the two officers. "Something else?"

"What room is Tanner Rosona in?" Thomas said.

"What you want him for?"

"We've got a warrant for his arrest." Brown sat the warrant on the counter. "Now give us his room number."

"358," Rubin said, "but I don't think he's in now. He's working."

"Give me the damn key." Brown put his hand on the counter, palm up, and wiggled his fat fingers.

Rubin hesitated then placed a keycard in his hand. The officers headed for the elevator.

"That's out of order," Rubin said. "You'll have to walk up."

"You fucking with us, shithead?" Brown punched the up button and the elevator door opened right away.

Rubin threw his hands up, pretending to be startled. "It's a miracle."

"We'll deal with you when we come back," Thomas said.

As soon as the elevator door closed, Rubin phoned room 358. He only said two words, "Run. Cops." He slammed the phone down and shuffled to the front door, disappearing out into the street.

Brown and Thomas got off on the third floor, walked to room 358 and tried the keycard. The lock beeped but the door wouldn't open.

"Bastard gave us the wrong card on purpose," Brown said.

"Think I heard the fire escape ladder drop," Thomas said.

They ran down three flights of stairs, out a side door into an alleyway, as Tanner dropped off a nearby fire escape ladder. He took off running, straight into a tall fence blocking off the alley. He was trapped.

The cops stopped about ten feet from him and drew their weapons.

"Get on the ground, pimp, or I'll blow your shit away," Brown said.

Tanner shifted his feet and looked at the distance to the cops like he was thinking of running.

"Last chance," Brown said, waving his gun at Tanner. "If you don't get on the ground with your hands over your head you're a dead man."

Tanner reached to the back of his belt to try and draw his gun. Both cops opened fire before he could. He fell to the ground, blood pooling around his body.

"I think he's dead," Thomas said.

"Good riddance," Brown said. "Leave him like he is. We didn't have a choice. I'll call it in."

Thirty minutes later, Sunday was taping off the area while Eddy and the forensics crew started doing their job.

Sunday walked up to Brown and Thomas. "You know we'll have to put you on administrative leave until this is investigated."

Both shook their heads yes.

"Will we get paid?" Thomas asked.

"Yes," Sunday said. "File your report. You said he drew down on you, right?"

"Right," Brown said. "We had to shoot."

"Thanks," Sunday said. "Go on home now."

Brown and Thomas walked back to their cruiser and left the scene.

"What do you think about their story?" Eddy asked Sunday.

"I believe what they said."

"Tanner's got a brother named Mario who's even worse then he is," Eddy said. "Don't have a warrant on him, though, he was acquitted on his drug charges."

"I called him," Sunday said. "He said he didn't have anything to do with his brother, that he wasn't going to bury him and to not ever bother him again. Didn't surprise me. Their father is doing life in prison for murdering their mother. They grew up on the street dog-eat-dog. Wonder why Tanner thought he had to shoot his way out?"

"Hard to figure," Eddy said. "Maybe he thought we'd link him to Annie's murder. Even if it wasn't him, we're likely to find his DNA on her."

"We need hard evidence, like the knife or whatever he strangled her with. If we find his DNA on Mary, too, we'll know it's him."

"That would do it."

"Find out what forensics has on this."

"Sure. You never know until you know." Eddy grinned and walked away.

Sunday stood there looking at Tanner's lifeless body, deep in thought.

"We're still chasing a ghost."

3

The next day, the buzzer at the morgue rang and a little man with glasses and a white coat unlocked the door and cracked it open.

A tall man with thick, black wavy hair and dark brown eyes was standing there, handcuffed to a uniformed police officer even bigger than he was.

"The cops made me come down here to ID my brother, Tanner."

The little man looked at the cop.

"Let us in, Billy," the cop said. Billy opened the door and they walked in

"Follow me," Billy said and they walked down a row of metal doors. He stopped at one labeled #39, grabbed the handle and pulled a body out on a tray.

He pulled the sheet off the face of the dead body. "Yeah, that's Tanner. Can I go now?"

"Sign the sheet and you can go," the cop said.

He scribbled the name Mario Rosona.

"Get the coroner to sign his John Hancock on that and send a copy to homicide,

Billy."

They walked back to the door. Billy unlocked it and let the two men out. The cop stopped in the open door.

"Why do you keep the door locked?" the cop asked.

"People steal bodies," Billy said. "Especially women."

"I'm sorry I asked."

Mario Rosona stopped at the Ritz hotel. Rubin was back behind the counter.

"I'm Tanner's brother. I'm here to get whatever he has left. What room was he in?"

"Room 358," Rubin said. "Someone already stripped it, though. Nothing left."

"You know who did it?"

"Not sure," Rubin said. "Someone did it before the cops came back when I wasn't here."

"Bullshit. You know word travels fast." Mario reached behind his back, pulled out his snub-nose and placed the barrel against Rubin's head. "Now, tell me who took his stuff or say hello to Tanner."

"The bitches from his stable must have. Wasn't me."

"I'll have a look anyway, give me the key." Mario lowered the gun and Rubin handed him the key.

Mario walked to the elevator and stepped off on the third floor. Room 358 was the first door on his left. He opened the door and walked in. All of the drawers from a chest and tables had been dumped on the floor. The mattress pushed off the bed and cut open. Nothing left of any value.

"Shit," Mario said as he kicked a drawer over and noticed a key taped to the bottom. He took the key off and looked at it. It had the words SURELOCK on one side and the numbers 34305 on the other side.

The first thing he thought of was a bank box with money in it. He stuck the key in his pocket and went back down to the front desk. Rubin put his hands up over his head.

"I told you I didn't have nothing to do with it."

"You ever hear Tanner say anything about a bank?"

"I don't know what you're talking about," Rubin said. "Never heard him mention anything about a bank, he always used cash from his whores."

"If I find out you're lying I'll be back."

They heard a woman's high heels and looked around. Shelly was walking in with an old man with a smile on his face. Rubin reached under the counter and handed her a key when she got to the counter.

"You getting an early start to the day, Shelly?" Rubin said. "Thought you would go to Tanner's funeral."

"He's not having one," Shelly said. "The state is going to put him in a pauper's grave soon. He didn't leave me nothing."

"You Tanner's girl?" Mario asked.

"Don't nobody own me," Shelly said. She put an arm around the old man and walked him to the elevator.

"After you turn your trick I want to talk to you," Mario said.

"I got nothing to say to you motherfucker," Shelly said.

Mario ran to her and slapped her down. The old man swung at him, but Mario gave him an uppercut and he fell to the floor out cold.

"You son of a bitch," Shelly said, kicking at Mario. He backhanded her and she hit the floor again.

"Leave her alone, Mario," Rubin said.

"Shut up or I'll kick your ass, too."

"I'm going to kill you," Shelly said, rubbing her face.

"You don't tell your target before you do, stupid," Mario said. "I might decide to do away with you first. Now, do you know if Tanner had a bank account or savings box at any bank?"

"No, I don't." Shelly staggered to her feet. "Look what you've done," she said, pointing at the old man on the floor.

"Why don't you just take his money and disappear."

"Yeah, just get out of here, Shelly," Rubin said.

Shelly stared at Mario then bent down and removed the old man's wallet from his pocket.

"I'll get even with you," she said, still looking at Mario. She turned around and ran out of the back of the hotel.

Mario walked out the front door, got in his car and started to pull away from the cub when a police cruiser blocked him in. Two young cops jumped out with pistols drawn, yelling at him.

"Get out of the car and put your hands over your head," one of the officers said. "Try anything and you'll end up like your brother."

Mario slipped his gun out of his belt and laid it on the seat so he wouldn't be armed. If they shot him it would be murder as last revenge.

He leaned up against the car, put his hands on top of it and spread his legs. He was very familiar with the routine.

"You're under arrest," the cop said. "We've got evidence this time."

They handcuffed him and sat him in the back seat.

"I want my phone call," Mario said.

They didn't answer so Mario repeated himself.

"I have a right to call my lawyer."

The cops still didn't answer him, just talked about which football games they would watch over the weekend.

Mario ran his handcuffs across the metal grill on the back of the front seat, making a horrible noise. The cop on the passenger side glanced back at him.

"Cut that shit out," he said and they went back to talking about sports.

4

Mecana and Sunday sat looking through the one-way mirror into the interrogation room. Eddy was in there speaking to Mario Rosona. Sunday thought they had a lead on Dewey's missing evidence room key.

"This guy is Tanner's brother," Sunday said. "We had to force him to identify Tanner at the morgue yesterday. He swears he found the key in Tanner's hotel room on the bottom of a drawer after someone had ransacked the room. The key had Dewey's numbers on it."

"I know of him," Mecana said. "That's where he belongs, whether he has the key or not."

"Him and his brother were sworn enemies," Sunday said. "We have a witness that will testify he was with Mario when he made a million dollar deal to buy cocaine from a cartel. It will be a retrial, his lawyer got him off the charge the first time when the drugs disappeared with the box we're looking for. We've got a witness this time, though. We know he's not the killer. He was in jail when both Mary and Annie were murdered."

"DeMax could be right," Mecana said. "Maybe Tanner got the key from Dewey, stole the box and someone else got the bag. The murders are so similar. If Tanner is a copy cat then we have two killers."

"We have a close watch on the Mary Kellys," Sunday said. "We should be getting the DNA report soon. Hopefully it's a match to someone in the database."

Sunday flipped on the microphone switch in the interrogation room. Eddy was speaking. "We've got a witness that was with you, saying you made a deal with the cartel," Eddy said. "Did you also steal drugs and evidence from our property room?"

"I told you, I found the key at Tanner's. That's all I know about it. I thought it was a bank key."

"Where did you get that idea?"

"I'm not saying another word. I want my lawyer," Mario said.

"Who's that?"

"Gipson Hayes."

Sunday turned off the mic.

"Hayes was the public defender for Rosona on that drug deal."

Sunday said.

"Have you run a check on the lawyer?" Mecana said.

"Yes, he's a well-respected attorney with a great record." Sunday opened a folder and read from it. "Only one conviction out of 75 clients he represented in the last five years. He was at the top of his law class, born and raised in Reesville. No arrest or connections to any criminals. No DNA in the database. He represented Rosona as a public defender pick. Not his choice but his obligation as an attorney."

"Just happened to be Rosona," Mecana said

"I have some men at Rosona's apartment now looking for evidence. We might need to convict him if something happens to our witness. We're going to try and get a confession before we jail him."

"Well, from what you said, you might need it if Hayes represents him," Mecana said. "I'll ask Darcie how that works."

"Mario had a .38 in his car. We'll run a ballistic check on it."

"I'm going to have a talk with Dewey," Mecana said. "Darcie had the department run a check on his days off and there were two. One matched the time the box and drugs were discovered missing. Trouble is, nothing was officially checked out on those days, so we don't have a suspect other than Dewey. Maybe he went in and no one saw him, or maybe he gave someone the key for money."

"We could use a break." Sunday flipped the interrogation room speaker back on and Mecana walked out to his truck. He checked Dewey's address in his notepad and drove that way.

The address was on a street with a row of old brick houses that had been kept up with over the years. Probably owned by the tenants. Dewey's house had a white picket fence around the front yard. Two cars were parked in the driveway.

Mecana walked up to the front door and rang the door bell. No one answered. He rang it again. Still no answer. He stepped over to a window and looked in. No one in the room. He tried the door bell again. No one came to the door. He walked around to the back of the house and saw the back door was slightly open. He drew his Glock and entered the house.

Inside was a foul smell he recognized. He walked down the hall to a bedroom, the smell coming through the cracked door was even stronger. He pushed the door open with the barrel of his gun. A woman was lying in the bed, a pool of blood around her and Dewey, who was draped over her lower body wearing nothing but pajamas and a hole to the head.

Mecana listened for any sounds and continued searching the house. When he didn't hear or see anyone he put his gun away. He went back to the bodies. No question they were dead. They were turning purple. Rigor mortis had already set in.

He reported what he found to the police and waited on the front porch. He wanted to check Dewey for the property key but knew it wouldn't be a good idea to leave any fingerprints.

By the time the first ambulance showed up, so did Robert Chandler and Kimber Blount. The two men walked up to Mecana. He noticed Chandler and Blount weren't as thin as they used to be. Work and marriage must have been keeping them from the gym, he thought.

"We heard your call on the scanner," Chandler said to Mecana. "You and murder are old friends."

"You may be my next victim, asshole, if you don't back off," Mecana said.

"You're talking to police officer. Mind your tongue before I arrest you."

Blount stepped between them. "What are you doing here anyway, Mecana? You're not a cop anymore."

"Her about the missing evidence. I found two dead in the bedroom. That's all I've got to say to you."

Chandler and Blount looked at each other. Blount motioned toward the door. They reached in their pockets and put on a sanitation mask and walked in the house through the open door.

Mecana stepped off the porch and walked out into the front yard and called Sunday.

"Hey," Sunday said. "We heard it on the monitor. Both dead?"

"Yes. They're turning purple. Now we know why Tanner was running. Think evidence will show he kill them. Tanner was the one with the key. No doubt he's our box thief. But who in the hell has the bag?"

"He was afraid Dewy was going to spill the beans."

"Seems to add up that way," Mecana said. "Chandler and Blount showed up. You going to leave them on this?"

"That's Walt's call. He probably will since they were first on the scene. Doesn't change anything with us, though. Barry and his crew will do the important work anyway and give us a report."

"Those two are dangerous."

"They think you are, too."

"That's not surprising," Mecana said.

"By the way, Mario keeps asking to call his lawyer."

"You mean Hayes?"

"Yeah," Sunday said. "We called but he said he doesn't want to represent him. Apparently last time wasn't his idea either, but a judge still might assign him as a public defender since he's represented him before on the same charge."

"I'll stop by."

Mecana hung up the phone and saw Barry and his forensic crew had arrived. Several headed for the bedroom. Barry stopped to talk to Mecana.

"Sunday said you called this in and to get in touch with her before giving Chandler and Blount a report."

"We don't want it messed up," Mecana said.

"Don't have anything to say about that. Except I got a call from my superior to send it to her first and that's what I'll do." Barry grinned and started walking away.

"Thanks, Barry. I saw a .45 casing lying on the floor, should match the murder weapon."

Barry nodded and kept walking.

Chandler hurried out of the house. "We're going to need a statement on this, Mecana," he said.

"I'm on my way to see Sunday now, we're going to talk all this over. I'll fill in the blanks for her."

"We need it now," Chandler said.

"Get out of my way. I'll give it to Sunday," Mecana said. "I still remember those trumped-up murder charges you tried to pin on me. You knew it was a clean kill. Those assassins were trying to murder Candy Kane. Thank goodness Robert straightened you out."

Chandler let his anger show as Mecana walked away.

"You're gonna fuck up one of these days, Mecana. And when you do, I'll be there to hang your ass."

5

Gipson was up late working on evidence for the Winmont case, trying to keep his mind off Mary Kelly. His phone rang, it was Margi.

"Glad you called," Gipson said. "I've been working on the case and we have a very good chance to win."

"That's great news," Margi said. "Really great. But...I can't work for you anymore. My mother has lung cancer and I'm going with her to Arizona for treatment. I'm sorry."

"Can't you make other arrangements? I need you. In more ways than one. I was counting on you."

"I have to go. We're on our way to the airport now. I'm so sorry."

Gipson stood up and slammed his fist on the desk.

"What was that noise?" Margi asked.

"You lied! It's like my mother said, a man can't trust a woman. Go on, bitch. If you come back you'll be sorry."

"I knew your mother was insane, Gipson, but it sounds like you are, too," Margi said. "Don't ever call me again."

Gipson grabbed his computer monitor and threw it against the wall, breaking the glass. Truffles jumped up and ran out of the room.

"She's like all the rest!" He flopped back down on his chair and put his hands to his face, crying. After a few minutes of sobbing he wiped his eyes and stood up, anger boiling over.

He walked to the bathroom and removed the Gladstone bag from the wall. He sat down on the stool and opened his makeup kit. He began to add wrinkles and age spots to his face, painted his eyebrows gray, and enlarged his nose.

He looked in the mirror and saw a septuagenarian looking back at him.

"None of you deserve to live," he said to the mirror.

With a change of clothes, a pair of gloves and a knife, Gipson walked to his car and headed for Berman's law firm.

Gipson pulled into a parking space that still had his name on it. Before he got out, he taped a trash bag under his jacket and adjusted it to look like a fat stomach. He walked out to the street and sat down at the bus stop. Once the next one came along, he rode for thirty minutes with no destination in mind, just looking for a woman of opportunity.

Several stops later, two young women dressed in waitress outfits sat in the seat behind him. They both were pretty, in their twenties. The blonde had the window seat and the brunette the aisle. He overheard them talking.

The brunette said, "I'm glad that shift is over."

"Your boyfriend home?" the blonde asked.

"No, he had to go to Chicago for a seminar."

"You want me to spend the night with you?"

"I'll be alright. I got a gun and know how to use it," the brunette said. "My stop's coming up, see you tomorrow."

"Yeah get some rest," the blonde said.

The brunette got off at the next stop and Gipson followed her off, but turned in the opposite direction. He walked down to the end of the block and stopped, turning back to watch her walk down the dark street. The bus had already headed for its next destination. No one else was on the street.

He turned around and followed her at a distance. She turned on the next street toward an apartment building and he began closing the distance between them. He watched her walk up to a door on the ground floor apartment with drapes drawn across a window. She unlocked the door, reached in and flipped on the light switch. No one else in view.

Gipson bolted around the corner and pushed her through the doorway. She dropped her purse on the floor. It flew open and a snub-nosed .38 fell out. He kicked the gun away and cut off the lights. The brunette tried to run through the open door but he grabbed her around the neck before she could get away, putting a choke hold on her. She screamed but his arms were cutting off her wind pipe and it came out as a whisper. He kicked the door shut and hung on with a death grip as she struggled to get free. He squeezed the life out of her and she collapsed in his arms. He dropped her on the floor, took the trash bag from under his clothes and pitched it away from her. He propped her up in a corner and stretched her legs out. He drew the knife from his belt, pressed it deep into her throat, sawing on it until her head fell off, blood covering her body, his gloved hands and clothing and shoes. He placed her hands in her lap palms-up and sat her head in her hands, pressing her closed eyes open with his thumb and index finger.

"That's better," he said, looking at her open, glazed brown eyes. He wiped his knife off on her uniform under her 'Tillie' name tag and stuck the knife back in his belt. He stepped away from her, removed his bloody clothes and very carefully folded them and placed them in the trash bag after removing the clean clothes. He put on skin-colored gloves and a gray toupee from his clean jacket pocket and adjusted them both, then made another fat belly by pushing the trash bag around under his clothes.

"Time to go. Can't wait for the cops to see you," he said, staring at her posed headless body. "Wish it was you, Margi."

PART FIVE
"Wish it was you, Margi."

1

In the wee hours after the murder, Mecana rose up in bed, wide awake.

"I'll be damned," he said, staring into his dark bedroom.

Darcie turned on the bedside lamp.

"You woke me up," she said. "What are you mumbling about?"

"DeMax mentioned someone named Shelly. Tanner's main squeeze, I think. If he had the key, then she would know how he got it and who has the bag now."

"That suddenly came to you in your sleep?"

Mecana stood up in his underwear, went to his closet and started getting dressed.

"What are you doing?" Darcie asked.

"I'm going to pick up DeMax and go look for Shelly. These are her working hours, after all."

"I'll go with you."

"No, the whores might attack you if they think you're the new competition."

"I don't know if that's a compliment or an insult."

"A compliment, naturally, because you're so gorgeous." Mecana smiled at her as he dialed.

DeMax answered the phone. "Something bad happen?" he asked.

"We need to find Tanner's girl Shelly."

"At two in the morning?"

"Tanner stole the box but someone else has the bag," Mecana said. "She would know who. I'll pick you up in thirty."

"Alright, but you're gonna have to explain to Mabre. She wasn't too happy about me spending all that time with the whores, not sure I'll survive a second trip out there."

"I may have the same problem," Mecana said and hung up.

He turned to Darcie. "Keep your Beretta in the bed with you, honey, until I get back." He gave Darcie a quick kiss and hurried out the door.

An hour later, Mecana and DeMax were walking in Suzy's Café. There was only one other person besides Sue in the restaurant – a young woman wearing skimpy clothes, slouched in a corner booth, head down and eyes closed.

"That girl okay?" Mecana asked.

"She's sleeping," Sue said. "What are you two doing back?"

"We're looking for Shelly, seen her?"

"Kiss my ass."

"Ain't that desperate," DeMax said.

"You seen Shelly?" Mecana asked again.

"Which one? Know several Shellys."

"You know who we're talking about," DeMax said. "Tanner's girl."

"Heard she quit the street," Sue said. "Buy something or leave."

"Where is she now?"

"What you want to know for, you're not a cop."

"We can find one if you don't tell us."

"I don't know, try Rubin at the hotel."

"What you think, DeMax?" Mecana said.

"She's been working the beds there for the last two years," DeMax said.

"Lets go then," Mecana said.

"Yeah, get the hell out of my place," Sue said.

"You got a real attitude problem, lady," Mecana said, shaking his head as they left.

Outside, the skinny sax player was still sitting on the street in front of the movie house, playing his saxophone.

"Let's take a walk over there and talk to Blaster," DeMax said. "Shelly was always giving him money."

"The sax player?"

DeMax nodded and they walked across the street.

Blaster took the reed from his lips when he saw DeMax and laid the sax in his lap.

"Well, well, well. You finally come home, DeMax," Blaster said. "Saw you the other day but you didn't come to see me. Heard you was a detective now, big shot. Too busy to say hi?"

"Yeah, sorry," DeMax said. "Been working."

Blaster coughed and wiped the perspiration from his face with the back of his skinny hand, then brushed his long hair back from his forehead. His legs and feet were twisted out of shape. A pair of crutches behind him.

"You seen Shelly today?" DeMax asked.

"Nope. She done quit us since the cops killed her man. Gonna try and be an upright citizen or something. She was kind of whored out anyway. If she had as many dicks sticking out of her as she had stuck in her she'd look like a porcupine." He gave a good laugh at his own joke then looked at Mecana. "Do I know you?"

"Not exactly, but you may have seen me," Mecana said. "Used to be a cop. Retired now, though."

"That's it," Blaster said. "Thought there was something about you I didn't like."

"He's a good friend. Saved my ass once or twice," DeMax said. "You know where Shelly went?"

"Think she said her mother's. Didn't get a name or town," Blaster said. "But I wouldn't tell you even if I did know. You're not one of us anymore, DeMax."

Mecana reached in his pocket and dropped a hundred dollar bill in Blaster's cap.

Blaster picked up his sax and blew the first five notes of the national anthem and sat the sax back in his lap. "There's your money's worth," he said and smiled.

Mecana smiled back. "Let's check the hotel."

"See you, Blaster," DeMax said.

Blaster picked up his saxophone again, blew a long, rough-sounding note and sat it back in his lap.

At the hotel, a working girl and a middle-aged, sloppy-looking John were coming out of the elevator. They both stopped and stared at Mecana and DeMax until they walked on by, then gave a sigh of relief and left the hotel in a hurry.

No one was at the front desk. A sign propped up on the counter read, "If you already have a room go on up. If you don't go away. Rubin."

Mecana walked around behind the counter and banged on the door behind it, but no answer.

DeMax stepped up to the door and took a turn pounding on it.

"Get your ass out here, Rubin, or I'm gonna huff and puff and kick your door down!"

Mecana grinned. "That should do it," he said.

The door opened and Rubin was standing there in his heart-covered boxer shorts.

"What the hell do you two want?"

"Where's Shelly Taylor?" DeMax asked.

"She left this afternoon, said she was done here and won't be back." Rubin was pushing the door, trying to close it.

DeMax stuck out his foot to block the door.

"Where did she go, Rubin?"

"I don't know. Let me get some sleep."

"She's been here at least two years," DeMax said. "You know where she goes when she's not working."

"To her mother's I think."

"What's her mother's name?" Mecana asked.

"I think she said Ruby. Ruby Taylor. Same last name as Shelly's. She's got a young daughter her mother keeps for her. I don't know where she stays, though. That's the truth."

"You're sure her mother's name is Ruby Taylor?" Mecana asked.

"Yeah that's it," Rubin said. "Now get your damn foot out of my door, DeMax."

DeMax looked at Mecana.

"If that's her name we can find her," Mecana said.

DeMax took his foot out of the door and Rubin closed it.

Mecana and DeMax left the hotel and Mecana called Darcie.

"Are you okay," Darcie asked.

"Yeah, what about you?

"Fine. What's happening out there?"

"I need you to look up a Ruby Taylor. She's Shelly's mother. Think that's where Shelly went to. Her mother's probably in the city somewhere. She watches Shelly's kid so it's probably not too far away. Unfortunately, Taylor is a very common name."

"Okay, I'll see what I can find and get back to you," Darcie said. "Couldn't sleep anyway."

2

Darcie came up with three possibilities. Mecana and DeMax left near dawn to check the first one at a trailer park. The name Taylor was on the mailbox. No lights were on in the small trailer. An old silver Toyota Corolla was parked in the driveway and a newer-model red Ford Taurus sat on the street in front of the trailer.

Mecana stopped across the street, turned off his headlights and left the truck running.

"What now?" DeMax asked.

"Thinking it over," Mecana said. "They could have us arrested if we break-and-enter and I don't want to call the cops until we find Shelly. This is a likely place. They're not going anywhere 'til daylight. Let's wait until dawn."

Once the sun was up, they decided to try the trailer again. A light was now on.

They walked up to the door and Mecana motioned for DeMax to step back and he knocked on the door. No one came so he knocked again. A woman pushed a curtain back on the door window and looked out with big blurry eyes at Mecana and quickly closed the curtain.

"We're looking for Shelly Taylor," Mecana said through the door. "Is she here?"

"What you want," a woman's voice said through the door.

Mecana smiled. They found her on the first try.

"Go away, asshole," a different woman's voice said.

DeMax stepped up to the door. "You need to talk to us before we have to call the cops. You don't really have a choice. It's us or the cops."

"The guy at the door a cop?"

"No, he's a private eye. We just need to ask some questions about Tanner," DeMax said. "If you come clean you may not have to go to jail."

"Guarantee me I won't be arrested and I'll talk to you."

"We can't do that," Mecana said. "But if you don't talk to us we'll have to call the cops."

"He's right, Shelly," DeMax said. "You're better off with us."

The door came open and Shelly was standing there in a red housecoat, her hair tied in a ponytail. She pulled the coat tighter around her and stepped back from the door. Mecana and DeMax walked.

"Okay," she said. "What do you want to know?"

The older woman picked up a pack of cigarettes off a coffee table and took her granddaughter to another room. Shelly sat down on a floral-patterned chair and Mecana and DeMax sat down on a small black leather couch pushed up against the wall.

"I'll get right to the point," Mecana said. "Tanner stole an evidence box and drugs from the police station property room. We know he had the key to the property room and there's a very good possibility he murdered the evidence clerk Dewey and his wife. You could be charged as an accomplice to murder. Tell me about it."

Shelly dropped her head and tears fell to the floor. She raised her head and wiped the tears from her eyes.

"If I tell you, will you help me keep my daughter?

"Give me the complete story as you know it," Mecana said. "We'll do what we can."

"That true?"

"His wife's a lawyer," DeMax said. "She saved me from all kinds of hell."

"Dewey made a deal with Tanner," Shelly said. "Tanner gave him ten grand for the key so he could steal the drugs on Dewey's day off. I got arrested that day on purpose, and Tanner came to bail me out. He was doing that for all his girls so it didn't look suspicious for him to be there.

"He went to the restroom and came out with a wad of wet toilet paper in his hand. No one was in the hall to see us. He stuck the toilet paper on the camera before we were in view, opened the gate to the property room and grabbed the box. He took the bag out and handed it to me and filled the box with cocaine. We never opened the bag.

"He told me to put the bag in the dumpster when we left the building. I couldn't raise the heavy dumpster door with one hand so I just sat the bag down in front of the dumpster. Then we hauled ass out of there."

"What time was that?" Mecana asked.

"About three that afternoon, or so."

"Do you know who picked up the bag?"

"No. It was sitting there when we left. That's the last time I saw it."

"What did he do with the drugs?"

"I don't know," Shelly said. "Sold or traded them, probably."

"Did Tanner kill Dewey and his wife?"

"He said Dewey wanted more money. I didn't know he was going to kill them, I swear. I wasn't even with him."

"You did the right thing, Shelly," DeMax said.

"I'll have to call the cops to arrest you for your part in this but I'll call my wife to see if she can get bail for you," Mecana said. "Can your mother take care of your baby until we can get you out?"

"I'll get dressed," Shelly said.

"DeMax, stay with her. I'll go outside and call Sunday and Darcie."

"Okay," DeMax said.

Mecana got up and headed for the door and they heard sirens screaming in the distance as he walked out.

Mecana hadn't been gone five minutes and came hurrying back inside.

"There's been another murder," Mecana said. "When I called Sunday she said they got a call to 4319 Dickens Street. Sunday and Eddy are on the way. The sirens we heard must've been heading there. I'm going to go and see what we have. Hold on to Shelly. I'll call you a ride and you take her to the police station for booking. Then wait for me and Darcie to get there."

"You got it," DeMax said.

Mecana hurried to his truck and drove away.

A crowd had gathered by the time Mecana got to the murder scene. It was taped off. Six police cruisers, an ambulance, the coroner's wagon, forensics officers, Sunday and Eddy's cars were all parked in front. Mecana walked up to the tape. A young officer was patrolling to keep people out.

"My name's Mecana," he said. "I'm working with Sunday, can I go in?"

"Not unless they tell me you can," he said.

"Would you tell them I'm here?"

"Can't leave the tape right now. Reporters trying to get past to take pictures."

Sunday appeared and waved him inside to the room.

Inside, a sheet was covering the victim, blood on the edges of the sheet. Sunday raised the corner up. Mecana took a quick look and she dropped it back down.

Mecana grimaced and shook his head.

"This is the worst one yet, but no doubt it's the same killer," Sunday said. "But not a Mary Kelly. Her name is Tillie Moncreate. Her boyfriend found her this morning when he got back from Chicago. By the estimated time of death, he was still in Chicago when she was murdered.

"As you can see there's bloody shoe prints, same size but a different shoe sole. That makes three different types. We're searching for where the shoes were purchased. Eventually we'll find him, but he may kill a dozen more before we do.

"We've got the DNA back from the hair on both victims but we can't find a match. He strangled her, cut off her head and posed her so when anyone opened the front door she would be the first thing they would see, holding her head in her lap. Most disgusting thing I have ever seen.

"If Shelly Taylor confessed to being with Tanner when he stole the box and bag, at least that's some progress."

"She did," Mecana said.

Eddy walked up. "Hey Mecana. Never seen one this bad. Having trouble keeping breakfast down."

"Sunday was telling me about it. He couldn't wait for a ripper victim. He had to kill now."

"It's so frustrating," Sunday said.

"Sometimes staying busy helps," Mecana said. "A lot of cases have taken years to solve."

"I know, it's just so incomprehensible that a human mind could be this sick," Sunday said.

"They have always been out there and always will be," Mecana said. "I'm going to run by the station and check with Darcie to see what the deal is with Shelly getting bail. I promised I would."

"Okay," Sunday said. "I'll call you when we get done here. No doubt it's the same killer. He just quit playing the Jack the Ripper game."

3

Darcie and DeMax were waiting in a courtroom for a judge to hear Shelly's request for bail when Mecana walked in. A door came open and a bailiff brought Shelly in, wearing an orange jumpsuit with her hands cuffed in front of her. The bailiff un-cuffed her and sat her down in front of a court bench.

Darcie saw Mecana and waved for him to join them.

"Looks like I got here just in time," Mecana said.

"She's been charged with theft, prostitution, perjury and as an accomplice to a homicide. She said she wasn't with him when he killed Dewey and his wife so I contested the accomplice charge," Darcie said. "Not going to be easy or quick but I know this judge, he has always been fair."

The door opened behind the judge's desk and a short gray-haired man in a judge's robe walked in. He had his glasses pushed down on his large nose, glancing at a paper he had in his hand and stepped up on the desk platform.

The bailiff said, "All rise." Everyone stood up waiting for the judge to sit down. When he did, everyone else followed.

The judge cleared his throat and directed his attention to Darcie.

"Well counselor, it's been a while since I've seen you in my courtroom," he said.

"Haven't been practicing, your honor, until this came to my attention."

"What I have here is a request for bail for Shelly Taylor."

"Yes, your honor."

The judge looked at Shelly. "Please state your legal name, young lady."

"Shelly Ann Taylor."

"Counselor, I see she has been arrested several times for prostitution and other misdemeanors. The charges this time are far more serious. Felonies, even. You may present your request for bail."

"Yes, your honor. She's a single parent and wants to find a legal and moral way to put her life together and raise her daughter. I believe she's sincere and will change her life for the better. Shelly denies having had anything to do with the murder and has an alibi. She was working at the time."

"Working?" the judge asked

"At her profession."

"Oh, that profession."

"Yes, she has no objection to reporting weekly for accountability and proof she's no longer pursuing that profession."

The judge picked up the paper from his desk and looked at it and laid it back down.

"Because some of the charges are felonies, bail will be set at one-hundred thousand dollars. Miss Taylor, do you understand the conditions of bail?"

Shelly stood up without being prompted. "Yes, your honor."

"If you are charged with any other crimes, or fail to appear for your trial, you will be arrested and confined. Do you understand?"

"Yes your honor," Shelly said.

"Very well. Good to see you again, counselor, you may post the bail by signature for Miss Taylor and she can be released immediately."

"Thank you, your honor," Darcie said.

The judge stood up, and everyone else did. He stepped down from the bench and made his exit out the back door.

"Damn you're good," DeMax said.

The bailiff removed the handcuffs from Shelly and walked over to Darcie.

"Get her bail posted and we'll release her," he said. "She can remain in the courtroom until you do."

"Thanks," Darcie said. "Mecana, you and DeMax hang out with her. I'll get her clothes and post the bail."

"Alright," Mecana said. "Shelly, come sit with us until she gets back."

Shelly walked over to Mecana and DeMax and sat down.

"Thank you," she said. "Will Darcie represent me?"

"I don't know," Mecana said. "That's Darcie's call."

"I thought of something I didn't tell you before," she said.

"What?"

"There was a new-looking black Cadillac Escalade parked in the alley behind us when me and Tanner went out the exit door."

"Anyone in it?"

"No," Shelly said. "I didn't pay much attention to it at the time. Don't remember any of the plate numbers, but I had seen it parked there before. Tanner always parked in the alley and we went out the exit door when he would get me out of jail."

"Kind of stupid to steal cocaine from a police station," DeMax said.

"I tried to talk him out of it," Shelly said. "He knew the drugs belonged to Mario and was going to show his brother how smart he was. What he didn't know was the cocaine was being held as evidence against Mario. And with no evidence, his lawyer got him off."

"His lawyer named Hayes?" Mecana asked.

"I don't know," Shelly said.

"You know who arrested Mario for the drugs?"

"A black dude named Blount. He's arrested me twice, too."

Mecana and DeMax looked at each other. "We'll pay him a visit," Mecana said.

Darcie walked back in with a piece of paper in her hand and Shelly's bag of clothes in the other.

"Okay, you're free to go when you sign the bail contract. There's a clause that makes you responsible for good behavior and to report every Friday here for visual contact. That means if you go back to prostitution they will revoke your bail and put you back in jail." Darcie handed Shelly a pen to sign the bail contract and she signed it.

"Will you represent me?" Shelly asked.

"I'll think about for a couple weeks, see how you're doing," Darcie said.

"I'll change, I promise."

"We'll talk later, go put your clothes on. Mecana and DeMax will take you home. I'll deliver your bail contract to the bailiff."

Shelly hugged Darcie's neck, then Mecana and DeMax. "Thank you." She took her clothes and headed for the restroom.

"You were great as usual," Mecana said, looking at Darcie.

DeMax nodded in agreement.

"Thanks," she said. "Now, Mecana, if you'll take DeMax and Shelly home, I'll meet you back at the house."

Shelly walked out of the restroom, dressed.

"I'll take you home Shelly," Mecana said.

"Behave yourself, Shelly," Darcie said and smiled.

4

As Mecana dropped off Shelly, her little girl came running out the door. Shelly picked her up and carried her in the trailer.

"Everyone should have a second chance," DeMax said.

"She will," Mecana said. "Let's swing by the police station and see if Blount's there. He may tell us something useful he doesn't know he's doing."

"Would have to be that way. Don't think he would if he knew it was to our benefit," DeMax said. "I'll call Mabre and let her know it will be a while until I get home."

"She working?" Mecana asked.

"No, she's home," DeMax said. "She starts her new network job next week. She won't have to wait tables anymore. We're thinking about getting us a house after we both get some money put away."

"That's a good idea," Mecana said.

He parked in the alley behind the homicide department next to a no parking sign. The dumpster was no more than ten feet from the property exit door. The alley was wide enough for the big garbage trucks to drive through. They got out and opened the dumpster door. It was heavy so it wouldn't blow open. It had miscellaneous trash in the dumpster. Nothing that looked like it would have come from the homicide department. They got back in the truck and Mecana drove to the pay parking lot in front of the building, parked, got a ticket and made their way up to the homicide department on the fourth floor, looking for Blount.

When Mecana and DeMax walked in, the only detectives were Blount, Chandler and tailor-dressed Bennie Modele.

Chandler saw them walk in and stared at them as they walked over to Blount's desk.

"What are you doing here, Mecana?" Chandler said. "Walt's talking to the police chief about that maniac killer you and Sunday can't seem to catch."

"Wanted to ask Blount about the arrest of Mario Rosano," Mecana said.

Blount leaned back in his chair. "What for?"

"Found out the drugs Tanner stole from the property room caused you to lose your Rosano case. May be some connection with Tanner stealing the drugs."

"His attorney was behind Tanner stealing the cocaine so we wouldn't have any evidence," Blount said.

"What makes you so sure of that," Mecana said.

"He even had the nerve to come by that day and ask us to cut a deal with the prosecution before we knew the drugs were stolen," Chandler said.

"Was that Hayes?"

"Yeah, must be one of your friends. Should be disbarred," Chandler said.

"You know what kind of car Hayes has and where he parked that day?"

"Take your misguided brother with you and leave us alone," Blount said.

"You keep DeMax out of this."

"Yeah, I may have to sic Darcie on you," DeMax said and grinned.

"I don't remember," Blount said.

"Chandler, you're a stickler for records and procedure," Mecana said.

"I could look it up but I won't."

Chandler looked at Blount and waved his head toward the door and they got up and walked out.

Mecana walked over to Bennie Modele's desk.

Modele was looking good after recuperating from the wounds he got helping Mecana protect Candy Kane from assassins. He was wearing one of his tailored suits with his usual sour-puss expression.

"I guess you were listening, Bennie," Mecana said.

"Didn't have a choice. I have to be on their side. You don't work here anymore, remember."

"You ever see Attorney Hayes here?"

"Don't get me involved in this, Mecana."

"Who saved your ass when you were shot?"

"You and Darcie," he said.

"How about returning the favor then."

Bennie shook his head and gave Mecana one of his signature frowns. "A few times as I remember." he said. "He was always in a hurry like he had ants in his pants and would leave from the property room exit door to save time and money in the parking lot."

"Have you mentioned this to Walt or Sunday?"

"No, why should I?"

"One more favor, Bennie, and we'll go away," Mecana said. "Pull up Gipson Hayes and see what kind of vehicle he drives. Give me the license number and his home address."

Modele turned to his computer and ran the check.

"Only one Gipson Hayes in the system. Has a 2018 black Cadillac Escalade. Plate TYB1028. Address is 23745 Terrence Heights, Dallas. Here, I'll write it down for you so you won't come back." He picked up a pen and notepad and wrote the information down and handed it to Mecana. "He works for Berman," Bennie said.

"Thanks," Mecana said.

Mecana and DeMax walked out to the parking lot and paid the tab. Mecana started his truck and checked the addresses on his navigation system.

"Are you thinking what I'm thinking?" DeMax said.

"Yeah. He may be the one who picked up the bag but not the killer. We have to keep an open mind," Mecana said. "No evidence, but a chance a comment might tell us a lot. I'll call Sunday. According to the agreement we made with Walt we can't arrest him. We need someone who can. I've got goosebumps just thinking about it."

"Me too," DeMax said. "You just can't see them as well."

"We'll check Berman's law firm first," Mecana said.

Mecana drove to Berman Associates law firm. It was after five so the office was closed.

"Glad we didn't call Sunday," Mecana said. "Would have been going to the wrong place."

Mecana dialed Sunday.

"We're still here," she said

"Found out the attorney, Gipson Hayes, used the property room exit when he came to the station on the day Tanner stole the box. I got the description of his vehicle and it matches what Shelly saw in the alley on that day. I need your help in case he's the one we're looking for. The law firm is closed. I have his home address, though."

"Holy shit, I would have never believed it," Sunday said.

"It might not be him but we have enough to follow it up," Mecana said.

"You don't have enough for me to call a SWAT team but me and Eddy will meet you as soon as we can get there. I'll have two cruisers accompany us and have them block off the street."

"The address is 23745 Terrence Heights in Dallas. We'll meet you on the corner before we go in."

"We have to go in first," Sunday said. "Don't want it thrown out in court for violating his rights."

"Sometimes it's better not to let people know what you're doing," DeMax said.

"Okay," Mecana said. "We'll back you up."

"We're on our way," Sunday said.

5

When Mecana pulled up to stop on the corner to wait for Sunday and Eddy, Gipson's house was in view. The garage door was closed. No way to know if he was home.

"You bring your weapon?" Mecana asked DeMax.

"I forgot it," he said.

"Sounds like shades of Mexico again. There's one in the glove box."

DeMax opened the glove box and took out a nine-millimeter pistol. He pulled the slide and pushed the safety off.

Mecana drew his Glock from his shoulder holster.

A black and white drove up behind them. Eddy and Sunday got out and drew their weapons and walked up to Mecana's truck.

"Have you seen him?" Eddy asked.

"Not yet. The garage was closed when we got here and we haven't seen any movement in the house since," Mecana said.

"Mecana, you and DeMax move around to the back," Sunday said. "I'll have cruisers block the street and the rest can join us in front and back. Don't shoot unless he's got a gun pointed at you."

Mecana and DeMax nodded. Sunday motioned for them to approach the house.

She walked up on the front porch to the front door and rang the doorbell, stepping to the side of the door. Eddy and the other cop took a prone position aiming at the house. No one came to the door. Sunday rang the door bell again. Nothing. Sunday motioned towards the door and

Eddy jumped up, ran to the door and kicked it open with a high martial arts kick. He rolled into the house and came up holding his weapon, ready to fire. Sunday and the cop followed him in. Eddy made his way to the back door and opened it.

Mecana, DeMax and the cop came in with weapons drawn. They all eased through the house, checking every room, DeMax checking the garage. No cars. A yellow cat came running by, scaring the hell out of them and ran out the open back door.

Mecana entered a bedroom with a busted computer monitor on the floor. One wall was covered with law books and horror novels. An O. Henry short story collection caught Mecana's eye. He took it off the shelf and showed it to Sunday.

"He knew," Mecana said and dropped the book on the bed.

"Yeah," Sunday said. "But where the hell is he?"

One of the cops yelled from the bathroom and they all charged in.

Mecana spotted the Gladstone bag on the floor right way with an open phone book sitting on top.

A makeup box was sitting on the sink, with one of the little drawers pulled out and a bright red lipstick tube in it. An empty wig holder was sitting beside the makeup box with several brown hairs in the sink.

They all stared at the items, trying to digest the reasons for them.

"He's disguised himself as a woman," Sunday finally said. "That accounts for the weird look from the first murder. He was disguised then, too."

Mecana picked up the open phone book off the Gladstone bag.

"Look at this," he said. "With all his things still laying out he's in a hurry to get there." He handed the phone book to Sunday. She looked at it and checked her phone for who was with which Mary Kelly and called the stakeout cops.

"Adams, are you and Waxman with Mary Kelly?" Sunday asked.

"No she's working. I'm parked in the lot at the VA hospital, watching her car. Waxman is with her on the fourth floor."

"Leave the parking lot, go to her and tell Waxman we think the killer may be on his way there disguised as a woman. Tell the nurses to move their patients to another floor and stay away from the fourth floor until we tell them it's clear. You and Waxman get Mary Kelly to the ground floor and we should be there by then. Do it now." Sunday put her phone away.

"She's working at the Veterans hospital on the fourth floor. Let's go," Sunday said. "I'll call a SWAT team to meet us there."

Everyone ran out of the house, jumped in their vehicles and headed for the hospital.

Across town, Gipson drove into the VA parking lot. He got out wearing his brown wig, makeup, blue dress and high heels. His legs covered with skin-colored hose, carrying a purse with the Ripper's knife inside. He walked to the elevator and went up to the fourth floor, got off and sat down in the waiting room watching the activities to get acquainted with procedures and to pick out his victim. All the employees had name tags.

A nurse with brown hair and eyes was walking down the hallway toward him, escorted by two officers. She had 'Mary Kelly' on her name tag. They knew he was here. He picked up his purse and went to the ladies room across the hall.

Sunday, Mecana and the cops drove up to the hospital entrance and got out.

"Smith, you and Downs stop anyone from coming in or going out and move them away from the doors," Sunday said. "We're going to the fourth floor. Tell Knowles when the SWAT team arrives to let hospital security know what's happening and secure all the ground floor exits."

"I got it," he said.

Gipson was sitting on the commode when he heard the door open and someone walk in. A mans voice yelled, "Anyone in here?"

Gipson raised his feet up and removed the knife from the purse and waited. He heard massive footsteps outside the restroom. The door closed and he left the stall and peeked out the door.

He saw nurses and aides pushing beds to the elevator, then Sunday and her crew stepped off an elevator. A nurse was running toward the restroom and darted inside. He turned away and she ran to an open stall. He opened the stall door and swung the Ripper knife, cutting her throat. He jerked her name tag off her scrubs as she fell against the stall wall, blood running down her clothes over her panties to the floor. He left his purse on the floor and put the knife inside his dress.

When Gipson saw a bed coming toward him in the hall, he opened the restroom door and grabbed the bed, helping push it to an elevator. Cops were checking everyone getting on the elevator. When he got to the elevator, he let go and another nurse was holding it, waiting to get on the elevator. He moved backwards slowly to the stairwell and opened the exit door. When no one saw him, he walked down one flight of stairs and got off with his new name tag on and walked down the hall in a hurry to an elevator no cops were checking. He got on the elevator and punched the button for the basement floor.

The elevator made a stop on every floor, but no one checked him with his name tag on. He looked like any of the other overweight middle-aged nurses.

SWAT team leader Roy Knowles got a call from Sunday.

"He's not on the fourth floor. Block all the exits," she said. "He knows we're on to him. He didn't get Kelly but he cut a nurse's throat."

Gipson got off the elevator on the basement floor and two cops were standing in front of him. He jerked the nearest one to him, stabbed him in the back, then dropped the knife and grabbed his gun. He mowed down the other cop with several rounds and ran out the outside door carrying the cop's M15 pistol.

He ran across the lawn and was spotted by members of the SWAT team who opened fire at him. He returned fire and they ducked down behind their cars. H kicked his high heels off and jumped over a fence, still wearing the dress, and climbed in his car. Bullets were ripping holes in the side of his car, missing the tires. He floor-boarded the Caddy's gas pedal, at least ten cop cars and Mecana following. Ten miles down the road, he made a quick turn through a neighborhood and they lost him.

"Where the hell is he going?" DeMax said.

Mecana put the pedal to the metal and called Darcie. "I'm in a chase with Hayes now, he's definitely the one."

"Oh no," she said. "You take too many chances, Mecana. You're going to make me a widow.

"Just too much at stake."

"I know. You never give up for the right reasons."

"See if he has a childhood address."

"Just a minute," she said. "Home town address was 421 Old Farrow Road in Reesville."

Mecana made a u-turn and hit the interstate, going west towards Reesville.

Five miles down the road, DeMax spotted Gipson.

"There he is," DeMax said.

Mecana followed as Gipson weaved around a truck.

"He's got a lot more power than I have," Mecana said. "I'll let him run and meet him there."

In minutes, a city limits sign appeared:

Reesville, Texas – Population 2219.

Mecana called Sunday. "I have him in sight. He's going to his old home address: 421 Old Farrow Road in Reesville."

"Okay," Sunday said. "We're on our way now. How do you know?"

"There's nothing else left for him," Mecana said. "He knows that."

Gipson turned off the exit and drove down to a side road to his old two-story house. He stopped at the gate, revving the motor like he was getting ready for a big race, Mecana getting closer.

Gipson punched the Caddy, tore down the fence and crashed through the front of the house into the front room, walls caving in on him. The fuel tank on the Cadillac exploded.

Flames shot up to the ceiling and within seconds he was trapped inside his car. Ceiling fire debris covered the Caddy. The house and car were burning like a college bonfire. The chase was over.

Mecana picked up his phone and dialed. "Sunday, you can slow down. He's burning alive, too late to get him out."

"How did that happen?" she asked.

"He crashed into the house. The gas tank exploded."

"We'll be there in about ten minutes. You can probably hear us now."

"Yep, I hear you," Mecana said and hung up.

"What are we going to do after this is over?" DeMax asked.

Mecana grinned. "You assume you're my partner whatever it is, huh?"

"How about we open a restaurant like Simon did. We could get killed doing this."

"Too hard of work for me," Mecana said, looking in his rearview mirror. "I see Sunday coming in with a herd. I bet there are twenty cars behind her."

"Good," DeMax said. "Mabre didn't want me to come but I knew I had to. I'm your partner, it's what I do."

"Thanks, DeMax," Mecana said. "After Sunday gets here we'll go home and think about what to do next."

"Sounds like a good idea to me," DeMax said.

6

Darcie was waiting at the front door when Mecana drove in after taking DeMax home. When he got out of his truck, she ran to him, hugged his neck and kissed him.

"Talk about a warm welcome," he said.

"I was very worried about you chasing that monster," Darcie said.

"We caught him more by accident than evidence. He killed himself, burned to death in his Cadillac. With his DNA, I would think several other cases will be solved. Shelly remembering the Cadillac is what made this all happen."

"Thank god it's over. Time to move on now."

"I've been thinking about that," Mecana said. "If our families can't come to see us we go to see them. We take some time off, think about what we want to do next and include DeMax and Mabre."

"They are like family now," Darcie said.

"I could spend some time with my kids, take you to Waco to see your family. You and Marcie could dress alike and see if I can tell identical twins apart. We may have a wedding to go to soon. Eddy's going to propose to Sunday."

"She knows. She's going to say yes."

"What I thought. I have some other things in mind, too."

"You always do."

Mecana took off his jacket and sat it on a chair on the porch. He unbuttoned his shirt and threw it on top of the jacket.

"What are you doing?" Darcie asked.

"Thinking about what else I want to do." He picked up Darcie and walked through the open door, kicked it closed with his foot and carried her to the bathroom.

Darcie rubbed her hand across Mecana's bare chest.

"You're a mind reader," he said.

"No, but I know you."

"I wouldn't want to be anyone else."

THE END
...but...
LIFE GOES ON

ABOUT the AUTHOR

John L. Lansdale was born and raised in east Texas. He is married to the love of his life Mary. They have four children. He is a retired Army reserve psychological operations officer and a combat veteran that served three tours in Vietnam with numerous medals and awards. He is a graduate of a Texas police academy and a state certified peace officer. He is an inventor, country music songwriter, performer and television programmer. He produced the television special "Ladies of Country Music" and several other programs. He goes back to the Sun Record days and was introduced to Elvis Presley by Mary on their first date when Elvis was a seventeen-year-old student at Humes High School in Memphis and a ticket-taker at Loew's State Theater.

John has produced a variety of albums and music videos for country artists in Nashville along with songs for movies, with one as recently as 2018 titled "Tremble" for an upcoming film. He has hosted his own radio shows and won awards for radio and television commercials. He was a writer and editor for a business newspaper. He has worked as a comic book writer for Tales from the Crypt, IDW, Grave Tales, Cemetery Dance and many more. He co-authored Shadows West and Hell's Bounty with his brother Joe. He is the author of Slow Bullet, the four-part Mecana detective series, Long Walk Home, The Last Good Day, Broken Moon, Zombie Gold and several others.

John's novel Slow Bullet was reviewed by Publishers Weekly as a must read page-turner with constant action and compared his work to that of popular 1950s author Mickey Spillane. The novel Long Walk Home was a finalist in the fiction category for the National Indie Excellence Awards. The novel Zombie Gold received great reviews including a Booklist review that praised it as a superb story with characters that came alive. Kissing the Devil received praise as a pulp novella. All titles are still in print with more on the way.

John was recently inducted into The Gladewater Museum.

His motto is: **<u>Never Give Up</u>**.

TITLES from JOHN L. LANSDALE

SLOW BULLET

Army veteran Clark McKay is searching for the truth behind his best friend's murder. This search takes him across the globe, where he meets a multitude of characters and is forced to wade through the murky Washington DC waters of corruption. Clark McKay wants to find a murderer... but what happens when he uncovers so much more?

LONG WALK HOME

The O'Rourke family lives on a fading farm in the small town of Angel Point, Mississippi. With family, friends and neighbors fighting overseas in WWII - and rising racial tensions back home - the summer of 1944 turns into a nightmare of murder and loss. Trenton O'Rourke reflects on those days and how his life was forever changed.

THE LAST GOOD DAY

As the Civil War draws to a close, Major Rance Allison is wounded in one of its last battles. He later awakens in an enemy field hospital only to find out he is now on the same side as those he was fighting. The war is over. Missing a limb, his home and his family, Rance sets out to find a new life for himself.

BEYOND IMAGINATION

An all-new short story collection spanning a variety of genres. Also contains the following fan favorites:

BOY AND HOG / BOY AND HOG RETURN

In the deep woods, anything can happen. A group of white-collar workers with a hand-drawn map trek into the wilderness for a hunting expedition. But out there, will they be the hunters or the prey?

EMERGENCY CHRISTMAS

Join the Albright family and the guest who surprises them just in time for the holiday. Along the way, they discover sometimes crisis brings a family closer together.

OTHER TERRIFIC TITLES
from BOOKVOICE PUBLISHING

<u>John L. Lansdale</u>
- The Last Good Day (Hardcover - eBook)
- Long Walk Home (Hardcover - Paperback - eBook)
- Beyond Imagination (Hardcover - Paperback - eBook)
- Kissing the Devil (Hardcover - Paperback - eBook)
- Slow Bullet (Hardcover - Paperback - eBook)
- Horse of a Different Color (Hardcover - Paperback - eBook)
- When the Night Bird Sings (Paperback - eBook)
- Twisted Justice (Paperback - eBook)
- The Box (Paperback - eBook)
- Zombie Gold (Paperback - eBook)
- Emergency Christmas (Chapbook – eBook - Audiobook)

<u>Joe R. Lansdale</u>
- The Magic Wagon (Hardcover – Paperback - eBook)
- Bubba Ho-Tep & Bubba and the Cosmic Blood-Suckers Double-Feature (Paperback)
- The Complete Drive In: A B-Movie Triple Feature 1/2/3 (Paperback - eBook)
- The Drive-In 1: A B-Movie with Blood and Popcorn, Made in Texas (eBook)
- The Drive-In 2: Not Just One of Them Sequels (eBook)
- The Drive-In 3: The Bus Tour (eBook)

<u>John L. Lansdale and Joe R. Lansdale</u>
- Hell's Bounty (Paperback - eBook)

STAY CONNECTED with
BOOKVOICE PUBLISHING

Follow us online at
www.bookvoicepublishing.com